GRIFFITH

Smoke on the waters

BY

Francis E. Reynolds

Sarge Publications
P.O. Box 1200, 351
Alpena, MI 49707

ISBN: 0-9618116-3-3
SAN 666-1327

Acknowledgements:
Historical Collections of the Great Lakes.
Bowling Green State University

Illustration... Lars Leetaru

Sarge Publications
P.O. Box 1200, 351
Alpena, MI 49707

Printed in the U.S.A., Model Printing Service, Inc.
Alpena, MI 49707

In Dedication

Hazel "Barney"…my life.

PROLOGUE

The Cleveland Weekly Herald
Cleveland, June 20, 1850

Tragedy struck Cleveland in such magnitude that has not been equaled since the sinking of the Steamers Erie and the Anthony Wayne. This Monday past the Steamer G.P. Griffith burned and sank off Willoughby with the loss of more than two hundred fifty German, English and Irish immigrants as well as crew members, many of whom are from the Cleveland area. It is believed that only thirty-one survived. The consternation and helplessness of the stricken passengers must have been overwhelming as they attempted by all means available to save themselves from their fiery and watery death. It is believed by a few survivors that the holocaust was caused by a fire starting at the base of one of the smokestacks. The flaming vessel crashed upon an unknown reef only a few hundred yards from shore and then become engulfed in roaring flames. As a large number of immigrants were from Germany and were bound for Cleveland, a leader of the Cleveland German community, Edward Hessenmueller, is asking for a hearing as to why the precipitous haste of burying their beloved countrymen and relatives in unmarked graves along the stark Lake Erie shoreline. Mayor William Case has been appointed as Chairman of a committee to investigate the cause of this most horrendous loss of life and limb.

CHAPTER ONE

June 17, 1850

The hunched figure of Bill Evans with his gaunt features and darting bloodshot eyes moved slowly in the shadows trying not to stand out from the immigrants huddled on the decking. Some were stretched out trying to sleep, others were in small groups unable to contain their eagerness for the days dawning. With a few exceptions, no one seemed to notice him as he moved to the forward locker where he had heard the Clerk tell the Captain earlier where the wine was stored. The whiskey was all gone and his craving for it was unabated. He had almost panicked when he finished the last drop, until he remembered when the two were talking outside his cabin window. Wine. Damn. He would rather have whiskey but he didn't have any choice until in Cleveland and he wasn't even sure then. So, the wine then was a Godsend and he'd get what he needed to tide him over. "Carrie!" he blurted. Why? What made me call her name, he thought, his senses confused. "Oh my God," he sobbed softly. He looked fearfully about. Nobody paid him any attention. Ah my Carrie. Indeed it will not be too long that again I'll see you. Not too long, he said silently. He paused. The keys! The thoughts of his dead wife vanished as he felt for and found his keys to the locker in his right front pocket.

He still had his keys. Ha, he laughed silently. The damn fools. They didn't take them from him. He shook his head. They probably never thought of it. So if it's locked! So what!

But, he had thought, would I be able to see if there were no lights? Ah, ha! He had that figured out too. He would just take his peg oil lamp with some loco-focos and make his own light. He was nobody's fool. He descended through the hatchway from the main deck to the locker forward of the crew's quarters. He looked about. Good. No one was about. He moved cautiously, feeling his way in the passageway to the closed locker door. "What do you know?" he whispered softly. "It's unlocked! Damn. If I was the captain and some dumbass left the door unlocked, I'd really raise hell," he added as he eased the door open and stepped into the darkness. He reached out and felt around. I'll need my light. I can't see a damn thing. He closed the door behind him and knelt on the deck where he placed his lamp and fumbled for the loco-focos. He scratched one on the deck and it burst into flame but then went out. "Crap!" he growled. He scratched another. This one lit. He cupped it and then touched it to the lamp. "Well, now that's better," he sighed in relief as he held the lamp high to see about the closed compartment.

The locker was filled with various Griffith's supplies of cleaning goods, spare parts, coils of rope and other items needed on a cruise. In the confined quarters, the lard oil lamp gave off thick fumes causing him to gag. "Ah. There's the wine," he said with a wide grin as he saw cases of wine bottles stacked in a pile. "Ah, what luck. A couple are already open. Ah, yes," he remembered that Henry had opened a few bottles to check for the supposed sabotaged wine. But not all the bottles, only a few. Hell, spoiled or not, they won't miss a couple. He reached into a case and took out a bottle, throwing the excelsior packing to the deck. Shit! The cork. He didn't have a bottle cork opener. But wait! Ah, my penknife. That'll do it. But it's in with my shaving gear in the cabin. The smoke and fumes from the lamp caused him again to cough. I'd better hurry and get a few and run, he realized as he pulled two bottles again casting the packing to the deck and atop a small keg of highly polished oak, bound

2

with bright copper bands alongside a number of others, all neatly stacked together.

He stuffed two of the bottles into his front waistband and carrying a third, moved with the lamp toward the door. One of the bottles slid down his pant leg causing him to stumble. The peg lamp fell into a loose pile of packing causing it to flame. "Damn!" he bellowed as he stomped on the fire. "I'd better be more careful. He checked the spot and was sure he snuffed out the fire. "I'd better go and get the hell out of here," he muttered as he made his way to the doorway in the near stygian darkness. He found the door and elbowed the door latch and cautiously eased his way out into the passageway; the door giving as with a twinge of pain as it creaked on its hinges. He gave the door a shove with his right foot to close it. He then moved out to return to his cabin and enjoy his new found bonanza.

The door did not close all the way allowing a draft of fresh air to enter into the locker from the passageway. It wafted its way around and about and settled itself into the excelsior where at its base were small glowing embers which were not stomped out. The embers glowed and grew as additional fresh air fed the now expanding burning of the highly inflammable long, fine pine shavings. In only moments the packing flared into full flame and spread its searching fingers to seek new tinder.

CHAPTER TWO

The Griffith

"Take her to four-seven degrees, Mr. Evans."

"Aye, Captain. Four-seven degrees, wheelsman."

"Four-seven degrees it is, sir," Richard Mann acknowledged with the turning of the helm to the right into a slow turn putting the steamer into an easterly course. The steamer, wallowing in a broad swell for a few moments then steadying with a thrust of power from its two side paddle wheels, the G.P. Griffith, with a foaming parting of bow waves, headed on another leg of its passage northeast on Lake Erie from its last stop in Cleveland, Ohio to its next port of call, Erie, and then to its final destination, Buffalo, New York.

Captain Charles Roby nodded to Bill Evans, his first mate, and proceeded down the stairway to the starboard of the pilothouse to the saloon deck where he was greeted by his daughter, Candace.

"Good morning, Daddy," she called to him as she half turned from where she had been watching two deck hands coiling lines and securing quarters from which they had just recently left the Stockley Docks at the foot of Columbus Road hill in the Flats of Cleveland. She took her father's extended right hand and the two turned to look back at the receding Cleveland shoreline.

Captain Roby was a tall, thin faced man in his late thirties, with a shock of thick black hair, sideburns and deep blue eyes.

His skin too was dark. His thirteen-year-old daughter was also dark, with brunette hair falling in ringlets about her shoulders. She was tall for her age but still as a young girl who was into the beginning of young womanhood. Her sailor-like blouse was white trimmed with black piping, and she wore a black skirt and black patent leather pumps. Her attire had been especially made for her first long trip to complement her father's uniform as captain: black coat and pants, black shoes and a white shirt.

The Cleveland shoreline, now about two miles to the south and west of the Griffith, was bathed in midmorning sunlight with the sky a cloudless expanse of azure blue. Two parallel wakes of the side-mounted paddle wheels spread out in the black-blue waters in almost straight lines back to the lighthouse at the mouth of the Cuyahoga River from which the turn had been recently made for the steamer's movement eastward along with a warm following southwesterly breeze. The lake waters were calm with an occasional swell from the northwest attesting to yesterday's storm that had blown in from Canada and caused the Cleveland layover of the Griffith to be extended.

"Daddy, that man." Candace pointed to a young man walking aft along the starboard rail, a frown on his bearded face. Captain Roby looked to his daughter's pointed direction.

"You mean deck hand Cooper, Jack Cooper. What about him?"

"He said to the other man that you were afraid to sail last night into the storm, and he's mad because he will be late in getting home to see his wife. He called her Amanda." Candace half whispered to her father so that the young man might not overhear her.

Captain Roby gave a quick smile. "The word he should have used was prudent, my dear. I was not afraid or scared or whatever. I was just being cautious, another word for prudent. It seems he wants to see his new bride in Buffalo. He was married in May and I am sure he would like to see her as often as he can. But the safety of the passengers and the boat as well as his

5

own well-being is my first responsibility. Especially now since I have my family aboard with me on our first long cruise this season," he added. "Are you enjoying yourself?"

"Oh yes, Daddy," she answered squeezing his strong hand in youthful exuberance. "Grandma and Mama were a little bit afraid that I might get seasick but I fooled them." She arched her shoulders with a giggle. "They are the ones who got seasick."

"Oh, my darling, I'll make a sailor out of you yet, you and your brother," he said with pride in his voice, giving her a loving look.

"Will Tom be a captain someday like you, Daddy?"

"Oh, honey, it's going to be a long time before Tom will be ready to be a captain. He's only seven months old." Her father smiled at the thought. "He will have to do a lot of growing up before he thinks of being a sailor or a captain or whatever."

"Maybe he'll be a president," she said with a quick smile. "Like President Taylor."

Her father gave a hearty laugh. "Well now, he would have to be of a different persuasion than President Taylor. The president is a Whig and I am a Democrat." He shook his head at the thought. His son a Whig. Oh no.

"Oh Daddy, I don't understand all about what you call...," she paused for the right word, "...politics."

"I know, I know, honey, politics are adult concerns and you shouldn't have to worry your pretty little head over such nonsense." He tousled her hair as they continued their way aft along the starboard passageway between the paddle wheel housing and the cabin's midship.

"Good morning, Captain."

"Good morning, Miss Hood," the Captain answered a cabin maid who was exiting a cabin carrying a basket of soiled linens.

"Good morning, Miss Roby." The maid, a girl in her late teens or early twenties greeted Candace with a nod of her bonneted blonde hair.

Candace smiled a return greeting to the maid and stepped aside to let her pass with her load. "She's pretty," she whispered to her father as they descended the stairwell from the saloon deck to the main deck and proceeded to the Captain's cabin.

"Good morning, Mother," the Captain called cheerfully to his mother who was attending to the needs of his infant son in a bassinet set in the corner of the cabin. "Did you sleep well?"

"Oh yes, Charles. This is a beautiful boat and the accommodations are just grand. Candace and I are very comfortable, thank you." The Captain's mother, Ada, an attractive woman in her middle to late fifties bent over the bassinet and continued with the needs of her grandson who was in the process of being diapered.

The Captain then crossed the cabin to his wife, Emily, who was preparing to nurse the baby. "How are you feeling, my darling?" he asked solicitously.

Emily Roby smiled a weak smile. "As well as can be expected I suppose." Captain Roby's wife of fifteen years was a most gracious lady with a sensual mouth and hazel eyes. Her hair was parted in the middle and drawn behind in a bun.

"You know I am very sorry, dear," he said gently, concerned as to her having been seasick along with his mother on what was to have been a pleasant and relaxing adventure for her, the children and his mother.

"I know, dear. It's beyond our control what the weather will be like from day to day, but I do hope that the bad weather is past and that we will really enjoy ourselves in Buffalo. I am looking forward to seeing Hazel Tiffany and her baby."

"As well as I seeing Albert," Charles answered, helping to adjust for the needs of the baby Thomas.

"Candace, dear," her grandmother said softly, "let's you and I take a turn about the deck. We haven't really had the time before and it seems to be a nice day for a stroll while your mother is busy with Tom."

"And I'll join you, Mother," Charles added, knowing that Emily would rather nurse the baby alone than have an audience.

Candace quickly gave her mother a kiss on an offered left cheek and touched the baby with a light tap of affection.

"On your way the three of you," Emily, smiling, nodded her head toward the open cabin door.

* * *

A warm following west breeze was invigorating as the three moved forward on the main deck to enjoy the warm summer morning.

"Captain. Captain Roby," a short, stout man in his early-to-mid-forties called to Charles, who turned to his name being called.

"Good morning, David," he acknowledged his chief engineer.

"Good morning, Charles, and to you too Ada and Candace." He touched the brim of his cap and nodded his head to them.

"Good morning, Mr. Stebbins." Candace smiled and gave a brief curtsy.

"Good morning, David," Ada Roby greeted him cheerfully.

"I am sorry to interrupt you like this, Charles. I was just below and Max asked me to have you come to see the shaft..."

"The same old problem?" Captain Roby, now back in command of his boat and not like a paying passenger, enjoying the whole scene, nodded, his face with a small frown.

"Yes, sir," the chief engineer again the chief engineer. "It's now requiring almost a full-time man just to keep adding the oil. I'll be glad when we get to Buffalo and get the new grade oil that I sure as hell..."

"Excuse me," Ada interjected, "Candace and I will continue our walk. You two can work out whatever problems you have. Come dear, we'll find Mr. Chitchester and see if he can't find you a treat."

8

Nodding adieu to the two men, she and her granddaughter left to seek the headwaiter.

"She doesn't like me to keep bringing up the problem with the shaft but the bearing has to be almost constantly oiled or it will burn out for sure, and there are no works to do anything on short notice in Buffalo. I have Max and both Ed and Howard on top of it working alternate watches."

"Good. But I am sure we'll be alright until we get back to Maumee next week," the Captain replied, he as concerned as his chief engineer about the bearing but more understanding of his brother-in-law's demands for profit. "We'll just have to keep after Bill to have it replaced."

"Aye, but with him and his demands for profit, he might just talk us out of it again," the chief engineer said, shaking his head.

David Stebbins was forty-three years old, a widower with no children. He was of short to medium height, a sturdy build with red hair and a somber air about him. His main concern in life it seems was the G.P. Griffith.

It was for him a labor of love, as he had designed the steamer and supervised its construction in the W.T. Harris Boat Works in Maumee City, Ohio. The owners, of which he was one and had one-eighth interest, were businessmen of the area, but William V. Studdiford, of Monroe, Michigan and Captain Roby's brother-in-law, owned controlling stock and called the shots as to the Griffith's enterprises.

"You build 'er, David. You sail 'er, Charles, and I'll see that we all make money," he had once told them laughing, but meaning every word. "And we don't make money sitting in repair yards," he added.

"Are you sure that this new lubricant can do the job, David?" Charles asked quizzically.

"Oh, yes. No doubt about it," David replied with enthusiasm. "The whale sperm oil . . . we have been using doesn't have the mobility, the consistency of the bituminous coal oils that have been developed in England by a James Young. These new coal oil lubricants will last much longer than whale oil. It's been proven and I want to see how they work on the Griffith."

"And I am with you," Charles agreed. "I'll be below shortly," he added, as he raised his right hand in a short salute to his ship's clerk who was approaching them.

"Yes, sir," David said departing.

"Good morning, Captain," the clerk greeted pleasantly.

"Good morning, Mr. Wilkinson," the Captain responded, as he glanced about the deck and took in his domain, the G.P. Griffith. The steamer named for a well-to-do businessman in Toledo, was of wooden hull, one hundred ninety-three feet long by twenty-eight feet wide, a draft of eleven feet and displacing five hundred eighty-seven tons.

Its appointments were modest but well designed and attractive. The hull was of Michigan lumber cut from William Studdiford's own reserves in southern Michigan. The hull was painted a dark brown with the upperworks white with red trim as were the two thirty-one-foot side paddle wheels. The two smokestacks were painted a brilliant black, standing out in contrast.

A beautiful steamer. One of the newer models developed through the genius of men the likes of David Stebbins. Ah David, a shame he has no head for business. He could own his own boat works and build and sell rather than design and build for others.

Charles was proud of this steamer. Proud to command. Not like the Indiana which had sunk after hitting a snag in Maumee Bay three years earlier. The Indiana was a scow compared to the Griffith. Good riddance. This is a Steamer. A steamer capable of carrying much more freight than the Indiana, such as lumber, grains, barrel stoves, cured beef and pork and wines from the lower lake ports of Toledo, Sandusky, Cleveland, Fairport and Erie Canal to New York, Boston and the world.

But it was in Buffalo that the Griffith paid for its keep. The immigrants who were swarming into the United States, especially New York and Boston, were in turn heading for the American mid-west of Ohio, Michigan, Indiana and Wisconsin. Some even to the gold fields of California. The Griffith had accommodations for forty-eight first-class passengers, a crew of twenty-six and deck space for two hundred thirteen immigrant passengers who would bed down on deck with a minimum of cover and other needs for the short day or two for the run down the lake. Its hold carried stores for the mid-west, primarily ports in northern Ohio and southern Michigan. But the final line for profit was the immigrant trade that could and did provide for the bulk of the Griffith's revenue and profits.

"Sir."

"Oh. Oh, yes, I'm sorry, Henry. I guess I was carried away for a moment." The Captain answered almost apologetically for seeming to ignore his clerk.

"Yes, sir. I understand," Henry Wilkinson allowed himself a thin grin, as he as well as others had noticed, the Captain's love for his steamer and how he would, on occasion, seem to be miles away from reality, playing with his imagination.

"What can I do for you, Henry?" The Captain smiled to his clerk as he turned to the starboard rail and faced south to the distant shoreline, which he guessed should be about in line with Willoughby, Ohio.

"The wine, sir. The wine we took aboard in Sandusky."

"Yes?" The Captain, back to reality, questioned mildly.

"I'm not sure, sir, but..."

"Well?"

"It seems, sir, that after it was brought aboard... that a few bottles were found broken in a case..."

"How?"

"Possibly rough handling by the winery people. They loaded the cases. As it is John thought..."

"John?"

"Our new barkeeper, sir, John Paulding. He came aboard in Toledo."

"Oh. Yes. Continue."

"John thought that they smelled... funny, at least one of the bottles that he checked."

The Captain turned to his clerk, a frown on his face. "And?"

"Yes, sir, it is as he thought the wine smelled funny so he asked my permission to tap another unbroken bottle."

"And?"

"I did and he said it tasted like... er... piss."

"Piss?"

"Yes, sir. It was spoiled before it was ever brought aboard in Sandusky."

Captain Roby rubbed his chin and glared at his clerk. "Tasted how?"

"Well, sir, I meant it tasted bad."

"Oh! Yes. I know what you meant."

"As it is, sir, we have thirty-five cases of this same wine. I don't know if each bottle is spoiled or..."

"Sabotage!"

"Sabotage?"

"Yes, Henry. As you know we have been carrying Glenn's wines these past two years and this year we are taking Avery's. It's a matter of business. My God, Henry! You know. I don't have to tell you."

"I know, sir," a peevish Henry answered. "But I was not in on the purchasing or transferring your marketing to another vendor. I came aboard only this past March."

"Yes. Yes," an exasperated Captain growled. "But James Glenn was quite upset with us last fall when we told him we would be buying Avery's wines instead of his. My brother-in-law said at the time, 'Look at the profits. We'll make more from shipping with Avery than Glenn.' It was as simple as that. Profits. His world revolves around profits."

"I. . . I don't know, sir..." the astonished clerk stammered.

"I know. Damn it, I know!" The Captain turned and with long strides headed for the pilothouse.

"How was your stay in Cleveland? Did you see George?"
Christine Hood wiped her brow with her left hand. "No, I
didn't see him. His sister said he had taken a barge to Akron
and was to bring back some horses. She didn't know when he
would be back."
"Aw, maybe you'll see him when we come back next week."
Marie Walrath, a big bosomed woman in her late twenties, smiled
as she fluffed a pillow and placed it on the bed she was making
with her fellow cabin maid.
"I hope so," Christine answered with a shrug.
"You say you haven't told him?"
"No, I've never told him. I really haven't seen him since I
found out."
"Is it his? Is he the father?"
"Oh yes. Yes."
"Did you tell his sister?"
"No, I want him to know first."
"Well, you'll have to be telling him soon for you're begin-
ning to show."
"Oh, I know but I hope not. Not so soon. I need the work so
badly. Mr. Dana would be furious, and I know he would fire
me."
"Oh, don't worry about Larry Dana. He seems tough. You
just have to know how to please him."
"Please him? How?"
"Oh, my God," Marie chuckled, tucking in a bed sheet.
"You're laughing at me," Christine said petulantly.
"Oh no. Just surprised. You didn't know Gail Arnett? No,
I guess not. She left us at the end of last season. Well, she sure
knew how to please Larry. So much so that it was the talk of
the boat. In Buffalo, when we would stay over for a few days
and we got a few days off, my Ollie and me would go to his
cousins in Landcaster but Larry and Gail... well, they would

13

just disappear, returning when we were ready to steam as if nothing ever happened."

"The Captain. What did he say?" Christine asked, surprised that he would allow such openness of the two.

"Ollie said he heard the Captain telling Mr. Stebbins that they could do anything they wanted to do ashore but not on the steamer. Now then," she continued gathering her things, "let's get on to the next cabin."

* * *

"We won't be needing only but eleven settings. Mr. Lovelace and his companion are staying in their cabin. He's not feeling well." First Porter Lawrence Dana informed his two assistants, John Paulding and William Tillman, as they prepared for the noon lunch of the first class passengers.

"Did you see how poorly he looked when he came aboard?" William asked, as he placed silverware on the table set in an open space aft of the pilothouse on the hurricane deck.

"Yes, like death warmed over, he did," answered John Paulding, at thirty-three, blond of medium build, an otherwise handsome rogue whose looks were marred by a gaping hole where two top front teeth were supposed to be. Puffy red lips and a tenderness about his left eye attested to the fact that he had recently, the last night in fact, been on the losing end of a fight in a bar on Irish Town Bend in the Flats.

"Mr. Dana says he's going back to England to die," William added, as he wiped a water goblet with a cloth and studied the sun's reflection in its etched prisms. William Tillman was twenty-eight, another young rogue who was in his second season as a bartender on the Griffith. Tall and gangly with a peculiar walk. He had originally come from Philadelphia by way of Wheeling, Virginia where he had worked in the coal mines but soon realized that his mother didn't raise a fool. Ha! He laughed at that as he had never known his mother but he liked the expression

14

and would use it whenever he could.

"What do ye think he has in them trunks?" he asked Lawrence Dana who was placing name tags to the seating places at the table.

Lawrence Dana, forty-five years young with curly auburn hair and a build of body to do a younger man justice, shrugged his shoulders. "Who knows? Who cares? All I know is that he wants to go back to England and die."

"And he has no family but the boy," William continued, pressing for information on the poor skeleton of a man who had arrived on board the night before accompanied by a boy of about fourteen or fifteen and four huge sailing trunks.

"And who is the young lad," John added, "his grandson? The old man is bent and gray but the boy is tall and he looks like an Indian..."

The discussion was interrupted by the appearance of Ada Roby and her granddaughter. "Is Mr. Chitchester about?" she asked of Lawrence.

"He's in the galley with the cooks preparing the lunch. Can I help you?"

"Oh, it's nothing. How soon will we be eating, Mr. Dana?"

"Oh, not for another while, Mrs. Roby. Not until eleven. Can I get you something? A snack for you, Miss Candace?" Lawrence Dana exuded charm for his captain's mother and daughter.

"Oh, I think we can wait," Ada said pleasantly. "Unless you would like a snack?" she asked Candace who was looking with interest at two men below on the main deck who had come from the engine room to get some fresh air and the rays of the sun. Their bodies were sooted and sweat made rivulets down their backs. The two men leaned on the railing taking in the fresh air and relaxing from their chores as firemen who stoked the boiler with firewood.

* * *

15

George Jefferson lit his brier pipe and blew a cloud of smoke from the side of his mouth as he threw his spent loco-foco into the wash of the bow waves cascading passed.

"Did you see Paulding when he came aboard last night?" he asked of his workmate, Hiram Faulks.

"Aye, I did, and a sad sort he was. He was spitting blood and puking at the same time."

"When will some of these young buckos learn they cannot take on the world of Fancy Dans who know a hell of a lot more of this world than they do," George continued. At thirty-six, he wasn't that much older than John Paulding, but he figured he had learned a long time ago that drinking, fighting and whoring could and did put many a young man in an early grave. To be thirty-seven on June 17, George was of moderate build, lean but strong as was required of him as a fireman. His dark hair was curly and his complexion fair. Except that he had no left ear, he could pass for almost any laboring man working the docks of Toledo, Sandusky or Cleveland during the hustling spring, summer and early fall of the shipping season of the lake haulers.

"Eh. Let 'em knock their sorry brains out! And for what?" Hiram replied as he cramped baccy into his brier pipe, then touching his loco-foco match to the bowl. He took a few short sucks and then exhaled a cloud of smoke into the wind as he cast his match into the rolling waters of the bow wave.

"I heered he was after a wench and met up with her boyfriend, and he a married man," George continued.

Hiram spat a black mouthful of phlegm into the lake being careful not to get it back in a returning wind. "Ah. I've seen them afor. Married men with pregnant wives and children and they on their own in the big city. It 'appens every time."

"Oh ho! And what about you?" George laughed as he leaned and spat over the rail, ducking as his sputum was caught in a tendril of wind and was cast above him to an upper deck. "You'v a pregnant wife and have three littlens; haven't you ever tried to show your mettle?"

"Aye. Oncet I did when I was twenty-two and it was in Sandusky on my first trip on the old Mac Gowan. An Indian girl, she was. It only took me one beating by the whore's pimp to never try it again," Hiram replied, as he wiped his neck and shoulders with a towel, blackening it from the grime on his body. "And what about you? And how did you loose your ear?"

"Oh, no! I'v niver tried. I can wait a week or more and as for my ear, it was chewed at by a rat when I was but a babe. It had to be cut off by my granny cause it was a-festering."

"Oh, my God! A rat!" Hiram shrugged his shoulders in revulsion.

"Ah, I was, as I said, only a babe. A few months old and remember nothing of it." George leaned over the rail and again sent a streak, this time downwind as best he could determine.

"Hey men. Hey George… Hiram."

The two turned at the approach of the chief engineer, who was calling to them. "I will be needing help of the two of you to stand an extra watch for a few hours each day until we return to Toledo."

The two looked at each other, both knowing of their favorite officer's concern for the drive shaft which needed almost constant attention in being oiled.

"Edward and Howie as well as Maxim are putting in extra time to help, but I need to relieve them. I have talked with Captain Roby and he said to assign you the extra time, but I wanted to talk to you first."

"We're putting in our twelve on and twelve off as it is, Mr. Stebbins. How much extra time do you want us to put in?" George asked, concerned with the possibility of the shaft's bearing burning out with no means of replacing it until returning to Toledo in another few days.

"Only to replace Howie and Ed when they go to eat," the chief engineer replied, pleased with the men's understanding of his need for all the help he could get.

"And what about Hugh and Karl on their watches?" Hiram added.

"They will share the time to keep on top of the oiling. Just as you two are helping," a frustrated chief engineer explained.

The two looked at each other, both knowing of the worry and fretting that the chief engineer had about his boat and now this problem with the bearing. They knew he had wanted it replaced after the last trip but that the cheapskate owner, William Studdiford, and his wanting as much profit as he could from still one more trip, had talked the Captain and Mr. Stebbins into another trip.

"We will do what we can, Mr. Stebbins," George said, knocking his pipe on the railing, the ashes flying with the wind. "But we do hope that the Captain and Mr. Studdiford will take the time and spend some money to fix the damn bearing and a few other things that need tending to on board," he said cramming his pipe into his right rear pocket. "We know that you have ordered a new kind of oil. Bitu… Bitum…"

"Bituminous oil. Really coal oil. Made from coal by an Englishman. It is really a tremendous step in engineering," the chief engineer added, sensing that the crew, at least the firemen, were aware of his problems and too felt his concerns.

The two of them then took deep gasps of fresh air and returned to their positions in the boiler room as David Stebbins put his right hand to a stubbled chin and looked to the Ohio shoreline from what he knew was at least three miles to the south and as best he could determine, was offshore of Willoughby.

* * *

"Why is Daddy so angry? He looked so mad talking with Mr. Wilkinson," Candace asked of her grandmother as the two seated themselves at the buffet table for lunch.

"I don't know, dear. He does seem to be upset about something. I suppose that being a captain of a boat he has to worry

18

about many things. It is part of his duties," Ada answered, as she surveyed the display of goods prepared by the cooks.

"Was it what Mr. Stebbins said about the oil?..." Candace wondered as she too took in the offerings.

"Oh, I don't think so. Mr. Stebbins is a cautious man and sometimes imagines things as more terrible than they really are. If it was the oil, I am sure your father and Uncle Billy will look into the problem when we return to Toledo."

"Ah, Mrs. Roby and Miss Candace," a beaming headwaiter greeted them, "did you have a nice stroll about the deck? It has turned out to be a beautiful morning and it looks like the rest of the day will be just fine as well." John Chitchester, at age forty, was a pleasant smiling type who seemed well suited as a waiter. Eager to please and enjoying his livelihood. He was of slight build, somewhat effeminate with thick curly black hair beginning now to recede. "Our cooks have gone to great pains to make your lunch fit for a queen and her princess."

"Oh, Mr. Chitchester, how you do carry on." Ada Roby laughed as she spread a linen napkin on her lap and helped Candace snug hers.

"As you can see, we have fresh strawberries and cherries. The cherries are from a first picking from a new orchard just south of Cleveland."

"Oh, Grandma," Candace said excitedly. "They have peppermint cake patties . . . and peanut brittle."

"Yes," the headwaiter said, as he nodded to two other passengers who were seating themselves at their place setting. "Our cooks, Mr. and Mrs. Gantry, are quite expert at little tidbits that make a lunch even better. They prepared these special treats on our stopover in Cleveland just for the two of you. I am sure you will enjoy them as well as our main lunch."

"Oh, I know I will," Candace replied as she helped herself to two peppermint cake patties. "I'll take these to Mother and Thomas."

"Oh, Thomas cannot eat peppermint cakes at his age,"

19

Ada laughed and elbowed her granddaughter in a kidding rebuke.

"I know. But I'll be able to eat them myself for my dessert." Candace giggled in reply to her grandmother's teasing.

* * *

First Mate William Evans, from his position behind the wheelsman and to his right in the pilothouse scanned the grape-blue waters ahead as the steamer Griffith steamed under a clear sky with the sun glistening on its resplendently colored super-structure. "There is smoke to the north," he said to the wheelsman, Richard Mann. "It is well out of our way so you can still hold your heading."

"Aye," the wheelsman acknowledged, checking his heading then quickly looking ahead and to his left finding a smudge of smoke on the horizon. About five miles, he thought. Safe enough.

The first mate moved to his right in the pilothouse and looked down on the forward deck and bow as the steamer moved serenely through the calm waters. A few passengers were strolling about and enjoying the sunshine and warm air. He looked to his pocket watch and checked it with the chronometer on the rear bulk-head. They agreed. He then went to the map table and noted the other steamers sighting in the log. While the weather was mild and promised to be better as the day progressed, the first mate wore a heavy knit sweater that gathered about his waist in a bulge of cloth. He turned his back to the wheelsman and deftly extracted a pint bottle of whisky from the folds. He took a glance at the wheelsman and then took a quick nip. Ah, good. He thought. Only another few hours and I'll be really ready to enjoy a drink and not on the sly.

Richard Mann, while his attention was directed to his respon-sibility of steering the Griffith, was also aware of the first mate's penchant for the bottle as was most of the crew, but it doesn't seem to affect his duties. He seems to be always in control.

20

The young wheelsman at twenty-two had only been a wheelsman since this past spring, this being his first full season having served as an apprentice two years prior. He was blond, tall and muscular as his Teutonic ancestry would have him. And already bronzed tan in late spring.

"Mr. Evans," the Captain's voice commanded as he entered the pilothouse startling both the first mate and the wheelsman.

"Sir," the first mate answered taken aback by the Captain's tone and sudden appearance. He thought he was about to have lunch with his family.

"You was aboard when we took on the shipment of wine in Sandusky?" the Captain asked.

"Aye. Yes, sir. I was." He wondered, What's up? The Captain usually doesn't get himself worked up like he seems to be now.

"I have just been told by Mr. Wilkinson that a number of cases had been broken and that upon examination of their contents, proved to be spoiled. Do you remember who was in charge of the handling of the shipment?"

Why is he asking me this? the first mate pondered. I am not responsible for the cargo. Henry is.

"Mr. Wilkinson."

"No. I mean from the winery."

"I don't know, sir. The shipment wasn't from Glenn's. I know Horace Ackerman; he's one of my cousins. A distant cousin. But..."

"I am not interested with your family relationships. I want to know who was responsible for the delivery of sabotaged wine."

"Sabotaged?"

"Yes. Sabotaged. The wine was evidently spoiled or adulterated so that when we took it aboard and then to Buffalo and sold it for transshipment east it would not be for weeks or months until an unknowing buyer would end up with a bottle of piss."

"Piss?"

"Never mind. I will take this up with Glenn's when we return to Sandusky. I'll even make a special stop."

21

"Er. Yes sir." The first mate nodded, not knowing of the events or why the anger of the Captain. But he did know that Henry Wilkinson could be in for some trouble by allowing the wine to be brought aboard and not finding out about the problem until after being underway.

"What is our heading?" the Captain asked. His anger now somewhat subsided as he returned to his role as a captain of a steamer not an antagonized businessman.

"Wheelsman?" the first mate asked.

"Still at four-seven, sir."

Captain Roby searched the now whitecapping waves from the northwest caused by a sudden wind shift. "The wind has shifted more to the northwest. Compensate for it, Mr. Evans."

"Aye, sir."

"I am going below. Keep an eye on the glass. The sky is darkening to the west. We may be in for some rough weather. Let me know, Mr. Evans."

* * *

"Now David. What do you have to show me?" Captain Roby asked almost shouting to be heard over the din of the pulsating steam engine, as he entered the boiler room where his first engineer and an oiler, Eddy Thatcher, were examining the underside of the waterjacket that girthed the base of the two smokestacks that extended up through the overhead.

"We're just checking to see how the jacket is holding. It is working well. The space between the stacks and the jackets is right, and we should have no further cause for worry on that count anymore," the chief engineer said, pleased as he backed off to let his captain observe his handiwork of which he was most proud.

"Aye, sir," Eddy agreed, leaning to the Captain's right ear. "You have really got a safe steamer here, sir . . . Mr. Stebbins can be really proud of his coming up with this idea." Captain

22

Roby bent his head and nodded. "I sailed on the Erie before she caught fire in 'thirty-eight, and I know that if she had them there waterjackets, then the fire on the Erie might never have started," Eddy added assuringly.

"Yes, I know, Mr. Thatcher. David has good reason to be concerned about his engines and the boat's safety. I am sure we will not have any undue worries." He gestured with his hand to the direction of the rear of the engine. "Show me the shaft, David," he said as they moved cautiously around two firemen who were feeding small lengths of wood into the boiler, the only illumination being the glare from the open fire box. They then rose up a steep ladder to a small walkway that sided the upper part of the engine. Here the light was gained by a small sperm oil lantern which cast its flickering, smoke-filled rays on a grimy, small featured individual who was in the process of adding sperm oil into a receptacle.

"I'm here to take over for a while, Howie," Eddy yelled over the clanging and hissing of the engine. The oiler, Howie Crown, nodded to him and also the Captain and the chief engineer, who crowded along side of him to see down the length of the turning shaft that led to a junction box where it joined the axle of the driving paddle wheels.

"How often do you have to fill the receptacle?" the Captain asked. The stench of the wood smoke with the acrid addition of the sperm oil almost nauseating him.

"About every ten or so minutes. Whenever I think it needs it." He shrugged his thin shoulders. "When it starts getting hot." He stepped aside and gladly accepted Eddy taking over his duties.

"You are sure that the bituminous oil will do a better job?" the Captain asked as they returned through the semidarkness of the engine room to the fresh air of the main deck being swept by a refreshing breeze from the west.

"Oh, yes," the chief engineer replied, wiping a sweaty fore-head with the back of his right hand. "All we will need are some new fittings. The sperm is thicker than the bituminous. Otherwise, it should do the job and better. Of course, we will need new bushings, but in the long run it is the lubrication that must be maintained."

"All right, David," the Captain agreed as they entered onto the main deck and its refreshing breeze and sunshine. "I'll make sure that Billy understands our needs. Give the men my compliments. I can see that it is a rough and dirty job to maintain the shaft. You have my thanks."

* * *

"You wanted to see me, sir?"

"Yes. I did. Come in."

Christine Hall entered the walk-in linen room where she had been told by her fellow cabin maid, Marie Walrath, that Mr. Dana wanted to see her.

"How are you feeling?" he asked, as he folded napkins on a small table before him.

"Fine," she answered, wondering why his sudden concern for her health.

He looked at her quizzically. "You're from...?"

"Cleveland... Forest City... the west side of the river."

"Oh, I thought you were from Sandusky."

"I was born there. I have lived in Forest City the past five years."

"Oh," he said touching his right index finger to the spectacles firming them to the bridge of his nose. "I really don't know too much about you. Are you married?"

"No."

"You should be."

"Why?"

"You are a comely young lady. I have noticed that about you. Most girls your age... er ..."

"Nineteen."

"Nineteen. Yes. Most girls your age are already married and have a child or two."

"I am engaged."

"Oh. And the young man?"

"George Tracy." Why this questioning? she wondered. It was none of his business. It was Mr. Wilkinson who hired me. He knows all about me. Why is Mr. Dana so asking?

"Where is your fiancé?"

"Mr. Dana, I am not at all sure what it is that you want to see me about. Is it my work? Am I doing what you expect?"

"Oh, your work is fine. You do a fine job," he said testily. "But I am not too sure if you will be able to do as you should as to the rest of the season. We need sure footed girls who can roll with the ship and not stumble and fall and hurt their unborn babies."

"Ah!" she gasped. "Mr. Dana, I… "

"I know. It's a secret," he said shrugging his shoulders as if in dismissal. "Marie told me about you and knows you need the work. Well so do I. If I thought you would not be able to continue, I would ask to have you discharged in Buffalo. But I do know that you can be a good, safe worker and I will not say anything to the Captain or Mr. Wilkinson."

"Sir." Christine bowed her head as tears saddened her eyes. Her heart beating a tattoo in her chest.

"Christine?" he asked, his manner softened.

"Sir," her voice almost inaudible.

"It's all right. Just do your best with Marie and maybe when we get to Buffalo, I can show you the sights. It really is a splendid city with a lot to offer a Forest City girl like yourself. Maybe we can get your George a souvenir."

The recollection of Marie's telling her of the girl. Gail? Yes, Gail. Why? What is he doing to me? She asked herself. She looked at him with a sense of fear and the unknown.

"Well?" he said with a slight cough, after a few moments of excruciating silence, as she stood before him as a repentant for

25

her sins. "We can talk about this at another time. I am sure you must get back to your duties. I will keep your little secret and you can keep your position." He paused. "We'll see how things turn out in Buffalo."

It was mid-afternoon as she left the linen room slowly and desolate. The sky to the west had been turned to a bank of slate-gray clouds that moved toward the east at a rapid pace while to the east the sky was still under a golden sun soon to be drenched by an early summer storm. "Oh, my God!" she said wearily. "Oh, my God!" She leaned against the handrail and looked out across the lake, a darkening gathering of clouds, only to see the tears in her eyes. What have I done?

* * *

"Hold her at four-seven degrees, wheelsman," the first mate called from the open pilothouse hatchway as he looked to the northwest. "A squall line is forming and we will be in for it soon. It looks like a small one but it can get rough."

"Aye, sir," the wheelsman replied turning the helm slightly to bring the Griffith back to its assigned course from which it had drifted.

"How does it look?" the Captain called above the rising wind as he ascended the stairway, two steps at a time, from the hurricane deck to the pilothouse.

"It will be a bit of a blow," the first mate answered, turning to the Captain as he entered the pilothouse.

"I saw it building up and thought I should be on the bridge when it hit. I am worried about shoals and sand bars this close in with heavy weather."

"Aye, sir," the mate agreed as he looked south to the shoreline about three miles distant. The heights of the shore showed greencapped in bright sunlight as they faced the approaching storm.

"Out here in the deeper water, I have no fear but it is offshore that we have many unmarked or transient obstructions. Beat as best you can, Mr. Evans, for deeper water."

"Yes, sir. Helmsman, prepare to alter course."

To the northwest was a line of rapidly approaching slate-gray masses of clouds with driving rain in its forefront. The lake waters, relatively calm a few moments ago now rose suddenly from the windsheer and turned into thick froth which beat against the now staggering hull of the Griffith. Heavy rain drops driven slantwise clattered against the windows of the pilothouse and washed against the steamer's superstructure, which gushed waters from flooded scuppers.

"Take her out deeper," the Captain barked to the wheelsman who was now fighting the helm as the winds of the storm were forcing the steamer in a sluggish fight for control of steerage way.

For what seemed to be many anxious minutes, the sudden summer storm, entrapped the Griffith and her human cargo in a stygian darkness mixed with flashes of green lightening and shrieking winds. The rain fell heavily on a now calmer lake as the cutting edge of the storm passed on to the east and south along the Ohio shoreline where now crashing waves were beating along the stony shores and unprepared dockages of the coastal villages.

Almost as suddenly as the storm arose, it ended. The wind subsided to almost none at all and a quietus calm settled over the waterway and the Griffith, as a hot-orange sun in a cloudless western sky, glared down on its glistening wetness.

"I will never get used to the sudden tantrums of this lake," the Captain stated as he opened the pilothouse hatch door to allow feted air, cooped up inside during the storm, to escape only to be met by hot, smothering humid air from without.

"I hear tell and have read," the mate said as he watched the wheelsman bring the steamer back to the original course. "Well done, wheelsman," he commented to a now relieved and smiling

Richard Mann. "I hear," he continued, "that of all the five lakes, it is Lake Erie that has most of these quick storms."

Captain Roby, stood alongside the wheelsman and checked the heading. "Two points port," he directed. "Yes. It will be a great day when we can understand more of this lake and the others and react to their wiles."

"Captain Roby! Captain!" a voice called from below on the saloon deck at the base of the stairway to the pilothouse.

"Yes?" the Captain answered and looking down saw a deck hand, he remembered as deck hand Cooper, standing at the base of the stairway.

"Sir," he called cupping his hands to his mouth. "Mr. Wilkinson would like to see you, sir. He says it's urgent. He is in Mr. Lovelace's cabin. Number eight, sir."

* * *

"Oh, Grandmother, I was so afraid during the storm," Candace said as she pumped the handle of the toilet in their cabin.

"You were very good. You are a good little sailor," her grandmother assured her, as she adjusted her bonnet and brushed aside a gray hair. "Your daddy can be proud of you. And even little Tom took it as a good little sailor."

Candace's eyes smiled at her grandmother. "He slept all through it," she laughed. "He will make a good sailor. Even a captain like Father." She paused and reflected a moment. "Mother was terribly worried and fretted so over him."

The two left their cabin and walked to where Emily and Tom were seated in the shade of a tarpaulin stretched between the two smokestacks to provide cover in the now intense heat of the late afternoon sun shining on the dazzling, silvery sparkling now calm waters.

"Can I get you something, Emily?" her mother-in-law asked gently to a nodding mother.

"Oh!" she started. "No, thank you. I'm sorry I just sort of

closed my eyes. I didn't hear you coming." She yawned with a weak smile. "I'm afraid that the storm took something out of me." "I know, dear," her mother-in-law reassured her. "We have had a few days of bad weather since leaving Toledo, but this is early summer and we may still have many weeks of fine sailing weather ahead. Months maybe."

Candace studied her mother. "Are you sure, Mother, that you don't want something, a glass of water or a snack?"

"No, dear. Thank you anyhow. You may want to get me a wet washcloth for Tom. His poor little face is red from the heat. It will help him cool off."

Candace rose and headed for her mother's cabin, the Captain's cabin. Other passengers as well as the couple who had sat at their table for lunch and the Indian boy were seated in deck chairs along the starboard rail just forward of the paddle wheel sponson where it was quieter because they found the noise from the paddle wheels turning in the water was lessened by the forward movement of the steamer allowing the noise to trail behind. She noticed and wondered why the Indian boy was sitting with his head between his hands, elbows resting on his knees and looking out over the railing to the distant horizon to the south.

* * *

"What do you think?"

"Old age certainly. Look at his hands, his hair. Ancient." Captain Roby sighed as he arose from the bedside after examining the body of Alexander Lovelace.

"How long has he been dead?" wondered the clerk.

"The boy said he went right to his bed when they came aboard. I would say he probably died shortly after," the Captain offered with a frown on his face. "This young boy, he isn't related to the old man, like a grandson, I mean?"

"No. He says he was a companion and that he lived with the

29

old man, and that he, the old man, was taking him to England to put him in school. To a place called Eton."

"Eton?"

"That is what he said."

"Well, it takes all kinds, Mr. Wilkinson," the Captain sagely advised as he pulled the bed sheet over the deceased apothecary's sunken eyes and bulging false teeth.

The clerk reached into a small black box and took out a brown stubby candle and inserted it into a blue porcelain plate-like bowl with a perforated cover. "The boy hardly speaks English and from what I know of the Indians from around here, he is not from Ohio. His features are so different. His skin is more yellow than red and his eyes are slanted."

"What's his name?"

"Mr. Lovelace called him Bear when he signed on, but on the manifest he is listed as Kuruk, Indian. No tribal designation."

"Oh, well. We will just have to put him ashore in Buffalo and let the Indian authorities take over. He's only a passenger to us."

"But what of the trunks? They must be holding something that has some value or why would he have spent so much time and money to take four large trunks as they are all the way to England?" the clerk queried.

"I really wouldn't know," the Captain shrugged. "Somewhere in his papers, I am sure there is a Will or some sort of disposition for his trunks and, yes, even for the care of the Indian. As I said, all we can do is report him to the Indian affairs office. I am sure they do not want an Indian loose in Buffalo, especially one who might not be a true native. They have enough trouble I understand with their own native Indians." The Captain looked about the cabin. He saw no papers or containers which might hold same. Two leather bound suitcases and a toilet kit, evidently the old man's, were at the foot of the bed.

"You might want to contact Albert Tiffany, our agent in Buffalo. Have you met him?"

"No, not yet but I have met Charles Lockwood, his partner."

"They will know what to do. This death is the first I have ever had as a captain. They can handle the legalities. We may have to return the trunks to Cleveland to his connections or family or put them in storage until something is determined to do with them."

A pondering clerk, nodded to his captain. "Yes, sir. I will do that."

"Also see that the death certificate says that he died of old age, not typhus or cholera or whatever. I don't want the Griffith to ever get a bad name," the Captain added as he looked about the cabin.

"Oh, no, sir. We don't want that." A now canny clerk formulating some of his own thoughts, nodded to his captain as they left the cabin, closing the door behind them leaving a covered incense candle to overcome the odor of already decaying flesh on a humid and hot late afternoon in mid-June.

"Our captain seems to have his hands full this trip," First Mate Evans said to his relief, Second Mate Sam McCoit, who with the wheelsman replacement for the evening watch, Robert Davis, entered the pilothouse.

"Oh? What's up?" he said as he checked the Griffith's bearing.

"Hold her at forty-five degrees," the first mate directed to the wheelsman.

"Aye," the wheelsman answered with a nod.

"Something about the wine, along with Stebbins worrying about the damn shaft. Henry must have found out something about spoiled wine."

"Oh, yeah. Johnny was just telling us about it at supper. He said Wilkinson was really ticked because the Captain blamed him for the screw up . . . "

"Aw, it wasn't his fault, but it might do him good to get some blame."

"Huh? Why?" the second mate asked quizzically, as he scanned the horizon round about for any shipping.

31

"Ah, he's a smart ass. It's only his second trip and he already knows all the answers. And the way he moons around with Marie while her husband, Oliver, is in a Buffalo hospital with a carbuncle on his ass as big as a house."

"So what? If he can make out with her, good for him. I'd like to be able to do it with her but my wife would have my hinder if she knew I had any such thinkings."

Wheelsman Mann, backed off from the helm as his replacement for the next watch took over and assumed the steering duties. Ach, he thought. Here we go again. Mr. Evans finding fault with everything. It's none of his business what Mr. Wilkinson does or whatever Marie does. It's only talk anyway. At nineteen, Richard Mann only knew of a few of the foibles that a man could get involved with and become entangled with a married woman. It was not yet within his range of knowledge or experience.

Richard Mann, as he was born and raised, had been brought from Cassel in Westphalia as an infant with his German immigrant parents and two older sisters. He did not remember or know too much of the passage across the Atlantic Ocean to Philadelphia from Breman, and his parents rarely spoke of the crossing. The family had moved to Ohio, to a village called Leipsic, in the western regions of the state. As a boy growing up, the harsh winters and sweltering summers soon diminished his interest in a farming future and at seventeen, with much anger and railing from his father, he left the farm and went to Maumee and eventually to Toledo, Ohio where he became a deck hand on various steamers in and out of the Port of Toledo. His alertness and attention to duty soon brought him to the attention of Captain Roby, then the captain of the Indiana, who brought him around as an apprentice wheelsman, when he took command of the Griffith. He exited from the pilothouse following the first mate, and the two proceeded to their respective quarters. Richard then to supper and later to his continued reading of Melville's, Typee. The first mate bypassed supper or any reading and took up with an Old Crow, aged in a cask.

* * *

"Who would have ever thought that after this afternoon's storm that the weather could be as beautiful as it is now?" Ada Roby, asked of her son, as the two stood at the taffrail on the saloon deck as the Griffith moved now through calm water, its two paddle wheels foaming the dark-blue waters with parallel wakes trailing behind to the west under a high sky aloft, filled with a fiery sunset.

"Yes. I know," her son acknowledged. "As I was saying to Bill Evans this afternoon just after the squall: the lake can really throw a tantrum one minute and the next be dead calm as if nothing had happened. It was luck that it was a small one. I hope it will be the last for a while. At least on this trip."

"Let's hope so. Emily is certainly not enjoying this trip as much as I or I am sure she would," the Captain's mother paused. "Has she said anything to you? Have you noticed anything about her?"

"Say anything to me?" the Captain asked looking to his mother with a questioning frown. "What do you mean? Oh, I know she hasn't been herself lately. She seems to be always tired and not at all her old self. It has been a long winter, and difficult for her with Tom being born during a blizzard and then with her mother dying in March. God rest her soul. I know, we all know, that she has had her problems, but we both hoped this trip, and maybe another later in the season, would bring back her spirits."

"Oh, Charles, let us hope so. She is just not the same Emily, our Emily. When we get back to Toledo…"

"Hello. May I join you?" David Stebbins asked as he joined the two as the setting sun, its rays now touching the western horizon with sparking glimmers, began its decent to signal the end of another day. The three stood silently watching a glory of God's creation manifest itself to their eternal wonderment.

"Well, David, one more night and we will be in Buffalo. I must congratulate you on your splendid steamer. It is a beautiful boat…" Ada Roby said with a smile as the threesome turned from the railing and began walking along the deck before turning in for the night.

The night lanterns were lit casting soft glows about the deck and cabin areas. Other couples and an individual or two were also taking in the pleasant summer evening.

"Yes," David answered. "I thank you for the compliment, and I must add how pleasant it has been having you aboard as well as Emily and Missy Candace and Master Thomas."

"That is nice of you, David. But now I must be saying good night to the two of you. I want to check with Emily and attend to Tom for the night," Ada said as she left them and entered the nearby captain's cabin.

"We should arrive off Buffalo Harbor Point tomorrow afternoon about four-thirty and be at dockside at five at the latest," the Captain reminded his engineer as he lit a cigaretto, now that he was out of the presence of a woman.

"Aye, I am anxious to see what that bituminous oil is like. I could get only six kegs, that is how much a demand there is for it," he said as he fanned the air of the cigaretto's smoke. "I also hope that the fittings are the right ones. The last order I had with Turner's was a mess and I had to have them send some of the order by railway to Toledo. Remember? And we who do shipping of goods ourselves."

"Remember! Ha. Oh, yes. Only too well. You were fit to be tied. But maybe they have learned a lesson with you."

"I certainly hope so."

"I'll take my leave now, David. I want to check with Samuel on the Erie charts. This, as you know, is only his second tour with us and I want to see how he does going into Erie at night. It can be trying to get around Presque Isle and into Thompson Bay in the dark. We should be getting in about midnight."

"He is a good man, Charles. I knew him when he crewed on the Troy. And Robert is a good man as well. You're in good hands."

"Aye. Good night then, David."

"Good night, Charles."

David Stebbins turned to the starboard railing. He stood for a few moments looking across the now gathering darkness along the south shore of Lake Erie. Huge cumulus clouds high in the eastern sky caught the last rays of a now reddened glow from the western horizon and in seconds it ceased the clouds losing their color in turn to darkness, leaving only the stars and a half moon rising in the heavens. He guessed the Griffith was about four miles offshore and from what he remembered of the few shore lights along this stretch of the coast, they were now off Pennsylvania just below Erie, about twenty miles, if Charles' guess for his arrival time for Erie was correct. Which he knew it was.

He yawned, stifling it with a fist to his mouth and headed forward to take his nightly turn about the Griffith.

My splendid steamer, a beautiful boat; that is what she called you, he mused as he descended the stairway between the saloon deck and the main deck. Ah, I suppose it is true. I designed you. I built you and now I am tending to you as a man attends to a woman, or wife. As I had once attended Celeste. God love her. You are mine, just like your sisters, the Troy and the Albion, and the others that I have worked on over these past twelve years as a shipwright and engineer. He stopped and stood before the port paddle wheel housing, the sponson as they were now called, he remembered, and listened to the rushing waters as the blades dipped into the bosom of the now calm lake, each grabbing a trough full of water and pulling it along the hull sides, its force thrusting the Griffith ahead at a speed of about ten miles an hour at its maximum flank speed. The sounds were reassuring to him as the shaft was still being maintained by the hard working crew who respected him as they knew he respected them. The shaft. Yes. In a few days we will have it replaced and an entirely new

35

lubrication method installed. At least if we can convince Billy of the need. But it is early in the season and we can make up for lost downtime if he complains again about his damn profits going out the window.

He looked up to the pilothouse and in the glow of its interior lamp saw Charles and the second mate, Samuel McCoit, in conversation. A good captain, one who knows his boat and its crew; that is what you are, Charles. A good captain and a fine husband and father.

"Oh," he said aloud. He remembered that he wanted to get a towel and washcloth. The maid, Christine, a sweet girl, he remembered had forgotten, evidently, to replace the ones she had taken from his cabin when she changed his cabin linens just before the squall hit. Well now he would go and get them from the linen room. He retraced his steps and soon was at the linen room door. He entered and stopped abruptly. The night light in the doorway illuminating a shadowy interior.

"Ah. I'm sorry," he stammered. "I didn't know anyone . . . I want to get a towel and washcloth. I am sorry . . . " He quickly turned and left the room bumping into the doorframe in his hurry. Slamming the door behind him.

Henry Wilkinson arose hurriedly and pulled up his pants. "Damn it," he growled angrily.

Marie sat up and pulled her bra around to the front and adjusted it to her bosom. "Help me up," she asked, offering her right hand to him.

"All we need is for him to spread the word," he muttered as he helped her up.

"I don't think Mr. Stebbins will be the kind to tell. He's been around sailing men too long to know to carry tales," she countered as she adjusted her garter belt and pulled her skirt up and tucked it around her waist.

"I know we should have waited until tomorrow night in Buffalo; but no, you wanted to have it tonight," Henry said listening at the closed door.

"I have to be with Ollie tomorrow night, you know that, and until we leave on Sunday," she said coming up behind him in the now complete darkness. The slamming door having blown out their lamp.

The clerk relaxed and turned taking her into his arms.

"Did you see the look on his face?" she asked as she molded her buxom body into his eager arms, his legs spreading to allow her closer entry.

"No, I was facing the wrong way," he tittered, as he nuzzled his head into her neck, her body smell of the earlier days work adding to his lust for her as he fondled her buttocks with both hands, pulling her close.

"We'll make up for it when we get back to Toledo," she purred, her hands groping at his crotch undoing his fly buttons.

"Why wait that long?" he said, his voice almost inaudible.

"Uh huh. Why wait?" she purred.

CHAPTER THREE

England
Robert Hall

"Up and about, my girls. It's that time for rising and putting your things in order," Sophia Hall called softly as she drew back the drapes from the window allowing the early morning sun's rays to enter into the bedroom of her two daughters, Margaret and Regina. She turned and looked at the girls now awakening reluctantly from their dreams.

"Dream, my darlings. Dream of your new life. Dream of your new lives in a new world," she said softly with a gentle smile. She, herself, had not slept a wink, or so she thought, the night before. She turned again to the window, the early April sun rising golden into a blue sky with clouds reflecting brightly upon a new day. At least the weather will be in our favor she mused remembering the past three days of heavy rains. She hoped this sunrise would be an omen of better things to come, in many ways.

She continued in her thoughts as she stood at the foot of the bed watching her daughters. It is a new day for you both, for the two boys, George and Stanley, and for herself and Robert, her husband. It is a new day for many of the villagers as well. She paused. Today is that eventful day that thirty-one of her fellow villagers in Ramsey will be leaving the only home that many of us have ever known. There are those who are adamant in going, her own Robert and William Waters, and those who are unsure like herself and most of the other women. And poor Richard Trimble wanting to go but ailing . . .

"Good morning, Mother," Peggy, the eldest child at sixteen, interrupting her mother's reverie, said as she rolled over shading her eyes from the sun. Regina, the youngest child at eight, sat up and squinted her pretty face giving her mother a mouthed kiss.

"Good morning, my dears," the mother replied leaning over and kissing each on the forehead. "Up now you are. We have to get ready as your father wants us on our way by ten o'clock so we can meet Grandma and the others at the crossing and be on our way before it is too late in the day. He wants to be at Hartford by nightfall. So hurry. We have many things to do and still have a breakfast."

"Oh, Mother," Peggy said with a touch of sadness in her voice. "I do want to go and I am happy for Father for wanting us to be happy and have a better life for us all in America but these past few days have been dreadful with wondering . . . " her voice trailed off.

Sophia sat on the edge of the bed. She looked into her daughter's brown eyes and brushed a stray hair from her left cheek. A quick thought flashed. How much you are like your Aunt Edith. A real beauty . . . A wonderful sister and friend. Yes, a second Edith, as she remembered her sister at this age.

"Yes, my darling. I know just how you must feel. It is how we all have felt these past days and weeks about our journey." Sophia, herself, nodded understanding her daughter's concern trying to reassure herself as to the enormity of what was to take place this day.

Her thoughts were interrupted by Robert's voice coming from the bottom of the stairwell that led to the second floor bedrooms of the children.

"Sophia. I have put the cow to the commons and am now leaving for Ned's to fetch his horse. I will be back before long.

See that the children have gotten their things in order as we talked yesterday. I want to leave as soon as possible right after breakfast. I'm off now," Robert's voice trailed off.

Sophia rose from her daughter's bed, she took a deep breath then slowly expelled it in a sigh. Oh, God, she thought, her eyes gazing in supplication to the ceiling. Oh, God. Her melancholy thoughts were interrupted this time by Stanley, her second son, eleven years old, talking in not too subdued tones to his older brother, George, at fourteen, in their bedroom across and down the hall from their sister's room.

"Father," she heard Stanley saying agitatedly, "said that we can only take with us what we really need. We have room to carry only what we can…"

"I know. I know," George replied, anger in his voice. "I know what Father has told us but this is my very own book given to me by Mr. Tomlinson. It's mine and I want to take it to America with me."

"Boys," Sophia tapped on the door and entered the room. "I can hear you all over the house," she joked, looking at her eldest son, a small lad for his age with dark curly hair and blue eyes of her people. In many ways resembling her in build and temperament.

"George, dear," she knew his dread of leaving all that he knew in his young life and sympathized with him. "You know we have been told to take only what we would really need. What is really necessary. We will be traveling in very close quarters on the packet and we also have a long walk to Liverpool and even with Uncle Ned's horse, Min, pulling our cart with our goods…"

"But, Mother," George said almost in tears, "I… I…"

His mother looked at him with deep affection. Here she thought is my claim to the future. My reader, my student, he who will see and do that which I can't do. Oh, the girls are wonderful but like me, their lives will be tied up in a man's world to do his bidding and bear his children. It is the way it is.

40

But George may be able to change that and would give any child he may have golden opportunities in a new, young world such as she has never seen or can even dream of.

"Yes, George. I know how you feel as I am leaving my books too. I love them all but we are limited. You know that and yes, this book might be your greatest treasure, a gift from your schoolmaster, but perhaps when we get to America... to Medina in Ohio, we can find a copy or send back for it if need be. I am sure they will have copies of it where we are going. Now then," she concluded saddened by her son's wishes, "let's be getting on with it."

She left the room and called down the hall over her shoulder as she descended the stairwell, "Girls, get a move on. We'll want a breakfast early. Boys, you have your chores to attend. Hurry now all of you."

Louisa Taylor

The morning sun rising as a golden orb in a clear, blue sky slowly eased its way into the eastern heavens over the village of Ramsey beginning a new day for its one hundred forty-two inhabitants.

Justin Taylor crossed the kitchen from his seat at the hearth and poured himself a cup of coffee and added cream from the pitcher. "How was your night?" he asked of his daughter Louisa standing in the open doorway leading unto the courtyard between the cottage and her father's workshop.

She turned her head to his voice. "It was fine, Father. I really don't know how much I slept but I feel fine and refreshed."

"Would ye like some more coffee?" her father asked reaching for her cup on the window sill of the open window fronting on the courtyard.

"No. No thank you." She turned fully toward him. She looked at him with a sad smile. My father, my da, she thought of her familiar name for him as a child. "No, thank you, Da. I must be gathering my things if I am to meet the Halls and William and Hilary at the crossroads at ten o'clock." She smiled more broadly and touched his right arm gently. She looked down into sad blue eyes as she was a good head taller than he. Justin Taylor, a weaver by trade, was in his early fifties though he looked older. He was bald with a fringe of white hair that set off a florid pockmarked face. He was of medium height and build, stooped shouldered from his years at the shuttle and his trade as a weaver had taken its toll on his physical being.

Justin in turn looked up into his daughter's pale blue eyes and saw in his mind's eye his bride Jeannine as she looked at Louisa's age, nineteen soon to be twenty. She has the same honey colored hair as her mother as well as her height above him. Oh, my darling, he thought with a catch in his throat. He swallowed and brushed tears from his eyes. Her smile… and her wit were bequeathed on her, he had said many times, by her mother, God rest her soul in heaven, who has been dead these past five years in June. They held together for a few precious moments then parted.

"Charles will be here shortly to help you with your baggage to the crossing," her father informed her as he took their coffee cups to the basin on the hearth.

"It is of no need, Father," she said gently, knowing that he had requested Charles to assist her as far as the crossing with her baggage. Her voice caught at the thought that these might very well be her last words to him.

"Oh, Father," she said her voice barely audible. She turned to the hearth, its glowing coals soon to be embers waiting to be resurrected for the evening meal, a meal she would not be preparing. "How can I leave you? You and Charles. What will you do? Who? What? …Oh, I am so confused." Tears came to her eyes, flooding her view of the kitchen with its many child-hood memories with her mother.

"Lou, my darling, hush now," her father again holding her. His own voice soft and consoling. His heart breaking now at their almost final time together.

"There is no future for you here. Oh, yes, you could marry Charles and begat bairns but for what future? The factories in Birmingham and in Cambridge can make our goods much faster and cheaper than I or Charles can make them… by the hundreds they can. Aye. They are not the same quality or have the love of the making them. But they sell 'um and we cannot. The factories in the cities are taking our children and young men to live in filth to make just enough shillings to get by on. Charles loves you, I am sure, and a fine and honorable man he is. But you need a young man. Charles is only a few years younger than myself and while he is strong, it will be only a few years that you will be taken care of. Then you will be taking care of two old men as well as any bairns and also his mother and his sister Mame. No my darling, you will go to America with the Halls and Waters. They are God-fearing folk and will take care of you on the journey."

Louisa stepped back, her eyes glistening. She nodded her head and gave a small cough. "Yes, Da, I know, but it still does not seem fair," her voice almost a whisper as she said from arm's length, "I know that Mr. Brunswick is giving me a chance, a great opportunity he said in his letter, to be with his family in Ohio. But to leave you, to leave…," she cast her arms in a waving circle about the room.

"Lou! What is done is done," Justin interrupted her in a strong tone of voice, if only to force himself to be strong to his daughter's leaving. "Today is the day and that's a fact. So it is off with you it will be, as I hear Charles with the barrow coming through the yard. You'd better get to the nettie as it is a fair walk to the crossing."

Louisa wiped her eyes with the sleeve of her left arm and stood tall before her father, her head high. "Yes, you're right, Da. What has been done has been done. I did make up my mind to go and now I will leave with the Halls."

"Lo. Lo." Charles' voice called from the yard. "I hope I am a not late. Mame had a turn last night and I was up most a it." He approached the kitchen door and touched his cap to Louisa.

"No. You're not late," she said looking to the Mudge Mantle Clock in the parlor adjacent to the kitchen, one of only three clocks in the village. Louisa was calm and in command of her emotions. "I have my valise ready and we'll be on our way," she said as her father came into the kitchen from the parlor toting Louisa's worldly possessions in a wicker valise he had made himself for the occasion of her leaving.

"They say ye have to live in the clothes on your backs for weeks at a time until ye get to America," Charles observed as he took the valise from Justin and placed it on the barrow. Louisa smiled, a forced smile, but indeed a smile for Charles' sake. "I have enough for three changes. I packed my valise three times and was finally able to get in what I think I will need."

Charles Braitwaite in his middle forties, was of medium height with broad shoulders already showing the effects of his trade as a weaver. Due to a childhood injury, when the village bully threw a stone that hit him in the left eye, he had been blind in it since. He never married as he cared for his mother, a widow who lost her husband in the Battle of Lake Erie in 1813, as well as his sister, Mame, known in the village as Lame Mame, who in her late forties was a burden to both Charles and his mother. Her scathing tongue and recriminations against the village peoples over the years had driven most of them to ignoring her and letting her brother and mother care for her needs.

"Well now, ye'll be getting to your walk to the crossing," Justin said placing the valise on the barrow. The men walked to the hedge gate leading out unto the roadway. Neither spoke, each in his own sad thoughts. Justin stopped and cocked his head and said, almost in awe, "Do ye know, I have never been to Thrapston in all me life and it's only thirty walking miles away and here my Louisa will see it, and Northampton, and Coventry... and... and... Birmingham and... Liverpool. And then across the ocean to America. Aye," he said to Charles with a sober air, his left hand pointing to the northwest, her direction of travel. "We live in strange and wondrous times."

"Aye, that we do indeed." Charles replied looking now to Louisa who was walking up behind them. She stopped at the gate and turned to look back at the only home she had ever known. Her life had been centered in the village of Ramsey and now she was to walk down the well-traveled village road, possibly never to return. To walk past her church and its cemetery with her mother and her mother's people buried there from the time

45

of the Romans, lying there in repose until judgement day. Her walk will take her still further to the turn of the road at Bart Mayhew's blacksmith shop. Beyond was a rise in the roadway with a copse of rowan trees bordering both sides of the road, beyond which lay a few miles, the village of Hartford where there at the crossroads she would join with the Halls and the Waters and then to her new beginning, to a new life in America... in Ohio, a village called Medina. She shuddered at her thoughts but then breathed deep and told herself what is done is done as her Da had said. No more feeling sorry for herself or her father ... or for Charles. Poor Charles. She had always known him as being like an uncle or an older brother. Always there when needed.

Justin, now looking and feeling as an old man, took his daughter in his arms and held her close. Tears ran down his cheeks. His throat so constricted, he had to clear his voice before he could speak. "I send with you your old da's love and will look to see you again in heaven where we will meet again and rejoice with your mother and dear Jesus."

Charles, standing aside, doffed his cap and stepped back to let the two clasp a last hold together. Tears moistened his eyes as well. Oh, Louisa, he thought. He had known this lass from her birth. Aye. Her birth to Jeannine. Jeannine, who he, himself, had loved since she was a wee one and he had seen her grow into a woman. It was she, why he had never married. Why he had stayed in Ramsey after Justin came from his village of Owensboro to start his own shop at weaving and taking on him as his apprentice and then later his partner. Because of his love for Jeannine, who never dreamed or had any indication of his love for her, he stayed on. She had been taken as a young girl to wed Justin who was a man of some means and had a trade while he was only a ploughboy working the old Hall farm until Robert came of age and assumed his role as master and took over many of the duties. It was fortunate that Justin came when he did to give me a trade and a livelihood but to what cost? Oh, yes Louisa, he continued nostalgically, as the father and daughter parted and Justin turned toward the house. Louisa looking aside to Charles gave a nod to move out onto the road.

"Oh, Louisa," Charles murmured softly, his heart breaking. "Your da will miss you and so will I. That I will."

Joseph Wildes

The morning sun eased into a bright April sky, its golden rays bouncing off the whitewashed cottage situated on a knoll surrounded by spring blooming daffodils, bluebells and primrose. The twittering and chirping of recently returned migratory birds carried across the River Severn that skirted to the west of the cottage as it moved, rain swollen, on its course to the south and then to the Bristol Channel and to the Atlantic Ocean beyond. The river gurgling along the shoreline below where Joseph Wildes was putting the finishing touches to the loading of his backpack.

"They ye are," his younger brother Jerome said as he snugged a cord into a half-hitch to Joseph's belt in the small of his back shoulder straps. "The bottom of the pack is tied tight to your waist; you should have no trouble with the pack shifting," he continued. "Julia will be able to make any changes that may be needed."

Julia Wildes nodded her head in agreement. "Aye," she chuckled. "He looks like a tin smith with his pile on his back but with no pots of tin."

Joseph tested the pack and shifted his shoulders to get use to the weight of it. At twenty-seven, he was of medium height, broad shouldered with blue eyes and auburn hair. His arms were thick and muscular as the result of his trade as a stone mason since a young lad.

"It will be only a few days on foot, so I should be able to make the trek," he said, motioning to Julia to undo the cord and take the pack off his back. His testing done.

"Are you sure you can handle the cart and Gwen?" A middle-aged man asked Julia as he positioned a makeshift cradle onto the piled goods of a two-wheeled handcart.

"Yes, Daddy," Julia replied wiping a stray hair from her forehead. "We have been practicing for a few days now and I can pull the cart with the baggage as well as Gwen."

"Ah... Julia, my dear," her father sighed. "Your mum and me will surly miss you and Joseph, but it be the babe most of all. If only ye..."

"Yes, Daddy, I know," Julia said sympathetically. "But, please, we have gone through this many times. We know that you will miss us as we too will miss you and Jerome and Maude and all the others. But what is a stone mason to do here in Stourport, while in America they are needed and at a good wage from what we hear? Oh, yes, Joseph could stay here, and do what? Or we could go to Birmingham. But for what work? Or at what wages? The poor houses are full there as in other towns and villages all over England... In America they want us. America is growing and needs men of Joseph's trade and others as well."

"I know. I know," her father shook his head sadly. "Maybe if I were younger I would go with you but your mum..."

"Aye. I know. Mum is not well to travel but when we get to America, to this Amherst in Ohio, we can send for the two of you and Jerome and Maude."

Julia Wildes faced her father and gave him a warm hug. She was slightly taller than he as she was also with her husband. With flaxen hair, blue eyes and a large bosom, she was an imposing figure of a woman. The crying of the baby Gwen called Julia's attention to the cottage.

Jerome examined the cart and cinched a cord securing a parcel to the front of it. "All should hold well for you," he said to Joseph. "Unless the roadway is too bumpy and rough to cause the load to shift."

"Between here and Bridgenorth the road is a little worse for wear from past rains, I hear. I know not how it is further north to Shrewsburg," Joseph answered as he gave the cart a last check to satisfy his concerns for the four days and nights travel to Liverpool.

"You'll make it to Cressage tomorrow night?" Julia's father asked.

"I hope so. Let's pray the weather will be with us. If we can make twenty miles a day we should be in Birkenhead on the third day and then the ferry to Liverpool on the following day."

"And your packet?" Jerome asked.

"It leaves on the fifth day, the seventeenth, so we will have a day in Liverpool to get ourselves ready for the ocean voyage."

"It is good that you have already your passage fare paid," Julia's father stated seriously. "I hear there are many a traveler who has been stuck in Liverpool because the packets to America are already full up."

"Aye. It is indeed fortunate," Joseph agreed. "But even then we still have to walk to Birkenhead to save money for when we get to New York and then on to this Ohio."

Jerome rubbed his chin in contemplation. "To think that only two months ago not one of us had any idea, other than, we would be here in Stourport for the rest of our lives as have our people before us and now tomorrow you will be leaving..." He stopped. His eyes looked to Joseph sadly, a lump in his throat.

"Aye, indeed. It is strange that we should be leaving." Julia answered as she returned with Gwen, her six-month old daughter. "It was the letter from Constance Howard that told us of the work in America and how grand it was living in Cleveland, Ohio where her husband, George, is helping to build a railway or something like that. My only fear," she continued as she placed Gwen in her cart cradle, to check it out for what seemed to Joseph, to be the hundredth time in the past two days, "is the passage across the ocean. I...We have never seen the ocean and from what I have heard it will take us weeks to cross."

"And that is my fear too," her father added. "I hear tell also that they be great storms and..."

"Well if it was, or is, all that bad, I am sure Constance would have told us of it in her letter," Joseph interrupted, himself not too sure of the perils that may lay before them, but pretending to not be afraid for Julia's sake.

"'Tis true," Jerome agreed. "If it weren't for the Drakes and the Hudsons of our own past and other of our ancestors who settled in the colonies, where would the world be today? You and Julia and the babe are only following what has gone on before. In a year Maude and me will be joining you and maybe Julia's mum and her da as well... God willing."

He looked to Julia and Joseph then stroked little Gwen's left cheek. "Now I must be getting to my chores," he continued. "Maude says our Bonnie will be calfing anytime now so I should be with her when it happens. We will see you later this afternoon if all is well to wish you God speed on your trip to America."

"And I too, must return to your mum," Julia's father said as he embraced her and then bent to kiss the baby on her forehead. "You will stop to see us later?"

"Yes, Da," she answered remembering that Jerome had used the old expression for dad— da. How that one word brought back a quick torrent of childhood memories. No! She thought. Not now! She closed them off. "Yes, Daddy," she continued shaken. "We must see Mr. Massey in the village to notary the papers of the sale of the property to Thomas and Valerie Allen. We will see you after that and visit until dark. We will bring our supper."

Joseph and Julia met together and held hands as they watched her father and his brother take leave down the path that led to the lane that took them to the village of Stour-port-on-the-Severn, the only place on God's green earth that any of them had ever known.

William Waters

"You promise!"

"But, Ethan, I..."

"You must promise not to tell."

"Ethan, I don't know. I cannot lie to Father."

"You will not lie if you don't tell."

"But he... they will ask me. I know..."

"You know nothing. I never told you a thing."

"But... but... Oh, Ethan, why cannot you go to America with us? Father and Mother will need you in the new land."

"He will need me only to beat and make do the work of three lads for one."

"Oh, Ethan, that is not true. Father needs you now and he will need you even more in America. He is firm, yes, but only 'cause he wants what is best for all of us, for you. He has said so many times."

"No. I have made up my mind. I will help you with the cart and help you with Shirley to Liverpool, but before the boat sails I will leave. I will go."

"Where will you go? You know no one in Liverpool. "

"No, not in Liverpool but in Wrexham, in Wales where Mother's Uncle Alec lives... but enough. The less you know the better it will be for you when I do leave."

"Ethan! Are you about?" a male voice called out, causing Ethan to put his right index finger to his mouth cautioning his sister Lorna to be still.

"Go to Mum," he said quietly nodding his head in the

opposite direction from whence the voice had entered through the barn door. "Yes, sir," he answered as Lorna scurried away. "I am here tethering the lambs so they will not run from Stanley," Ethan explained to William Waters who had just entered the dimly-lit cow barn. "Your mother needs you to help secure the cart. Here, take this twine to her," he said as he tossed a small roll of twine to Ethan. William Waters was a man of small to medium height, wiry with great strength for his size. His hair was prematurely gray with sideburns. At forty-two he was the father of three adopted children and newly wed to their mother Hilary. The union had been in effect only this past half year. His first wife, Rose Ann, had died childless two years past, at Easter, of the flu that ravaged the countryside at the time. While he was considered a successful farmer, with a good business head for figures, it was to America he had set his heart on going after receiving a letter from his first wife's brother, Loren, last fall from a place called Litchfield in Ohio. While the claims for farming seemed wild and extravagant, especially for an area still on the edge of wilderness, it was to America he had set his mind on going.

"Hurry now," he continued. "We're to meet the Halls and Louisa Taylor at the crossroads at ten o'clock. As it is, we might be late. So get a move on."

The preparation for departure on this Wednesday, April 10, 1850, had been underway since daybreak after weeks of planning. At the meeting on Sunday in the parsonage of St. Alban's in Ramsey, it was finally established that thirty-one souls from the surrounding area of Ramsey and nine from Ely would be meeting at the crossroad at Hartford to go by foot and hand drawn carts, except for the Halls who were having the use of a horse-drawn dray to Liverpool.

William Waters had sold his farm to his older brother, Stanley, who was to hold the property until he received word from William as to the situation they would be in after two years, two seasons in America. If all went as well as they expected, Stanley would then sell the farm to Squire Gratten of Brekland Manor who wished the lands of William and Stanley to round out his holdings to the east of Ramsey. If all did not go well, William and his family would return to Ramsey and regain their rightful property. Stanley was to gain all that was garnered in the two years as compensation for his efforts in maintaining the farm.

It was for his business acumen that William was so highly regarded by his neighbors. While being a farmer born and bred, it was his understanding of market trends and his willingness to experiment with various products not necessarily native to the fens of East Anglia, that put him forth as one of the more successful farmers and businessmen in Ramsey and the surrounding villages.

Ethan carried the ball of twine to where his mother and now Lorna, and their younger sister, Shirley, were putting the finishing touches to the handcart and its piled goods.

"Mr. Waters sent this to see if you might need it for securing the load," he said as he showed his mother the twine and a pen knife.

"Ethan... son, please for my sake and the sake of your sisters, please call William father. He really is, you know. As my husband, he is your legal and dutiful father and it would be so much easier for all of us if you would..."

"I know, Mum, but maybe someday, sometime, I will regard him as my da, but until then I will show him due respect but I have only one father and he is dead. Just give me time to know the difference. Here let me help you," he said as he knelt to the side of the cart and helped her secure the twine to the load.

Hilary Waters at thirty-four was small busted with honey blond hair braided under a beehive bonnet in preparation for the next few days' travel. Her eyes were blue, as were those of her three children. Ethan Wilcox, who by law was now Ethan Waters, sixteen years, stood fairly tall at five feet ten inches with a lithe build and brown hair with a patch of white at his left temple.

54

"The Wilcox Streak" it was called as his father and his father before him had the same genetic characteristic.

The village of Ramsey had been shocked and dumbfounded only one year ago, almost to the day, when Miles Wilcox was found dead beneath a millstone of hundred-fifty weight that he had been transporting from Ramsey to Oakham for Mr. Paddington, the miller, who was building a new mill in the town. It was believed that the horses must have bolted tipping the wagon carrying the millstone, throwing Miles under the load as it careened into a gully along side the roadway at Traverse Lane just outside of Peterborough on the road to Oakham.

"I believe the cart is now ready as it will ever be," Ethan said as he coiled the unused twine and placed it on the cart's left-hand shaft.

"Aye. And I hope we are about as ready," his mother answered as she viewed the surroundings of the farmyard, the home of Wilcoxs since early times now the property of Stanley Waters. The orchard to the west with its pear and apple trees and the stream that meandered through to the Little Ouse River to the east and then to the North Sea, of which she had never seen.

Lorna and Shirley were just returning from the nettie and joined their mother and Ethan as they surveyed the only home they had ever known and wondered if they would ever see it again.

55

John Northy

"And you still insist that you are going to America... to California?"

"Yes. I do. I have made up my plans and I am to leave Plymouth on the twenty-seventh of this March," a subdued but determined John Northy, a young man of nineteen, answered the question of his questioner, Mr. Richard Milne, the Rector of St. David's Episcopal church in Ashburton, Devon, England.

"Do you have the wherewithal to pay for your food and passage?" the Reverend Milne frowned and gestured toward the plain furnishing of the rustic cottage that John shared with his recently widowed mother and his younger brother, Arthur.

"Aye. I have saved from my earnings over the years and believe that I have enough to carry me through on my travels."

"Oh, ho, and is that right?" the Reverend Milne guffawed as he raised his eyebrow and glared at John. "And who will care for your mother and your brother? Their needs are still to be met. The parish..."

"Their needs will be met!" a now peevish young man replied firmly interrupting his pastor. "Mother has her seamstress shop and Arthur is to be apprentice to Mr. Merrimen as his charge until he is sixteen, another three years. I hope by that time that I will be able to return home a rich man or else have them join me in California."

"You are sure then that you will find the streets of gold in California. Streets of what I have heard are paved with gold by the devil himself for such as you to be tempted by his wiles."

"I do not fear the devil and his wiles as you say, no more than my pa did. He was a God-fearing man who sought his Bible as he needed it. As do I," John replied, his voice tight.

"Your father lost his way and but for your mother and me, you and Arthur would have followed in his footsteps. He is dead now. Not buried these three days, and you are all ready to leave your home and hearth, your mother and brother, to go on a wild goose chase to another land, another world. To America... to the United States... to the God-forsaken California."

"Yes, and others have gone as well. Jamie Alcott only a fortnight ago and Terry Ambrose earlier. Why am I no different? The rush is on to California. Why shouldn't I be able to be part of those who hope to improve our lot in life by seeking riches planted by God and not the devil?" An enraged John now eyed his pastor at eye level never believing he would be talking to his religious mentor in this manner. "I was my pa's apprentice since I was a lad of nine. I toiled for him and at my trade and for what? He is now dead, the result of his head being crushed and now I am to go to Poole and slave for my Uncle Dermot for my keep. No, by God! I will not. I will take my future in America."

The Reverend Milne blanched at John's outburst.

"I will go to California," John continued feeling a strong release of repression that he had for a number of years now at last his feelings being stated, "to seek my fortune as the posters at the town hall say and let the devil take the hindmost!"

The Reverend Milne stepped back from John, stunned by his tirade. "You are like your father. One who professes to believe in God only when it serves your own purposes," a now thoroughly irate minister stammered, wiping his chin of spittle. "Such blasphemy... I... I..."

"John... Reverend Milne... Please stop!" a distraught Amelia Northy arose from a bench beside the hearth, her right hand reaching for balance on the mantle, her left to her forehead, her legs trembling.

"Reverend Milne, listen, please, to John. He made up his mind to go to America away before his pa, Paul, was killed in the accident. We, his pa and me, knew of John's wanting to leave many months ago. But now that Paul is dead, there is no reason for him to stay. As he says, I have my seamstress trade and Arthur will be well taken care of by Bruce Merriman as his apprentice. We had a good life here in Ashburton, our home and our parents before us, since early times. But now with Paul dead, John has to seek a new life. Ours here was a moldering. Paul knew that, I know that and John knows that. And in time, I am sure Arthur will also want his release. He is but a lad now but a man to be."

The Reverend Milne started to speak.

"Wait, hear me out. Please," she raised her left hand as if to ward off his words. "With Paul dead and carpentry not what it once was, John must seek a livelihood elsewhere. My brother, Dermot, has only a limited need for John's help. And no, not a slave as he may think, but Dermot has his own family to think of and John would be an imposition." She looked to John who was listening with his eyes now closed. Hearing his mother's voice releasing him from an unwritten pledge made as a young nine year old boy.

"Yes, I agree with John. If he wishes to go to America and seek gold in the streets of California, so be it. So much the better for him, and I pray for us as well."

John moved to the casement windows that looked out upon the cold, damp late March afternoon as it spread a mist across the moors and craggy tors of Dartmoor which was his heritage. The home of his ancestors, both his mother's and father's, since the time of the Normans and earlier.

"Well then, I am sure that he has his plans well in hand," a now chagrined Reverend Milne said as he straightened his shoulders, his hands on his hips, looking to John's back framing the window. He turned to Amelia who seemed faint. He thought a moment of what he wanted to say. "As you know, our parish and the Board of Guardians funds are limited to help those who are truly destitute. The whole of England is financially strapped and with the demands from the starving, ingrate Irish. When will it ever end?

John turned and looked to Reverend Milne, his pastor, his God-hand since a child.

"Reverend Milne," he said in a firm steady voice wanting to be as sure as possible for what he was about to say. "I am aware, sir, of the plight of the poor in our own parish and of the God-forsaken Irish. Wouldn't my leaving then help you with money from California to my mother and Arthur to ease your need to maybe care for them if times and conditions worsen still? I do not fully understand why it is that you do not want me to leave, to find a better life for me and maybe one for them. We have always had a fine relationship, you and I. I, then, find it hard to understand why you are so against my wanting to leave."

A now downcast Reverend Milne scratched his right ear lobe and cleared his throat. "I. . .I am not against your leaving for America. I am against your leaving your mother and Arthur and," he paused, a lump arose in his throat, "and Mrs. Milne, and I have. . .had hopes that perhaps in time that you," he paused again, "that you and our Marcella might, er would. . ." He stopped with an embarrassed giggle.

John turned his back to the casement ledge, crossed his arms and looked to his pastor in almost total disbelief in what he had just heard. He looked then to his mother who was slowly shaking her head.

"John," she sighed, backing into her bench feeling with her left hand for the armrest for support, "your father and I both had hope for you and Marcella," she groped for words of explanation, "eventually marrying and we just thought that. . ."

"Marcella!" John interrupted with almost a shout of her name. "My God, Mother, she is a child! She's no more than fourteen. . ."

"Fifteen," Arthur interjected from where he sat in the far

corner of the room next to the pantry doorway from where he had been observing the entire debate in quietude and concern.

"Fifteen then," John acknowledged sarcastically. "She's more for Arthur than me," he continued, his eyes rolling at the idea of his marrying a child and an ugly one at that. Four years younger than he and he had his mind set on Eleanor Nelson, the potter's oldest daughter, who was a real looker and just turned seventeen.

"Well then, I suppose all that has to be said has been said so I will take my leave and wish you well." The Reverend Milne nodded to Amelia and turned to John, "And you as well."

Arthur handed the pastor his hat. "You will then be leaving for America on the twenty-seventh? Wednesday a week?" his mentor asked to reassure his own understanding of John's intent.

"Yes," John now contrite and sorry for his reactions to his pastor's concerns for him, his mother and brother, "I sail on the Ambrose, a packet, directly for New York. I have already paid for my passage as well as my rations."

The Reverend Milne extended his right hand to John who accepted it gratefully. "I wish you well, John. I really mean it and trust that God, in His infinite wisdom, will care for you." He turned and bowed to Amelia and nodded to Arthur. A thought flashed. Arthur?... Who knows?

* * *

An ornate mantle clock of the Italian baroque style, an heirloom from his mother's Uncle Thadeus, struck the time at three o'clock on the afternoon of Tuesday, March 26, 1850. The melodious tones carried through the cottage to where John Northy, his mother and brother Arthur, along with a vivacious Eleanor Nelson, sat over a lunch prepared for John's departure that afternoon for Plymouth and his sailing on the morrow with the outgoing high tide. The gathering was subdued, the weather adding to the gloomy atmosphere of the cottage. The fireplace in the main room glowed with embers which took a chill off the wind blowing from the Western Sea but left no assurance of happiness for those within. John made an attempt at levity by telling Arthur that he was the man of the house now and maybe when he came home from America in a few years, Arthur would be married and John an uncle.

Arthur smiled a weak smile at his brother's humor and Eleanor simpered at his wit. Amelia, too, gave a weak smile but no more.

"John," Amelia interrupted another attempt by him to try to be funny, "you must be serious. You are leaving at a very trying time. I know that you want to and we want you to go. Many of our young men are going to other lands, as you said the other day of Jamie and..." she paused.

"...Terry Ambrose," John said filling her loss of the name of the young man in the village.

"Yes, Terry Ambrose, the orphan boy. They are going to America and to Australia and, yes, to New Zealand, wherever that may be." She nodded to Arthur who arose from the table and went to a wall cabinet where he extracted a parcel and brought it to his mother. John knew what it contained.

"John, I want you to have a tie with us. A tie to your father and his family, the North's and his mother's people, the Trevelyans of Fowey in Cornwall. Aye," she said to his arching his brows at the name of his distant cousin on his grandmother's side, Sir Charles Trevelyan, the Assistant Secretary of the British Treasury. Tears welled in her eyes as she untied a cord on the parcel. Her adept fingers over the years needed in her sewing, now took to fumbling as she tried to undo the cord. Eleanor reached and helped her with it. From a small pasteboard box she took out a bulbous silver pocket watch and a silver chain.

"These," she said to an astonished John, "were, as you know, given to your father as a boy by his great-uncle, Paul Trevelyan, a sailor man, for whom your father was named. I want you to have them now. Your father wanted you to have them when you were to wed but I suppose he would let you have them now."

John looked at the offered watch and chain with both pleasure and sadness. Pleasure that they were his, as he knew they were to be as a young lad. With sadness as it was a fulfillment now attained and not as he and his parents had ever dreamed of it happening in this way.

"While your father never wore them—he had no need—he did love them and wanted you to have them for your own boy. But…," Amelia wiped her left eye with a finger, her eyes downcast.

John shook his head and wiped the back of his neck. He was actually sweating. Aye, he thought, it was a beautiful gift from his father but did he really have a need for them now. Would not Arthur have better use for them in his near future? And then, I have only so much to carry me over to California. Do I really have enough? He pondered.

It is a long way to California and what if I have not planned as I should and be stranded in some gulch or canyon in the wilderness with the heathen Indians and the wild men of the mountains. Watches and silver chains could be changed to cash if need be and if I didn't need to sell them I would always see that Arthur would receive them someday for his first child. Yes, I will take them but only as a safeguard in case I need cash in America. Aye, I'll take them.

* * *

That evening in the stark darkness of the thatched roofed loft bedroom, as heavy gusts of northerly winds scathed across the Bristol Channel then overland across the wild heather-clad moorlands of Exmoor and thence south over the Dartmoor tors to the village of Ashburton, a wondering John Northy lay under heavy covers. Oh, what am I doing? he thought. My God, what am I getting myself into?

Ireland
Pierce Hill

....A cock's crow to the awakening day carried over the pall of turf smoke in the vale of Cherryville as Pierce Hill winded his way from the stream toward his cottage tucked in the waning grasp of night. Earlier, before light, he had gone to the stream to check his nets, set the night before, and found three trout, small but adequate and a medium sized pike. Enough to broil and give us a start for the day, Pierce mused as he approached the cottage door, his home these past two years along with his wife, Honora, and their three-year old daughter, Noreen. It was not really his cottage, he was only a cottier tending to the three acres of wheat and cabbages and with the potatoes rotting in the fields, had only milk and cheese, and his netted fish to sustain them. But not for long, yesterday was his last day to do the work for others. To toil on their lands while his needs had to wait... No, by God, today is the day we leave for Naas and then to the Dublin docks at Clontarf Port for passage to Liverpool and from there to America.

In the growing sunlight under patchy gold-tinted clouds, the whitewashed cottage now showing signs of the ravages of the past damp and cold winter, hedged in scarlet fuchsia, stood out against the other such black thatched cottages that formed the village of Cherryville. Not a village in the sense of a town square with shops or a church but rather a line of cottages with their goldengorse and purple heather bordering and facing the

63

Kildare Town Road, which winded its way between Kildare Town and Naas and then on to Dublin, thirty walking miles away to the east.

A commons of sorts was situated between the holdings of Ben Doherty and Seamus Byrne where a roadside statute to Saint Brigid, the Patron Saint of Kildare stood for passerby to pray. Here was the meeting place of the area for gossip or news. It was here that Pierce Hill had heard that a price was on his head in Tipperary and that while he was known as Pierce Hill here in Cherryville, he was known by his birth name, Michael O'Connel, in Tipperary where he had taken part in an ill-fated rebellion two years earlier against the British rule of Ireland when he had joined the Young Ireland movement with its cause of revolution and separatist nationalism. Their cause failed against better trained English landsmen and lack of support from most of their fellow Irish, many of whom had left or were leaving Ireland for America and wanted no part in further bloodshed with the English overlords.

Knowing that he was a marked man if his real identity were known, he had his cousin Francis Ronan, living in Dublin, contact his old friend and coconspirator, Thomas Meagher, now living in Boston, in America, for aid in assisting him and his family to secure passage to New York. For almost two years, Pierce had worked as a cottier at an almost subsistence existence. Toiling on others' lands. Working for almost no wages and saving that which he did receive, hoping to hear from his cousin and friend. Then three weeks earlier, the information and additional funds he needed arrived in Dublin to Francis. A hurried overnight trip to Naas where he met Francis, to firm up plans and a date of April 15, was set for him and his family's passage from Dublin on the packet Achill to Liverpool for connection to America.

His wife, Honora, met him at the doorway and took the fish from him while he attended to putting two oblong brownish-black peat lengths onto the fire in the hearth. The buttery fragrance

64

of the fuel permeated the cottage and with the other cottages, the entire countryside as well.

"Is the babe any better?" he asked about Noreen, who was still in her crib in the far corner from the hearth. "Is she able to travel? Will she be able to stand…"

"Aye, she seems much better, her cough has stopped a bit, but she still has mucus but not as bad as earlier," Honora replied as she dressed the fish with a deft hand at quickly scaling, then beheading and filleting them.

"'Tis a shame that she has to be taken with the croup at this time. It'll be bad enough to travel without her ailing," he said softly with a concern for his child, his alana…

Honora straightened herself from her chore with the fish at the cutting board over the water tub. She turned and looked at her child, her second, also with a concern for her. Honora Hill at twenty-four was of medium height, big busted with dark brunette hair in a bun and with pale-blue eyes. As a young girl she had spent four years in a convent preparing to become a sister. While her mother was praiseful to God for her to be a nun, her father thought else and when she was sixteen, just prior to her first vows, he brought her home reasoning that as the only girl of six children, her place was at her home to care for him and her mother and her two younger brothers still at home, which one, Liam, was lame and had fits. At nineteen she met Michael O'Connel, an itinerant printer and ran off with him to Tipperary where he had a position promised with one Anthony Fahy, Printer Extraordinarily.

"The fish are ready," Honora said to Pierce as he adjusted the grill over the coals from an earlier fire for boiled eggs. "I'll take the innards to the chickens at Hennesey's. I've packed and all we will need is for you to fetch the trundle from him."

Pierce nodded to her and placed the fish on the grill. "They'll be ready when you return. I'll be getting the babe up and ready for you." He then crossed the room to Noreen's crib where he saw she was awake. Her pale-blue eyes, like her mother's, were now red and swollen, from both her condition and the almost constant turf smoke in the cottage.

"Good morning, my alana," he said with a smile as she raised her arms for him to pick her up. She answered him weakly, her voice muffled by the infection in her throat. "Yes, my macushla, I know you are in pain and here we are taking you away, to a new land over the sea and you know nothing about what is happening. Ach, my babe, do any of us know what we are doing? Do any of us know what is happening or..." His one-sided conversation was interrupted by a sharp call from Honora.

"The fish! Watch the fish!" she called sharply to him as she entered the cottage. He turned and saw that the fish had slid from the grill to the coals beneath and were blackened with the turf ashes.

"You tend to the fish, I will tend to the babè!" she said exasperated.

Pierce handed Noreen to her as he turned and groped for the fish in the coals.

Damn! Damn it all, he thought. Honora is upset with me again. These past three weeks have been hard on her. Aye, and me as well. But what is our choice but to leave? To stay here is to maybe for me to be returned to Tipperary and be sentenced to be hung... or shot. Oh, my God! Why did I ever join in that wild—crazy action. Maurice Coady and Lawrence Coleman dead and a constable killed and for what? To prove we were men! Boys we were! Not men! Boys who listened to orators, to politicians, to everyone but to those who warned us, and yes, begged us to give up our high hopes of overthrowing the English with our pitiful pitchforks and spades, while the English had cannon and rifles. Ach! What have I done, Honora? What have I brought you to? To this! To exile from our own land. To be going to a new world with only a few shillings and misguided hopes for our daughter. Oh, Honora. Oh, my darling. Here we are with a sick child, and on top of it, your grief for baby Angela.

Only seven months, she was, and dying of a fever, from what no one still knows. Oh, my...

"We will want to be getting on, fish or no fish," Honora interrupted his melancholy thoughts, she now subdued and sorry for her outbreak.

"Aye," he agreed. "I'll tend to the loading of the trundle. We can have bread and butter on the road. We must be in Naas by the noon hour if we are to meet Francis," he added as he poured water on the turf coals, the steam filling the cottage with the acrid smell of steam and hot ashes causing Honora, with Noreen in her arms, to race for the door and the more fresher air outdoors.

CHAPTER FOUR

Griffith

The Griffith, gray smoke billowing and sparks spewing from her twin stacks, slowly edged her way along the south shoreline of Presque Isle Bay, giving Misery Bay, an area of foul ground to the north and on the port side plenty of clearance as it approached the cut into Thompson Bay and Lake Erie beyond to the east.

"This is where it gets tricky," Captain Roby said to Wheelsman Mann, as he pointed ahead to a gap between two spits of land that almost closed off the bay as a small lake adjacent to Lake Erie.

"Aye," he answered nervously glancing to both starboard and port, gauging the space as well as getting the sense of clearing the narrows cut and still watching for the turn buoy that lay, what should be, dead ahead when they cleared the cut and entered the larger Thompson Bay. "Coming in last night with Mr. McCoit and Robert and you was really exciting and fun too," he added eyeing his captain quickly.

"Where were you? I didn't see you," the Captain wondered.

"I couldn't sleep and I did want to see the port at night. I was on the main deck bow. I was able to follow all you did."

"You could have been with us in the pilot house."

"I know, sir, but I didn't want to bother you with another person in the way. I was able to follow what went on though. It was exciting."

"You're a good man, Richard. At least the lake was calm as it is now. Luckily we had no wind or combers to put up with," the Captain added as he turned to the first mate who stood quietly at the rear of the pilot house during the exit from Port Erie.

"How do you feel now?" he asked a pale William Evans.

"Much better, sir."

"You are sure you can handle this leg to Buffalo?"

"Yes, sir. I just got a little dizzy when I got up this morning. But I feel much better now."

"Very well. Set the course for fifty-five degrees, Mr. Evans," the Captain directed as he checked the chart and putting his calipers in the drawer in the map table. "With the weather the way it is we should have no trouble between here and Buffalo. You will want to watch for shoals off Van Buren Point so stay well out and circle round."

"Aye, sir. I remember the shoals well."

Captain Roby turned and looked at the wheelsman and with a wink gave him a thumbs up. The wheelsman smiled and gave him a nodding thank you.

First Mate Evans wiped his chin stubble and blinked his eyes. Oh, God, he moaned to himself. What a night. How many more will I be able to take? He took a quick look at the wheelsman who was intent on following the course set by the Captain, steering against a longshore current that kept his attention. I wonder how much Charles really knows. He's seen me like this before. He must know something. Shit! I have to have something to eat. Or to drink. "Mr. Mann, I will be leaving for a few minutes. I have to go to the crapper and be gone for a few minutes. Hold her steady at fifty-seven degrees."

"Fifty-seven degrees?"

"You heard me."

"Aye, Mr. Evans."

The wheelsman inched the helm to fifty-seven degrees. He thought... I really didn't hear what the Captain said when he gave Mr. Evans the bearing. He shrugged. Oh, well, Mr. Evans has been here before. He knows what he is doing.

* * *

"What will happen to the Indian boy?" Candace asked her grandmother as they stood at the bow of the Griffith on the main deck, the bow rising and falling with a gurgling and splashing of white water racing back along the water line.

The wind carried Candace's voice away and her grandmother had to bend toward her to hear her. "I don't know. It is a pity that he cannot speak English as well as we would like him to. He is not a native to these parts. Mr. Wilkinson thinks he might be from Mexico or some other place in the west."

"What? I cannot hear you!" Candace yelled.

"Never mind. Let's leave. It's too windy here. I cannot hear you too well either."

The two left their position and returned to the relative quiet of the foredeck on the main deck and took seats on a bench against the port bulkhead away from the bright late morning sun.

"I wonder if Mr. Chitchester has a special treat for us like he did yesterday at lunch," Candace said as she adjusted her bonnet ribbon about her chin.

"Oh, I am sure he will have something nice again today. Maybe ash-pone and cocoa."

"Oh, Grandmother. Ash-pone. I don't like ash-pone," she paused knowing her grandmother was teasing again. "But I do like cocoa."

"I don't know, dear, what he will have. We will just have to wait. Oh, here comes your father and Mr. Stebbins. Hello, Charles. Hello, David," she greeted them gaily.

"Good morning, Ada. Good morning, Miss Candace," a frowning Chief Engineer greeted the two.

"Good morning, Mother, Candace," an equally frowning Captain greeted the two.

70

"Good heavens. Why so glum?" Ada asked. Surprised at their unusual attitude when the two were together.

"Oh, it's Mr. Lovelace, or whatever is left of him. He is putrefying much faster than we had anticipated and it is creating some problems with some of the crew and passengers," her son answered.

"You placed the incense candles?" his mother asked, now knowing the reason for their glumness.

"Only one," he answered lamely.

"Only one? There should have been at least three or four."

"I know, but Henry could find only the one in the stores. It seems the others have disappeared or have been used for other purposes."

"Oh, Grandmother, what a terrible thing to happen to Mr. Lovelace," a shocked young lady said with a grimace, her right hand to her throat.

"The exceptionally warm weather these past few days isn't helping matters, and it looks like we are in for more of the same today." David offered as he wiped his brow with a large green handkerchief.

"We'll just have to keep him sealed as best we can until we can get an undertaker to take him when we get to Buffalo," the Captain offered.

"And what undertaker would want to come aboard and take a stranger? And who is to pay for him if one does take him?" David added.

The Captain frowned and cupped his chin in his left hand. "It's about another six hours to Buffalo. At least to docking. That will put us there about..." he looked at his watch, "...four-thirty or at the latest, five o'clock." He paused. The others watched him, wondering what he was getting at. "Maybe we could have a burial at sea for him."

"Charles! Oh, Charles," his mother exploded. Appalled at her son's thought.

"I am serious, Mother. I have the authority to marry and I

71

have the authority to bury. It is strictly my decision," he paused again. "If I think his body would cause a pestilence, I would be able to have him buried at sea. It is done every day on the ocean packets from Europe. I have heard, as have you, of hundreds of corpses being dispatched overboard on many ships to protect the others from the spread of disease."

"But, Charles," an agitated mother admonished her son, "Mr. Lovelace died of old age. You, yourself, told me that."

"Do I really know that he died of old age? It was only a guess on my part. He could have had any number of contagions that could spread to my other passengers and crew, and yes, to you."

"Charles, he was an old man. He just died of old age. Of natural causes," Ada offered petulantly.

"Charles is right, Ada," David said, not to sure of his own feelings on the matter but supporting Charles' right to protect his ship. "We could put him in a tarpaulin bag in a few minutes and over the side a few minutes later."

"But what of his family? What of a minister? or priest?" a now thoroughly disturbed Ada burst out in near anger.

The two men stood silent as Ada wiped her eyes and tried to compose herself after her unusual reaction of one who normally would never argue with a man, especially her own son.

Captain Roby stood silent and then realized that during their discussion, a small crowd of passengers and crew members had gathered. The couple who sat at Ada's and Candace's table looked at the Captain with fear in their eyes while one of the bartenders, William Tillman, looked with great anticipation at the possibility of seeing a burial at sea, or at least a burial in the lake.

"Oh, I guess you're right, Mother," the Captain conceded, realizing that they had made a spectacle of themselves before a number of people. He gave a short wave of his right hand as a signal of dismissal to them. "The ethical and business questions might be too much. It's true, we know nothing of his family or business associates and there is the Indian boy to be considered," he shrugged. "We will just have to take steps to contain his condition and have Albert Tiffany take over for us when we get into port. I guess that could be considered part of his responsibility."

"Oh, Charles. Yes. I am sure that he can take this matter off your hands," Ada, now relieved, agreed with her son.

David with a pensive look, nodded his head. "You are right, Ada. As usual. It would be too much for us to take this matter into our own hands. It could have led to great problems and I am sure Billy would not be happy without being tied up with possible legalities down the line." He thought for a moment, "What little ice we have left, I will have some volunteers pack him in a shipping box that can be lined with canvas to hold him and the ice, at least for the next couple of hours."

Hearing this, a few of the group who did not leave at the Captain's dismissal, began to leave. The old couple nodded their heads in agreement with Ada and looked palefully to the Captain. William Tillman said, "Damn."

A silent Candace followed her grandmother as they headed back to the cabin, there to prepare for the approaching lunch hour. When they got inside, she started to cry softly, then more loudly. "Oh, Grandmother," she was finally able to whisper between sobs, "would Daddy have really buried Mr. Lovelace in the lake? That poor old man. And the Indian boy, what will become of him?"

"Oh, my dearest darling," the grandmother said slowly, her heart near breaking for her granddaughter's concern for an old man and a boy she had never really met. "My darling, no, I am sure your father would never have carried out his thoughts. But you must remember that your father has many worries being a captain and this is just one example of his many responsibilities he must contend with in the course of any day on his steamer."

Candace sniffled and sighed a long sigh. She looked at her grandmother with wet but now sparkling eyes. "I knew he wouldn't. He is my daddy and my daddy is a good daddy."

* * *

73

"Marie! How could you?" a distraught Christine asked petulantly as she entered the linen room where Marie Walrath was sorting soiled linen to be washed upon arrival in Buffalo.

Marie looked up from her chore with a shrug. "Oh, so Mr. Dana has spoken to you," she said matter-of-factly. "He would have had to know soon enough. You are beginning to show and if you want to finish this trip and make one or two more, he can help you," she tossed her head coquettishly, her eyes fluttering, "Besides, he has taken a liking to you."

"To me! He hardly knows me," a now angry Christine exclaimed, upset that Larry Dana had taken a liking for her and for only one reason.

"Oh, don't sell Larry Dana short. He can do an awful lot for you. You, yourself, said you need the work badly."

"I do. I really do. But I don't want to be indebted to anyone, much less Mr. Dana."

Marie placed a basket of sorted napery on the floor and started sorting through another. "He said he'd like to show you the sights in Buffalo. He can be very nice," she paused and looked knowingly to a now less angry Christine. "He was nice to Gail Arnett. So nice that when she left last fall after the season was over, she told me that for the first time in her life she had some savings."

"What you are saying is that this girl, Gail, was sleeping with him whenever they came to Buffalo."

"And when we were in Detroit."

"But everyone knew. Even Captain Roby. It was common knowledge."

"True. But everyone left them alone. It was their business. He was, is, a grown man and she was a grown woman. Just like you."

"But I am engaged."

"With a ring? I don't see a ring," Marie said mockingly, raising her left hand showing her wedding ring.

"George could not afford one," Christine said defensively. "Besides, it really isn't necessary."

"Oh, enough! I'm sorry if you are upset because Mr. Dana knows of your condition." Marie's voice showed irritation. "Be glad he is giving you a chance and it would be damn nice if you showed him some appreciation."

"I can. I can work harder," Christine answered, now subdued by Marie's support of the first porter's intentions. "I can do extra work. I can help in the galley or setting the tables. . . ."

"That isn't what I meant," Marie interrupted archly. "Larry Dana is a man! You are a woman! Figure it out!"

"But I am pregnant with George's child," a now beaten Christine said wearily.

"So. That is much less you have to worry about Larry Dana. Does anyone else know but you that it is George's baby?"

"Only you and Mr. Dana."

"Well it's up to you," Marie said as she picked up the sorted linens and headed for the doorway. She stopped and turned. "Life isn't easy. Not by a long shot, honey." Then she was gone.

A forlorn Christine leaned against the shelving and shook her head slowly. "Oh, George. I do need the work so badly," she whispered, "and for you and the baby."

* * *

Hiram Faulks leaned toward the open firebox door, shading his face from the glare with his left forearm, and squinted into its raging inferno. "It should hold for a while," he said as he closed the fire box door with a long poker. The heat in the fire room was intense to the average visitor but to Hiram and George Jefferson, they could, and did live with it. The two shuffled to the exit door onto the main deck where they once again gasped in the fresh midmorning air as it wafted its way over cobalt-blue waters of the lake, now calm and serene under a bright sun.

Hiram placed the knuckles of his grimy left hand to the side of his left nostril and blew a gob over the side, watching it arc into the passing wash of the paddle wheels. "The Cap'n seems surely worried about the shaft," he said to George as he extracted his pipe and began tamping in a coarse tobacco.

"Aye. His coming to see it in the shaft well shows it," George nodded in agreement as he too filled his brier pipe.

"I'm glad we are only filling in for Ed and Howie," Hiram continued as he stood with his back to the wind as to light his pipe. "I gets the willies bein' cooped up in that place too long doing nuttun but to watch the shaft turning and see that the bearing is oiled."

"Well, it'll be for only a few more days, next Wednesday I was told by Mr. Stebbins," George said as he exhaled a blue cloud of smoke that smelled and tasted like burned sumac leaves.

"I hope we can make it. It's taking us and the others and Mr. Stebbin's frettin to keep it oiled and working," he continued as he spit over the side, the sputum being caught up into the air wash from the hull and disappearing upward onto the saloon deck.

"Watch it, you lummox," an agitated John Paulding growled as he came up from behind to the two who had their backs to the wind.

"Oh, I'm sorry. I did na see ya coming," George said embarrassed if the bartender had been streaked.

"How are ya feeling this morning?" Hiram asked, noting that the young man seemed to be much better off than the last he had seen him.

"Oh," he paused, "better." He remembered vaguely a group of the steamer's crew were at the dock when he and Bill Tillman came aboard the other night just one step ahead of the Cleveland police patrol. He guessed these two were part of the group. He placed a small wicker basket at his feet and took a half-smoked segar called a long nine from his jacket and hunched over to light it against the wind.

"Whatcha got in the basket?" Hiram asked.

"A surprise," John answered, picking a particle of tobacco

from his still tender mouth and lips. He looked out across the watery expanse between the Griffith and the distant shoreline where the sky was bright blue with thin high cirrus clouds stretching far to the south and west.

"A surprise. And for who?" George questioned.

"Miss Candace. The Captain's daughter. It's from Mr. Chitchester and he asked me to take it to her cabin while she is at lunch."

"Do you know what the surprise is?" George asked again.

"No. I don't. Mr. Chitchester asked me to do him a favor and that I am doing. I don't know and really don't care. It's no one's business but his."

"Well, I suppose it is no one's business but Mr. Chitchester's," George said coolly, feeling put down by the smartalec bartender. He really didn't like the fellow. Too cocked sure of hisself. Evidently, someone else had felt the same the night before and it showed then and still does.

"Well, Hiram, I guess we have to get back to work. At least some of us has to," George said knocking his pipe against the railing.

"Ah, yes," Hiram agreed, knowing of George's implication about those who had to work and those who could play delivery boy. The two took their leave, their pipe ashes flying in the wind as the bartender threw his segar stub over the side and resumed his errand and headed for the Captain's mother's cabin.

* * *

Abraham Gilpin wiped his hands in his apron and then proceeded to ladle his prized Saturday special gumbo soup into pewter bowls lined up on a sideboard in the galley. "Soups on," he called in his quaint Creole dialect to his assistant cook, Marshall Gantry, who then passed them through a hinged partition out onto the deck where his wife, Clara, served them to the dining passengers. The Saturday lunch was always looked forward to by the crew, especially when the dish of dish of dishes by the Chief Cook was salmagundi soup.

The lunch tables were filled except for the places where old Mr. Lovelace and the Indian boy were to have been seated. The Indian boy, now known and referred to by his name of Kuruk, was now seated across from Ada and Candace. Ada had requested a change of seating for the boy so that she and Candace would be able to confide in him as someone whom he could relate with. Which the three were now doing now quite animately.

As the assistant cook and his wife were serving the passengers, Abraham tended to the stove, a large cast iron six-holer with a water reservoir on each side for the preheating of water for cooking and washing of dishes and pots and pans and other utensils. It was fueled by corn cobs which devoured them at a prodigious rate. Being of almost no ash, the cobs allowed for less in the way of cleaning as did wood or coal. Abraham at thirty-three as best he could figure, was a heavy, thick shouldered black with a ready smile and a hearty laugh. He was born and raised on a plantation in the lower reaches of the Mississippi River and trained as a boy to be a household cook and for that he was eternally grateful. While toiling in the fields under a blazing Gulf of Mexico sun was not his want, he did sympathize with the field hands and when two years ago he was whipped at a post for inciting a small uprising against his master's refusing to let a female slave keep her boy child when she was sold to another slave holder out county. It was then that he was determined to head north, hopefully to Canada through the underground railroad. He wasn't all that sure of his reception in the northern states as many escaped slaves were returned for their reward money. As it turned out, he did get to Cleveland, Ohio and found his reception to be wonderful and all he had hoped for and he made it his home since.

Taking the empty kettles that had just held the gumbo, Abraham with Marshall began filling them with warm soapy water to be heated more on the stove burners for washing later.

"Stoke the fire," he asked of his assistant. He ladled the warm water from the reservoir on the left of the stove. He looked out the serving space and saw Mrs. Roby and her granddaughter talking with the Indian boy who was such a topic of conversation last evening at the crew's mess. He stopped and studied the three, their heads bent in close conversation. He was especially interested in Mrs. Roby and knew that her being with the boy could only mean well for him. He liked her. A nice lady who has always been nice to him. He had met her when the Griffith had returned to Toledo from a trip to Cleveland where her son, the captain, had taken him from the church group who had supported his long and arduous trek from the south. When his cooking skills became known, she had her son hire him as the cook for the Griffith and on any number of occasions had him prepare dinners for the partying of the Captain's and her friends when in Toledo. She especially liked his southern version of a Christmas dinner: roast suckling pig, oysters on the half-shell, hot rolls, onions in cream and his specialty, vanilla ice cream as well as many other trimmings. He chuckled at his remembering the past three Christmases he had been with them. Ah. Such good years. What a fine lady.

He returned to the task at hand when he let out, "Ma Gawd!" as the cookstove behind him made a jerking, jumping movement, the kettles tipping and crashing to the deck with the hot waters splashing all about. The stove lids flipped out and the hot ashes and burning cobs and smoke filled the enclosure. On deck the tables lurched and crashed, tipping food and passengers helter-skelter in piles as the Griffith made a ninety-degree turn to the port. The smoke from the stacks hung low over the steamer as it came to almost a complete stop, the port paddle wheel feathered while the starboard wheel labored under flank speed. Ada, as with the others, was thrown from her chair to the deck with Candace falling atop her as the two slid on the canted deck toward the port guard rail, to be pinned against the pavisade by the Indian boy who was knocked unconscious. Shrieks of fear and crying rent the air as the Griffith righted itself and the two paddle wheels again were synchronized, the starboard wheel's paddles churning mud and bottom debris in voluminous amounts as the Griffith skirted a shoal, almost having cast itself upon it.

"What the devil?" Hiram Faulk yelled as he was thrown off his feet as the decking under his feet swerved in a tight turn to his left. A lump of firewood flew from his hands and crashed against George Jefferson, who was also thrown off his feet unto the wood pile they were fueling from.

"We've crashed!" George screamed as he tried to stand but couldn't as his right knee buckled. Hiram reached for him but realized the fire box door was open and that the burning embers in the fire box could be strewn out onto the wooden decking of the fire room. He staggered to his feet, fell, and tried again, the Griffith now rocking to an even keel and reaching over George slammed the door shut. The two huddled for a few moments getting their bearings and trying to figure what might happen next. Without the glare of the fire box giving its limited light, the fire room was in near complete darkness with only a lard oil lamp over the exit doorway giving limited illumination.

"Come, George. We'll have to get out," Hiram grunted as he tried lifting George from the wood pile.

"We didn't hit anything?" George questioned, wondering as the steamer seemed now to be on a steady course and the paddle wheels back to their monotonous thumping.

"We seem to be still moving," Hiram answered rising and trying to help George.

"Oh, my knee. Oh, Jesus. It hurts like hell," George moaned with pain.

"We'll take it easy. I'll get some help. If I can," a worried Hiram replied as he wondered to what extent George was injured. "I'm goin to leave you. It seems that we are all right. Stay. I'll be back soon. I'll bring back some help." He then stumbled to the exit doorway.

Emily Roby arose from the bed and crossed over to the water closet where she looked into the mirror on the bulkhead above the toilet and saw a strange image of herself. At thirty-three years of age, she knew she was still a young woman but what she saw was a fast-aging, much too early, woman who already had streaks of gray in her auburn hair, now loose and falling over her shoulders. She quickly turned away, not wanting to see any more of the stranger with dark circles under her eyes. "Will you please tend to Thomas?" she asked of her husband who was sitting at the edge of the bed putting his boots on. "He is fussing and I have to rinse."

"Aye. I will," Charles Roby answered as he stood from the bedside and crossed to the bassinet where Thomas lay crying weakly in a diaper and blanket now sodden with pee.

"He is really a little pisser," Charles said somewhat proudly of his child's dubious accomplishment.

"Oh, he is regular. But he is a boy and they seem to pee more than girls I've been told. I don't remember Candace as always being so wet as he is." Emily offered as she wiped herself and pulled on a clean pair of pantalets.

Captain Roby looked to his wife with deep affection. "You are still a most beautiful woman. It is with great love that I hold for you," he said, his eyes taking in her splendid body, the body he had just ravished.

"Oh, Charles. I love you too so very much! It is just that you and me... We... You and your needs. Me and mine. Whenever for you," she shrugged, "me in my time." She paused and began undoing her blouse. "I am dripping; I will nurse him now. Please hold off Mother and Candace for a while."

"I will. I must be leaving anyhow. I want to check Bill. He has the bridge. He wasn't quite himself last night and this morning and I hope that he isn't falling back on his missing Carrie."

"Is he..."

"Yes. I don't think he will ever get over her. Her death was tragic but he must realize that life goes on. He is an intelligent man and one of the finest first mates any captain would want. I also want to check on Richard Mann. He has the helm. I would like to get him his papers after this trip.

Emily leaned over the bassinet and began to pick up Thomas. "Charles!" she shrieked as she fell backward and the bassinet tipped and catapulted the baby atop her on the floor.

Charles did a stumbling jig as he tried to maintain his balance as the cabin swirled to port and he crashed on the floor beside his wife.

"What? What? Charles," Emily gasped as she held fast her baby now in the throes of terrified screaming.

"I don't know! I don't know!" an anguished Charles spouted as he tried to extract himself from his wife and baby and make his way to the cabin door.

* * *

Richard Mann yawned and blinked his eyes. His reading into the early morning hours was taking its toll of his not getting enough sleep he knew but the book he was reading by Herman Melville, Typee, was to him most fascinating. He thought of what it must be like to be on a whaler in the South Seas—Tahiti, Samoa, the Carolines. Ah. What it would be like to sail around the Horn. To see a whale harpooned and thrashing about with its red blood spurting. What an adventure to be able to write about. The monotony of the course, fifty-seven degrees, under a clear sky with high cirrus clouds to the south being replaced by cirrocumulus, was beginning to take its toll on the sleepy Richard. He looked to starboard. The coastline, which he knew was along the New York shore was much closer than he really liked. While the lake water was calm, he could see white caps along the shoreline. He turned his gaze forward. "White caps!" he gasped. "Mr. Evans!"

"Eh. What?" First Mate Evans aroused himself as he raised his head from its nodding over the map table.

"Shoal water! White caps!"

"Shoal water? Where away?" the startled First Mate called out as he made his way to the wheelsman.

"Dead ahead!"

"Damn it!" Thoughts raced through the mates sodden head. "Dead ahead. Almost due east. Shoal water. To port, deep water. To starboard, shallow water and shoals and reefs." He almost screamed, "Hard to port!"

Wheelsman Mann spun the helm hard to the left as he had never done before. The Griffith, at almost flank speed, surged against itself as it swung into a tight immediate left turn, the entire equilibrium of the vessel being thrown into utter confusion creating violent reactions throughout the steamer.

CHAPTER FIVE

Robert Hall

"It is getting late and we should be on our way now," Robert Hall said to William Waters as they adjusted the belly-band on Min, his brother's hackney mare. "From the sky it looks that we will be having more rain and we must be in Hartford by nightfall if we are to make our time to Liverpool."

"Aye," William agreed. "Do ye suppose something is wrong? That maybe someone is sick or has changed their mind?"

"I dunno. But we had best be ready to go if they do not show in the next few minutes." Robert grunted as he gave the band a last chinch. The two men hunched together beside the mare tending to its harness making final adjustments with the horse as well as the wagon piled high with goods of their two families.

Sophia Hall leaned against the wagon and rubbed her slightly puffed left ankle. "I hope that my poor feet are equal to the walking to Liverpool," she sighed to her daughter, Peggy.

"Yes. And we have only begun and already my feet are aching too," she agreed with her mother. "Stanley seems to be doing well. He is keeping up well with Ethan who has set a good pace for us from Ramsey to here at the crossroads."

Sophia turned and sought out her son George, who was talking with Lorna Waters. She smiled. Lorna was just twelve this past Sunday but seems much older in her ways than her age would tell. Sophia thought as she compared the two. George, her bookish, serious son of only fourteen, who too seemed much older than his years. The two were well suited, she continued in her musing. What future do they have now? What would they have if we weren't on this journey? Twelve and fourteen. She about the same as I when I was pledged to Robert. Now what? We are moving to a new world. Yes, with many of our friends and family. But to what? She shook her head slowly and looked to Peggy who had her right brogan off and massaging her toes. Oh, Robert, she continued in her lamentations, are we doing right? Is Peggy right in her concerns of this morning? She turned to the roadway at the sound of a voice calling.

"Here they are!" She saw her brother Murdoc pointing down the road to a group approaching with their barrows and packs.

"Hello," he called to them. "We have been worried."

"It was Hester Kent," a tall lean man in about his middle fifties said as he approached Murdoc with an outstretched right hand.

"Hester?" Murdoc questioned, shaking the man's hand.

"Yes. She decided she did not want to go after all and at the last minute. So we had to settle with her for her share of the costs and her passage money."

"We are late and we must make time." A worried Robert Hall said as he came up to the group from Ely. "The road to the north has been under heavy rain these past three days and we must move out as soon as possible if we are to make our time schedule."

"Aye. We know and we are sorry," the man agreed adjusting a pack on a younger man who resembled him in his rangy, rural appearance.

The early spring weather, while sunny and almost cloudless in the early morning, now was taking on a typical rainy and blustery day in the Fens area of southeast England. The wind had picked up and rain had begun falling in gusts from the northwest, causing a number of the travelers to add on more clothing to ward off the chill.

"Abram," Robert Hall said to the leader of the nine people from Ely. "We have worked out a way that each day of our travel we will alternate with a lead group to set the pace."

Abram Clement, a surveyor, with a promise of a livelihood in a growing and expanding area of northeast Ohio in America, nodded in agreement as he took a drink of water offered to him by Hilary Waters, who had just filled a bucket from the nearby stream that flowed under a stone arched bridge. "Yes. My son Hosea and his wife Geraldine set our pace this morning. I just hope we will be able to follow."

"You must. We all must. Our packet leaves on the seventeenth and we have to be there at the dock the day before," Robert said to emphasize his concern. "It will be tight but we can make it if we all try and help one another."

The crossroads beyond the village of Ramsey found on this April morning, at a little after ten o'clock, thirty-one souls from Ramsey and nine from Ely, the Cathedral City, queing on the Oakham Road under gray skies with blustery winds.

"Come Stanley… Regina. We are to stay together as close as we can," Sophia called to her two younger children. "Stay by me and do not wander off the road."

Stanley who earlier had kept pace with Ethan now walked with his younger sister and mother behind the horse and wagon that were being led by his father. Peggy and George took up the rear of the Hall family group, each toting small backpacks of personal belongings.

Sophia surveyed the landscape about the road to Oakham. The road was rutted and uneven from the past winters ravages as well as the heavy rains of the past few weeks. The countryside while beginning to green and blossom with the onset of spring still was within the grasp of winter. The farm fields and fallow land were still to feel the ploughs and the turning of the sod for the summer's crops of oats and barley as well as rape and clover.

Ahead of the Halls were William Waters and his wife Hilary and their three children. The two older children, Ethan and Lorna,

86

helped William maneuver the borrow over and around puddles and ruts. Hilary kept Shirley moving and not to dawdle.

Sophia turned and observed Louisa Taylor who had joined up with her mother. Her brother Edward and sisters, Laura and Edith, behind her and Robert. The other brother, Murdoc, was at the end of the caravan along with two men from Ely, George and Albert Reynolds, who would be of any assistance to any of the party in need of help in their travel.

All in all, Sophia guessed that the line, in pairs of two, extended for a distance of over a hundred yards, as best she could judge from the road markers along the way on the side of the road.

The wind began to subside a little before noon and soon a heavy somber gray mist settled over and followed the procession blotting out only the immediate passageway at their feet. About mid-afternoon, after head-down, monotonous plodding, Sophia heard a frantic almost hysterical voice call out.

"Halt! Stop! Help us! We must stop," the voice was from the couple two ahead of the Halls.

"It is Brendan Foster," Robert called out to Sophia. "Here take the reins," he said to George thrusting the reins to him. "I will see what it is about. I do not see Emma."

Sophia told Regina and Stanley to stay with George and Peggy while she joined Robert and others who went to answer Brendan's call for help. They came upon Hilary Waters bending over a crumpled figure in the road. It was Emma Foster.

"William," Hilary called to her husband. "Call for Peter Gray. He is up in front. He has his medical box with him." William hurried around a gathering of onlookers from both their own group and other road travelers as well, to get help from the only one in the group who thought to bring a medicine chest, small and limited as it was.

"What is it? How is she? Oh my God! Sophia heard various questions and pleas as she joined with Hilary in turning over Emma Foster's limp body in the rain soaked road.

"She just fell. She just fell over," a lamenting Brendan wailed.

"Here help us move her to the verge," Hilary called to two men standing by as she and Sophia struggled to lift the heavy woman.

"Oh my God. Oh my God," Brendan moaned as he wrung his hands in despair and wept.

"Is she?"

"Yes."

"From what, do you suppose?"

"From what I know of her past, it was her heart. She had dropsy," Hilary said to the questions asked of various ones in the group, as she helped the men move her body from the roadway to a grassy knoll a few feet off the road.

"What'll I do now? We were going to America to see our son, Lawrence, in Ohio," he shook his head. "What will I do now? Oh Emma. Why?"

Sophia rose and went to Brendan who by now was in a state of shock after losing his wife of thirty-eight years to a sudden attack of what? A heart attack? A stroke? He wondered.

"Oh, dear God. Why now?" he murmured as he knelt beside her body and wiped a smudge of the road from her forehead.

Peter Gray arrived with his medicine chest being helped by Robert. "How is she?" he asked of Hilary, who was adjusting Emma's legs before rigor mortis would set in.

"She is dead," she answered. "She just dropped. It had to be her heart. She was awfully heavy and the walking and the weather must have been too much for her to take."

"What will we do now?" a concerned Robert asked to no one in particular but to all surrounding the body, now covered with a blanket on a gloomy afternoon in the middle of nowhere. "We have no plans for such as this. A burial at sea perhaps but nothing for our walking."

"Will Brendan continue on?" a male voice asked.

"He was determined to go to begin with," another said.

"Aye. He and Emma were determined to go to America to see Lawrence," another voice, this a woman's, stated.

88

"Well, we will have to do something," a discouraged Robert said. "We cannot take time for a service or a showing for three days. Our time schedule will not allow it. We must decide now. This minute."

He looked at the faces of the group and received no suggestion as to what to do at this unanticipated situation.

"Brendan," William asked of the distraught husband who was kneeling at his wife's side holding a plump limp left hand and crying into her rain sodden gray hair, "Brendan," he continued. "We must make a decision as to how we are to dispose of Emma's body. As you know, we are under a very tight schedule to get to Liverpool or loose our shipping time for maybe months as well as our passage fees." He looked at Brendan who now stood up and blew his nose in a voluminous green handkerchief.

"I know," he nodded. "I know. We had never thought of only seeing our son and his wife, Haley, and their three bairns then maybe we would be happy to die in America," he sniffed; "but this, this was not in our plans. Oh, my Emma," he blurted as he turned to her again.

"We do have an out. A slim one," Robert said to the somber, thinning group as each member returned to their station in the procession. A few stopped and returned to the gathering.

Robert began to unroll a map he withdrew from his wagon that had been wrapped in a waxed paper covering. "This is my map of our overland journey to Liverpool. It has the names of the villages and hamlets we have been through and will be passing through and I remember two of the villages that we passed through having public cemeteries."

A murmur came from the group.

"Yes, maybe we can have her buried in a public cemetery until such a time as Brendan, or his son, can send for her body to be shipped to America," a woman's voice said.

"She should be buried with her people. Her own in Ramsey. Not with strangers in a land she has never known!" an angry male voice challenged.

"Aye. True. But we have naught the time to take her back to Ramsey. It would be another day back and another day to rejoin us here or further along," Robert stated firmly as he passed a corner of the map to William. "Have hold there," he said to him who took the map while Robert took the other side, spreading it out for the others to see.

"See here," Robert pointed. "This is where we are. And look there is March where we passed through only an hour ago. I will hitch Min and have her carry Emma's body and have six of us as pall bearers to return with her and see that she is buried, properly."

"I don't like it!" the same belligerent voice stated firmly. "It is blasphemy!"

"No. No. Please," a subdued but still shaken Brendan entered into the debate. "I know that Emma wanted to see our son and his bairns as much as I, but…" he paused and took a deep breath, "…to take her back to Ramsey and be buried at St. Albans, our church and our forebears church, would be too long and only hold up the rest of you on your journey." He shook his head as to clear his thoughts. "I agree with Robert. If we can have her buried post haste, today or early tomorrow in Marsh,"

"March," Robert corrected.

"Er… Yes. March. Then I am for it and only hope it will not delay our going to Liverpool." He paused and looked down at his wife in death's repose with her hands crossed on her huge bosom. "I think she would understand," he whispered as he backed off and turned away.

90

Louisa Taylor

"Did you sleep at all?"

"Oh, I suppose I did, but not as I would have liked," a yawning and stretching Louisa Taylor replied to the question of Elly Hall, Robert's mother, as the two were preparing the daily morning portion of crowder for the families.

"Nor I," Elly said as she placed more twigs on the fire beneath the kettle boiling on a wrought iron tripod stand that William Waters had made especially for cooking the meals of the day while on the journey. "The past three days have been more than even I expected with the rain and all. Robert had been told that there would be way houses that we would be able to stay in but the shed we stayed in last night was not my idea of a way house."

"No. Nor mine," Louisa said, nodding in agreement to Elly's assessment of the near hovel that they and twelve others had called home for the long night, as she placed handfuls of oats into a large wooden basin set along side smaller wooden bowls and a tub of butter on the dropped tailgate of the wagon.

"Here. The water is ready," Elly said taking the kettle to Louisa who stirred the concoction vigorously while Elly poured the water into the basin. "Will we have enough oats and mutton for us to get to Liverpool?" she continued her conversation.

"Robert thinks so. He had it all measured out at three handfuls a day for each as well as three slabs of mutton," Louisa said as she doled out the porridge into the smaller bowls. "Here is your breakfast," she called to some of the group who were returning from across a grassy rain drenched field where in a small wood beyond, they had made their morning toilet. "As far as I can tell, we will have enough but Robert said that he was worried that the Ely group didn't seem to have enough and that we may have to share with them in a day or two. But maybe they will have enough. It is their having problems with their loads that also has him worried," Louisa answered Elly as she scrapped the basin clean, not wanting to waste a drop.

"Robert was wise in getting Min from his brother while she is old and near her end. He said we could take more food and personals in a wagon and then sell both in Liverpool," Elly said with a touch of pride in her son's thinking as she passed a bowl of the oaten porridge topped with a dollop of butter to her granddaughter Regina, the youngest of her grandchildren of Robert and Sophia, she was small with curly brunette hair and pale blue eyes like her mother.

"Stanley and George were arguing in the woods," she said motioning with her head toward the two boys who were gathered with the others in a line waiting their turn for a bowl of the breakfast food.

"Oh, boys will be boys," her grandmother laughed as she passed a bowl to her daughter Laura, who asked of her niece.

"What were the boys arguing about?"

"A book," Regina answered matter of factly.

"A book?" Elly asked quizzically.

"Yes. A book that George brought with him."

"Why would they argue over a book?" Laura asked taking a bowl from her mother.

"Because Father forbade us from taking only what we really truly need," Regina answered with assurance.

"A book shouldn't be too much," Laura offered knowing of the restrictions placed upon her and all the others. But a book? Sometimes she thought Robert was too demanding of his children, especially George. But a book. Huh. She forked a slab of mutton into her bowl.

The discussion was interrupted by Robert and Sophia joining the family gathering for the breakfast. "The weather bodes well for us this morning," Robert said as he took a bowl from Louisa, handing it in turn to Sophia. "I would hope we can make Coventry by nightfall," he continued to the group. "Today will be our longest leg but the road is much better I have been told and we should be able to move on in good fashion. Our delay with the burying of Emma can be made up if we all move along."

An early morning sun hung low over a rising mist as the entourage of Ramsey and Ely migrants to the New World moved out onto the Northampton-Coventry Post Road. By noon, under a bright, warm sky with a few patchy clouds, the procession was moving through rolling countryside with farmers in their fields attending to another spring growing season. Along the way an occasional "Hello" and a waving of arms was exchanged between the farmers and other travelers heading in the opposite direction. A stop would be made on occasion to allow a brief rest and a toilet break if the area allowed. Robert was pleased with the pace being set by Ethan and Louisa as well as the group moving along in good spirits due to the change in the weather.

"We are all moving well now," Louisa said as she stepped over a dropping of horse manure which along with others littered the cobblestone highway.

"Yes, and by the mile stone, we are making better than five miles an hour. If we can keep it up, we should be in Coventry well before nightfall," Ethan stated, pleased at the pace that they were setting and that the group was doing as well as it could. "I just hope that Min can keep her strength," he added.

"Yes," Louisa agreed. "She seemed quite restless at the last town, in Kettering, when she was being watered. She had been out to pasture when Robert got her. Maybe this trip might be too much for her."

"Let's hope not. We need her all the way," Ethan said as the two sidestepped around another mound of droppings.

Joseph Wildes

"Joseph, we will have to stop. I must rest," a nearly staggering Julia pulling the baby Gwen and supplies in the two-wheeled cart, called to her husband who was plodding ahead of her on the Bridgernorth-Cressage Road.

Joseph Wildes stopped and turned to take the left-hand shaft to assist his wife. "Only another mile and then we can both rest. The signs show that Cressage is only a mile and we will be able to spend the night and you can rest then."

Julia took a deep breath and nodded her head in agreement with her husband. "I didn't know the roadway would be so rough," she sighed as she looked at her palms, both beginning to blister. "I wish that we had thought to bring gloves," she added.

"Aye. And better walking shoes," Joseph agreed. "We thought we had it all figured out. But it takes the being on the way to tell what we should have done."

It was late in the afternoon on their first day out. The weather, while partly cloudy and windy, was mild. The roadway was narrow with a Hawthorne hedge on both sides, not allowing for off-road stopping or resting. The Shropshire Hills to their left rose as a shield against the western sky now beginning to clear for what promised, Joseph knew, would be a cold night.

"As soon as we find a widening of the hedges, we will pitch our bedding and I will set a fire to boil the water for supper," he said, as he bent down to assist Julia in her pulling what they now knew was an overladed cart. Already, he thought, Julia is suffering from the heavy pulling. Maybe this trip to America was too soon after the babe was born. Only six months she is and Julia not really as well as she had hoped to be for the journey.

"We will stop now," he said to her as they approached a bend in the road that provided for a small roadside space on which they could spend the night. He looked about and saw that the hedge would provide them with necessary kindling for their night fire and cooking of their porridge in the morning.

The Hawthorne hedge along the roadway was over shoulder height to Joseph and served as a bulwark between the roadway and stone-strewn fields that lay beyond. He could see, in the now gathering dusk, that the hedge had occasional gaps through which one could possibly crawl through from the roadway into the fields.

"It seems that we are all alone on this road tonight. We haven't seen anyone since before Bridgenorth," Julia said as she turned the cart from the roadway onto the small space of grass hugging the road's edge.

"I was told by Matthew Penny, that this road would be longer but faster than the Whitting Road, which is heavier with traffic. I would have thought that we would be seeing more travelers such as ourselves," Joseph said undoing his shoulder straps and kneeling to allow Julia to help remove his backpack. "It will be dark soon and I must get to the tending of the fire."

"I will set out the bedding," Julia replied lifting the baby's hamper and placing it on the ground alongside the cart. The stopping of the cart's jostling, which had been as a rocking for little Gwen, awakened her and she let out a cry of hunger for her mother. "I will have to feed her," Julia said. "She needs also to be changed. She is soaking wet." A now throughly exhausted and discouraged Julia sighed, as she began to open her jacket and undo her left shoulder strap.

Night soon drew down upon them; a half moon arose in the east and added a touch of loneliness to the darkened hedge and small campsite among its leafy shadows. Into the small hours the three slept exhausted from the day's toils.

"What is it?" Julia asked as she turned in the cramped tent, a layer of two bedspreads she had sewn together as bedding for their travels. Constance Howard had written that only loose straw was available on the packet and that they would want bedding and a pillow of feathers, if possible, for the long voyage.

"I don't know," Joseph whispered. "But the sound came from beyond the hedge. There," he pointed in the darkness to a gap in the hedge row reflecting in the stars of the clear night and a descending moon to the west.

"There it is again," Julia said nervously.

"Aye. It is something moving. I will tend the fire. Then we will see what it is," Joseph said as he eased out to the stoked fire they had used to cook the evening meal of porridge and salted mackerel. He crept to the fires embers and added a handful of dry twigs and leaves, blowing on the coals to fan a flame. He looked to the hedge and found a gap from where he guessed the sound had originated. He added more twigs and leaves as the fire caught and expanded its illumination to the direction he was looking at into the hedge. A pair of yellow-gleaming eyes, reflecting in the fire's glow showed him that an animal, perhaps a dog or a fox was lurking beyond the hedge. Another pair of jaundiced eyes joined the first pair, then the two backed off and disappeared with the crackling of dry leaves under their feet.

"It is only some dogs or foxes," he called softly to Julia. "They probably saw the fire and smelled the fish from earlier. They are gone now. I will stay up and tend the fire in case they come back and it is also getting daylight. The sky is lighting," he said to a now fitfully sleeping Julia with baby Gwen cradled in her protective arms.

John Northy

The packet, Ambrose, pushed through a rolling sea, its white sails taught from a steady wind and glistening from the early morning sun, as it swept past Lizard Point leaving the English Channel to enter the vastness of the Atlantic Ocean on its long fetch to New York by way of Cabot's route to Newfoundland. John Northy, standing with his feet braced and hands gripping the starboard handrail on the rear quarter deck looked back upon the Cornwall Headlands now receding rapidly to the east. He wondered how soon he would be seeing other headlands. . .those of America. . .New York. He had been told earlier by a seaman that it could take as few as twenty days or as much as two months, depending on the weather and the Captain's ability to read winds and currents. His eyes still held to the east until the last visage of England and all he knew of his ancestral home disappeared over the horizon under billowing clouds.

He turned and looked about him to see what his home to be for the next few weeks, he hoped, was to be like. The packet, a barque-type sailing vessel, he had been told when he had traveled to Plymouth the day after his father's burial, was a hearty ship. It measured over one hundred seventy feet from stem to stern and measured over one thousand tons. He marveled at the timbers of oak and the white pine masts, each as straight as a die, towering as much as seventy feet above the decks supporting voluminous folds of sails. He liked what he saw.

He had arrived to the Plymouth Docks, at wayside the night before just as dusk, having walked from his home in Ashburton by way of the Exeter Post Road. His brother, Arthur, had accompanied him but turned back at his suggestion when the weather worsened and a dark, heavy mist settled over the land. John was able to board the Ambrose as soon as he arrived and was shown his cabin which he was to share with three other men. As he was the last to arrive, he had to take a lower bunk and stow his belongings, few as they were, beneath the bunk with only inches to spare.

He was intrigued by the arrival, late that evening, by the steerage passengers who were permitted aboard after the cargo of crockery, textiles and pewter ware and the cabin passengers, fifteen in all, had been secured and in their places. As best he could determine, the steerage passengers were composed mostly of English, well over one hundred that included a large number of children. A contingent of French speaking people, perhaps numbering fifty or so, and also with a large number of children. He heard a smaller number speaking a tongue he did not know. They also had a large number of children.

From his vantage point this morning, on a roped off section of the quarter deck reserved for the cabin passengers, he was able to look into the waist of the ship and observe the steerage passengers as they moved about the deck entering and leaving their compartment below decks through a small house-like structure over the companionway leading below. As he learned later, this housing was called the booby-hatch and could be secured in heavy weather. Along the bulwark, he saw huge water casks, he knew them to be called tierces, which were filled with fresh water on the long ocean voyage. He hoped there would be enough.

What really caught his attention was the cooking grate, a large range of crossed iron bars that was to provide the steerage passengers their cooking at sea. This was located just forward of the regular ship's galley on the main deck and provided, as best he could see for about six cooking at one time, three on each side. For his own food, which he had paid a princely sum, he thought, to assure his eating regularly and the ship's cook had promised a wide variety of delectable foods.

The call had been made at four in the morning for all hands to attend to departing. The tide was at flood and the ship was to leave post haste. The sky, in the early morning darkness, held a wide swath of glittering stars under a full moon. John hastened on deck to see the preparations for and the leaving the port of Plymouth. He wanted to instill in his mind forever his possible last sight of his homeland, this port of Drake, this isle of Shakespear. Soon a rising sun over the English Channel found the Ambrose coursing under full sail, angling to catch the offshore winds, keeling to port and determined to reach the North American shores as soon as possible.

IRELAND
Pierce Hill

A winding narrow lane of a road passed through the spring greening, rolling hills of Kildare County under an expanse of a clear blue sky that reached in all directions. The Kildare Town Road was filled this day with a multitude of traffic going in both directions between Kildare Town and Naas. While Pierce was able to make good time with his trundle, Honora, carrying Noreen, first on one hip and then the other, kept straggling behind so that eventually he placed Noreen, precarious as it was, on the load on his trundle, and then proceeded on their journey east to Naas to meet their fate.

"Do you suppose that Francis will want to go to America someday too?" Honora asked as they stopped for a rest in a small copse and a drink of water from a stream that paralleled the roadway.

"He did not say when last I talked with him. He is still too much with the Confederation."

"Ho! The Confederation! Once it was the Son's of Ireland, then the Hearts of Steel, now The Confederation. Dear God! When will it ever end?" Honora exploded. "He still has to learn, as we, that they cannot continue this battle with the English with so little and them with so much," she said testily to Pierce's seemingly support of Francis' still being in the spell of a lost cause as she arose from a crouch from where she had peed and adjusted her skirt angrily.

"Honora, I know," a contrite Pierce continued in almost a whisper, taken aback by his wife's outburst. "But he is still young and I am sure he still follows Lalor's beliefs, as wild as they seem to us now, and John Mitchell's thought as well."

"James Lalor and John Mitchell. A pair indeed. James as far as we know is in hiding, like yourself and Johnny in Tasmania to serve a life sentence. And for what?"

"Come, my alana," Pierce interrupted his wife's favorite topic of conversation of late, her tirades against the lost cause of independence from the British. "Here, my macushla, let me hold you," he said to Noreen who held her arms to him from where she was perched atop a bedroll on the trundle.

"She'll be needing a change," Honora said now calmed down as she helped Noreen into Pierce's arms.

"Aye. I can feel," he nodded.

"I will rinse out the others. We have only two more dry," Honora said as she lifted a wooden pail from the trundle and extracted soiled diapers and other soiled linens from a small wicker creel attached to the side of the trundle.

"Away! Away!" the sudden thunder of horses hooves on the cobblestones road and the yelling driver of a careening stage-coach sent all three into a wild dive back into the copse along with other passersby.

"Bastard!" a young man called after the driver as he brushed his knees from detritus from the roadway. "Why in God's name do these draymen have to feel they own the public roads. I will never know. Here," he continued, "let me help you," the young man moved to aid Pierce who was helping a shaken Honora to her feet.

"Are you all right?" Pierce asked anxiously of her while the young man attended to Noreen.

"Yes, I am all right. I just landed on my bum," she turned to see Noreen. "How is she?" she asked the young man who was placing her on the trundle.

"Fine. I believe. With no thanks to that driver of that coach. He must be mad to not care for those on the roadway."

"He has a schedule to meet," Pierce offered as he checked Noreen's position on the bedroll.

"Let me help you. I will take her or you can take her to carry and I will push your wagon," the young man offered. "I have only my small pack and I am going in your direction as well."

The young man in his middle to late twenties, was of medium build with a fair complexion and red hair of the western Galwayan. "My name is Fergus Kilbane," he said nodding to Honora and extending his right hand to Pierce, "and I am on my way to Dublin, to the Clontarf Port Dock."

"And I am Pierce Hill and this is my wife Honora and our daughter Noreen. And we too are on our way to Dublin, to Clontarf Port as you and then to Liverpool."

"Hah. A small world," Fergus said, pleasantly surprised. "I am to take the packet Achill on Wednesday, tomorrow, to Liverpool."

Honora feeling better but her tailbone sore, entered into the conversation, pleased with the young man's offer of help to Pierce as well as his caring for Noreen. "It is indeed a small world. And we too are to sail on the Achill," she agreed. "It will be nice to travel with you. Where are you from?"

"From Galway. The village of Derryrush. What with the recent famine and no means of livelihood in the west country, my brother Hugh in Cleveland, in America, has sent for me."

"Ah, that is good. That is grand," Honora said as the three adults and young Noreen reentered the roadway heading east.

"We must be in Naas by noon to get our ride to Dublin," Pierce said taking Honora's left arm and supporting her walking.

"Aye. And me too," Fergus agreed. "Our boat then is the Achill and we sail with the tide tomorrow and if I miss it, it will be a catastrophe. At least for me."

"Well, with the two of us to share the trundle and to help Honora, we should make it on time," a now relieved and thankful Pierce said as he led Honora around a dropping of horse manure on the roadway.

CHAPTER SIX

Griffith

"Bill! What in the hell happened?" Captain Roby almost screamed as he burst into the pilot house.

"A shoal, Captain," the first mate answered as he clung to the compass binnacle and pointed with a waving hand ahead. "Not one showing on the chart. It may have come about from a recent storm."

Captain Roby strode to the map table and looked at the chart. He then looked to the compass, now reading seven degrees almost due north over deep water. "Bring her to one hundred ten. One-one-zero degrees," he commanded a trembling wheelsman, Mann. "Bring her gently, we have a boat full of shaken and surprised passengers and crew and I don't want any more of the same." He looked again to the chart. "We should be off Van Buren Point by now. The chart shows a shoal and a wreck at two-and-one-half miles. About how far from shore were you?"

A still shaken but recovering first mate answered, "I would say at least three miles. I was giving it a wide berth."

Wheelsman Mann blanched. Three miles! It was more like a mile. He remembered the bearing given to him by the mate, a five-seven which he knew brought them closer inshore than the fife-five the Captain had given. Now he remembered the reading the Captain had given.

The Captain leaned forward and scanned the waters ahead and then made a wide search of the surrounding horizon. He turned to the wheelsman Mann and said, "I want to congratulate you for your fine response at the helm and both of you," he nodded to his first mate, "for your quick reactions, which may well have saved the boat from serious damage or sinking." He turned again to the chart. "Mr. Evans, make a note on the chart of the shoal as best you can recollect. You know the procedures. We will inform the port authorities in Buffalo as soon as we get in." He studied the chart and looked to the now closer shoreline.

"Aye, sir," a throughly relieved first mate answered softly, as he caught the glaring look from the wheelsman. So what you bastard, he thought. So I made a degree or two in error in reading. It was caught in time and no great harm done. Don't you look at me like that.

"Take her now to five-zero degrees," the Captain told the wheelsman, directly bypassing the first mate. "I must check with the passengers and crew and see what damage, if any, has been done. We might be delayed in our entry to Buffalo, but with the weather as it is, we should be able to make up for lost time. I will leave now to see how my wife and baby are doing as well." He passed the wheelsman and gave him a wink and a thumbs up sign.

Oh, Jesus, the first mate thought, if only I could get some sleep. But no. Not last night or other nights. This damn loneliness with only a bottle. My God. Why can't I let it go? Why do I need it? He remembered when there was a time he never needed it. When he and Carrie . . . Oh, my Carrie, he groaned silently to himself as he began making notations on the chart of the waters off Van Buren Point, offshore of the state of New York in the waters of Lake Erie at a depth of a good forty or fifty feet, he now noted a shoal of about five feet below lake level. He shook his head in dismay. His captain really believed him.

* * *

"Are you all right?" a nervous, but now in charge, Ada Roby asked as she wiped the brow of Kuruk with a damp cloth. "Candace," she said to her granddaughter who was supporting the Indian boy's head in her lap, "we will want to get something for the bruise. It is quite swollen. I will go to find Mr. Stebbins and see if he has any ice left." As she arose from the deck along the bulwark, the old couple approached them and asked if they could be of help. "Yes. You may help my granddaughter with the young boy. She, herself, is shaken. I will see if we can get Mr. Wilkinson or someone to take him to his cabin. Oh . . .," she remembered. His cabin was under quarantine. "We will have to take him to my cabin. I will be right back. Dear," she looked to Candace, "I must see to your mother and Thomas as well," a stoic Ada said as she took leave of Candace and the Indian boy and the old couple.

Candace winced as she shifted her right shoulder to ease the pain where it had struck against the bulwark. "How do you feel?" she asked looking down into the face of Kuruk, who was now awake with glazed eyes.

"I. . .Wh. . . I . . .," he tried to speak.

"Shh. No. Never mind," Candace said softly, realizing that he was still in some sort of shock. She remembered once when her cousin Clarence, her Uncle Billy's oldest boy, was thrown from a horse and was unconscious for three days. At least Kuruk was awake and maybe he would be better in a little while. She gingerly wiped the swollen area above his left ear. He shook his head in pain. "I'm sorry," she said. "I don't mean to hurt you but it is bleeding a little. I'll try to be more careful."

Other passengers and crew members began to put their tables and chairs back into a semblance of order. The assistant cook and his wife helped Abraham Gilpin clean up the mess in his galley.

Fortunately, some of the fire from the galley was doused unintentionally by the hot water that splashed about and with Abraham's quick thinking of throwing bicarbonate of soda on the small fires those that did catch.

The bartenders, John and William, threw a half-filled keg of beer over the side when it had burst its bung and beer sloshed all over the deck engulfing the headwaiter who suffered a sprained left ankle in the upset.

* * *

"Hold on Hiram. Mr. Stebbins is coming with some help. We'll get you out of here in no time," George Jefferson assured his mate. "I've got to get back to tend the fire and put on more wood. We have to get up steam."

"What happened? Did we hit something? Another boat?" a still wondering and confused Hiram Faulks asked as he sat with his back to the bulkhead across from the now open fire box door, nursing his right knee which he felt swollen at least twice its normal size.

"No. We just made a sharp turn. Someone said we were in shallow water and the quick thinking of First Mate Evans, saved the boat from crashing on a reef." George said as he began stirring the fire bed with a poking iron. He then began feeding two-foot lengths of split maple into the demanding mouth of the furnace. "It is lucky we had no great upsets here but on the hurricane deck, they had lots a tipping and people getting hurt. At least we are safe now and the boat did not sink," he continued loudly, looking over his shoulder to Hiram who was biting the knuckle on his left hand to counter the pain in his now throbbing knee.

* * *

"Look at this mess. It will take us all the rest of the day to just put it all back in order," an agitated Marie said angrily, as she and Christine began picking up the strewn linens about the linen room. "How did you do? Did you fall down? You didn't get hurt?"

"No, I was on the toilet when it happened and I was able to brace myself."

"The baby is all right?"

"I think so. I feel all right. Just scared. It was really something to be seated one minute and the other, spun around. And what about you?"

"I was in that old couples cabin and I was thrown onto the bed. Lucky I wasn't hurt," Marie answered as she handed Christine the end of a bed sheet to hold so that they could fold it.

* * *

"Are you all right?" David Stebbins called to the oiler, Eddie Thatcher, as he worked his way through the drive shaft alleyway.

"Aye, I think so," Eddie replied peering into the gloom of the space. "God, almighty. What happened? I lost my oil cup and had to crawl all over before I found it. Luckily the lamp didn't go out or we'd be in real trouble."

"You did fine. The shaft seems to be all right. Though it does seem to be running a little more noisier," the Chief Engineer said with a new concern.

"It comes and goes," Eddie answered nodding as he gave the receptacle another filling from the oil cup. "I think it depends if the boat is running with or against the waves."

"That could be. We are now running against an offshore current. It could be laboring because of that," a somewhat relieved David Stebbins allowed. Hoping he was right. "We will have it looked at and replaced in a few days."

"Mr. Stebbins," a voice called from below the ladder.

"Yes," he answered.

"You are needed in the furnace room. Hiram Faulks has been hurt and they need you."

"I'm coming," he called as he edged his way back along the walkway. "Keep up the good work, Eddie. I'll see that you and Howie get a bonus when we get back to Toledo."

"Thank you, Mr. Stebbins," the oiler replied, pleased that his devotion to his job was being recognized.

* * *

"The first thing I checked on was Mr. Lovelace's cabin. I was afraid that the incense candle might have tipped and could cause a fire but it was still upright and smoldering. God! What a smell! I didn't stay only to check. His body lying there gave me the creeps," an ashen Henry Wilkinson explained to Lawrence Dana, as he rinsed his hands and face with a washcloth.

"I just wonder if there really was a shoal or a reef," Larry Dana offered as he changed into a fresh shirt as his other was spotted with burn holes that he had gotten in helping the cooks put out the fires in the galley.

The two men shared the same cabin, just two forward of the Captain's that also served as office space for Henry's duties as ship's clerk.

"What makes you think that?" Henry asked, wondering why the negative attitude of the first porter.

"I've sailed this run now for two years, since forty-eight, and I remember no shoals or shipwrecks or anything five miles offshore of this part of the New York coast as Evans claims were here."

"But I understand that a shoal or a reef can be built up very quickly as in a storm with heavy winds and seas," Henry offered as a possible reason.

"We sailed this way three weeks ago and nothing then," Dana said. "And to my knowledge no storm of such consequence has been in this part of the lake since the likes of which could have caused such a shoal."

"Well, what do you think then?" Henry asked agreeing with Dana's assessment.

"I think that Evans screwed up."

"Well, everyone knows he has been drinking quite a bit since his wife got killed last spring when they were in Cincinnati visiting her folks. Even the Captain knows it, but they are good friends and either he doesn't want to say anything or he is ignoring it."

"I don't know," a still skeptical Henry frowned as he selected a boiled shirt and socks for himself. "He seems to be sensible. He's always on duty and I have never seen him as to what I would call drunk."

"You wouldn't say that if you knew what he says about you. Being sensible, I mean."

"About me!" Henry blurted, looking askance at Dana.

"Yes. About you. Words have a way of getting around," Dana shrugged and pulled his shirt over his head. "A word here and a word there. A wheelsman, a cook," he paused for effect, "a cabin maid."

"What has he said about me?" a now aroused Henry asked angrily.

"Oh. You're kind of prissy. A know it all."

"Shit! I don't even know the man. Why would he want to say or talk that way about me?"

"I don't know. Some say things about others to make themselves look good. Have you ever had words with him?"

"No. Never."

"Then it must be his drinking. If it isn't you, it would be someone else. Maybe me."

* * *

"How is Thomas?" Charles Roby asked his wife as he entered the cabin, noting it was back to its original state of orderliness.

"He is fine. I don't think the fall did more than to scare him, as it did me. He landed on me and I broke his fall."

"And you? Are you all right?" the Captain asked quietly as he raised the coverlet on the bassinet and looked into his man child's face with eyes of a father's affection.

"Yes, I think so," she replied. "But I will not be happy until

110

we get to Buffalo." Emily Roby moved to the bassinet. "This voyage has not been the most pleasant for me. For us," she motioned to the baby.

"I know," her husband agreed. "It has been a bad one all around. But we will be seeing Albert and Hazel tonight and I am sure our spirits will be renewed seeing them."

"Oh, yes. I am sure that our being with them will make some of our discomfort worthwhile," Emily said, hoping that what she was saying was true. "How is the boat? What happened?"

"It was an unmarked shoal. Fortunately, William was able to see a water disturbance above it and made an emergency turn in time to avoid running aground," Charles said knowingly lying of his first mate's near destruction of the Griffith.

"Thank God for William," his wife said with a soft smile as she bent and kissed the baby Thomas on the forehead.

CHAPTER SEVEN

Robert Hall

"You can be proud of your efforts in getting us to Chester," William Waters congratulated Robert Hall as they maneuvered Min toward a roadside watering trough on the approaches to Chester from the southeast by way of the Stoke-On-Trent Chester Post Road.

"We can all be proud." A modest and happy Robert smiled in reply. "It has been a long and wearisome eight days, but we have met our daily goals, even with Emma Foster's death."

The two found a place between two other wagons from caravans from other regions heading for Liverpool. "How long along?" A gray haired, beefy, red-faced man in about his middle forties, asked of William as he adjusted Min's brow-band and winker-straps, as she drew water in copious draughts into her parched, demanding throat.

"Eight days and tomorrow is our last," he answered rubbing Min's ears and forelock. "We have come from Ramsey, Cambridge way. Where do you be coming from?" he asked in turn.

"We are from Leeds, to the north. A three-day walk," the man answered.

Robert joined the two in their conversation. "It would seem our biggest problem now is to be able to find lodgings in Liverpool for the night as we leave tomorrow with the tide. God willing."

"Aye, and we too," the man answered brushing flies from his horse's head and eyes. "What packet do you sail on?"

"The Primrose," Robert answered as he checked Min in her ability to draw water from the crowded trough.

"We sail on the Highlander, bound for Philadelphia."

"And we for New York."

"Well, God speed to you and yours," the man said, nodding to both as he backed his horse, slapping her on her rump as they made off to make room for another driver and his horse from still another group of weary travelers.

The contingents from Ely and Ramsey were all gathered on the roadside, overflowing into the field alongside the edges having long given up trying to grow crops due to the heavy crowding along the main road between Liverpool and Birmingham. To compensate for crop loss, a number of farmers, or their agents, set up road side stands for selling items for which the traveler either forgot or would be needing in his trek to the New World and paying the top price for them.

"We will take a short rest here. Then we will proceed to Birkenhead and take the ferry across to the Liverpool Docks this afternoon." Robert said aloud to his group, to as many could hear him, as another group was passing by with carts and wagon wheels squealing, people calling, children crying and horses neighing under overloaded wagons.

* * *

Ethan Wilcox buttoned the fly on his trousers and returned to the group with others who had used the privy of a local church that was set back from the road behind a cemetery.

"It is lucky we have come so far, for our food is about out," Hilary Waters said as she handed him half an apple she had just purchased from a vendor. The other half she gave to Lorna who took it and looked at Ethan quizzically, who caught her look and turned away and walked to the rear of the caravan. She left

113

the side of her mother who, with Hilary, was passing out apples to the others of their group, and followed him.

"Ethan. Please wait," she called.

Ethan looked over his shoulder. He turned to her. "I know what you are going to ask," he stated. "And I have told you before. The little you know, the better you will be."

"But Ethan," she met up with him, "it has been a fine trip. You have been a great help to us all, even being a pallbearer for Mrs. Foster and helping Mr. Gray with his medicine chest part of the way. And even Father." She paused, "Mr. Waters has spoken of your being so helpful to the others. He has made no demands on you that you have not done willingly." Again she paused. "What of Mother and me? And Shirley? We love you. We will miss you terribly." She bowed her head. "We will need you in America."

Ethan took a bite of his apple and looked with sad eyes to his sister. "I know and I love you all as well. And I have given it much thought. I have also talked with Louisa . . ."

"Louisa Taylor? She knows?"

"Yes."

"And?"

"She wants me to stay and make the crossing. She left her father, her da, as she calls him, from the old ways. She told me I would never forgive myself if I were to leave you and Mother and Shirley. But . . . " he stated firmly, ". . . as soon as I can, I will strike out for California, in America, where they have found gold lining the streets."

"California? Where?" a pleased but surprised Lorna questioned.

"Aye. California, in America. The United States. I saw a notice on the post board in the town hall when we went through Stafford Town the other day. It seems there is a great discovery of gold in this California, a state in their union, which is halfway around the world from here and if I can get to New York, I should be halfway there from here. And as William is paying for my passage to New York, then I will be able to oblige him by staying on until then, but no later," he emphasized, throwing his apple core to a roan mare who gobbled it after its first bounce.

"Oh, Ethan," a relieved but still perplexed young Lorna exclaimed happily. "I am so happy that you will be with us on the crossing and maybe stay with us when we get to New York." She took his hand. "And maybe to this Medina."

"I didn't say that. I said to New York. My mind is made up."

Their conversation was interrupted by Robert Hall. "It is time that we move on." He called to his group who had taken the time to toilet and rest and to visit with one another.

* * *

"One more night." Elly said to Sophia as the two arose from where they had been sitting on the ground along side the Hall wagon.

"I only hope that all I have to do on the boat is to sit. My poor feet are going to be the death of me." Sophia grimaced as she put her full weight upon them.

"And me too, with my back," Elly added, using the wagon side to brace herself as she arose.

Min, her head bobbing and swaying from side to side, made a valiant effort to move back under Robert's gentle pulling of the reins, but she only stumbled and fell into a dead heap. A long sighing escaping from her lungs as her weight caused a collapsing of them.

"William!" Robert called excitedly.

"Aye! I see, Robert!" a distraught William answered as he hurried to the stricken horse.

"Damn!" an agitated Robert blurted. "One more day and we would have been able to have made it with her."

William nodded in agreement. "Ah, we did know that she was old and we were not too sure she would make the entire journey. She did better than I thought she would do," he said as he reached to undo the curb-bit as Robert began unhitching the breeching strap from the wagon.

Members of their group began gathering about the fallen horse and the two men as they began stripping the trappings from it. "What will we do now?" Elly asked aloud. "The wagon load is much more than we can handle. It is much too much for a human to try to pull."

"We will have to have teams of pullers," Robert answered. His main concerns now being: How would the carcass be disposed of and how to get it off the roadway?

"Ethan," he called seeing Ethan and his sister, Lorna, gaping at the dead horse.

"Aye?"

"Do you remember the vendor that we bought the apples from this morning?"

"Aye."

"Go see if you can fetch him. We will see if we can get something for Min and her trappings or how to get rid of her, a knacker perhaps. We have to keep moving and be on the ferry by this mid-afternoon or we will be late and maybe miss our sailing on Wednesday. Go! Hurry!"

Joseph Wildes

"What did he say?"

"He said we have only about twelve miles and we will be at the ferry in Birkenhead and that one crosses every two hours in the day to Liverpool Dock."

"We will make in time to our boat?" Julia said as she adjusted her bra to a snug fit after nursing the baby, Gwen.

"Oh, yes. He said that we are taking the same packet, the Primrose, and that if we wished, we could follow along with his group."

"They are a large group," she commented as they began gathering their belongings.

"Aye. He said that they now number thirty. One of them died on the road, a woman it was."

"It will be well that we get to the ferry when we do." Julia grunted as she placed Gwen on the cart and cinched the cord holding her hamper. "I hope they have some food," she added.

"I know. With you nursing the babe, we must get something. Our planning for our travel was well thought out except for how much victuals we should need."

"And for gloves and better shoes," she interjected.

"It seems that the others..." Joseph pointed to the Hall's entourage as they were reorganizing for the last leg of the overland portion of their trek after taking a rest and finishing what food they had, "...have just about used up their food supplies as well."

The village of Ellesmere Port, overlooking the Mersey River that flowed on its northern edges, was where the river, between it and Liverpool, was at its widest in its course from its origin above Manchester in the Yorkshire Highlands, and was the focal point of the Hall's and other groups that had converged from the far corners of the island on this 16th day of April, 1850.

The afternoon had turned from three days of intermittent rain and blustery winds, to one of bright sunshine, the wide sky above and arch of blue with just the touch of puffy clouds to the southeast. A feeling of well being and accomplishment trickled through the group. The warm sun energized them and the group from Ely, who had just eked out their last supply of food, began singing ditties to express their new enthusiasm which was then picked up by the others.

"It will be grand to spend the night in clean and dry surroundings," Murdoc Hall said to Albert Reynolds, as they took their accustomed position at the rear of the caravan.

"Aye," Albert coughed a reply. "I have caught a cold and my chest is in pain from the hacking these past days."

"I have heard you and others. But with the sun on our backs this day, we should do well." Murdoc offered as he turned to call to the two Hall boys who were running to catch up with the group.

The two boys, Stanley and George, had detached themselves from their group, with their mother's permission to do so but to stay in sight, when they had arrived in Ellesmere Port to go to the river's edge along a gravel path that followed along its steep banks.

"This is the River Mersey," George said as he looked across the wide expanse of moving water to the far shore. The river, swollen from the heavy spring rains surged by them as it moved toward the west to empty into the Liverpool Bay and then into the Irish Sea beyond.

"It is a big river," Stanley said in awe, as with his brother, the largest body of water he had ever seen.

"And it goes to the ocean," George added. "We will soon be sailing on a great ship to cross to America. Tomorrow."

"Mother is worried and I know Peggy is scared," Stanley noted as he threw a stick into the water and watched with fascination as it whirled and bobbed at a great speed, soon out of sight.

"Are you scared?" George asked.

"Yes." Stanley replied nodding his head, following a drifting log in its journey to the sea.

"I am too. But Father knows what is best and says it will be only a few weeks, at the most, and we will be in America, in New York." George added as he threw a stone into the water, its splash erased in an instant in the swift moving turbulence.

"He still doesn't know about your book?"

"No. I don't think so. It really hasn't taken up any needed space. I have it hidden in the clothes hamper. I think Mother knows I have it but she has said nothing."

"What do you suppose it will be like in America?" Stanley asked, a questioning frown on his young face.

"I don't know. But I have read of the colonies and Drake and Raleigh."

"What about Indians? Will we see any?"

"We could. Mr. Tomlinson told us once in session about them. He said that there were many tribes and that in warfare they ate their enemies."

"Oh!" Stanley shuddered.

"I think he was only teasing us though. I don't think they really do." George said smiling at his young brother's reaction.

The two brothers stood gazing across the wide waters looking to the north shore and the hills that lay beyond, now under a cover of bright sunshine, the green of spring tingeing the landscape.

"You know, Stanley," George offered solemnly, "I am glad we are going to America, to this place in Ohio..."

"Medina," Stanley added.

"Yes, to Medina. I have been thinking and from what I have read and what Mr. Tomlinson had told me and the others of things in America, other than Indians..."

Stanley nodded in understanding his brother's meaning.

"I would like someday to become a missionary to help the heathen Indians give their souls to Christ."

John Northy

The Ambrose was on a direct line toward the setting sun on a starboard tack. The sun, a huge crimson disc, just beginning to touch the horizon, threw a magnificent brilliance upon the packet as it pushed its way through cresting seas now abating from an earlier storm. John Northy wiped his eyes of salt spray, as he clung to the rigging in the mainmast, the sting of the salt spray and the taste of it on his lips, invigorated him. For the past three days, he had ridden in the lower shrouds midship on the mainmast during the daylight hours feeling firsthand the vicarious experiences of the sailors of the ship without their responsibilities or the hard toiling they had to undergo daily, foul weather or fair. As a paying cabin passenger, he was allowed a few privileges, such as playing sailor and enjoying the best of food. He did not regret the money he had paid for the crossing as a cabin passenger. He could have come steerage, and had even thought of doing so. It had cost him dearly of his limited funds but he knew and was learning more, day by day, of the privations the steerage passengers had to undergo and was content that he was not with them.

For the past three days, no steerage passengers had been allowed on deck and thus no cooking on the grates had taken place. He did not know exactly what went on below the booby-hatch but he did see the first mate and various seamen at times making sure the clogs were secured on the hatch covering and that no souls from below could venture out into the inclement weather. "It is for their own good." The first mate, a Mr. Holiday, told John when he, John, had wondered out loud as to how the steerage passengers could be held below decks for such a long period of time without the sun, water and fresh air. "They would not know of the ship's sudden movements in the heavy seas and could be tossed overboard with the slightest list," he laughed. "Also," he added, "the conditions they are under, and they are only temporary, are really no different from where they have come from. Many were tenement dwellers. On this trip, most are from Bristol. And the Frenchies, ha, they think they are in heaven. At least for these first three weeks, it has only been these past three days that the weather has been so uncooperative," the first mate laughed again as he turned and called to a seaman in the rigging to shake a leg and get the lead out of his ass.

John returned to his cabin, the ship settling down to a more leisurely run into the coming seas and the sun, now below the horizon signaling the end of another day. The ship's bell struck seven, telling John, who had learned the bells meaning, that it was now nineteen hours and thirty-minutes by naval time or seven-thirty to a landsman and that the ship's cook had a dinner special this night for the Captain's birthday party in the ship's saloon to which all cabin passengers had been invited. The three other passengers in John's cabin were an elderly man, a Mr. Lindsey, grumpy and secretive, who had little to do with the other three. A boy, George Talbot, not much older than John, who was to meet an uncle in New York who was then to take him to a place called Louisville in Kentucky. "Wherever in God's name that is!" he once stated to John and the third member, a man in his mid-thirties, Maurice Lynn, who said he was in imports. Just imports with no further explanation. With the exception of old Mr. Lindsey, the three got along and ate their meals together. The meal this night was actually a continuation of the afternoon's dinner but with special attention for the Captain. The meal was presented in the dining saloon which was ornately done in green and white with gold trim. The linens and silverware were of French Provincial motif and a miniature Oriental candelabra dominated the saloon.

A small spinet piano secured to the decking, was played by one of the lady passengers, a middle-aged prig of a woman, whose main renditions were French minuets which John felt put a damper on his enthusiasm for the special occasion. The main course consisted of consommé, clam chowder, and lentil soups, breast of lamb, chicken casserole, dry cider, coffee or tea, mixed nuts and hot rolls. To add to the festive occasion and add sparkle to the repast, Spanish wines were consumed during the meal and topped off with French champagne for the toast to the Captain. The Captain, Ezra Gray, was a portly red-faced, bald-headed man in his mid-fifties, who barely spoke to the passengers. He arrived late and left early. The Ship's Purser, a Mr. Marlett, informed the gathering that the Captain's haste in departure was due to his having gotten word late this afternoon that some of the steerage passengers were evidently unhappy with a few things and wished to speak with the Captain. "Not to mind," the Purser assured the cabin passengers. "Problems do arise with those who know nothing of what it is to be like on a ship, especially for weeks on end. Our Captain understood their concerns and he will meet with them in the morning and their problems would be taken care of immediately. If not sooner," he added with a smile as he noted that the cabin passengers had no concern at all for the steerage passengers.

The hearty meal with the Spanish wines, topped off with his having three goblets of French champagne, proved to be almost too much for John who rarely drank and had never had such a sumptuous meal in his life. He excused himself from his dinner mates and took a turn around the deck. The Ambrose was now on a port tack, wind from the southwest chasing frothy whitecaps that splashed against the hull with rhythmic beats.

The sky was clear with bright moonlight glowing on full sails. John worked his way gingerly along the slanted starboard spar deck pulling himself along the railing. He looked out over the blue-black waters moving in a constant heaving to the northeast to eventually crash upon the shores of Cornwall, and there to separate: one branch to the north to the Celtic Sea and then on into the Irish Sea, the other to the south and east into the English Channel, past Plymouth on to meet the waters of the North Sea. John shook his head and drew deep breaths. He grabbed and clung tight to a shroud line and wondered again, as he had each night since his leaving Ashburton and his family, if he would ever see England again.

Pierce Hill

A gray wall of sky with rumbling thunder and sheet lightning followed the Achill across the Irish Sea as it beat its way under full sail off the Carmel Head of Anglesy, Wales on its course to Liverpool Docks, still a good twenty leagues to the east. Fergus Kilbane and Pierce Hill stood at the starboard bulwark of the main deck, the wind to their backs coming in a steady gale. "I never knew that a boat trip could be so exciting." Fergus called to Pierce who bent his head toward him to hear over the roaring wind.

"Aye. Nor have I and it's not too well I feel with this rising and lowering of the waters." Pierce called back. His stomach churning and his mouth watering.

"A seaman told me when we came aboard that we could expect a rough crossing at this time of the year. The wind, he said, could be quite heavy and changing directions at all times." Fergus looked to a heaving following sea white foam scudding from wind driven crests. "And I believe him," he said turning his back to the first stinging pelts of rain as the cloud formation that had been following them all afternoon, finally caught up with the Achill, as a great blackness overtaking the packet as it shuddered under the weight of a torrential downpour of a spring storm reaching its peak after its trans-Atlantic crossing from its origins in the far Caribbean Sea and moving with the Gulf Stream into the far reaches of the North Atlantic.

"Everyone below. Return to your quarters," a Bosen Mate wrapped in foul weather gear, yelled into the wind as the Achill dove into a rising trough of seething sea. Others about the deck, cabin passengers and the few steerage passengers who could make the venture onto the limited space for their recreational walks, beat a hasty exit from the ship's deck for their compartments.

"And to think that we must put up with such as this again in our crossing the Western Sea in just a few days. And we will be going against the wind not with it. I have been told." Pierce said wearily and discouraged as he followed the others down through the booby-hatch into their steerage quarters, "'tween decks" as he heard them referred to by the sailors in an almost derogatory referral.

The Achill was a smaller type packet that plied between Dublin and Liverpool on a regular basis, weather permitting, as opposed to the trans-Atlantic packets. By comparison to them, the Achill could carry only two-hundred steerage passengers and twenty-two cabin passengers. But its small size, speed and mobility, with which larger ships could not compete, gave an edge on the inter-shipping between Ireland and England as well as an occasional side trip to Norway and Sweden for their American bound immigrants by way of Liverpool. Everyone wanted a piece of the immigrant pie, and the Achill was not to be denied. It would then sail twice a week between Dublin and Liverpool with a full load of passengers and food stuffs to England and mercantile goods back to Ireland, especially to Belfast, in Ulster, where it made a side trip about every other week, as the trade demanded and the weather allowed.

The two staggered through the dimly lit passageway, bent over as the height between the deck and the overhead was only about five feet. A swinging lard-oil lamp cast moving shadows in proportion to the heaving and rolling of the ship as it followed over the wind-blown sea. The stench of vomit and excrement met them as they approached their assigned quarters where Honora and Noreen were huddled together in a cramped three-foot by six-foot space enclosure atop the same space for Pierce and Fergus,

126

who used it only to make room for Honora to stretch when Pierce took Noreen to the head to wash and change her sodden clothing.

"And how do you feel now?" Pierce asked quietly of Honora as he knelt beside the opening into the trap-like compartment that was her sleeping and living quarters and passed for a bunk.

"Ach. It is my back. My tail bone," she gritted from the pain.

"You really did get hurt when the drayman caused us to jump out of his way?" he asked, realizing that she had been hurt more severely than what she first showed or admitted.

"How is Noreen?" she asked, moving her legs with pain trying to find a comfortable position.

"She is doing well. Fergus is tending to her." He helped her by moving her hips and putting his jacket under her legs to raise her knees. "Does that help?" he asked.

"Some."

"She has taken a liking for him," Pierce added.

"Aye. I can see that. It was indeed a very lucky day when we met him."

"But not under the circumstances," Pierce commented.

"No. It is true. Will he be able to join us on the next transport?" Surging seas heeled the Achill in a great angle causing Honora to roll violently against the side of her bunk. "Oh, Mother of God." She wept as the pain centered in her lower back. In another instant the ship righted itself, then rolled in the opposite direction throwing her to the other side of the bunk.

Pierce, almost at a loss as how he could help Honora in her back and forth motions, crawled into the bunk with her to have his body act as a buffer between her and the slatted sides and to wedge her in from the to-and-fro, up-and-down, wild movements of the boat. They clung together as the heavy seas began abating from the onslaught of the cutting edge of the storms fury as it passed over them and moved ahead to seek out other unfortunate ships lying in its path.

They lay holding each other for what seemed interminable minutes.

Pierce raised on his right elbow. "It seems we are settling down now."

"I have been praying that it would." Honora smiled. "And Jesus heard me," she paused. "I asked you before. Will Fergus be able to stay with us when we sail to New York?"

"I don't know. We will find out when we get to Liverpool and see our boat."

"How will we know what boat is ours?"

"Francis said that it is called the Primrose and it is at a dock called Prince's Dock. We are to look for a tavern called the White Swan on Waterloo Road where we are to meet a Mr. Gallagher, Terrance Gallagher, who is to have our papers and passage for the travel to New York."

"Can we be sure?" Honora braced herself and tried to shift herself to take pressure off her left hip.

Pierce shifted himself to allow her to move. "I'll back out and let you have the bunk to yourself now."

"I have to pee," she said softly. "I will need the bucket."

"Fergus took it with him and Noreen. Can you wait?"

"No, but I'll be all right. I'll have to be," she said resignedly, as she again shifted her body to accommodate her new discomfiture. "Can we be sure that this Mr. Gallagher will have our papers and passage? Can he be trusted?" she continued.

"I don't know for sure. We can only trust the man. Francis said that he has sent others who support the confederation and are on the run and has helped them to get to New York and Boston."

"And what of Fergus? Is he a member of the confederation? Will he help him as well if he is not and keep us together?"

"Ach. I don't know. We have not talked politics and I really don't want to know. I. . ." Pierce shook his head, "I . . ." The ship suddenly heeled again and listed to port with a sudden lurch as a maverick wave caught the Achill and tossed her almost on her side.

"Oh! Jesus, Mary and Joseph!" Honora cried pleadingly, as she rolled again against the cage of her bunk. Others in the quarters were also tossed about from their rickety bunks, those on the top being thrown to the deck in heaps. The overhead lamp swung wildly. The light cast grotesque shadows along the passage way, only to be blown out by the violent motion, casting the steerage compartment into almost complete darkness save for an enclosed wall lamp near the hatchway that led up through the booby-hatch and topside.

"Noreen! Noreen! Where is my baby?" Honora wailed, again in pain only to be compounded now with worry of her child.

"She is all right." A shaken Pierce arose from where he had been thrown and went to his wife. "I see them now. They are making their way to us. She is fine," he lied as it was too dark to really distinguish anyone in the gloomy semi-darkness.

"Oh, Pierce! My God! What have we gotten ourselves into? What have we done wrong?" a now thoroughly distraught Honora sobbed uncontrollably.

CHAPTER EIGHT

Buffalo

At 4:18 P.M. on the afternoon of Saturday, June 15, 1850, one of the pilot boats in the Buffalo harbor took up a line from the steamship G.P. Griffith, and a Mr. Peter Lassiter, Pilot, came aboard and directed it into its berth at the Main Street dock. Port Buffalo on this sunny, mild mid-June afternoon, was the host to a large number of sailing vessels, both sail and steam. A break in a bank of the Erie Canal near Lock Berlin created an eleven-day delay in transients coming from New York City via Albany, which in turn caused a shortage of passengers scheduled to leave earlier. While some vessels sailed to meet their regular requirement schedules, others held over and caused a backup of shipping in the harbor and great demands on the capabilities of the port and its facilities, until the influx of more than the usual immigrants on a given day could be accommodated.

"Charles, how good to see you, and you too, Emily. How wonderful you look. And little Thomas. My, what a handsome lad." Albert Tiffany greeted the Griffith's Captain, his wife and baby boy at the passageway ramp leading from the main deck to the dock.

"Albert, how nice it is to see you again. It has been too long a winter." Emily greeted her best friend's husband. "How is Hazel?" she asked, giving him a hug.

"She is well and sends her regards. She is sorry she cannot

be here to greet you but her mother is not too well and she has been spending time with her as much as she can. But she will join us later at the Mercer Hotel where we have reserved rooms for you and Charles and for your daughter, Candace and Charles' mother, also, a milk nurse for Thomas."

Albert Tiffany at forty-two was a tall, gray at the temples and thin to almost being called skinny example of a transported New Yorker who had to always bear the comparison to his renown cousin, Charles. As a co-owner of the firm of Tiffany and Lockwood, Shipping Agents, Buffalo and Toledo, he was aware and alert to anything that had to do with the shipping on Lake Erie and the other lakes as well.

"I have a number of concerns that you will want to know of." Charles Roby said after the two had said adieu to Emily, his mother and the children as they took a brougham coach to the Mercer Hotel to prepare for the evening's activities set up by the Tiffanys. But first to rest and relax after the day's ordeal.

The two men returned to the Captain's cabin and opened a bottle of apple brandy that Albert had brought aboard for the welcoming occasion.

"Here's to the Griffith, as fine a vessel as has ever been. A toast!" Albert said raising his glass.

Charles nodded and met the glass with his own. "We had a scare, just this afternoon that could have been the end of her or at least done some severe damage."

"Eh. What?" A wondering Albert sipped his drink.

"A near miss of our running aground on a supposed shoal."

"Supposed?"

"Yes." Captain Roby nodded as he sipped his drink. "My First Mate William Evans…" He paused. "You've met him?"

"Yes. A most pleasant fellow. He's been with you for a while." He thought a moment. "Isn't he the one whose wife died quite unexpectedly?"

"Yes. Carrie. A most tragic accident."

"Um. Tell me about the shoal."

"It was on his watch and I believe he gave the wheelsman a wrong call from one that I had given him."

"He gave the wheelsman a different call than you gave him?"

"Yes."

"Then he must be.reprimanded, or released."

"Yes. I know. I intend to do just that tomorrow. I do not want to disgrace him, however, in front of the crew. He was, or still is, an excellent officer. There has never been one better. But," Charles paused as recollecting better times. "I know that his wife's death has taken a toll on him both mentally and physically."

Albert Tiffany looked sagely to his friend and business partner. "Charles, I know that you will do what you have to do. We can...."

"Wait. That isn't all. I...We still have other problems." Charles said as he took a long pull at his drink.

"Oh, what more, pray tell?"

"It seems that we have a problem of disposing of a corpse. A very decomposed corpse."

"Charles, what in the hell are you talking about?"

"I have had our Chief Engineer, David Stebbins..."

"Yes, I know David."

"He has packed an old man's body, a Mr. Archer Lovelace, who died just after coming aboard in Cleveland. Actually only a few minutes after we left Cleveland."

"Charles, I don't know," a now puzzled Albert offered.

"We have him packed in ice, our last lot from last winter. We are now out of ice and we need you or someone to get an undertaker to take his body and dispose of it."

"Well. I don't know," a bewildered agent said as he added a touch to his drink. Not sure what his responsibilities was in such a situation.

"He is in his cabin wrapped in a leaking tarpaulin. We need someone to come and take him away. Now!"

"Charles," an exasperated Albert said after a long silence as

132

he weighed his Captain's statement. "This is Saturday afternoon and to be honest, this is the first time I have ever had to contend with a corpse…"

"And a discomfiting one," Charles added. "Something must be done. I have an upset crew and passengers who can spread the news ashore faster than a wildfire." He paused. "And that isn't all."

"Oh, my God."

"We also have his ward, an Indian boy named Kuruk, as well as four trunks belonging to the old man."

"His ward? An Indian boy? Trunks?"

"Yes, but that is too much to go into now. I need… We need someway or somebody to get him off the boat. Now. As soon as possible!"

"Charles, you are giving me a handful. I…"

"Hah! That isn't all."

"Oh, Charles, what more could be wrong?"

"Thirty-five cases of piss-poor wine. That's what's wrong."

The Griffith's agent looked at Charles with a deep, questioning gaze. "Piss-poor wine?" he intoned slowly.

"Aye, and while it is not really your concern, it was a side business venture of mine. I will still need your help in deciding what I am to do with them."

"What happened? What do you mean…" he paused, gesturing, "piss-poor wine?"

"Oh, crap!" A now near tipsy Charles laughed testily. "This hasn't been the best of voyages by any means."

"No one has ever said they were to be," Albert gestured with his glass.

"I know. I know." A now suddenly tired and self-effacing Captain Roby muttered, wishing that all this were behind him.

"Well, now," a staid agent said as he finished his drink. "I'll see what I can do about your pariah. That will be my first order of business, then we will discuss the Indian boy…. Er…"

"Kuruk."

"Yes. And what about the sailing trunks?"

"I am having my clerk, Henry Wilkinson... You know him?"

"Yes. I met him when you were here in May."

"He is to contact you or an attorney to see about their disposition. I want him to see you first and he should be contacting you any time now. As soon as he sees to the unloading of our cargo."

"Except for the wine."

"Yes, except for the wine. It should be stored separately."

"I'll see to it."

An exasperated Charles looked to his friend, tipping his glass to him in a salute. "Why does one have to put up with so much? I only wish to sail, to see the beautiful waters of this inland sea. Why do we have to put up with such tripe just to make a living?"

"Charles," an understanding Albert responded, "if we knew the answer to that, we'd all be as well off as your rich-bastard-brother-in-law, Billy."

* * *

"Mr. Winslow, you wrote in your reply to my inquiry of the bituminous oil being available that I could have six kegs at two dollars a keg. As it is, I have only received five kegs and you raised the price to three dollars a keg. Where is the sixth and why have you raised the cost?"

An embarrassed Geoffrey Winslow, of the firm of Turner and Sons Wholesalers, brushed his slight grey hair with his right hand as he held his pince-nez glasses to the bridge of his nose with his left. "Yes, I see that we had six kegs reserved for you for delivery on the fifteenth of this month. That means that we should have six of them here for you to have received."

"So. Where is the sixth? And why a change in its price?"

"I'm sorry but it seems that all we have are but five for you. We have to meet other orders as well. There was also a break in the canal..."

"A break in the canal? Where? When?"

"Near Lock Berlin, in Wayne County, just above Seneca Falls. We heard of it only five days ago when the last barge before the break came through. It happened on the fourth and the barge traffic has been backed up for miles in both directions ever since."

"What has that to do with my receiving only five kegs?" an impatient and near disgusted David Stebbins asked icily.

"There is more coming and we hoped to add one from the new order to your order to make it your sixth keg."

"When will this new order arrive?" a now fidgeting David asked as he looked out of the office windows and observed the crowded dock and adjacent streets in the harbor area on this now late Saturday afternoon in a bustling and dynamic Buffalo. All manner of traffic was moving to and fro in a festive atmosphere.

The Griffith and two other steamers were disgorging their cargos of mostly farm goods and lumber from the western reaches of the lake that took in the agricultural regions of eastern Indiana, southeast Michigan and northwestern Ohio, while other steamers and sloops were loading immigrants as well as manufactured goods for shipment west from as far east as Boston, New York and New Haven, all to sail yet this balmy and beautiful June late afternoon or early evening. The weather was ideal. A light cooling rain had fallen in the late afternoon, just before five o'clock but it did not dampen the excitement of the throngs of multinational immigrants to the New World with their multiple of tongues as they milled about seeking their transports to the west and a hopefully promising future in this bounteous and beautiful land.

"We hope that the oil and other of our wares will be in yet this evening," the wholesaler offered as he sorted through various billings on his desk. "You are concerned, sir, as to the raise in our quoted price to you earlier," he added.

"Yes. I thought it was a set price," David responded.

"It is an immutable law of economics that supply and demand controls the cost of an item." Mr. Winslow almost lectured. "With this shortage, due to the break in the canal, we do have a shortage and thus an excessive demand. We must meet then the demand with those who will pay for the product."

"I am well aware of the immutable laws of economics as you call them," an offended and a put-down David replied. "And I think I can understand your trying to meet the needs of other users of the oil as well as myself and I will applaud your trying to make an extra dime, but my steamer, the Griffith, sails tomorrow morning at ten-thirty sharp. I am sorry about the break in the canal but I am also determined that I get the six kegs of the bituminous oil by nine-thirty tomorrow, at the latest, or there will really be hell to pay. Please see that all six kegs are on the dock no later than that time."

"I am sorry, Mr. Stebbins," the wholesaler said almost fawning, "but sometimes we have to take from Peter to pay Paul as the saying goes. We have other clients as well as yourself and we try to meet all their needs. I hope you understand."

"Yes, Mr. Winslow, I think I do. But," he jabbed his finger, "if you had to take from Peter to pay Paul, please put me down as Paul Stebbins. Good day, sir. I have other business to attend to."

* * *

"Aunt Barbara?"

"Surprise, Henry!" A smiling wisp of a woman in her middle to late fifties and attired in a red jacket over a white crinoline skirt greeted her sister's son as he returned to his cabin to gather shipping papers and the steamer's manifest for the port authorities.

A taken-aback Henry hugged his aunt leaning toward her and over the extended hoop of her skirt. It was the latest in style of the well-to-do and his aunt proved to be a fine model of its popularity.

"I saw you working with your men in your unloading of the cargo. I didn't want to disturb you while you were working so hard so I asked a sailor boy where your office was and he gave me your cabin number. I hope you don't mind if I made myself at home."

"Oh no. It's just that I didn't expect to see you on this trip. We are only in and out. Tomorrow morning we leave at ten o'clock precisely."

"Yes, I know," she giggled. "I am going to join you on your trip back to Toledo. I want to surprise your mother and father as I have surprised you."

"Oh, you have, Aunt Babs," Henry said calling her by her family nickname. "And I am sure they will be pleasantly surprised. But … How? When…"

"I made arrangements through Mr. Lockwood, one of the companies agents. He is an old friend of mine and your late Uncle Ernest, God rest his soul," she said as she reached into her reticule and brought out a yellow passage ticket. "I am in cabin eight. I will need someone to bring my belongings aboard from my carriage that is waiting around the corner from the dock. It is so busy here. I couldn't get any closer."

"Yes," Henry nodded. "I understand that there has been a break in the canal and it has caused quite a problem here with a backup of shipping and barge traffic." He looked to her ticket. Oh, God, he thought. "Ah, I'm afraid that the cabin you have been assigned will not be ready for another couple of hours. Let me check the passenger list and I will see about another cabin." He added, "I'll also see about your belongings and that they will be brought aboard to my cabin in the meantime."

His aunt nodded understandingly.

"You may stay here if you wish," he motioned to his surroundings, "but I am sorry, Aunt Babs, I must meet now with our attorney and the port authorities to go over our boat's register and our passenger list. We are having immigration problems with Canada and we have to show citizenship of all our passengers."

"Oh, I know, Henry," his aunt motioned with her left hand. "You are busy with many things to do. I will stroll about and stay out of your way and the other's as well."

Damn, Henry thought. Not angry but perturbed as he left his aunt and proceeded to the dock and his meeting with the company's lawyer. He had earlier sent a runner asking for an emergency meeting at their office, Andrew Putnam on Front Street, a few blocks from the dock to discuss Mr. Lovelace and the problems of what to do with the Indian boy.

He was mostly perturbed because his aunt, now being in attendance, put a damper on his hoped for plans that he had for his night's stay in Buffalo. If Marie couldn't or didn't want to be with him, he would make plans to visit a whorehouse on the south side he had heard Bill Tillman and John Paulding talking about on the last trip to Buffalo. He asked them a few innocent and leading questions to find where the place was and the two were most zealous in their describing it and where it was located. Now he had to spend some time with his aunt. Damn. Damn. But now to the business at hand, he thought. Old Man Lovelace. His ward, the Indian boy... and... he paused in his thinking. The four travel trunks.

* * *

"I am Homer Westinghouse. Your runner said that there was an emergency."

"Yes. We certainly have an emergency," Albert Tiffany answered a tall but slightly stooped shouldered individual in a dark green frock coat and a black top hat who had just come aboard with two assistants. Albert, himself, had just returned to the steamer from his office after his talk with Charles Roby earlier from where they separated. The Captain to the hotel, Albert to his office·and a check on an undertaker and then returned to the Griffith. He wasn't too surprised the way the man was dressed as he realized he was an undertaker and was attired in his professional garb.

"We have had a death. An old man died just after the Griffith left Cleveland, and with the age of the individual and the humid weather, we must get him off the boat and disposed of as soon as possible."

"Yes, I can understand," the undertaker replied as the two and his two assistants walked to the Lovelace cabin.

"We would like to be as discreet as possible," Albert cautioned. "While some passengers and crew know of the death, they don't know of the problems we have had with his rapid decomposition."

"Yes, that can be a problem, especially in this warm weather," the undertaker agreed. "The gentleman's name?" The undertaker then asked as he took a pencil and a pad from his frock coat pocket and touched the pencil tip to his tongue.

"Archer Lovelace. He was an apothecary in Cleveland for many years." Albert offered not really knowing why he added that information.

"His age?"

"Quite elderly I understand. I really don't know. Is his age really necessary?"

"For our records. Merely a statistical requirement." He paused. "Who will be responsible for the cost of the..." he ahemed, "disposing of the deceased?"

"My office, of course. We will handle the costs. You can bill us at 146 Canterbury Court."

"Oh, yes. I know of you and where you are. But this is a Saturday afternoon." He looked to his pocket watch. "Actually early evening and if we have to do as you ask, we will have to expedite our usual procedures of interning the deceased."

"You have a place? A cemetery?" Now wondering about this undertaker's scruples, Albert asked.

"A place? Yes and we need to be paid in cash. Now."

"Now?"

"Now."

Albert was in a stew. He could understand the undertaker's demand of cash on the barrelhead as it was, but he always wanted any business transactions in writing and accounted for. He cleared his throat. "How much are you asking?"

"Twenty-five dollars."

"Twenty-five..." a surprised Albert gulped.

"Yes, and if he is as bad as you say he is, it might cost you even more when we see the cadaver," a now-in-command-of-the-situation undertaker explained to a hesitant and confused President of the Tiffany and Lockwood. "As it is, even as we stand here without the cabin, I can smell the rotting. It can be an odious task just to get him off your boat, much less of disposing him ashore."

An astonished Albert felt for his purse. Twenty-five dollars! He thought. Twenty-five dollars! For that much he could have him embalmed with a full showing as well as a minister or a priest, or even a rabbi, to eulogize him.

As the four were talking at the cabin door, a number of passengers, including the old couple, as they were all leaving the steamer, slowed their pace as they listened to the conversation. Albert looked about. He had no choice but to nod his head in agreement. He withdrew his hand from his purse, cash in hand. "Sold," he said.

* * *

"Ah. There you are. I was wondering if I would get to see you and know what your plans are for the evening," a dapper Larry Dana greeted Marie and Christine as they were carrying a basket load of soiled linens to the dock where they were to pile it with others on the tailgate of a laundry company's buckboard.

"It'll be me to the hospital to see Ollie for a while, then back here to our cabin," she nodded to Christine, as she answered, puffing from the exertion of carrying the weight of the clothes basket between them as they moved down the ramp.

"And you," Larry smiled at Christine, a gleam in his eyes.

"I..." she hesitated, looking to Marie for guidance.

"She's a new girl in town," Marie said with a knowing look of raised eyebrows to Larry. "A girl has to be able to say she saw Buffalo at night. It is a great town and has a lot to offer. Don't you think?"

"Yes, it does and if I may," he gazed at Christine with a grin, "I would like to escort you on the town tonight. We can even get your friend that souvenir we talked about."

Christine wiped her brow with the back of her left hand after they set the basket in the back of the buckboard. "I have not the clothing or have had a wash." She hoped that would deter Larry's wanting to be with her. "I had planned on just staying on board the steamer and get a full night's sleep."

"Oh, that won't do." Marie countered, looking to Larry with a motion of her head. "I have a dress you can wear," she said to a silent and subdued Christine. "It is a little too small for me. Maybe a bit big for you but we can tuck it in here and there and I am sure we can have you ready in no time."

"I can wait," an anticipating Larry stated though as he realized Marie was helping him in his wanting to make out with Christine.

A beaten Christine answered solemnly, "Give me time to wash and fix my hair. I have no bonnet except my . . ."

"I have one. That's no problem," Marie said. "It's old but it will do."

An elated Larry exclaimed, "And I'll be here at the ramp," he checked his pocket watch, "in one hour."

"That will be fine." Marie smiled, a feeling of accomplishment overcoming her. Hell, she thought, if it wasn't for Ollie, I could be meeting with Henry and maybe the two couples of us could make a foursome. The four of us! Ah. What a thought. Then she pondered. Henry? The last she saw of him was when he was talking to an older woman dressed in a red jacket top with a white crinoline skirt and a cute Armena toque, outside his cabin. Who was she? And where is he? He's been gone a long time.

* * *

"You say the Indian boy...?"

"Kuruk. No tribal designation."

"You say this Indian boy, Kuruk, is or was a ward of the deceased," he looked at his notes, "Archer Lovelace, and that you are concerned as to what must be done with him legally." Andrew Putnam, Attorney at Law and the Studdiford Shipping and Transit Company's legal representative in Buffalo, asked Henry Wilkinson.

"Yes. We feel that we are only the means of transportation for the lad and that the death of Mr. Lovelace does not impose a legal requirement upon us." Henry explained as he replaced his coffee cup on its saucer and wiped his lips with a napkin.

"Yes, of course." The attorney paused for a moment. "If this Kuruk was a ward, then there must be legal papers attesting to such. Have you seen them?"

"No. Why should I?"

"No matter. If there are legal adoption papers that is one problem. If he were a ward in name only, that is another story. From my experience, limited as it is in these situations, most of the wards are just in name only and have no recourse in the courts if being decided upon to be disposed of at a later date by the sponsor." The lawyer brushed away a fly that was flitting about his desk. "That has been the case in a number of instances of runaway slaves who have come north through the Underground Railroad and had been taken under the wing of an antislavery individual or group, well intentioned as they may be, only to find that after a while they have neither the wherewithal to feed and clothe the individual or have lost their interest in the movement, and then turn on their own and eventually they become a drag on society."

"Then what should we do?" Henry asked.

"As you said, turn him over to the Indian Affairs Authority. You do not know his tribe?"

"No. No one does. He doesn't look like any of the Eastern woodlands Indian types that I know of."

"Where is he now?" the lawyer said as he offered Henry a glass of sherry from a decanter that he had taken from a cabinet behind his desk, and took one himself.

Henry accepted the glass and raised it to his nose. "He is still aboard the Griffith. He was being tended to by the Captain's mother."

"Tended to?"

"Yes. He was injured in a slight accident when the boat made a sharp turn to avoid something or other. Nothing serious. A bump on the head I understand."

The attorney shrugged. "And you leave tomorrow?"

"Yes. At ten-thirty."

"Then the Indian boy must be placed in a home or a situation where he can be looked after until at least Monday morning at the earliest."

"Yes. I understand, but…"

"Don't get yourself upset," the lawyer cautioned. "That is what I am here for. I will see that he is placed in the care of the Ursulin Sisters at St. Patrick's. They take in waifs and transits until somebody takes them in, or other arrangements are made for them. But…" he emphasized with his drink held high, "we must get him there as soon as possible."

"When?" a relieved Henry answered hoping for another offer of sherry as he finished his glass.

"Tonight. Now. You leave in the morning. Then what?"

"I don't know. This is new to me and the Captain. He, Captain Roby, put it to me and now I put it to you."

"This Mr. Lovelace? What papers did he or do you have of his?" Mr. Putnam changed the course of the conversation and tipped the sherry decanter to Henry's eager glass.

Papers? Henry had to bide his time, he had to think. "He had a small travel case as did the boy, the toiletry type. I don't know if they held any papers. But he had and we have them now, four large travel trunks. I am not at all aware of what they may hold. They are heavy, I have been told." Henry thought. Maybe this lawyer would know what to do with them. Can I trust him with my idea. I will need some help. He seems to be quite knowing which way the wind blows or which way it should blow.

"To whom were the trunks addressed in England?" the lawyer asked as he offered the decanter toward Henry's again empty glass.

"To himself." Henry remembered, nodding for a refill. "A place called Chipponham Gloucestshire, England. I have no idea where that may be, however."

"Who would know if they arrived or report them if they did not?" a now willing accomplice asked of the clerk. His innuendo not lost to Henry.

"The boy maybe? Although he could hardly speak English so I really don't know if he can even read." A now relieved Henry replied, knowing that he had a professional to help him in his developing devious plan for the ultimate destination of old Mr. Lovelace's four heavy trunks.

CHAPTER NINE

"What does it say?" a fatigued Albert Reynolds asked William Waters as they stood before a poster board outside of the Emigration Office on Waterloo Road, three blocks from the Prince's Dock.

"It says it is a warning. A notice, I believe." William replied adjusting his reading spectacles as he peered at the rainwater-splotched notice being exposed to a mid-afternoon thunderstorm brought in from the Irish Sea, dousing an unwanted and unneeded torrential storm on what had earlier been a sunny and serene landscape, now dark and dreary.

"It speaks of cholera," he continued. "It seems to be a problem."

"Cholera?" Albert questioned, with a hacking cough. "Here? In Liverpool?"

"Yes, evidently." William read silently for a few moments. He then read aloud to Albert and others of their group who gathered around. "Her Majesty's Colonial Land and Emigration Commissioners feel that it is best to recommend to the parents of families..." He stopped to again wipe his spectacles.

"What does it mean?" A man's voice from the group asked as they huddled in a bunch to get mutual protection from the rain.

William turned and faced the questioner, "It would seem there is fear of a cholera outbreak and the authorities are asking not to sail to America until a milder season is upon us, especially if we have children or someone who is ill."

"Bosh!" another male voice grumbled. "We have been on the roadways best over a week now and they tell us we canna go on when we are ready to board our boat."

"No, not really," William tried to explain. "It seems to be only a notice of what could happen. I don't think we have to worry. We have a cough or two among us but they will be gone when the weather changes as we travel across the ocean. We are all in good health otherwise and I am sure when Robert and Abram Clemont return with our place to stay this night, we will be well on our way tomorrow."

"I don't know now," a woman's voice stated uncertainly. "I hear this cholera can be a terrible thing. Only a year or so ago in Belfast, in Ireland, I was told, that the cholera caused many deaths."

"I am sure they are only being careful. After all they are not saying we can't sail. They are just asking us to take precautions and eat well and dress for the weather." William replied to the "doubting Thomas." "I am sure," he continued as he saw Robert and Abram returning from their visit to the Emigration Office, "that if all was not well, they would not allow us to proceed. Hi, Robert," he called waving his right arm to him and Abram as they rejoined the group.

"And where do we spend this night?" a subdued and spent voice asked of Robert, its gender muted.

"We are to go to the White Swan, a tavern and boarding house on Merkel Street, no more than a ten minute walk, I have been told." He looked at a paper in his hand. "We are to go north," he nodded to his left, "on Waterloo Road until we come to the Regent Bridge, cross it and take the road to the right and go straight until we see the sign, a blue with a white swan painted on it."

The last day of the overland trek was drawing to a close as the weary and weather-beaten caravan of Ramsey and Ely migrants to the New World took up their wares and began the last leg for a good night's lodging and sleep for tomorrow at dawn they board the Primrose and with the flood tide, depart for America. The good Lord willing.

A heavy, dampening mist now took over from the heavy rains that had plagued them since they earlier boarded the ferry in Birkenhead, as Sophia Hall gathered her four children about her. "We want to stay close together. While it was bad enough on the road, it can be worse here," she admonished them as the group began to mingle into the mainstream of traffic on Waterloo Road with its multitude of humanity moving in all different directions with seemingly little or no direction or control.

"Ethan," Lorna Waters called to her brother.

"Yes, I am here," he answered as he picked up Shirley to carry her as her feet were soaking wet from the rain water still flooding the roadway.

"Ethan. I am so tired." Lorna said almost weeping.

"Aye, and me too. As well as others. Mother too. This day has taken its toll on many of us. All of us really," he acknowledged as he took her left hand helping her along.

"It would be so nice if the weather was as it was yesterday," Louisa Taylor said gloomily to Edith and Laura as they sloshed through the roadway that knew nothing of catch basins. "My Uncle Joseph," she continued, "once told me when he had been here to Liverpool when he was a boy that it was beautiful small town that looked out on a place he called Bidstone Hill that overlooked the river where it entered into a bay. He loved it and said he always wished he could go back and live there. But he never did. He died and is buried in Ramsey. I just wished that it could have been like that today. Oh, what a terrible place to have to live in now.

"Yes, and we are to spend only the night here. I do miss our village." Edith said wiping her face with a well-worn cloth.

"We must not dwell on what we would like or what we will miss," a little irritated, Lorna chided her sister. "We have made our commitment and we must live with it."

Edith looked to her sister and shrugged. "Yes, I know. I am sorry. I think this past week has taken so much from all of us."

"Well, I only hope that all goes well with our sailing tomorrow," Louisa said as she noticed a small lad inching his way along side her. She was appalled by his clothing and appearance. He was a small fellow with a pinched face and a pug nose. His clothing looked to have been passed down as they fit loosely and his shoes were much too large for his feet.

"'Ello," he called to her. "Kin I elp ye wi your baggage? Ony a pence. I'm strong, I am. And I can ease yer lod. Ony a pence."

Louisa could hardly understand his English, if that is what he spoke. It was almost like a foreign tongue not at all like her native Cambridgeshire. She looked to him as he pranced about her. It was nothing like she had ever heard or seen before.

"Hi! Move on you little scut! Git!" A strong voice called out from the crowd to the street gamin. "Git or I'll kick your... Oh, I am sorry, Miss," a contrite and apologizing young man in his early-to-middle twenties nodded to Louisa, white teeth flashing in the dimness of the afternoon, said as he joined her from the passing crowd. "You will have to forgive these little dirty beggars. You can't trust them. Not a one! They will steal you blind if you are not careful."

"Why, thank you," Louisa said, pleased that a gentleman had come to her aide in her coping with the urchin and what might have been a bad situation.

"And now," the blade asked, pleasantly, "I seem to be going your way. May I have the pleasure of assisting you in your journey to... " He paused.

"I...We," she motioned to the group about her, "are going to..." she hesitated not really sure where they were heading.

"To the White Swan on Merkel Street," Edith answered, eyeing the young man cagily.

"Ah. How grand. I am going by there, myself, and if I can be of any help with your luggage, I will be only too happy to oblige."

"Why, thank you," Louisa replied, glad that she would be relived of having to carry her wares since the demise of Min. "How very nice of you."

The young man, a dandy type, was clothed in a round hat with a broad brim tilted at a rakish angle. He was wearing a brown coat with wide lapels and black trousers. Hessian boots, decorated with golden colored tassels, now soaked and blackened from the rains, set him off.

"My, you certainly have a load," the young man commented as he took Louisa's wicker valise, her da's parting gift to her, and hoisted it on his left shoulder.

The milling street throng pressed upon the Ramsey-Ely group as they tried keeping together. "Here, Stanley, keep with us. George, watch out for your brother," Sophia's voice could be heard. A number of travelers from other caravans as well as the city dwellers mixed with them. A drizzling rain began bringing on a chill that Albert Reynolds felt only too well as he bent over in a coughing spasm to be aided by his travel companion, Murdoc Hall.

"Do you suppose Peter Gray has something for my cough in his cabinet?" Albert asked, almost pleading.

"I dunno. But we should soon be at the boarding house. We have already traveled to the bridge." Murdoc pointed. "And it is just on the other side down away. Come," he added taking Albert's right arm, "I'll tend to you till we get there."

Robert Hall looked over his right shoulder searching for his charges in the gathering twilight, mitigated by the drizzle and now foggy conditions.

"We are here now at the bridge," he said to those near him. "We will take a time to see that all of us are together. Ethan," he called to Ethan Wilcox, who was attending his younger sister, "circle among our people and see if all is well and that we are still together. This crowding and milling about of so many is almost too much for our people."

"Ramsey!... Ely! Here by the bridge." Ethan called aloud

as he waded into the crowd of passersby, many who gave him dirty looks for his intrusion into their walking space.

"Make way. Let me through," a heavy set man, attired in great coat and a hat pinned with a badge of a lamplighter, to give him authority, called as he edged his way into the group about the base of a lamppost, carrying his ladder and a lamp. They parted and he was able to attain his goal and commenced to set his ladder on the lamppost at the approach to the bridge which held three separate burners enclosed with dirty glass prisms. He placed his ladder on the lamp irons and proceeded to his task.

The Ramsey-Ely groups milled about in the semi-darkness until a flickering gleam, then a steady glow from the three lamps cast a pale but luminous light upon them.

"We are all here," Ethan told Robert as he joined them leading a somewhat dazed Brendan Foster. "I caught him just as he was about to turn down a side road. He seems to be very confused."

"Aye. We will have to keep a close touch with him," Robert said. "But we are still all together. We will want…"

"My valise! Where is my valise?" a near hysterical Louisa Taylor cried out. "It was here only a moment ago. The man… The young man… He is gone with my valise." She stood on her tiptoes to see above the astonished gathering to see if she might be still able to see the thief. A murmur arose from the group. "The dirty sneak." "Good heavens." "What next?" filled the damp air.

"Oh, ho," the lamplighter cackled as he stepped down from his ladder, turning to Louisa. "You lost yer valise you did. Ha. Be glad it wasn't yer life."

"Eh! What do you mean?" Joseph Wildes questioned, as he and Julia and the baby Gwen, joined the group sidling up to Louisa. "Why do you say that?"

"Ye are from the country. I can tell," the lamplighter nodded to the group as a whole as he surveyed the gathering of pale, gaunt faces under his limited lamps illumination. "May I give ye all a word of warning?" he said as he lifted his ladder to his right shoulder. "Be aware and not trusting of any stranger. Anyone here in Liverpool! Yer young lady," he nodded to Louisa, who was almost beside herself with reproach, "has been taken. Oh, we have too many of these sneak thieves who are quick to take advantage of anyone who is foolish enough to give them a lead and think of them as a friend. No so." He pointed his left index finger up.

"But he seemed so nice. So much of a gentleman." Louise tried to explain. "We had a grand talk along the way."

"Ah, yes," the lamplighter agreed, nodding. "And may I ask? Did you see a young lad about? A wee boy," he said placing his left hand out for height.

"Yes. He wanted to carry my valise, but the young man..."

"Ah, yes," the lamplighter shook his head. "I know of them. They are a pair. A team of thieves as ever there was. Some call the tyke, Noddy and the older one is called Reggie. No one knows their real names. Maybe not even themselves."

"Do you mean to say," Lorna entered into the conversation, astounded at the lamplighter's accusation of such a young boy as being a thief.

"What I mean to say, my dear," the lamplighter said testily, angry at her questioning his information, "is that you must remember and be aware that not all men or women..." he paused for effect, "or little uns, are your friends. You are from the country and know your own. It is not true in the city or towns beyond your village or hamlet." He shrugged. "Oh, there are them who you can trust and who wish you only the best but they are few and far between." He added and worked his way through the crowd.

"Well, bad cess to those two then," a voice said. "It is bad enough we have thieves among us but what I want is something to eat."

"Aye," another voice agreed. "It has been since morn that we have eaten."

151

"Robert," the first voice asked, "is there food at the boarding house?"

"Yes. I would believe. It is part of the tavern and that means that there must be food served. But Abram and I just passed a street vendor selling sausages and he was heading our way."

"Here he is coming now," still another voice called to the group, all heads turning to see a small donkey pulling a large wagon fitted with high racks with strings of sausages covered now with a sheet-like cover to keep them from the weather. On the wagon's tailgate was a brazier on which was a large frying pan, over which was an overhang to keep the now subsiding rain from inundating the cooking facility.

Covered boxes of bread and rolls as well as assorted condiments lined the sides of the wagon. Attending to the selling was a middle-aged matronly woman dressed in a long coat with a cowl hood, who took a spate of orders and fetched up the sausage sandwiches in newspaper wrappings. A man about her same age, also with a long coat but wearing a brown felt cap, tended to the cooking of the sausage with a toasting-fork and held forth with jokes and jovial laughter as the group from Ramsey and Ely, surged around the wagon for what many knew might well be their last meal in England.

* * *

"My God, this is to be our stay for the night?" A perplexed and upset William Waters said to Robert Hall as they entered into the White Swan's third level dormitory. "I've had better for my hogs."

Robert looked about their quarters, their assignment on the top floor of the decrepit building. "Aye, it does leave something wanting. While I have not been to Buckingham Castle to compare, I would have hoped for better than we have here."

"I can see why we had to pay our shillings in advance." William offered as they assisted others who were trooping up the steep, rickety staircase with their limited toiletry wares for the night's stay.

"If we saw this sty earlier, we surely would have tried elsewhere." Robert commented.

"Elsewhere! From what I have seen of this town, elsewhere looks to be the same as here." William grunted as he helped Albert Reynolds up the last step where he had knocked his right shin on the riser which was much higher than the others.

"Maybe we should be glad that we have what we have. It is only for the night and a short night it will be if we are to be at the dock at sunrise." Joseph Wildes added to their conversation as he assisted Julia and their baby toward the tier of bunks along a wall. "And it is well that we have your son," he motioned to William, "and Murdoc to watch our goods while others of us sleep."

"Yes, it is. We will work out a relief for them after midnight. The clerk said he will wake us at that time and we can decide then who will take the next watch." William explained to Joseph and others who were milling about deciding where to stake their claim for a bunk. He sighed as he surveyed the low ceilinged, dormitory-type room. Twenty-two, two-tiered bunks lined the side wall. He counted. Forty-four. Enough to meet their needs with some to spare. Good. In the aisle between the opposing rows of bunks, were three tables with benches. Overhead of each was a gas-jet light fixture giving out a minimum of light glare.

At the far end of the dorm was a sink with a water barrel aside it and a cooking stove with a rusted metal pipe leading into a grimy chimney, from which he guessed was to provide for heat and what cooking there might be. A small four-paned, dirty window over the sink with a faded blue curtain provided the only light from the outside in the entire room. The opposite wall, behind him, had the stairwell from which members of the group from Ramsey and Ely were still streaming in tired family clumps, all weary and worn.

"I can understand why there are no amenities with this being a place for us to stay only over night." Sophia Hall said as she placed her toilet case on her chosen bunk. "But this is no better than the hovel we stayed in the night near Coventry."

"Oh, it has been indeed a long week and then some," her mother-in-law, Elly, sighed as she slumped into her top bunk. Edith crawled in below.

"Are you all right, Mother?" Sophia asked aside as she pointed out two bunks, one atop the other next to hers for Regina and Peggy to occupy and then pointed to a tier directly across the aisle from her for George and Stanley to bed down in.

"Aye, I think so. It is just that my age, it can be very demanding. Poor Emma, she certainly would never have made it even if she had not died when she did. And the weather. It was so nice and like our spring back home yesterday but look what can happen in only one afternoon here in this part of England. And what of tomorrow?" She shook her head.

"At least we will be on our packet and inside for a change," Sophia offered as a consolation, as she placed her sodden cape on a wall peg at the head of her bunk, hoping it would be dry in the morning.

"It was lucky that we met with the street vendors when we did. We'd most be starved now what with the way the tavern's food serving was from what I saw as we passed through to get to the stairwell." Elly stated as she too placed her sodden cape on a peg at the head of her bunk.

"Yes, but it took a bit of our savings that we had not counted on." Edith interjected into the conversation, as she sat on the floor next to her bunk and was taking off her soaked shoes and hose. "How is Louisa doing?" She asked raising her head to see down the way to where Louisa was doing her best to accommodate herself to her situation of having only the clothes on her back to get her to America and her new beginning.

"She is still upset, and well she should be," Sophia answered. "She is angry. I offered her a cape but she refused."

"She said she was silly for falling for the young man's glib tongue and trusting him with her worldly possessions, except, thank God, she held her purse. She called him a thieving pirate and that she deserves to pay the piper for her folly."

"Ah, we have so much to learn." Elly said as she stood and stretched. "I must find the nettie. Is there one here on this level?" she asked, looking about the room for signs of a toilet.

"I saw one on the ground level and it was in full use from the line I saw waiting to get in." Edith offered as she joined the others in their preparations for what she and they knew was going to be a long night.

"Wait for me. I'll join you."

* * *

"You are Terrance Gallagher?"

"I am that."

"I am Pierce Hill. This is my wife Honora and our daughter, Noreen." A smiling and relieved Pierce Hill said doffing his cap as the three and Fergus Kilbane entered a small cubicle of an office off the main hallway entering into the White Swan tavern and boarding house on Merkel Street. "We were told to meet you here for passage to America, to New York, by a Francis Ronan of Dublin."

"Aye. I have his letter and his warrant for your passage on the Primrose docked at Prince's Dock." He smiled. "You have just made it. It sails on the tide tomorrow. I have been waiting for you." The man in his mid-to-late forties, took off his top hat and extracted a folded, wrinkled paper and opened it up. "Ah, yes. You are Pierce Hill," he nodded, the paper evidently giving a description. "And you are Honora," he nodded to her. He paused. "There is nothing of a child."

"But!" Pierce blustered.

"No matter. It happens all the time," the dealer in human passage raised his right hand in a cautioning manner. "The babe

155

can be fitted in with you." He looked over his spectacles to Fergus. "And who is this lad with you?"

"He is…" Pierce started to say.

"I am Fergus Kilbane of Derryrush, Galway," Fergus interrupted. "I am on my way to a place called Cleveland and I am alone. But," he added looking full to the agent, "Pierce and his wife have been very kind to me as to let me travel with them."

"Do you have the passage money?"

"Aye, I do," he paused, "Within reason."

"What do you mean within reason?" a taken aback Terrance Gallagher questioned angrily. "Do you know how many want to leave? And could take your place! Do you want to go or not? If not, move on as I have others who are willing to pay the going rate and pay well."

"Ach. I meant no offense," a taken back Fergus excused himself as he realized that he had misspoken and surely would have to pay whatever was being asked. He realized that his brother Hugh would have sent ample. "I just hope I have enough, that is." He said as he reached to his right hip pocket for his purse.

Pierce and Honora looked to each other. What if he did not have enough for the passage Honora wondered? Do we have enough of our own to help him? Oh, so close. So close.

"The cost of passage is three pounds, five shillings." The agent looked to Fergus, who seemed to be calculating the cost in his mind.

"Aye, I have it," Fergus replied with a look of relief on his face. He drew out his purse and took out the exact amount and placed it on the table in front of the man.

Pierce and Honora smiled to each other in relief.

"Here, sign the contract. It will be, as with the Hills, on the Primrose lying in the Prince's Dock. You will spend the night here at the tavern. It is all part of your cost. He checked a list. You are all on the third level."

"Aye. And I thank you."

156

"And," the agent continued, "as with the Hills," he nodded to them, "that along with your own food and other provisions you have brought with you, the packet will provide you with adequate fresh water each day as well as bread and rice. But, here," he said handing Fergus his contract to be signed. "It is all on your ticket. It is spelled out... Can you read English?"

"Aye. I can. Some. I can get by," he said signing his name with a flourish.

"We will be able to stay together on the packet?" Pierce asked, motioning with a circular movement with his right hand to the three of them and Noreen.

"You will be assigned by your ticket number. The living spaces are numbered. You will be shown your quarters when you board the packet. Now you will have to move on. There are others behind you." The agent stood up as he placed the payments into a metal box and pointed with his quill pen to a milling group in the hallway.

"I wish to thank you for your service to us," Pierce said as he backed away to leave. "May God bless you and the Confederation for your help."

Terrance Gallagher blanched and gave a quick look about, glad that the next clients were still without the office door and out of hearing. "We do not speak of the Confederation," he almost whispered, "here or anywhere else in England. Take heed also on the packet and mention it not. The walls have ears and the ceiling eyes. Now go! And may God bless you too. You will need it!"

CHAPTER TEN

A warm gentle late afternoon shower gave way to the sun's slanting rays, now a bright orange, reflecting from fleecy strings of clouds low on the western horizon. The city of Buffalo on this early evening was in the throe of Saturday night party fever with happy throngs milling about the dock area, some coming, some going on the various steamer and sailing vessel that were entering and leaving the harbor as Christine and Larry made their way from the Griffith and headed up Ferry Street to take in the city's night life. A ragtag black boy and girl were entertaining at the street corner of Jefferson and Ferry: Dancing and singing to the accompaniment of a white-haired elderly Negro playing a banjo. The songs were lively and quick and the singing by the two was snappy and fast. Wide toothsome smiles greeted each passerby who would contribute coins for their efforts into the old man's straw hat set at the curb. Traffic along the way was busy as coaches hurried back and forth, pulled by prancing horses to be skirted around, by others with pushcarts or smaller wagons or just walking and dodging.

Christine was impressed by the noise and the holiday air of the evening. In Cleveland, she knew, it did get noisy and hectic on a Saturday night, especially in the Flats area of the Cuyahoga River below the Columbus Road Hill and the shanty town known as the Angle above Whiskey Island. But her little village, Forest City, which was on the western heights above the river valley, would now be turning in for the evening. Larry Dana led her through another gathering at a street corner which was enjoying the antics of a monkey, attired in a fez cap and spangled jacket with matching spangled short pants, which was doing back flips and other gyrations to the tunes of a melodeon, played by a young, dark skinned man of a Mediterranean type who also wore a fez with a spangled jacket, but with long spangled pants rather than short ones.

"Well, we have been walking all over the town's center. I think it is about time for us to find a meal and decide what we want to do with ourselves this evening." Larry said as they backed into a doorway of a storefront now closed for the evening.

"I have no idea," Christine offered, not really knowing how soon or to what extent he might be wanting to be paid for his attentions to her.

"I know you don't. That is why this evening is my treat," he smiled as he closed in on her, looking down into her face in the shadows of the store overhang. "I think you might enjoy, first, a dinner at a fine restaurant I know of only a few blocks from here. Then if you like, we can attend a minstrel show at the Capital Theater, again only a few blocks from here. Does that sound all right?"

Christine felt trapped. Yet she was enjoying their walk through the streets. Seeing the sights of a strange city she had only heard of. She liked what she saw. She was excited. It was her first time away from her little knot of friends and now, comparing Buffalo with dinky little Cleveland. A minstrel show? She had never seen one. It could be fun from what she had heard of them. And eating in a restaurant. Only once, really, she thought had she ever ate in a true restaurant when she and George... George. Oh. She bit her lower lip.

"Well? What do you say?" Larry asked, impatient at her delay in answering.

"Yes. I think that will be fine. I only hope I am dressed well enough. I have never been to a minstrel show and have eaten

159

only once in a restaurant."

"You look grand." Larry assured her, not really being excited about her borrowed bonnet, as he again leaned into her and tried for a kiss. She stiffened. He backed off. Damn. Plenty of time for that later, he thought. He took out his watch. "If I remember right, the second show starts at nine-thirty. We can stop at a saloon I have been to before in which ladies are welcomed. We can bide our time there until dinner with a drink or two. It's now only six forty-five, and we have plenty of time."

While she did not object to having a drink, in fact, it sounded good as she felt the need for a belt as much as she ever did. But . . . She remembered it was because of her drinking more than she should or could handle, that she got herself into her present condition. She gave a short cough. It was at the party on Gerlach's boat, the Lynn, docked at Whiskey Island. Captain Gerlach had a party for his crew on the boat and his canawalerps from Akron to celebrate the opening of the new shipping season in March.

George had not wanted her to go but the captain insisted that wives and girlfriends be invited. So, she and George, a canawalerp for the captain, went and . . . Oh, damn! She thought. I can use a drink now. She nodded her head to Larry and with a tight smile put her arm through his and said, "Lead on. I'll follow."

* * *

The Mercer Hotel on Delaware Avenue just a few blocks north of Ferry Street, was considered by many to be Buffalo's finest hotel. It was only five years old and was already talked of in New York and Boston as the place to stay when in Buffalo. Albert and Hazel Tiffany arrived at the third floor room of Charles and Emily Roby at half past seven and by eight o'clock were gathered with Candace and her grandmother in a private dining salon off of the main ballroom where this evening a reception was being given by the local Whig Party for its favorite local boy-made-good, Vice President Millard Fillmore. The Vice President of the United States was in town for a long fourth of July holiday visiting constituents, shaking hands and mending political fences.

The salon was richly furnished in the French tradition with wallpaper depicting historical scenes of French history, highlighted by a finally carved molding of polished black walnut. At one end of the room was a fireplace of white paneling with a mirror that rose to the ceiling above its mantle.

On the opposite wall a large window, draped with peacock colored-chenille curtains, overlooked Delaware Avenue below. The carpet was of a rich pile on which was centered a Hepplewhite table of mahogany with sandalwood veneer. On the table was an arrangement of flowers around which was a succulent dinner from which the gathered friends were enjoying.

"I heard in Cleveland, that the connection has been made from Jamestown to Dunkirk, New York by the Erie Railroad. Just these past few weeks. Have you heard anything of it?" Charles asked Albert as they enjoyed a taste of Candace's surprise cookies, macaroons, she had received from the headwaiter on the Griffith that she had wanted to share with the Tiffany's as her part of the reunion and the evening celebration.

"Yes. It has been the talk among some of the shipping people. I believe the railroads are here to stay and will soon be giving our canal people a run for their money."

"Oh," Charles mused. "And what about us?" shaking his head no to Candace who was offering him another macaroon.

"No problem. There will always be a need for lake steamers. The west is opening up as you well know and it will require shipping to move the heavy goods back and forth over the lakes. But as I said the railroads are here to stay but they have a way to go to accommodate passengers," he smiled to Candace and took a proffered macaroon. He continued, "I have heard tales of boiler explosions." He nodded, "Not unlike some of our steamers. And of passengers being burned and clothing ruined by sparks from the engine as well as catching fire to the country side. And on top of it, the damn rides are so bumpy and swaying."

Charles thought for a moment. "I suppose they are on land as we are on water. In many ways the problems are the same. We had our problems when we started out."

"No bumps though." Albert laughed.

"No. No bumps but a lot of waves and swells," Charles too laughed.

"Charles. Albert. Oh, you two men. Whenever we get together, you two get your heads together and there is no pulling you apart." Hazel Tiffany interrupted the men's conversation. "Albert," she looked to Emily who was joined at her side by Charles, "and I thought you would be interested in attending a minstrel show this evening at the Capital Theater just a few blocks from here. It will be our treat for all of you." She nodded to Ada and Candace.

Charles looked to Emily who nodded with a grin then to his mother and Candace, who returned the same. "We saw a show in Cincinnati last winter with the Evans...." He stopped.

"Oh, yes," Hazel said understanding his reason for pausing. Knowing of their close relationship with the couple and the woman... Carrie... her death but not the details.

"But ..." Charles continued "...it sounds like fun."

"Then it is all settled. We'll send a runner to the theater to secure a tier of seats as we can still be there by nine-thirty." She questioned Emily. "It would not be too late for Candace?"

"Oh, no," Candace answered for her mother. "Father said once that he would take me someday to a minstrel when I was older and that was some time ago, so now I am older." She giggled.

"Ah, my darling," Charles said as he hugged his daughter, pleased that at her expressing herself. He backed off and looked to Albert with a motion. "But first, Albert and I have some final business to discuss," he nodded to Hazel, who smiled at his meaning. "So if you will excuse us for a few moments, we will return and all get ready for a night on the town."

The women smiled and returned to their catching up on the news and each other's ailments while Candace went to the window and observed the traffic below.

"Now," Charles asked of Albert as the two retired to a corner of the room. Charles lighting a cigar, and Albert taking a chaw. "Any idea on the wine? I haven't seen Henry to talk to. He left the Griffith for something or other and I wasn't able to see about taking the shipment ashore. And what about Old Man Lovelace?"

Albert looked about for a spittoon and brought one from near the fireplace.

"Old Man Lovelace, as you refer to him, has been taken care of by a Mr. Westinghouse, an undertaker. I am not too sure of the details and really don't want to know. As for the wine, I suggest you return the entire lot and get back what you paid for it or at least something. I would think that Paul Avery would want to know of the situation and that his wines were tampered with. That is his problem and it can get very touchy. Try to stay out of any problems between the two. It is fortunate that you found out when you did or your name would be mud down the line as a steamer that can't be depended on."

"Yes. You're right." Charles agreed. "I'll take it up personally with him. I'll make a special stop in Sandusky and unload it."

Emily, uncomfortable with her engorging breasts, looked to Charles still in animated discussion with Albert. Business. Always business. But then again, as a boat Captain he always has to be on top of things that relate to the boat.

He is the company's representative. Her brother's company, she was proud to say. Others belittle Billy for his ways. Money hungry, she had heard him referred to once when she overheard a conversation at the church social in May. But why not? Little does anyone know of our childhood. Of our near starving with a drunken father on a hardscrabble farm in Connecticut. Let them deride Billy. He has come a long way and still has a long way to go. He is young and with the need for lumber and his owning acres upon acres of it in Michigan. Oh, Billy. I am so proud of you and what you have done for Charles and me and …"

"Emily." Ada interrupted her reverie. "Are you all right? You look so pale."

"What? Oh. No, I am fine. I was just thinking of … Carrie." She said for no reason.

"Carrie?" Hazel asked surprised also concerned at Emily's moment of detachment. "Will our going to the minstrel show bring back some sad memories of your friend?" She asked. "If it does, I am sure we can find another entertainment for the evening. I know we can find something else to do."

"Oh, no. I think the show would be fine. I know Candace and mother will enjoy it, as well as all of us. I guess we all need a good laugh." She said realizing that she had been caught in one of her recent moments of forgetting where she was or even who she was with. And she was so uncomfortable. Her breasts hurt so. Oh, she wanted to nurse Thomas so bad. "The trip up the lake wasn't the most pleasant," she continued. "I am sure that the dancing and singing and the jokes of the interlocutor will take our minds off our troubles. Please excuse me. I must take care of myself and see to Thomas."

"Yes, certainly." Hazel said looking to Ada who wore a frown on her face. She waited until Emily cleared the room then asked Ada, "Just what happened to her friend, Carrie? All we have heard is that it was quite a terrible thing to the poor soul."

Ada looked to Candace, now quiet and attentive to the adult's conversation, finishing her last macaroon. "Oh, it was, indeed. And it was because of her death that you will never get me to wear a crinoline dress again."

"A crinoline dress?"

"Yes. From what I know and have heard, it was last January, just after Thomas was born, that Charles and Emily decided to take a break and visit with William and Carrie in Cincinnati. Just to get away for a week or two. Our winters in western Ohio can be quite bleak you know." Hazel nodded. Also in Buffalo she added to herself. "So they took the stage to visit. Part of their visit was to see a minstrel show that William had spoken so highly of that was to visit in late January. They went and from what they told me, they had a great time. It was only after they were home for a week that they learned from a letter, a special delivery letter from William, that Carrie had been killed by a runaway horse."

"A runaway horse. That happens all the time."

"True. But from what William wrote, and later told us, when he returned to Toledo in March, for the opening of the boating season on the lake, it was a crinoline dress that she was wearing that got caught in the steps of a carriage she was getting into when the horse bolted and ran off, dragging Carrie along. The driver, who was helping her get into the carriage was thrown to the ground and couldn't get control of the horse. It was finally stopped by others but not until she was dead."

"Oh, God. How terrible," Hazel said softly.

Candace, who stood with her eyes downcast, had heard the details before but could never get used to the idea of such a way to die.

"She died of a crushed skull and other damage to her torso," Ada finished, wiping a tear from her eye.

"I'm almost sorry I asked," Hazel explained, now understanding. "I can see why Emily could be so upset. The show reminds her too much of Carrie's death."

"As she said," Ada added. "It would do us all some good to see a silly show now. Now then," she said firmly, standing tall, "Candace and I will prepare ourselves and meet you in the lobby in a few minutes."

"Take your time. We can leave almost any time. It is a short walk and the evening is warm. It will help us get our minds off many things. Ah, here are our men now." Hazel said as she gave a curtsy to the two as they came to rejoin the women, now only Hazel left.

"I will be going directly too, Hazel." Charles said, taking his leave. "We will meet you in the lobby in fifteen minutes."

"Fine. That will give us all time to prepare for the evening." Albert said, checking his watch. "I must take some bismuth. I've got a touch of dyspepsia from eating Candace's macaroons." He laughed.

"Oh, Albert," Hazel chided as they left the room passing into the main corridor which took them past an open doorway that led into the ballroom where they were able to see and hear the Vice President of the United States at a podium in some sort of exhortation to an applauding audience.

* * *

"I'm sorry, Gertrude, but I can't spend the night with you and Ray. By the time I visit with Ollie here at the county home for indigents as it's called and get back to the boat, it will be late and we leave at ten-thirty tomorrow morning. And I have a lot to do until then."

"Ah, Marie. We would love to have you stay over with us. We have been looking forward to your visiting with us but we know your boat is only in overnight."

"It has been nice and thoughtful of you to have visited with Ollie while I was away. He seems to be better. The infection is down some since I saw him last but I was told by a nurse that he is too frail to travel and maybe the next time I can take him back to Toledo."

"He certainly has been through quite a bit. The carbuncle was as big as a fist I have been told and being so close to his butt hole, made it all the worse for the doctor to lance. As it is, he is still in pain and taking his laudanum like a good lad, but it makes him sleepy so the times we did come he hardly knew us."

"Well, it was lucky for me that you were here today for me to see you."

166

"Eh. We had to come to town anyway. Ray has promised me for a long time that he would take us to see a minstrel show the next time one came to town. So here we are. You're sure you wouldn't want to join us. It will be our treat."

"Oh, no. Thanks anyhow. I'll visit with him until dark then I'll return to the boat. We are expecting a large crowd of immigrants first thing in the morning to come aboard. I was told that the canal had a big break and that many people have been backed up and all the barges are filled up with still more to come. I must be back then and get ready and make sure we have enough linens and such for our cabin passengers. Forty-five we are expecting."

"Forty-five. That's a lot."

"Oh, yes. And as I was leaving I saw many of the immigrants all ready to get aboard waiting for the first class passengers and cargo to go on first."

"They will sleep on the docks tonight? The immigrants?"

"Yes. I'm told by others and by themselves that we have carried, that it is not uncommon. Most have said they have seen worse in England. It's terrible. It is no big thing unless it is raining too hard or it is snowing. But our trip is short and they put up with the weather. They have no choice. And to boot, I promised the Captain's mother, a really sweet lady, that I would look after an Indian boy..."

"Indian boy? Why would you have to look after an Indian boy?"

"Ah. It is a long story, but no matter. He was hurt and she has him in her cabin and as she is ashore for the night, I said I would look in on him from time to time. As I said, it is a long story."

"Well, Marie, you know what is best. Me and Ray will take our leave as they say. The show starts at nine-thirty and we have not yet had anything to eat since noon. So we will say our goodbys now." Gertrude held out her arms.

"Ah, Gertie," Marie arose from where she had been sitting along side the bed of her husband and met with Gertrude. They hugged as old friends. "It has been nice seeing you and Ray again, if only for such a short time. But this is one of our in-and-out trips. I am just glad that I got to see Ollie even if he is sleeping."

"Well, then we'll say goodnight. Take care of yourself. We don't want two of you sick."

"And thank you, Ray. Maybe the next time we get together you and Ollie can go bowling again." Marie offered a hug to Ray, a somber, reticent soul who only nodded his head to her and moved off with his wife.

Marie turned back to her husband as he laid comatose, from what she understood was in his third day. "Well, Ollie, I guess I'll head back to the boat. You don't even know if I am here and if you did, what? What is there to say or to talk of? We have no children. No families. Just Gertie and Ray and only when we are in Buffalo and not always then. Just the two of us and now you're out of it."

She walked to the window that looked out on an enclosed courtyard with a high fence. A number of patients, inmates she thought would be a better word, as they were confined as in a prison, were sitting on benches or wandering about biding their time for what? She wondered. A hospital it was called or is it an asylum? Well, whatever. She knew that the next time she came, she would be expected to make some payments for his care. So, I'll try. They can't get water from a stone. She turned and looked about the room, a ward it was called. Six beds. Six souls in a bleak and dreary existence. Two others like Ollie, were in deep sleep or comas. A fourth was sitting on the edge of his bed picking his nose, his bare feet dangling. A fifth was curled up in a ball with his hands covering his face, while the sixth was in a corner singing and praying to a chair. A hospital or an asylum? She shook her head in almost total belief in what she was witnessing. She cleared her throat. "Goodnight, Ollie, honey. Sleep tight and don't let the bed bugs bite."

"As best I can determine, we should be back here in Buffalo in two weeks, three at the most, barring any unforseen problems with the damn shaft being replaced and the new lubricating system installed that Stebbins keeps harping on. That should give you plenty of time for whatever paperwork you will need to show that the trunks are mine... Er... Ours." Henry corrected himself as he tried focusing his eyes a little better to the attorney's face as he sat across the desk from him. His face a fuzzy image caused by the excellent sherry and aromatic cigar he was enjoying.

"Yes. Ours." The attorney corrected. "It can be a little tricky but it is done every day with lost or misplaced shipments. They could be lost or stolen as many are every day on the docks, especially now in the height of the shipping season. The canal barges are full of them and I am sure it is not uncommon on the steamers as well." Andrew Putnam explained knowing full well that Henry was aware of such a situation and thus his reason for making the attempt of stealing the old man's trunks.

"True. True." Henry agreed. The face still a little fuzzy around the edges.

"Now, then. The Indian boy. You say he is on the Griffith?" the attorney asked as he started putting the sherry decanter and unused glasses back into the wine cabinet.

"Yes. He is in cabin six, the Captain's mother's cabin. But she, as well as the Captain and his family are ashore for the night at the Mercer Hotel. He should be alone. Oh, yes. One of the cabin maids is to look in on him once in a while but we'll have no problem with that. Her husband is here in a hospital and she will be with him..."

"Hospital?"

"Yes, he had some kind of infection the last time we were here and it was quite serious so he had to stay over. I don't know if he will be returning with us or not. She was going to find out."

"I know where you mean." The attorney nodded knowingly.

"It is not a hospital, though we are trying to get one worthy of the name going. It is our Erie County Home as we call it. We take in indigents, most of them drunken sailors or Indians. And do our best to keep them off the streets and not bother anyone."

"I believe he is one of the sailors," Henry quipped.

"I will have one of my assistants draw up the necessary papers so that we can legally take the Indian boy from the steamer until Monday when we will bring him before the authorities."

"Who will pay for all this?" Henry asked as the attorney locked the wine cabinet and pocketed the key.

"Why, the Studdiford Shipping and Transit Company of course," the lawyer smiled. "Who else? I am sure Bill Studdiford would not want to have a case of an illegal Indian on his hands. No. I will get my recompense from his firm." He paused realizing his cohort was more than just a little under the weather. "What now of your plans for the rest of the evening?" He said looking to a wall clock over Henry's left shoulder. "It is now almost six-thirty and I must leave as my wife and some friends and I will be visiting with our Vice President this evening at the Mercer Hotel."

"Vice President Fillmore." Henry's eyes opened wide.

"Yes, he is an old friend. We were boys together. Can I drop you off somewhere?"

Henry thought. Vice President Fillmore. Wow! He turned to the clock. It's getting late. Damn it to be alone. Oh, Aunt Babs. No. The whorehouse? No. Not tonight. Marie? Nah. She's with her husband and a cousin of his. "No, thanks. I'll work my way back to the Griffith one way or another. I have piles of paperwork to do and should get at it. Thanks anyway."

"As you wish...You are feeling all right?"

"Oh, yes. Never better. I'll walk. It's not too far to the docks. The fresh air should do me some good."

"Fine. Now if you will excuse me, I will say adieu. My best wishes to you..."

"And you." Henry acknowledged with a nod of his head.

"…on our new found friendship. May it be of value to both of us."

* * *

"Wh… Where am I?…It is dark…I am…in a room?…I cannot see…It is so dark…I…I am on a bed?…Oh, my head, it hurts…The room…I remember…Mr. Lovelace's room…No. …That nice lady…Oh, my head…It is wet…I must get up…I will rest…a moment…damn, I cannot see…What? The edge of the bed?…My clothes?…My shoes?…Where are they?…My feet on the floor…Yes…Oh, I am so dizzy…Oh!…I fell…Where am I?…I am on the floor…A chair?…Yes, a chair…Let me think…Oh, my arm. I hurt my arm…when I fell…Oh…I'll call for help…the English word…HELP!

…My head…Oh…let me think…In Mr. Lovelace's room… the chair was across from his bed…on the wall…Oh, my head, my arm…If only I could see…the chair across the room from the bed…Ah…HELP!…The chair…I can feel the chair…behind the chair, a wall

…Yes…What?…What is it?…A table?…Yes, a table…Yes, there was a small table

…That noise…a crash…Uh…Broken glass…No…a broken bowl…Ah, a chamber pot

…Yes, there was a chamber pot on the table…I broke it…Let me feel…Ah…Oh, my knee…I have cut my knee…I have knelt on a piece of the broken pot…Let me feel…the wall…Yes…The door …HELP!…It is so dark…Wait! …I must take it easy… Take my time…but my head, oh, it hurts… My arm… I am wet … my leg, my knee …it is bleeding from being cut… HELP! …The door …Yes, the door…Good …Now the latch

…Ah … Yes, yes… Uh … Uh … Ah … Ah … Fresh air! I have it opened…HELP! Where am I? …I cannot see… Mr. Lovelace's cabin…It was by the big wheel …Ah, I am on the deck they call it … but I still do not see …What has happened? …Why can I not see? … HELP! Which way to go? …I am so dizzy…my head …I hear a noise … A boat? …Yes, a boat … What they call a steamer…HELP!…What's this?…A rope?…Yes, a rope. Ah… If I could only see … It is so dark …Ah, yes, I will try to stand … Ah, yes …I will stand …Aaaaaah… "

* * *

"So, here we are, my darling, just the two of us in Buffalo," William Dana raised a tumbler of whisky to the Daguerreotype of his wife, Carrie, in a frame above the headboard of his bed. He stood with his glass raised and staggered just enough to catch himself. "Oops! Gotta be more careful. We don't want this boat moving about without us knowing about it now do we?" He giggled. He then took another drink and sat down with a thud into a chair at the table attached to the wall. "Yes, here we are in Buffalo… All alone! Who gives a damn?…Who really cares? No one!…Where are they? All gone!" He waved his right hand about the room. He sat gazing with drooping eyelids, trying to focus on the sepia toned picture of a young, vivacious, dark haired woman, who, he remembered, was only twenty-nine years of age when the picture was taken four years ago on their honeymoon in Detroit.

"Ah, well," he groaned, then belched a burning bile. "We'll soon be back to Toledo and our home in Rossford. Our little vine covered cottage, the one you wanted to stay the year around in, as well you shall ever be now, my darling, instead of our going each season to Cincinnati in the winter months so that I could sail the river steamers to New Orleans. Ah, shit!" He shook his head.

"Well, my dearest. We don't have to worry about that anymore, do we? I am through. I am sure Charles will soon learn that my information on the shoal off Van Buren Point was a lie. And then what? Ha! I know what! I loose my ticket! I lose my job to that boy… Um… Richard… Mann. That's who! The German boy. He could take my place in a minute. Oh, well. Who cares? You do! I know you do! But who else?" He yelled at the picture. "Oh, if the Captain and his wife would be here... But no! They are out on the town by themselves or with their Buffalo friends and here I am... We are... All alone."

He reached for his tumbler, knocking it over, spilling the last dregs onto his pillow. "Damn it!" he snarled, taking a swipe at the glass, sending it crashing into the wall next to his night stand. "Oh! Whoa. Wait! My God. Wait!" He laid his head on the table top. "Oh, Jesus. Dear Jesus. Bill . . . Take it easy. Settle down. This is not you. You're drunk. Settle down." He raised his head now swirling, and wiped his drooling mouth, his stomach gurgling with vomit as he lurched for the toilet.

* * *

"Shush" George Jefferson put his right index finger to his lips. "What's that noise?"

Hiram Faulks looked up from the checker board and glanced at a passing steamer. "I hear only the Foreman going by with its squeaky paddles. She is a noisy boat."

"No. I didn't mean that. I heard a voice. A cry." George explained.

"There are many noises to be heard." Eddie Thatcher said as he looked over Hiram's left shoulder trying to figure out his next move.

"No, damn it! I heard a voice calling. Here," he pointed to Howard Crown who was sipping a cup of coffee in the background also wondering what Hiram's next play might be. "Go take a look. I cannot. My knee, damn it! I am certain I heard a voice call for help."

"I'll take a look. I am through anyhow." Richard Mann stood up from the table where he and the others had just finished their supper. Hiram and George eating as they played for the championship of the crew of the Griffith. "I, too, heard something," he agreed with George.

"Take a lamp." George called. "It is getting dark." As Richard put on his cap and left taking a peg lamp.

Any number of the ship's crew did not go ashore this night as they felt it unnecessary as they would only have to be back aboard early in the morning and also that it cost money to stay in a lodging which would have been no better than their own quarters aboard the Griffith, as well as not having to buy meals. The only place the cook, Abraham Gilpin, ever went ashore was in Cleveland. He was not always treated well in the other cities that the Griffith stopped.

Richard stepped from the crew's mess to face a pellucid western sky. The late sunsets of the approaching summer season allowed for daylight until late in the evening, now almost at the maximum. He looked out across the Niagara River to the Canadian shore alive with the coming and going of all types of water craft. He stretched, feeling a pleasant tingling of his muscles. He sighed. Ah, he thought. A good night's sleep will bring to the end the hectic past few days we have had. He would not even read tonight. He looked to his left, then right, fore and aft, down the deck. The deck was deserted. Maybe he did only guess that he had heard something. There were all kinds of noises along the dock. Even now he heard the chugging of a tug as it pulled a barge of cotton bales all the way from Dixie on a steam paddle wheel through to Toledo over the canal from Cincinnati by barge and then up the lake to Buffalo on the side wheelers for the mills in Massachusetts and Connecticut via the Erie canal again by barge. No one in sight. Just his and George's imaginations running wild. He raised the lamp.

"What the . . ." He paused after he had walked by a number of the cabins. He looked to a door ajar in one of the cabins. The one that Mrs. Roby was in. Where the Indian boy was staying. He noticed a smudge on the door jamb by the catch. He looked closer. Blood! "Oh, my God." He looked again and then saw blood tracks on the deck, one a distinct hand print. Then another heading toward the railing across from the cabin door. It was a

174

section of the deck where the railing was merely a rope with a snap from one post to another about six feet wide. It was where on occasion a ramp would be placed from there to a dock and so no reason for a secured railing. He approached the rope, lowering the lamp toward the deck edge and looked down into the river waters flowing by about ten feet below, north to the Great Niagara Falls. "Oh, my God." He gasped. "That poor Indian boy. Blood to the very edge."

* * *

"Good evening, Henry."

"Good evening Aunt Babs. I am sorry I couldn't get back sooner but I have had a lot to do. A lot of business to attend to and it took me longer to get to than I thought." Henry explained as he came panting up the dock ramp as the late afternoon sun was casting a burning orange glow on the west facing windows on the eastern shore of the Niagara River. "Have you had your supper?"

"Yes. Of sorts. A nice man, Mr. Mc… "

"McCoit. Yes, he is a nice man. His name is Samuel. He is our second mate."

"Oh, how nice. He sat with me in the dining saloon. We had a very nice talk. Is he married?"

"I don't know."

"Where is his home?"

"I don't know that either. Some place near or in Toledo. I suppose."

"Oh, well. He was nice and pleasant."

"Aunt Babs, I have had a very long day. A trying day, and will have an even busier one tomorrow. I'm . . .." he said trying to edge past her.

"Oh, I know, Henry. It is getting late and I am also tired. My ride in today from Spring Brooke was quite demanding and I think I will retire now as well. My old bones can't take it any more like they used to when Ernest was alive. God rest his soul."

"You have your cabin?"

"Yes. Mr. McCoit," she nodded now with a knowing smirk, "carried my bags from your cabin to mine. It is number sixteen. On the main deck."

Henry remembered, number seventeen was David Stebbins' cabin. If his Aunt Babs thought Sam McCoit was something, wait until she met the chief engineer!

Henry with his return to sobriety after his walk from the offices of the attorney and enjoying the freshness of the night air, left his aunt and entered his cabin. "Good," he said aloud, looking about and not finding his roommate, Larry Dana. "Larry's not here. I don't know if I want to put up with him any longer. I'll see if I can't get in with McCoit from now on. I need more room anyhow. How the old fart before me managed in this shared cabin, I'll never know. He went to his desk and withdrew a bottle of New York Sherry. Ah. He could really use a touch now. The sherry was dry and tasty as he drank from the bottle. He never did know how to tell a good sherry from a bad but someone once told him that dry sherry was best so he always bought the best. Dry sherry.

"God, what a day! What a long day," he said aloud. "I never thought that being a clerk on a steamer could be so demanding. But . . . it was better than clerking in McGraw's haberdashery in Perrysburg. Hell, anything is better than that! I should ask for a raise," he said with a laugh, but meaning every word. "Now, what about today?" He thought as he started taking off his shirt. "What does it all mean to me?" He took off his shirt and began undoing his pants. "Oops!" he tittered. "Better get my boots off first. Let's see." He thought as he took another swig from the bottle. "That old fool Lovelace, dying at the most inopportune time. Hm. Charles said . . . Whoops. The Captain said," he corrected himself. "Albert Tiffany would take care of him. Good. But he left the trunks up to me. Andrew? Can I trust him? Hell! I have to. I have no choice. I don't know all the legalities involved with people dying or having heirs and such. And just what is in those trunks anyhow? Maybe the riches of Croesus. Or maybe just crap! But there has to be some value to them or why has Andrew become so interested? Why indeed! Damn! And I won't be back for a couple of weeks..."

He sat on the edge of his bunk rubbing his stocking feet. "Ah, it feels so good. Oh, I've got to get me some new boots. These are too tight. I'll check with Schlegels when we get back to Toledo. I can use some underwear as well. The Indian boy? Hey, no longer my problem. It's now in the hands of the attorney." He made a check in the air. He paused. "Someone should have been here for him by now to take him to the sisters. Who has the duty tonight? Hell. McCoit! And where is Evans?" He took another slug of the sherry. "And the Captain? Shit! He's on the town and I'm stuck with all his problems. And they wonder why I want a raise? Damn!"

"What's that racket?" He rose and went to the cabin window and drew the curtain over it aside. It was dark out but he heard voices calling. "What the hell? I'd better see what this is all about." He returned to his bunk and bolted on his pants and boots as he heard running on the deck. "Damn! Something's up!"

"Mr. Wilkinson! Are you there?" an excited voice called from outside his cabin.

"Yes. I am here. I am coming!"

"We need you, sir. Something is wrong and we cannot get Mr. Evans or Mr. McCoit. Come to cabin six. Something terrible has happened!"

Cabin six? Mrs. Roby's cabin. Henry remembered. She and her granddaughter? No. They went ashore for the night . . . The Indian boy! "Damn. What now?"

* * *

"How do you like your Napoleon?" Larry asked of Christine, who was in the process of downing her third glass of brandy within the hour.

177

"It tastes good. I never had it before. We always drink whiskey. Or rum. This is good." She pointed to the three empty glasses on the table before her in the corner of the Cooney Tavern on Elmwood Avenue. "How do you like yours?" She asked, now a more convivial young lady from when they had entered for a few drinks and dinner before attending the minstrel show in the next block.

"I'm doing fine." He said raising his glass as in a toast to her only. The second drink he had, nursing it.

"I'm hungry. These pretzels aren't enough," she said fingering some from a bowl into her mouth as she looked across to another table where two middle-aged couples were enjoying a dinner of fried chicken with all the fixings and sharing a bottle of wine. "When can I get something to eat?"

"Ah, later. In due time. We'll find plenty of time later. Here, I'll get you another drink."

"No. I'm hungry… Well …Maybe one more," she raised her right index finger, hiccuped and giggled.

Larry looked around. No one seemed to be interested in them. It was about time now he made his move. She was well on her way but he didn't want her drunk so as to show here in the restaurant. One more brandy should do it. It always worked with Gail. Gail? She drank gin. Gail? I wonder where in the hell she is? Well, all it will take now is to get her in a hackney and take her to Maud's place where we spent some pretty good times. Gail. Damn, I miss her. With the supply of morphine he had picked up in Cleveland, he was now more than prepared to seduce this little wretch who thinks herself to be above him. Ah, you little bitch. You're mine tonight.

The waiter, a young black boy about Christine's age, at Larry's gesturing, brought her another drink. Christine, who now, with few inhibitions, thanked the boy saying he was cute and gave him a wink.

"Shit!" Larry blurted angrily in a low tone under his breath. "You don't say such things to black boys." He glared at her. She had a puzzled look. "Do you want to get us killed?" He looked quickly about the faces who only a few minutes ago seemed oblivious to them; now with dark looks and murmurings. Jesus! That's all I need now is to have a southern sympathizer for their right to hold slaves, get on his high horse. Yes, even here in Buffalo. Dumb bitch! She should know better. "Come, we'll leave now. We have only a short ride and it might do us good to get some fresh air. We'll get a hackney and will soon be at the show. Hurry."

He paid the bill. Leaving the change, anxious to get out and away from what he felt was a hostile atmosphere. "Here. I'll help you," he said as he led her from her chair. "Holy shit! She is drunk." He said to himself, surprised as to how far along she was. The two threaded their way through the crowd of tables and made for the exit doors.

The Saturday night crowd was busy on the sidewalk as well as the traffic in the street. It was still early and no hackney's were to be seen or else were already with fares.

They walked along the sidewalk. Christine shrugging his arms from holding her as she felt only a little giddy and didn't want his attentions. She was all right damn it!

A delivery wagon pulled up along side them. "Hi. Can we be of help?" a young man at the reins called from the driver's seat, as another emerged from the back of the wagon.

"No. We are fine." A now frightened Larry replied, not liking the looks of either one. Damn it anyhow!

"Ah, me bucko. But the young lady seems to be in a bit of a problem," a burly fellow with a short red beard stated as he jumped from the wagon as it pulled to a stop at the curb.

"No. She is all right. We will not be needing any help. Thank you."

A fourth fellow came from the wagon and circled behind Larry. "You mean to say your sweetie-pie is able to walk? She doesn't look that way to me!" the burly fellow hissed to Larry.

"Fellows! Wait!" Larry pleaded. "You don't know what is

179

going on. She... She's drunk. I am taking her home. She will be all right when I get her home."

"Yeah. We can see. You pimping son-of-a-bitch!" the fellow behind him shouted as he chopped Larry with a hand across his neck from behind.

"Oh, my God! Help!" A shocked and terrified Christine screamed as she saw Larry fall to the sidewalk in convulsive kicking.

"And as for you, slut!" the fellow turned to her and struck her full force to her face with a ham fist. "The next time you want to be cute, be it to a white man."

CHAPTER ELEVEN

Liverpool—at Sea

"You all have to provide your own guard for your goods. We cannot have a twenty-four-hour watch. So you must provide your own till morning."

"Aye. We know. That is why we are here," Murdoc answered the bar steward of the tavern as he accompanied him and Ethan to a large shed-like attachment to the rear of the tavern bordering on an alleyway. They were also joined by strangers from other groups bedding down for the night. And hopefully, some sleep if only for a few hours. Like the others with their own arrangements, Murdoc and Ethan were to be relieved at midnight by William and Joseph. The meager supplies for the ocean crossing and their final destination were piled neatly in a heap along side others with only a small space between for identification as needs be and a walkway. Other group watchers, as well as individuals on their own, were trying to stay awake—all having gone through the same travails in finally reaching Liverpool from all over England, as well as Ireland, Scotland and Wales, and now watching for sneak thieves who, it seemed, lurked just outside the shadows of the meager lantern's gleam.

Ethan and Murdoc took one of the small trunks, Laura Hall's, to sit on it with their backs against the rear wall of the shed so that they could see anyone coming and going before them.

A young redheaded fellow wearing a dark green woolen pullover, nodded to them as he took a position along side of them to keep an eye on a much smaller pile than theirs. Others in the shed did the same with their piles with a nod or a perfunctory remark to their neighbors for the night, soon to be silent or talking in low tones to their own.

Ethan counted six lanterns hanging from cross beams which gave a limited coverage for the shed which, as best he could guess, was about one hundred twenty feet long and fifty or so feet wide. Ha, he laughed to himself. William's hogs had better light at night than we do now. He looked about, those only a few feet distant from him and Murdoc, they were fortunate with having a lantern only a few feet to their left, were in a twilight between the dark and the light, their guards were no better off than if they were not there at all. As it was, most of them were already asleep letting their unknown neighbors keep on the alert for them.

While Ethan and Murdoc had known each other in Ramsey, their ages put them into two different social casts and they were not close. Their talk was small talk. Murdoc was wondering about his future as a farmer, which was all that he knew. He could read a little, thanks to Mr. Tomlinson, a transient teacher-type who came to the village on occasion. He had no wife but hoped he would get married when he had land for growing crops and then children. He was not inquisitive and did not press Ethan for his plans, although he knew that as the stepson of William Waters, he too would be going into farming.

Ethan kept his own council. He did not say a thing about his leaving the group when they would arrive in New York. No, it was his own, and now Louisa's and Lorna's secret. He knew it would all come out in due time.

"If you would like to take a nap, you can," Murdoc told Ethan as he stifled a yawn. The quietness of the shed was almost too much for both of them. The mustiness and the small of present and past occupants of the shed added to their being so uncomfortable that maybe only sleep could quell. Others on watch were taking to napping, as snoring or snorting at being awakened with a start was heard throughout the shed. In the distance the muffled noises of the streets about told of not all humanity was sleeping this night and that the docks of Liverpool were still full of life.

"No, I'll stay awake with you. We can talk and keep each other awake," Ethan replied, glad to have been given the chance but realizing it was not fair or wise as maybe Murdoc might, himself, drop off. They again talked of little things. Of things they saw on the trek. Of Murdoc telling of when he was a small lad seeing the Duke of Wellington, the Prime Minister at the time, in a great coach with a horse guard, as it passed through Ramsey on his way to Ely to visit the cathedral and maybe meet the king for lunch he laughed.

As they were talking, they noticed the young man, who seemed so Irish to them now, with his rough clothing and a hair style typical of the Irish laborer who by the thousands descended upon the English cornfields each summer to help with the harvests. The young man tried his best to stay awake, but kept dropping off, his head slumping but then catching it with a start.

"Maybe we should include him in our talk," Ethan asked Murdoc, feeling sorry for the young man. "It might help to keep him awake."

"Not if he is Irish," Murdoc whispered in reply.

"Oh. And why not?" Ethan answered, having an idea but not to sure.

"It is not done, to become too friendly with them, I have been told. Most can hardly speak English and that is their required tongue and they have wild tempers to boot."

"But I have heard him speak to the steward and he seems pretty tame to me." Ethan explained as he too was fighting sleep.

"I don't know. He seems quiet enough. . ." Murdoc began.

Their discussion was cut short by an explosion of shouting. "Thief! . . .Catch him! . . . Catch him! . . . The bastard! Get him! . . ." as a figure came running through the narrow aisleway between the piles heading toward an earlier closed rear door to the shed behind where they were setting. The door was now open and a small lad was beckoning to the figure who was carrying a box of a sort.

"Here! Stop!" Murdoc called as he jumped up and placed himself between the figure and the open doorway.

Ethan too, arose quickly and stood helplessly as the figure and Murdoc collided head on. The force of the meeting sent Murdoc staggering backward into their pile; the figure bowling into the direction of the Irishman, who having heard the calling and seeing the commotion, was on his feet, now wide awake. The figure rose and dove to his left trying to pass the Irishman, who bracing himself, threw a right-cross catching the thief flush on the mouth with teeth and blood spattering, then chopped him with a left behind his right ear. Ethan turned and saw the lad in the shadows, his eyes wide with fright, even in the dim lantern light, then turn and bolt into the direction of the dark alleyway and the streets beyond.

A milling crowd of the other watchers quickly gathered around Murdoc and Ethan as they looked to the thief who was unconscious and bleeding profusely from the mouth.

Ethan took a closer look, and checked the figures clothing. "It's the... He said as he then turned the man's face for a better look.

Murdoc, too, took a closer look at the man, really a young man. "Aye." He shook his head agreeing to Ethan's guess. "It is the rake who stole Louisa's valise. He seems to be a busy one at stealing other's goods."

"It will be awhile that he will steal again, a well-dressed man holding a lamp, bending over the figure, said. "He is out of it for a while." He rose and turned to the Irishman. "We thank you for your brave act in stopping this thief. This riffraff," he paused. "Are you all right? Here, let me see." He went to the Irishman who was holding his right hand, pain showing in his eyes. "Oh, damn. It looks like you broke your hand. The bone there." He pointed to the young man's middle finger knuckle.

"It will have to be set."

"I don't know. It is only a bump. I can get by," the Irishman said wincing in pain.

"It should be attended to. And you are bleeding," the man, now in the lantern light said as he turned to Murdoc. "And you, how are you? You, yourself, took quite a bump."

"I am all right. I fell into the pile and it broke my fall. I am all right. It is this young man I am worried about," he pointed to the Irishman.

"Well now," a voice from beyond the light injected. "I guess this tells us that we cannot ever ease up on our guard from thieves and cutthroats who will want what we have. It happened to us earlier on the street, only it was a young lass, no more than a child. A sneak-thief she was."

"Murdoc! Ethan!" a voice called as the crowd began to disburse back to their piles with renewed effort to stay awake and watch their belongings while the steward, with two cronies, whom they called arrived, and carried the still unconscious dandy back to the tavern with not a word said.

"What has happened?" an excited Robert Hall asked as he and Joseph Wildes approached Murdoc and Ethan who were tending as best they could to the young Irishman's needs.

"It seems that the thief who took Louisa's valise has been caught. He was stopped by this young lad here." Murdoc explained as he led the Irishman to the trunk where he sat with a thud and a sigh of relief.

"Fergus! What happened? Are you all right?" another voice called to the gathering as Pierce Hill joined them. "I was just called to relieve you when I heard of a fight." He looked to Robert and Joseph, his eyes questioning.

"It was not a fight. It was too one-sided," the man with the lamp added sensing Pierce's concern but not knowing why. "It seems a sneak-thief, who, evidently, some of you had dealings with earlier, was apprehended after he tried to steal from some drowsing countrymen and was seen. With a hue and a cry following him he tried to escape and ran toward an escape door," he pointed to the still ajar door into the alleyway, "only to be met by this brave lad who flattened him with a one-two punch worthy of David with his sling, himself."

Both Pierce and Robert turned to Fergus. "Well done," Robert said, putting his right hand out for a shake. Fergus smiled a weak smile and raised his left. "Well," Robert said realizing that the lad had hurt his right hand. "While we probably will not be getting back Louisa's belongings, at least we know the thief has been taken and will pay for his crimes."

"Oh, ho, don't be too sure of that," the man cautioned. "They don't always work alone. He had an accomplice on the outside. And I'll wager, unless I am wrong, that he is either or will soon be on his way back to where he came from to try again another day."

"You mean that…" Pierce asked in almost disbelief to what he was hearing.

"Oh, yes," the man continued. "They work in pairs or teams. They have a mentor. It could be a bar steward, a bar maid. Anyone here at the tavern who knows of the habits and weaknesses of the likes of yourselves."

"We have a man among our own," Robert interrupted seeing, Fergus in pain. "A man of medicine, not a doctor, but one who knows his ways. Can we have him attend to your injury?" he asked Fergus. "It is swollen and he may be able to help you with a poultice or give you something for your pain."

"Aye. Thank you. It will be grand of you." Fergus replied with a grimace.

"Come, let me help you," Robert said as the man with the lamp held it for Robert to lead Fergus through the piles toward the stairway which led to the dormitory as he remembered now having seen Fergus and Pierce earlier when they had all arrived at the tavern for the night's lodging and the Irishmen and a women and a child took bunks at the far end of the room near the water barrel.

Ethan, who had taken in all the excitement and was impressed by the young Irishman's agility in striking down the thief after nearly being asleep, was now wide awake and knew he would sleep, backed off into the shadows as the others left and Murdoc stayed until Robert returned or sent a replacement for him.

If the thief had had a weapon, a gun or a knife or whatever, a club, he could have possibly killed the Irishman. . . Fergus, Ethan thought reflectively. And Fergus, he didn't have to stop the thief. His goods were not being pilfered. But he did it to help someone else who was maybe not even an Irishman. He pondered: When will we ever let bygones-be-bygones? Wait! He caught himself. My own relationships with William! I have seen on this journey that he really is a good man. He is good to mother and Lorna and Shirley. He is respected by the others. Maybe I had better rethink my own thoughts and let bygones-be-bygones and stay with him and the family. "Aye, I have some thinking to do."

* * *

The rising sun came with a brilliant blue sky promising clear skies to the west while the setting gibbous moon to the west preordained a high tide to be reached at 6:46, which would open the flood gates at the Prince's Dock and others on the Mersey allowing pent up packets and other great ships of the sea to break out of their confines as horses from a racing gate to stretch out to the west, in a halter-shelter, almost hell-bent race, each ship having a course to sail and a destination to be arrived at in due time. The sooner the better.

Aboard the Primrose, Captain Aaron Devine stood with his First Mate, Anthony Grayson, beside the fiferail of the mizzen-mast on the spar deck observing the loading of the immigrants from a safe distance. "Ah, another one," the Captain said. "Another six or eight weeks of earning our keep. How do they look to you?" He waved with his left hand to the mob below on the main deck and those coming aboard.

"As with the others before. We will have to keep them under a tight line. Every trip is bringing more of them that makes greater demands," the First Mate stated as he too observed the immigrants only he was being more selective and was looking to the young girls and women who, while he figured most to be country bumpkins, might prove interesting at a later date. He knew he had plenty to choose and pick from if and when a time came.

"Letters from the new world?" the Captain laughed.

"Aye," The mate nodded. "It seems they are hearing more from the others who have gone on before and what they had gone through and they are now making more demands on their quarters and provisions."

"Well, let them," the Captain stated as he searched the deck, looking for inspectors who were supposed to be giving medical checks to the immigrants. "I don't see any of the port people. Who is to examine these people? Have they been seen ashore?"

"Some. But with so many they cannot all be checked out. They look all right to me. I did see them take a screaming Mimi back ashore earlier."

"Ah, well. Once we are at sea, we will be in control and keep them under a tight rein. He turned and glanced at the stateroom passageway where he saw two men, first-class passengers, exiting their quarters and move foreword to the mainmast halyard post and take a position looking down on the milling throng below on the main deck. One, he noted, was carrying an ear trumpet.

"The cabin passengers, they are all aboard?" he asked turning away, his attention now to other things.

"Aye. All but for an old woman who died last night at the Green Parrot. Her family is aboard and all the others as well."

"Very well. Now just as soon as Galaxy gives us her line when we leave the gate, we will be underway. Carry on, Mr. Grayson.

* * *

188

"Hilary! Stay close. Have the children close nearby," William called over the noise of the hundreds of immigrants who were now crowding the small space of the main deck that wasn't taken up with water casks, piled up baggage and hurrying seamen seemingly running in all directions at the same time.

"Where in the hell do I go!" a voice called. "I have a ticket but no one seems to know where it is for."

"My ticket," a young man said to an officious-looking ship's officer, "my ticket is three hundred eighteen. Where do I go?"

The officer, the Ship's Purser, looked disdainfully at the man. He pointed. "Follow that man with the blue hat. He will direct you to your quarters, your hatch way."

The immigrants as cattle, even to being prodded by sailors with marlin spikes to get a move on or get out of the way, were led aboard in two long meandering lines from the dock to the steep gangplank which led midship and continued on to the fore and aft passageways, each with a little shed-like covering on which numbers were posted. It was here that much confusion arose as some in the foreword line had ticket numbers for the aft passageway and vice versa.

"Are we still together?" Robert Hall called to anyone who would listen, as the group from Ramsey-Ely filed one by one up the steep ladder-like steps of the gangway from the dock to the main deck of the Primrose.

"I don't know," Sophia called back as she checked her four children who were ahead of her. Peggy and Regina having a more difficult time with their long dresses and still carrying their straw padding trusser.

"I don't see Brendan. He was with the Wildes, but I don't see him now," Elly grunted as she mounted the steps. "My God. These steps are worse than the stairway at the White Swan," she gasped, pains stabbing at her thighs and calf muscles.

"When will we know where our goods are?" a frightened voice begged.

A voice answered, "They are numbered as is your ticket of

passage. They match. And we will get them when we get to New York."

"I am sure we will be able to get to our goods once we are at sea and the crush of our all being here on board together at one time eases up," another chimed in. More with hope than conviction.

"Ah, I am sure they know what they are doing. I was told there is no room below in the quarters for extras so they must stash many things above on the deck until we get into port," still another voice added its bit of wisdom.

"Ethan!" Robert called to him as he was helping Shirley up the ladder. "Have you seen Brendan?"

Ethan shook his head. "No. I have been too busy with my own. I last saw him at the tavern."

"Robert! Come help us," Sophia demanded, upset as they were approaching the small opening of the booby-hatch to their compartment below.

Robert stood looking over the heads, as best he could, of the now docile and herded Ramsey and Ely group. He looked in vain and did not see Brendan.

"Come!" Sophia almost screamed. "He will be all right. He will be found. It is now that you must worry about us. Your family. You brought him here to Liverpool, now let him find his own way."

Robert looked to his wife in a new way with a feeling of the unknown about her. But then he thought, her main concern is our own family. Not Brendan or Ethan or... "Aye, Yes. I am coming."

* * *

"I am not yet over the feeling of being off the Achill and already I feel the motion of this boat," Honora said discontentedly as she and Pierce and the baby followed in their line across the deck toward their booby-hatch that showed the number as the one they were to enter.

"Ah, ha. And we are standing still," Pierce looked to her. "And you are already feeling the waves as I am sure we will be feeling them again but I do hope better than before. This is a much larger boat and it should ride better."

"Have you seen Fergus?" Honora asked as she scanned the faces of those about for his now familiar face.

"No. His number was two hundred thirty-eight, I think it was, and ours is four hundred twelve. So there is a large space between us and where he might be."

"There are that many among us?" Honora questioned in almost total disbelief at such a number being in one place at one time and on a boat at that. "I am worried about his hand," she continued as she shifted Noreen on her right hip to make way for a sailor who was cutting through the crowd to man a line with two others hurrying to their sea stations for departure from the dock.

"Ach. And me too. The man who helped set his bone said he would need better attention but he did the best he could do for him. When we are at sea, I am sure we will be able to get together with him and get some help from the boat's doctor."

The two with Noreen, now being carried by Pierce, wended their way with the others along the deck. Pierce looked about and compared the Achill, the only boat he had ever sailed on to the Primrose, the second and the last he hoped. The Primrose was a much larger vessel. It was called a barque, he had heard as was the Achill but this was much larger and safer he thought. He looked to the masts, three of them. With names and sails he knew nothing of. They were furled with so many lines of rope about as vines on a cottage wall, all a jumble and in seeming great disarray. He saw to his left a large grated metal structure set on bricks imbedded in the deck someway, which were once covered with ashes as best he could figure. They were blackened from earlier use. A stove of some sort he guessed for cooking although he couldn't imagine how.

A sudden shouting took his attention to other matters as he

saw sailors running to the gang way and other parts and throwing off ropes to the dock while others were pulling ropes up from the dock. Many of the immigrants who were as wide-eyed as he, were shouldered and elbowed out of the way by the working sailors who bustled about at the orders of the First Mate, a mean looker, Pierce thought, as he called directions through a hand held mouth piece which looked like a cone with its tip cut off. Other sailors were busy now storing the gear of the immigrants, too large or cumbersome to take below to the quarters, into piles on the deck, covering them with canvas and tieing them into unshapely mounds. Also taking much space on the deck were large water casks, actually old wine casks which had been procured by the Ship's Purser at only pennies to hold the fresh water brought aboard in Liverpool from upstream in the River Mersey. The casks also known to Pierce as tierces, were lashed together then to the bulwark and they, with the unsightly mounds, dominated the deck space leaving only little, narrow aisleways between for the sailors to move about.

"All right now! Hurry along! We've got to clear the deck before we can sail. Hurry along, damn it," a beefy sailor jostled Pierce who was evidently moving too slow as he tried to take in the sights and activity of the departure from Liverpool. He gave a last look out and across the railing to the bustle and noise from other craft with hundreds of stick-like masts waiting for a signal to move with the tide and hoist their sails once clear of the river mouth and out into the Irish Sea. How anyone could make any order of the situation, he could only guess. It was not only the Primrose but other boats, dozens of them he could figure, were also preparing to get underway when the tide was right and the leaving was good.

Honora, who was also taking in the scene and the activities about the deck followed the man in front of her into the confines of the booby-hatch, a little shed about four feet, which had a steep ladder leading into a hole for a passageway with only a glimmer of light to find her way below.

192

* * *

The steam-tug Galaxy, a new addition to the Liverpool Port
Authority, proceeded into the Mersey River and headed for the
open water with the Primrose in tow. The tide had lifted her
from her berth at Prince's Dock and was now floating her until
her sails could be unfurled in the openness of the Irish Sea which
lay beyond the point at New Brighton, two miles to the north.

The wind was fair and from the southeast which would be
in good staid. The sea beyond was mild with a slight rising and
falling with no waves of any consequence. On the spar deck the
cabin passengers were enjoying the mild weather and being able
to stretch their legs as they promenaded about. A table had been
set up with various offerings for their selection and enjoyment
along with assorted wines and cordials. Two of the cabin passengers were in conversation. One a short fellow, middle aged, who
held a hearing trumpet to his left ear into which the other, a
younger man, was addressing himself. The two had positioned
themselves to be able to observe the Galaxy as it cast off its
lines from the Primrose and proceeded to return to its station
off Liverpool and pick up another packet in need of a tow to
deep water and a fresh wind westward. From the port side, they
were able to see a small sloop slipping alongside the Primrose
which still hadn't unfurled its sails. They saw that on the deck
near where the port side gangway was positioned, now secured,
a number of flats consisting of assorted boxes, barrels and mixed
packages numbering quite a number of goods which were being
readied to be transferred to the sloop, now with lines attached
to the Primrose. The sloop's sails were slacked to enable the
two ships to come along side and make the transfer.

"Ah, yes. It is as Whyte wrote. The sloop is coming to pick
up the food stuffs the Captain had to show to the authorities that
were available for the steerage as according to regulations. "The
younger man explained to the other, who was nodding his head
in understanding. "They will be bought back from the Ship's

Purser most likely by the charlatans who will in turn sell them to still another ship's captain or his cohorts in crime to show he too is meeting the requirements of the law. Who will again sell them back when he is out of sight and well on his way at sea, or sell them at high prices later when the time demands aboard his ship.

"Ah, Oswald. It is a sneaky and underhanded thing they are doing to the poor souls who know no better," the older man of the two said as he tucked his ear horn under his left arm and looked to the Primrose unloading to the sloop.

"Yes, and as it was last night at the White Swan. All planned ahead to steal from the poor beings so innocent and trusting with their picayune resources and to be later at the mercy of the ship's foul fellows. Ah, then," he continued, "we must keep close track of what we see and hear on this voyage. What we will accrue in our notes can be very incriminating to those who trade in such despicable acts against their own kind."

"I am not too sure of the Captain regarding the immigrants, most at least, as his kind."

"No. Maybe not. It would seem to me he is even lower than they to take such action against them."

"And how do you suppose our fellow cabin mates regard such an occurrence which I am sure many have observed as we these past few minutes. They can see with their own eyes what we have seen."

"Oh, I am sure they could care less or even have any idea of such nefarious activity is taking place before their very eyes," the younger man turned his face into the wind and breathed deep. "As it is, we have a long voyage ahead of us and I am sure that what we have been witnessing will only be the tip of the ice berg as the saying goes. I will go now and write my notes."

"Aye. And I will mingle with the cabin people for a while. It will be interesting to get their views as the voyage progresses. I will be in shortly."

* * *

"Now hear this! Ye all! I am Bo-sun Fanshaw and am to be in charge of your care and well-being for the next few weeks. You have been asked by your own people to represent them at this meeting so I can explain to you the rules and regulations while at sea. Rules and regulations you must obey for your own good!" Boatswain Elliot Fanshaw, a thin, wiry looking middle-aged man with gray sideburns wearing a dark blue pea-jacket with light blue trousers cut at the knees, stood at the base of the mainmast on the spar deck and looked down into the unturned faces of about twenty-five steerage passengers assembled on the main deck who had been selected among their own to represent them and in turn report back to them of the Captain's or others orders to them for their care and well-being.

The wind of the Irish Sea coursed from the southeast and drove the Primrose at a tilt to starboard, wave crests chasing along with it. The white sails in full bloom in the clear morning air, stretched to their maximum as she and other packets fanned out, each to seek its own course for delivery of its wares. The wind was from behind the bo-sun and caused him to use a megaphone to direct his words to the men below who strained to hear, some with cupped hands to their ears to catch his voice as the words swept past them to the west.

"As best we can figure, and it is all in God's hands, it will take us the better part of six weeks to reach New York." Faces turned to one another, with wondering looks of disbelief. Others nodded knowingly and understood that any number of their fellow steerage mates had been misled by shipping agents as to the time it would take for passage just to get their fares. "Many of you have your own rations. We have rations for all but we may be limited as the cruise we are on and we may have to ration later on. We will have to wait and see."

He pointed to the grating. "This is where you will do your cooking. You will have to set your own schedules among your-

195

selves. Only eight can cook at a time. Wood kindling for your fires can be bought through the ship's cook."

A murmur of anger arose. A voice called out. "Only eight at a time can cook! My God! It will take us all day and night at the fires to be able to feed ourselves and to have to buy our fuel as well. I was told it was provided. And who is to know when it will be our turn to cook?" an upset angry young man wailed to those about him.

"Hush! Listen!" an older man stopped and motioned to the Bo-sun. "We have enough water," the Bo-sun continued, knowing of and seeing the reaction to his statement, "for each adult to have three quarts of water a day. That is based on a six weeks' trip. You will have to share with your children your allotted amount."

The Primrose rose in a rising mount of sea and rolled to port then back to starboard. The sudden motion, while known to a sailor, was not known to the assembled representatives who were picking themselves up from the deck. "God almighty!" a voice grumbled, "and this is only our first day at sea."

"Aye. And we have another month or so of still more to come," another voice added.

"As ye know," the Bo-sun continued, the wind now gusting more to the south, "each of you will be provided with an ample weekly allowance of hearty food stuffs. It will be doled out each Thursday beginning tomorrow here on the main deck. Be sure you have your containers for them and watch over them during the week. We will not open our stores otherwise."

From the southwest over St. George's Channel and whipping over Anglesey, a distance of about ten miles, a rain squall line moved rapidly approaching the Primrose and the other packets now beating to the west in the lee of the distant shoreline protection. "We will allow for on-deck visiting as the weather permits. We have toilets," he pointed forward to the forecastle deck where on each side where the bowsprit extended, a seating arrangement of rough planking was erected over the side of the bow with four holes each for voiding into the open waters below.

Robert Hall looked at the facility and wondered: Eight holes for about, as best he could determine, five hundred steerage passengers. Almighty God! There would have to be a continuous line for twenty-four hours a day on the deck to accommodate all who would have a reason to use them. He thought of the lines as they came from the dock to the boat in Liverpool. What will it be like now? He shook his head and looked about him. The Bo-sun's voice was now totally lost to him as the wind shifted and blew it away in another direction.

"It looks like we are in for some bad weather," a small man stated pointing to the coming squall line of heavy rain moving over the surface with low flying scud in its vanguard.

The Bo-sun waved his arms and pointed to the two booby-hatches, as if to tell the gathering that his talk to them was over and they had better get moving below. Robert joined the others. All in a hurry to get below before the onslaught of the weather change would be upon them. He worked his way down the hatch and entered into the accommodations for his family and others from the Ramsey-Ely group. He made his way through thickening odors of sweating bodies in heavy clothing, ship's mould and already, feces. He knew that any number were having problems now, including himself and it was just the first afternoon out. The only ventilation, he knew of, was from the hatches now being closed and sealed from above. In the dimness of only a few hanging lamps, he judged the area of space of the confines of the 'tween decks,' he heard a sailor call their quarters earlier, as about seventy feet long and about twenty-five feet wide with row upon row of bunks, berths the same sailor had referred to them. Each berth was about six feet long, a foot and a half wide with about two feet between the three berths in a tier for headroom.

A middle aisle separated the two halves of the area into a port and starboard, much as it looked in the White Swan, he thought, only the ceiling is so low here, so much so that he had to bend over to move about or strike his head on the overhead.

The hanging lamps gave only enough illumination, again only to those in its immediate vicinity. In their new situation each, instead of having their own berth, they had to double up: the boys together, the girls together and he with Sophia. He saw any other number of families with having to put up with even more. The tickets they had did not add up a one-to-one ratio as they had thought as some avaricious agents were concerned more with cramming than with the comfort of their fares. Even so he saw that some of the younger children thought it fun and laughed and giggled at the arrangement. He saw that Ethan and his sister Lorna had to share the same berth and that Shirley was to be with William and Hilary. Ants! "Oh, my God! Yes, ants! That is how we are to live these next few weeks. Months?" He was almost overcome with the enormity of their undertaking. It would have to be well worth it he consoled himself as he approached Sophia now his only claim to humanity and sanity.

"I am not feeling well," she said as the packet heeled so that the hanging lamp swung at a grotesque angle from the flimsy decking beneath which the sloshing of water was heard.

"Aye. And me as well. It is what they call a sea sickness," he answered as he crouched and spread the straw truss on his and Sophia's top berth. "How are the children taking things?" The ship's rolling giving him a queasy sensation in his stomach.

"They seem fine. They are young. They can adapt," she replied as she sat as best she could on the edge of the middle berth, where Peggy and Regina would hold forth in their sleeping hours. Already she knew that they would all have to have staggered hours for sleeping. "And what did the man, the Bo-sun, have to say?"

"He said just about what the tickets say for our victuals. We are entitled to only so much and we will have to be very careful with our water use. We will get our food rations on Thursdays. The netties are on the front deck up high..."

"There is a three-holer at the end of the room here," Sophia informed him. "Already it is being used as was the one in the White Swan, a long line awaiting. Have you seen the others?"

she added as she moved to make room for Peggy who was returning from visiting the nettie with her younger sister.

"Some. I will gather them after a bit. When we have all settled in," Robert answered as he tried to shake off the near sensation of having to vomit. "I will report to them what the Bo-sun said," he said as he arose from the berth's confines with a stagger as the Primrose dropped into a trough, heeled to port and rumbled in surging gasps to right itself. "I will have to report to them of what the Bo-sun said and we will have to make arrangements for us all to cook and eat together. The Bo-sun said we must agree to a time with others so that we can cook and eat on a schedule."

"Robert!" a voice called over the droning noise of the hundreds who were now in the process of bedding down and trying to understand their new plight in life.

"It is me, Brendan," the voice called out. Robert now seeing him approaching in the dimness. He smiled at seeing his old friend.

"Ah, yes Brendan. You did find your way back to us after all. We were worried about you. We thought you might have missed the boat."

"No, but I was about the last to board," he showed Robert his passage ticket. "My ticket number is two hundred eleven. I should be with you in this area," he peered into the shadows at the bunks, all full.

"Aye. We are all to be ticketed for a berth but such is not the case. I see none empty. But we will look." Feeling much better than he had earlier when he was lying down and the fear of being sick, Robert joined Brendan as they sought out the berth to correspond to his ticket number.

While the Ramsey-Ely group was as a whole together, there were a number of spaces in the assignments so that they were not all together as a common group.

"Ah, here is my bunk," a happy Brendan nodded as he matched his ticket number with a berth. A middle one. "I'm sorry, mam," he said to a middle-aged woman who lay curled up in a ball in the unmade truss. "Mam...Mam . . . I am sorry, but . . . " he closed in on her.

"Leave her alone! She' sick. Go to the bastard who took hers. This was empty so she took it. If you want one go to the hedon who took hers," a man in the berth above her railed at Brendan. A cold look in his eyes, a fist raised.

"I don't understand," Brendan began. "I..."

"Come, Brendan. Come," Robert said quietly as he led him away realizing that it could only lead to further problems if they tried to pursue the issue any further at this time. "We will find out more about the berth assignments when we meet again with the Bo-sun. I am sure that there are other mixups that will be corrected. It is only our first day out."

"But where?..."

"Hush now, Brendan, we can make arrangements in our own way. We can take turns sleeping and resting," Robert tried assuring him. "We will work something out. Come, sit by Sophia. You look tired."

* * *

"This is what we get our water in? This tin?" Joseph Wildes asked the sailor who was doling out the water from a cask into an open gallon tin container. "It says we get three quarts of water a day for each adult. A gallon is not six quarts and we have a babe."

"Well, then you'll just have to make do then. Won't ya?" the sailor said sarcastically, as he handed a like-tin to the man behind Joseph, who in turn had a mark made on his ticket by another sailor with an indelible marker. "Move on, damn it!" the sailor swore. "We haven't got all damn day!"

Joseph took his tin, net even near full, as it sloshed about and moved cautiously across the deck to the booby-hatch way.

The Primrose, now on a beat to port was tacking into a head-wind from almost due west. The weather now was pleasant with the earlier storm now past. The sun now in a warm glow under a clear sky.

"It has taken me almost three hours just to get our tin of water," he growled to the young fellow passenger who was assisting those who had water tins to pass them down to another lad in the compartment below. A number of others had stumbled or fell loosing their daily supply, to a sudden ship's motion or by being bumped by another in similar straits. While the babe, Gwen, did not need water for her food needs, as she was nursing, Julia did however. He could . . . He would try to minimize his daily needs but he did know he would also need water. He looked to the casks stored along the bulkhead not yet opened and in reserve for when the deck casks would become empty.

"Ah, Joseph. You're back. I have been so worried. Elly and Edith are so sick," Julia said as she swung down from their top berth where Gwen was wrapped in a blanket almost stuffed into the straw truss, her clothing soaked from pee.

"It is a long line for the water and I am sure it will get even longer if the weather gets worse as I have been told it will get." He set the tin down on the deck and wedged it as best he could to the berth. "If Elly and Edith are sick, it is the sea sickness that has them, as well as others," he added as he looked about the area and saw many of the passengers gagging and holding cloths to their mouths. A few tried to rise in their berths but fell back exhausted.

"How do you feel? He asked Julia.

"As they," she said nodding to the others. "We were told nothing of this by Constance in her letter. Only of the work on the other side," she paused as she took a small cup of water offered by Joseph. "Each journey is an experience and a reward in its own way I suppose."

"It is not the same water that we had as from our own well back home," Joseph said as he took a sip from the cup.

"No. I suppose not," she replied, adjusting the baby's blanket. "I don't suppose anything will ever be the same again."

JOHN NORTHY

"Forty-two days, six weeks exactly," John Northy said with a knowing wink to George Talbot, one of his cabin mates, as they heard the call of 'land ho' from the lookout.

"You had it guessed pretty well," the young man acknowledged as they made their way to the spar deck from the saloon where they had been eating the noon meal.

The Ambrose rose and heaved in a rolling sea, the wind from behind in the southeast, giving it a starboard tack and a fast approach to the distant horizon where almost dead ahead was the coastline of North America and somewhere along its shores, New York City, the journey's end. John looked round about the horizon and saw that the Ambrose was not alone in the haste to get to the docks on the Hudson and East Rivers as he saw any number of other vessels beating their ways on their own tacks. He counted seven others of varying distances from the Ambrose and marveled that for six weeks he had seen only one other ship and it had been heading eastbound now all of a sudden, all converging out of nowhere it seemed.

"It certainly has been an experience," George stated as he turned his attention to the now milling steerage passengers who were emerging from the booby-hatches to see now with their own eyes, the land for which many had given all their meager fortunes to arrive at. For the past three days the weather worked for the ship's crew and passengers. It was warm and the seas relatively calm allowing the sailors to direct the steerage passengers in cleaning and washing their compartments and themselves for their entry into the quarantine station on Staten Island upon their arrival. He also noted that the Captain had been rather lavish in his distribution of food stuffs the past week and that the steerage passengers seemed well fed and a happy lot compared to the first two weeks at sea.

"Aye," John agreed, "and as a whole I have enjoyed my experiences." He then turned his attention to the distant shore now taking on a configuration of height and width all along the horizon with signs of habitation. The day, a warm spring May early afternoon, brought with it across the narrowing space of the waterway, the smell of the land with its earthy greenness now taking still clearer forms and color. He took deep breaths. "Ah. My God. America. I can smell it. It is sweet and has the smell of apple blossoms." He shook his head in the wonder of it all.

The two's attention was now directed to the Captain and First Mate as they made their way to the starboard railing on the quarterdeck where they overlooked the now massing immigrants who were all trying, it seemed, to get their first and most memorable view of the new world. The crowding together was compounded by the ship's heeling from the tack, the starboard railing only a few feet above the waterline.

"Here there! Stay back!" the Captain called angrily. Then yelled, "Stand back. It is there! It will not go away! Stand back, damn it! Give yourself some room." The immigrants now in the hundreds kept pouring out onto the deck in an almost holiday mood, his voice lost to them. "Mr. Grulke! Where about!" The Captain ordered his helmsman. "The damn fools will kill themselves and us and drown within sight of the Narrows. Where about!"

The ship's crew anticipating the Captain's order, as the event of storming the railing had happened on earlier sailings, raced to their stations as the Ambrose swung its stern into the wind, the sudden abrupt movement catching the sails on the other side as the ship's direction was reversed causing the unsuspecting and unknowing immigrants to go tumbling back from the starboard railing and away from falling or being pushed overboard. "Mr. Grulke, bring her back about," the Captain ordered the helmsman. "Mr. Finch," he ordered the First Mate, "get those people back to their compartments and hold them there until we tie up. I want no more dancing on the main deck until they are ready to go ashore."

"Aye, Captain," the First Mate answered, smiling wryly in reply as he knew the meaning of 'dancing on the deck.'

John, from his vantage point on the spar deck above and behind the commotion, looked down as the few sailors who could be free from the task of righting the Ambrose herded the immigrants back down the booby-hatches for their final confinement. He mused that as a whole the mass of immigrants seemed to be quite jovial and not at all upset by the Captain's rash action. He released his grip on a shroud line that he had clung to in the sudden action by Captain and joined his friend.

"Well, now," he said to George. "It is now our time to get ourselves ready for our departure," as the two made their way to their cabin. They entered the cabin to be met with a tirade of abuse toward the Captain by the sudden maneuvering of the ship, by Mr. Lindsey, who during the action had been thrown to the deck and had broken his spectacles. Maurice Lynn, who had stayed in the saloon for after lunch drinking, was now packing his limited belongings into a small shipping trunk that John had not seen before.

"Are you still planning to go to this place of the gold rush?" George asked of John. "In California."

"Aye. I still have my plans. But I will have to know more of how to get there and hope some gold will be left for me," John answered lightly as he extracted his belongings from beneath his berth.

George looked to Maurice. "And you. What plans have you for in the new world?"

"My plans?" he shrugged his shoulders. "As I have said before to you, I am in imports. I will visit my clients in New

York and Boston and then in another six weeks or so I will return to Liverpool. It is as simple as that."

"You never have told us what it is that you import." John asked, having wondered on occasion over the past month of his fellow passenger's occupation.

Maurice looked to John with a snide look. "Oh, a little of this and a little of that. Whatever my clients want or need."

"Well, anyhow," John said feeling put down by Maurice's flippant answer, "I wish you good speed."

He turned to George. "And to you, George. I wish you well." The two clasped hands in a firm double handshake. They both turned their attention to Mr. Lindsey, who by this time had quieted down when he saw that no one seemed to care of his predicament.

"And you, sir?" George nodded to him. "I wish you the best in this new land." He added, "Do you have family or friends to meet you?"

The old man looked up from where he was sitting on the edge of his berth. "No. I have no one to meet me. No family or friends," he paused. "I have come here to die."

John stopped short. Both Maurice and George looked to the old man in amazement.

"To die?" John asked incredulously.

"Yes. To die," the old man stated matter-of-factly.

"How do you know?" George began.

"Oh, I know. I have been told and know it in my bones that I am dying and have only a few weeks or months to live at the most."

"But why the ocean voyage? Why not have stayed in England?" John asked, still amazed at the old man's revelation.

"Because I once lived here in America. In Rhode Island. In a little town called Tiverton." The old man wiped his nose with the back of a sleeve. "I was a young man then," he looked to George, "about your age. I was married." He lifted his eyes to look upon John. "I was married for four years to Brenda." He paused, his eyes blinking and wet. "Then she died in childbirth. It is to her and our little babe, Cassandra, that I am returning to be with them again. I promised her that I would return and now I am after all of these thirty-five years. I am keeping my promise to her and our baby girl so that we will be together in eternity."

The three young men's eyes focused on the old man, who instead of being an old grump, was now looked upon with respect and awe. John cleared his throat. "Er . . . Ah . . . " He turned his back to him and wiped a tear. The other two returned to their packing without another word.

* * *

The Ambrose, being the first in the line of a succession of ships, was met by a harbor pilot who maneuvered her through the Narrows into the Upper Bay of New York Harbor dropping anchor midstream off Castle Gardens at the tip of Manhattan Island. There were three quarantine and two customs officers came aboard for inspection of passengers and crew. John, along with three others from the cabin passengers, was singled out by the Purser to answer questions and be given a physical attesting to his well-being and good health after the ocean voyage. His questioning quarantine officer was a young man not much older than himself. He seemed bored and routine-oriented and asked his questions in a perfunctory manner.

"Your name?" he asked.

"John Ham Northy."

"Where was your place of origin?"

"Plymouth. In the West Country. From the village of . . . "

"I know. I know. How do you feel?"

"Feel?"

"Yes. Are you well? Do you feel ill or out of sorts?"

"No. I feel fine."

"How are your fellow passengers? Are any of them feeling not well?"

"No. Not that I know of." John thought a moment. "Mr. Lindsey is old but he seems well." He stopped, wondering how much he should say about the old man soon to be dying. He thought better to say no more.

The quarantine officer then peered into John's blue eyes. "Let me see your tongue," he said as he made a note on a card and handed it to John. "You are fine. You may go." He said as he turned to another passenger for his questions of him regarding his health and well-being.

John was then put upon by the Customs Officer who posed a gruff and brusk manner.

"What is your name?"

"John Ham Northy."

"How old are you?"

"Nineteen. Soon to be twenty."

"What is your work?"

"I am a carpenter. I was my father's apprentice."

"How much money have you?"

John hesitated. He wasn't to sure if he wanted those about to know of how much money he had. "Twelve pounds, three shillings," he near whispered.

The official nodded. "Do you believe in anarchy?"

"Anarchy?" John answered puzzled at the meaning of the word.

"Rebellion against one's government."

"No, sir! God save the Queen I say."

The official smiled a wry, weak grin at John's reaction. "That is all," he said and moved on the another passenger.

John backed away from the group and winked to George who had not been one of the examinees but stood aside to see the proceedings.

John looked then to the main deck where a number of steerage passengers had been brought forth to be interviewed. He saw that they were alert and answering questions with heads nodding, arms and hands gesturing, all with wide smiles.

John also noticed the Captain and the First Mate standing on the quarter deck at the accommodation ladder visiting with various individuals who had come aboard with the others when he saw Maurice and another man, a little older, who had been a cabin passenger and he had seen about the decks but had never really talked to. He noticed they both were carrying small trunks as they passed the two officers and descended the accommodation ladder to a small boat awaiting them.

He must be some kind of an importer to get such treatment as that, John guessed, as the small boat took off and headed for the shore of Manhattan Island a few hundred feet away. The view now caught his attention. It was a shoreline but not a shoreline as he knew one to be. This shoreline was entirely of piers, warehouses, berthed sailing vessels and a few steamers. It bustled and moved almost as a living thing. He looked up the river, the Hudson with its many moving small boats heading to and fro across its waters. He liked what he saw. It was as a stage and from his view on the spar deck of the Ambrose he saw such a wide scope of activity as he had never seen before. He thought of Plymouth. Pitiful little Plymouth.

His thoughts were interrupted by the almost rapid departure of the examining committee, as they abruptly left the quarter deck quickly shaking hands with the Captain and First Mate. Ah. They certainly know their business, he thought. Checking a whole ship for those who might be sick and on and off in only a matter of a few minutes. His thoughts were once again interrupted as he heard the blasts of a small steam tug forging its way to the Ambrose. He saw lines being thrown from the Ambrose to the tug as the crew members of both vessels moved about agilely as the anchor so recently dropped was now being raised as the tug began taking up slack in the lines to the Ambrose and headed for an opening at a pier at the foot of Wall Street.

John felt exhilarated. "Ah," he said aloud, his arms outspread, "America. Here I am."

* * *

"Bastard! Son of a whore!" John Northy raged and stormed. "I could kill him! I. . .I. . . Damn him anyway!"

"John. Settle down. Your screaming and calling names will not get back your father's watch or your money no more than it will get me back my mother's rosary and my money." George admonished John a distraught and upset John who had just found out that his father's watch and most of his money had been stolen sometime on the ship's voyage. It was when he and John checked their belongings after they came ashore and found that someone had very cleverly replaced the watch with a cheap imitation and the rosary in its pouch was only some pebbles and most of their money gone.

"My God, George, how can a man stoop so low as to steal a family treasure from another," John gasped almost crying.

"I don't know. It must take a certain type," George answered, just as perplexed as John at their losses.

John paced. "I will go back to the Captain. I will demand that he or the shipping company pay me . . . us . . . for our losses. I. . ." he smashed his right fist into his left palm so hard it hurt him.

"John. John . . . Come sit down. You are in a terrible state," George cautioned him as he led him to a small dining table at the rear of an eatery they had entered to examine their losses and regain some composure.

"I've only a few shillings and a pence," John lamented.

"And I have only about the same. But we have enough to pay for a small meal. I see they have an equivalent board for American and English monies and others as well. We will have enough for now and until I contact my Uncle Martin. I am sure he will help you."

"Your uncle. He is here in New York?"

"Yes. I have his address. His office. At least that wasn't stolen. He took a folded paper from his inside coat pocket. "Yes, here it is." He read an address. "I will check with the proprietor and find where it is and we will go there for his help."

"Oh, God," John sighed, slumping in his chair. "What am I to do? I have no place to stay. No money. I do not know a soul but yourself and you will soon be gone to . . . "

"Louisville. In Kentucky. My uncle has a business there and wants me to work for him," he looked to John, deep concern on his face. "As I said, I am sure my uncle will be able to help you get started. He is my mother's youngest brother and a very fine man." He then sat back in his chair and in a now more jovial manner said. "Well now. You are a bright lad and I am sure once you get back onto your feet, you will later laugh at today's misfortune. I am sure something will turn up for you."

"I hope so," John nodded as he fingered his bag and withdrew the cheap tin watch that was placed in the original watch's small box wrapped in a silk cloth. He looked at it. He held it to his right ear then wound it. He held it again to his. "It's ticking. At least it works. Now we will see if I can."

* * *

CHAPTER TWELVE

Buffalo

The desk clerk looked with disdain and a bit angry when he saw an unkept middle-aged man hurriedly enter the lobby of the Mercer Hotel and approach the desk panting.

"Sir," the man gasped. "Sir, is Captain Roby about? Is he in his room?"

"Captain Roby? Who wants to know?" the clerk asked wondering what this being would want with Captain Charles Roby, who with his family was in suite 312A.

"My name is Eddie Thatcher and I am an oiler on Captain Roby's boat, the Griffith tied up at the Main Street dock. I was sent by Mr. Wilkinson, our Clerk, to fetch the captain back to the boat. There has been an accident . . . "

The clerk put up his right hand to stop Eddie's questioning and pointed to the stairway leading to the upstairs rooms where at that moment the Robys and Tiffanys were descending and heading for the lobby exit.

"Captain, sir!" Eddie turned and called to his captain. "Captain Roby!"

"What?" the Captain stopped and looked to who had called him recognizing his oiler. "Eddie, what is it?" he asked seeing a concern in his eyes as he crossed lobby doffing his cap.

"Sir, Mr. Wilkinson sent me to fetch you right away. There's been an accident . . . "

"An accident?" Albert Tiffany asked as the two men left the

211

women and took the oiler aside from others in the lobby.

"A fire?" Captain Roby asked.

"No, sir. No fire. The Indian boy, he's disappeared and there is blood all over . . . "

"Disappeared? Blood?" Albert asked aghast at the implications.

"Aye. There is blood from the doorway to the edge of the boat."

"Charles, what has happened?" Ada asked as she joined the three who were getting stares from others in the lobby, and seeing the shocked expressions on her son and Albert's faces. "Is the Griffith all right?"

"Yes, Mother. It is Kuruk. He has disappeared and there seems to be blood all about."

"Charles, we must get back to the boat. I feel responsible for his safety and . . . Oh dear. Come quickly . . . "

"Mother, wait! If there is blood about, I do not want Candace or Emily to see it."

Emily, Hazel and Candace, by this time had joined the others. "I will stay here with Emily and Candace at the hotel tonight," Hazel stated as she realized that something serious had happened and that Charles did not want the two to be involved.

Charles took Emily's right hand, "There has been some sort of accident and I must return to the Griffith."

"I'll join you," Albert said looking to Hazel.

"And I," Ada said as she started to head for the doorway.

"Eddie said it was Kuruk?" Emily questioned as she put her left arm about Candace's shoulders, drawing a very frightened daughter to her.

"Yes. Something has happened to him, but I must go now. Hazel will be with you and you must check on Thomas. Perhaps you can still go to the . . . "

"Oh no!" Emily retorted firmly. "We will stay here at the hotel. We do not have to see the minstrel show." She paused and looked to her husband. "I hate minstrel shows!"

* * *

"Who are you?" David Stebbins asked a young man, accompanied by another of about his same age, both dapper and polished and in the latest clothing styles.

"I am Leslie Truman," the young man answered. "And this is Alfred Booth. We are from the Law Office of Andrew Putnam, Esquire . . . ," he looked to David for a reaction. He did not get one. "Ah, yes. We are here to pick up a young Indian lad." He looked at a memo pad he had in his hand. "Kuruk."

"He isn't here and we don't know where he is," David stated as the three stood at the base of the ramp from the Griffith to the dock.

"But we were told to pick him up and take him to St. Patrick's nunnery for lodging . . . " the young man tried to explain.

"That may be true, gentlemen. But there has been an accident."

"Accident?" Leslie questioned.

"Yes, an accident. It seems the lad has fallen overboard and probably drowned."

"Sir," the young man said trying to explain his situation. "This is terrible. We were told that he had been injured and was confined to a cabin." He looked at his pad. "Cabin Six."

"Yes, that is true. But I have been told by my captain, Captain Roby, that no one is to come aboard until the police and port authorities finish their investigation which they are doing now."

"Mr. Stebbins," a voice called from up on the main deck.

"Yes, Mr. Wilkinson?" David answered as he turned to the Clerk coming down the ramp.

"Are you from Putnam?" Henry asked of the two.

"Yes, sir," Leslie answered.

"I'm sorry," Henry said motioning them away from hearing of David, who looked at them in a quizzical way. "I am sorry for taking your time on a Saturday night but the boy evidently fell overboard. You will have to tell Mr. Putnam of the circumstances.

213

In some ways I am sure he will be relieved."

"Yes, I suppose he will be," Leslie said with a shrug. "These things happen all the time here on the docks. Mostly drunken sailors." He turned to his partner. "Well, at least it's early enough that if we hurry we can still make the minstrel show at the State. Let's go."

Henry shook his head at the two's thoughts of still having a fun evening on the town after hearing the bad news of a young boy drowning. Oh well. To hell with them, he thought as he turned back to Chief Engineer. "I'll be damn glad to get back to Toledo," he said as he gave a stretch.

"Yes. You and me both. This has indeed been some trip." David agreed, winking his right eye. Henry thought, good no big deal about me and Marie. "What do you suppose happened to the boy?" David continued.

"Oh, I suppose he came out of his coma or whatever it's called and found himself in a strange place and must have broken the thunder mug and cut himself while prowling about on his hands and knees."

"Then found his way out, only to fall overboard in the dark," David finished.

"That's about it," Henry yawned, nodding in agreement.

"Hello, Sam." David greeted the Second Mate as he approached from under the gas street lamp to the left of the ramp.

"Who were those two dudes who I just saw in a big hurry?" Sam asked.

"Ha. Dudes is right." David laughed. "It's a long story. Where have you been? You've missed a lot of excitement this night."

"Eh. I just went ashore for some tobacco and took a walk around town to see the changes since I used to live here." He sucked on his pipe. "What excitement?"

"Oh, you'll know soon enough. The Indian boy drowned."

"Oh? When?" a piqued Sam asked as he drew puffs.

"We don't know. A few hours ago maybe."

"Well, that's interesting, 'cause I just saw them take a body out at the foot of Porter Street a few blocks from here."

"Was it the boy?" David asked.

"I don't know. I was back a ways from the shore. It was just a body wrapped in a net."

"Henry! Stay here and let no one aboard but our own people. Captain's orders. I must tell him and the others of this," David stammered as he raced up the ramp.

"Mr. Wilkinson, may I see you?" Albert Tiffany called from where he was standing on the main deck at the ramp's rail.

"What now?" a miffed Clerk wondered.

"Yes, sir. Well, I guess it's up to you," he said to Sam, "to keep an eye on who in the hell can come aboard or not."

"I will," the Second Mate replied pointing his pipe in acknowledgment.

"Yes, sir. How can I be of help to you?" Henry said shaking Albert's extended right hand.

"Captain Roby and I have come to the conclusion since the Indian boy is evidently dead that we will take the old man's trunks back to Cleveland. The old gentleman must have had some business contacts there that might have some idea of what should be done with them."

"Sir..." A throughly surprised Henry stammered, "...ah...we...Mr. Putnam and I, we have already talked of them and he was to have them picked up in the morning and have them transhipped to England as the old man wanted them to be."

"No. We will take the trunks back to Cleveland..."

"But... sir..."

"We will also be sending back the shipment of wine to Sandusky. The Captain said he will make a special stop on the way back to Toledo."

"I...I just don't know. Everything is happening so fast these past few days," a discouraged and downhearted Clerk lamented.

"I know," Albert said realizing that the Clerk had gone through so much trouble to do his best to get the trunks sent to the old man's address in England and also his concerns about the spoiled wine. "A lot has happened these past few days and I am sure you are as worried as we but those are the Captain's decisions and he is the boss. Right?"

"Right."

"Now I must go to be with him and his mother and the authorities. Good night, Mr. Wilkinson."

"Good night, sir," Henry muttered almost seething. God damn! Who is he to tell me what to do? His mind racing at the thought of losing what might have been something special in the trunks. "He's only an agent. He's not my boss. Captain Roby? Yes. He's my boss and I guess I do what he says I have to do. God damn!"

He went to the railing and looked down into the now crowded dock area filling with the immigrants who were now allowed into the area in preparation for boarding after sunrise. In all of the hectic afternoon and now into the darkness of the night, he had almost forgotten the business at hand—the immigrants now milling about with their pitiful baggage and children, always children. He looked to them and remembered his first few times in seeing them waiting to come aboard here in Buffalo at the same dock. He had been impressed by them: stoic, a good word he had heard once that he thought best described them. Stoic but dumb. Now in looking at them from a now jaundiced eye of losing the trunks, they seemed only like so much cattle to be brought aboard and placed here and there until they reached their cities of destination down the lake and then to God knows where. Shit!

He looked to the base of the ramp and to his surprise saw Marie with Christine in hand, who was bent over and holding a cloth of some kind to her face, with Larry Dana shuffling behind them as they made their way through a cordoned walkway set aside for the ship's crew and cabin passengers to use in coming aboard.

216

Well. What do you know? Damn. What do you know? He asked himself fishing for his pocket watch. Hmm. A little after ten. The young lawyers will be a little late, but . . . Marie is back early and no husband and so are Larry and the maid. What the hell. Marie. Al. He smiled. Maybe it's just as well I didn't go to the whorehouse. Who knows?

* * *

"That about takes care of it," Captain Roby stated as he shook hands with Police Sergeant Paul Robinette of the Buffalo police department and George... of the Buffalo Port Authority. ..."The body found a short while ago has been identified as that of the Indian boy, Kuruk. It is a terrible shame and he being so young with a great future ahead of him by going to school in England, at Eton."

"Eton?" the Sergeant questioned.

"An old man's whim. I am sure." Captain Roby offered:

"We will have the necessary papers for you to sign in the morning, Captain," the Sergeant added as he gathered his notes and placed them in an envelope. "It is now only a formality and you should be able to sail as scheduled at your appointed time. Good luck to you, sir."

"Thank you, Sergeant. I certainly hope so," the Captain agreed. "We will start loading the immigrants at daybreak and we should be underway by ten-thirty," he said as the two officials left the cabin, leaving Charles, his mother and Albert to contemplate the day's events.

"Oh, Charles," his mother sighed almost in tears. "That poor boy. To die so horribly and bleeding. Oh . . . "

"Yes, Mother. I know how you feel, but we can't let it burden us with that we cannot control. He and the old man were passengers. You see them now and then you didn't. Like ships that pass in the night as the old saying goes."

"I know, but he was so nice. He took so to Candace and she

217

to him. It will be very upsetting to her."

"I believe I had better return to the hotel and let Emily and Hazel know just what has happened this evening." Albert interrupted.

"Oh, yes. Yes, Albert. I will stay here. I must," a now exhausted Captain Roby acknowledged as he studied his mother who suddenly seemed so old to him.

"Mother, I want you to go with Albert and stay at the hotel with Emily and Candace, as well as Hazel. Your cabin will be ready for you and Candace in the morning."

"Yes, Charles," his mother agreed. "I will go now with Albert. I must be the one to tell Candace of the situation and hope she will understand. I'll be with you shortly, Albert," she said as she turned from Charles and left for the ladies toilet.

"Well, Charles. I will take my leave and see you in the morning. Try to get some sleep and think only of the future. The old man and the boy are history. You did what you could for them. That is all anyone could ask."

"I don't know about being able to sleep or even think about the future. But I will try both. Good night, Albert." Charles followed his friend to the ramp where he kissed his awaiting mother good night and bid both adieu.

Instead of returning directly to his own cabin, he went to the pilot house. He entered the dark quarters and looked out from its high vantage point to the dock area below and the night lights of Buffalo near about. Below in dock area he saw many of the immigrants doing their best to bed down for the night. At least it wasn't like it was in April when a spring snowstorm blew in from lake Erie and blanketed the entire harbor and most of the Buffalo area with more than seven inches of snow on the huddled masses of immigrants waiting to board. He had allowed those with babies and young children to board the Griffith but many had to stay huddled among themselves to keep warm. He turned and looked out across the Niagra River to the Canadian Shore not too distant. In the western sky a streak of sunset merged into semi-darkness even as he watched. He turned again to the humanity on the dock below.

Why?...Who?...He asked himself. Why have these people spent so much of these past months on what surely must have been terrible experiences at sea? I have them for only a day or two, three at the most and yet most of them have already spent weeks and months on the packets. And the stories he had heard. My God! Again. Why? And who are they? From what he could tell they all seemed to be family loving people who from their appearances were hard working, determined people, regardless of their point of origin. The English, the Germans, the French . . . They all seemed to be industrious and pleasant to be with. He loved the Irish sense of humor. He thought of his own people. His father's side, the Roby's. His mother's side the Shafer's. The Roby's from England before the American Revolution. The Shafer's his Grandfather, his mother's father, a corporal in the Hessian Army that fought against his father's people and yet here they are all together trying as one . . . His thoughts were interrupted by the sound of voices below at the foot of the pilot house stairway. He went to the door opening and looked down into the growing darkness and saw David Stebbins and a woman he did not know walking together. He was going to call hello to them but thought better and held his tongue. He really didn't want to talk to anyone just now. He only wanted to be alone with his melancholy thoughts.

* * *

"You say that you actually designed and built this boat?" Barbara Gaynor asked of David Stebbins as she stood with him at the bow sprit of the Griffith on the Saloon deck as they looked out westward over the Niagra River, now under the last remnant of a late June sunset.

"Well, I did have some help," David laughed. "I had my own ship building company in Maumee. But, yes, it is my own design

219

and I did have some of my own money in its costs."

"But you don't own it."

"Oh, no. I don't have that much money," he rolled his eyes. "I do own a share though. An eighth. Just enough to get by on."

"And where is your home?" she asked loosening a light shawl from around her shoulders, the night air being warm and pleasant.

David thought a moment. "I suppose here. On the Griffith," he offered, not really too sure.

"Oh, silly. You cannot live on it during the winter. You must have a home? . . A wife?"

David pulled at his left earlobe. "I am a widower."

"Oh."

"My wife, Celeste, died five years ago. In September."

"And your children?"

"No children."

"Oh."

"No wife. No children. Just my Griffith. My boat."

"But you do have a home?"

"Well. Yes and no. I live in the off-season, the winter months, with my niece Carol and her family. She's my brother's daughter, in Curtice a little village east of Toledo." He turned and looked to her silhouette against the waning sunset. He liked what he saw as well as earlier. "And you?"

"I am a widow."

"Oh. I am sorry."

"Yes, my late husband, Ernest, God rest his soul, died three years ago this past March."

"Children?"

"No."

"Oh. Well… Ahem, do you have a home?"

"Yes. In Spring Brook just east of Buffalo. It is a big home. Too big for me alone. Ernest was a miller and did right well for us over the years. But," she sighed, "he is gone and as life goes on, it can be very empty rattling around in a big house all alone."

"Ah, yes. I know what you mean." David said as he still studied this person who only an hour or so ago he did not know. But now... "You will be visiting you said, your sister, our Clerk's mother, in Toledo?"

"Yes. It is a surprise visit. It has been three years since I've seen her. A few months after Ernest died. I just hope she will be glad to see me and put up with me." In an instant she realized she had not used her standard add-on whenever referring to her husband's demise since meeting this man. Why? She wondered? " Her husband, Keith," she continued a little flustered, "is rather a ...dud but I will stay only long enough to be wanted."

"Oh. I am sure you will be wanted," David said reassuringly as a strange feeling came over him. This Barbara? It was so odd that he should meet her under such terrible circumstances, the death of the Indian boy and her being questioned as to what she might have known of the tragedy. She seemed up to it and was relieved when he had told the authorities of his information from Sam McCoit about the body being found only a few blocks away and Sam's verifying it later.

The two now moved out some from their position and ascended the stairway to the hurricane deck passing the stairway to the pilot house, only now they were holding hands.

* * *

"What in God's name happened to you two?" a dismayed Marie asked of Larry Dana, as she assisted him into his cabin. "You look like you've been through a war. It's mighty lucky I found you two wandering the streets when I got off the accommodation trolley or you'd still be out roaming the city."

"It's her. The dumb bitch!" he swore as he shucked off his shirt and trousers. "Her and her smart mouth and wiles. She just about had us killed flirting with a black waiter."

Marie picked up the shirt and trousers from the floor then

221

poured a kettle of water into a wash basin. She soaked a wash cloth and then held it to the nape of Larry's neck.

"Ouch! Damn it. Be careful!" he bellowed.

"I'm sorry," she apologized, "but I must get to Christine. She looks terrible. Her poor face. My God!"

"To hell with her. I need attention too. I'm your boss. You tend to me first. Let her rot in her own misery."

Marie couldn't understand it. Here it was only a little after eleven and they were back this early from what she had expected to be an all night stand at Maud's place.

"Is my neck broke? It feels like it is."

"No. But you'll have a hell of a welt for sometime I think. What hit you?"

"There were four of them. One got a lucky punch when I wasn't looking."

"Well, I've got to get to Christine. She is in terrible shape. You'll be all right. Take some of your opium and then get some sleep. We all have a long day ahead of us tomorrow and with more than two hundred-fifty immigrants and the rich-bitches in the cabins, I just can't get too excited and still have you and Christine to tend to as well."

"Ah. Get the hell out! I'll take care of myself," he looked about the cabin. "Where's the creep Henry?"

"I saw him when we came aboard talking with the copper on the beat."

"Well, when you see him again tell him not to make a big deal when he comes to bed. I don't want a bunch of crap about what happened."

You shit, she thought, now angry at him rather than sorry. Something screwed up your plans with Christine and now you're taking it out on others. I'll bet Henry could care less as to what in the hell happened to you. She looked at the sad case before her. Well I guess this is it for Christine on this boat and now I have two or three days hustling for the two of us. Damn it anyhow. She looked at him as he winced in pain as he applied the washcloth to his neck. You're the creep. "I'll be back later to see how you're doing."

"Yeah. Goodby and do not slam the door."

Marie left the cabin and proceeded to her and Christine's cabin. God! What could have happened? A fight sure, but he blames Christine for it and over a Negro waiter. Well, maybe Christine would tell her what really happened. Damn but he was hurting. The sound of a chugging tug passing to the south rent the air as she made her way to the linen room for washcloths and towels for tending to Christine's bashed face.

"Ah, honey. I'm so sorry," she said as she entered the cabin and saw Christine sitting on the floor, a wash basin beside her filled with bloody water. Marie's dress in a pile beside her, crumpled and spattered with dried blood.

"Oh, Marie," Christine sobbed uncontrollably. "I have no teeth. They are all gone. Look." She pointed to the wash basin where four of her front teeth lay. "My beautiful teeth!" She burst forth in a long groan.

"Here. Here, honey. Take it easy." Marie tried to console Christine but knew that no kind words would ever bring back her teeth. How in the hell, she thought, do you console a person, especially a girl as young as Christine, who has lost four of her front teeth? And how in the hell did it happen? Who did it?

Larry never had a problem like this before. Not that she ever knew of.

"How am I to explain this to George… Oh my God…George. He will hate me. He'll never marry me now. Oh my baby, my poor little innocent baby … George's baby." Christine cried into the washcloth, her shoulders shaking.

"No, Christine, no. Please settle down. You'll have to settle down. What has happened has happened. You must calm yourself. You need rest. You have lost a lot of blood. Oh my God! Calm yourself! Hell! I'd kill the son of a bitch who'd do this to me." Marie raged in her own mind.

Marie helped Christine to her feet and walked her to the bed.

"Here, honey, lay down. I'll get you some hot water from the galley and wash you. Let me help you undress."

Christine held a washcloth to her mouth, sobbing intensely as she lay down with Marie lifting her feet onto the bed. "Oh, Marie, I want to die…"

Marie stood and brushed a stray hair from her face. "Jesus, what a mess!" she exclaimed angrily. How much did I have to do with this? Aaaaargh! Nothing! They are both adults. Well she is almost, but still she should know better than to try to make out with a Negro waiter, if that is what she did. Or even to tease one.

"Here, honey, take this," she said handing Christine a small packet. She hadn't wanted to use her opium pills but thought that if anyone ever needed one or two, now was the time. "Here take two of these. They will help you sleep and take away your pain." She drew a cup of water from a water pitcher and helped her take two of the pills. "I want to get hot water from the galley. I'll be back to give you a bath and put you to bed for a good night's sleep. Let the pills work."

Christine lay moaning and sobbing, holding the washcloth to her swollen gums. She looked up to Marie, her eyes filled with bitter tears. "Oh, Marie, I want to die. I really want to die."

* * *

"Here they go again. The same as the other night. Drunk as hell and dragging ass. The both of them," Hiram Faulk muttered to George Jefferson, as Bill Tillman and John Paulding plodded by the open doorway of the crew's mess on their way to the crew's quarters.

"Ah," George grunted in agreement. "They'll never learn until it is too late. When they're dead. They are a team they are. God forbid that they keep up their act." He struck a match and held it to his pipe. "I would hope Captain Roby would take notice of their actions and make demands on them." He blew a cloud of smoke toward the ceiling. "It is a sorry sight to see them as they are and as young as they are."

"But," Hiram yawned as he knocked ashes from his pipe, "they know their stuff as bartenders and helpers to Larry. And their little asides to us don't hurt. Ah well, what the hell. I'm going to try and get me some sleep. How about you?"

"Ah, me knee is giving me fits," George said touching it gingerly. "It's not as swollen as it was but it is still touchy. I'll sit up for a while and see who comes and goes. Take care. I'll see you in the morning."

Hiram waved his right hand and took leave. He walked softly and slowly taking in the sounds and sights of the night which had settled into now almost midnight. A crescent moon was high in a star filled sky, clear in all directions. He stopped and looked to the immigrants on the dock doing their best to, under trying conditions of crowding and no beds or cots to sleep on, to try to get sleep and rest for what he knew would be the last two or three days after many long weeks and months of weary travel to their friends and families waiting for them in Cleveland or Toledo or any of the other stops between. He noticed, as with others in the past, that they were quiet and well behaved with perhaps an occasional baby's crying or a tinkle of laughter. Nothing rowdy or boisterous, just hundreds of souls waiting for the dawn and the last leg of their journey.

He heard the sound of Mr. Stebbins' voice, low but able to be heard, on the saloon deck above his head. He heard a little giggle of laughter. It must be that woman he had seen talking with him earlier. A nice looking woman. Well good for him. He needs a woman. Good luck to him.

He moved slowly along the deck in the semi-darkness of the flickering gas-jet lights from the dock area and the occasional cabin lights behind drawn curtains. He paused at cabin 14, Mr. Evans'. It was dark. He moved on. A steamer's whistle carried across the Niagra River. He worried about Mr. Evans with the talk of his drinking and the crews comments: some

225

kind, some not so kind. He wondered too about the near grounding on a supposedly unmarked shoal. But... I'm only a fireman. He's the sailor. The next cabin, number 12, Mr. Dana and Mr. Wilkinson. It too was dark. He cocked his left ear and listened. Snoring. Someone in there was really sawing a log. Which one?

"Oh, I'm so tired," he half whispered to himself as he entered the opening to the crew's quarters below and foreword of the main deck where the working people live it had been referred to by those who dwelt within. He entered into a scene of mixed emotions. Abraham Gilpin, the cook, was at a small table in the middle of the compartment reading from a small Bible by the dim light of a small smoking candle, while between him and the starboard wall a bed sheet was hung to keep what feeble light there was from imposing itself on the pallid features of Bill and John asleep in their bunks, both dead to the world.

Hiram looked about and saw that Richard Mann's bunk was empty as was Jack Cooper's but he knew Jack's home was here in Buffalo so no reason to wonder. He saw too that Eddie Thatcher and Howard Crown were asleep. "God, what a day!" he said in a tired voice to the cook as he headed for the toilet. "I'm bushed. Let's hope our trip home tomorrow will be a lot better."

* * *

The cook looked up from his reading, his usual white eyes now red rimmed from the candle smoke, nodded and replied, "Amen, brother."

"Not tonight, Henry. Not tonight," a harried Marie informed the clerk in no uncertain terms. "If you knew what I have gone through with my Ollie and Christine and Larry, you'd want to crawl into a hole and hide, not into a bed, especially with me."

"Yes, I saw you when you came aboard with them in tow. Jesus, but he looked whipped. And her. God! What happened?"

226

"It happened that's all I know. Larry said something about four of them and something about a black waiter. I don't know and Christine hasn't said her side and she's out of it now. The opium did its trick and she's in never-never land at least for the time being."

"Well, I can see that you have your hands full with her. What's with Ollie? I thought he might be coming back with us."

"Oh, Henry," she sighed, almost beaten in spirit, "he's still in a bad state. He's still in great pain." She paused. "They are giving him a sedation they call it. He was sleeping all the time I was with him.

"Well, I'm sorry as hell, Marie, but this has been a bitch of a day for me too."

"Oh. Tell me about it! We can cry on each other's shoulders," she said flippantly.

"Really. It has been a bitch. You know about the Indian boy..."

"Oh, my God!" she gasped. "Oh! I forgot all about him with Ollie and Christine. Oh, Mrs. Roby will kill me. I promised...What? What about the boy?"

"He's dead."

"Dead! Jesus!" a stricken Marie slumped into a chair. "Dead. How? Oh, my God what have I done to Christine? What have I done to the poor boy?"

"Nothing! If I remember, you were asked only to look in on him when you had time. It was Mrs. Roby and the Captain's responsibility along with that Tiffany guy, to see that he was being looked after. Don't blame yourself for their being off having a good time on the town."

She waved her hand as if dismissing what he said. "How did he die?"

"He drowned. He fell overboard evidently."

"Drowned? How could he? He was unconscious when I left. That's why I left. He was out of it."

"Well, I sure as hell don't know all the sordid details and to be honest, I don't want to know. What I do know is that this is my last trip on this boat! I didn't ask for any of this shit!" Henry now on the rebound of emotion stalked out of the cabin slamming the door.

Marie staggered to stand and leaned her head against the door, her lower lip quivering. "Ollie. Ollie," she spoke almost inaudibly, tears brimming her eyes. "If only I could stay here with you and take care of you instead of those who bring terrible things on themselves. But I've to go along with them for the money." She wiped her running nose with the back of her right hand. "Oh, Ollie. I don't know what to do." She now sobbed uncontrollable.

CHAPTER THIRTEEN

At Sea

"What do you get?"

"As best I can determine, forty-six degrees, thirteen minutes north and thirty-nine degrees, twenty-seven minutes west, using the Greenwich system."

"And I got about the same," Captain Devine agreed with his First Mate, Grayson, noting the fix on the map on his map table and the time and date and latitude and longitude in the ship's log. "That puts us about half way, which means if we can keep this up, we will be in New York in three weeks."

The First Mate nodded, "And not too soon. This heavy weather has been taking its toll. The rains this past week have not let us vent the steerage and its beginning to stink."

"How are they taking it?" the Captain asked as he checked the compass bearing and lit a cigar.

"Like all the others: Some complain over nothing; others say nothing. It all depends on what they were used to," the Mate too lit a cigar. "The water is getting strong and I'm having them add vinegar."

"What does Fanshaw say about the stores?"

"If we get to New York by the end of May as hoped, he thinks we'll have enough—just enough. Not being able to use the grates this past week has saved some. We're low on oatmeal and rice but have adequate biscuits and potatoes."

"Any signs of sickness?"

"The usual. They take care of their own. One of the cabin passengers has the runs and is taking doses of Dover's powder. I've been told."

"Ha! And so have I. For three days now," the Captain exhaled a cloud of smoke and coughed. "And it doesn't do any good. Damn! Like now!" he gasped as he made a dash past the First Mate and headed for his cabin, his distress showing.

The First Mate gave the helmsman a glaring look for his laughing at the captain's discomfort. "Don't think it is funny for one moment," he growled at the helmsman, now giving his attention to the compass on its binnacle before him. "You have sailed enough to know the consequences of the shits. It could be nothing or it could be a hell of a lot worse. What is your course?" he demanded abruptly.

"Two hundred fifty-two, but hard to hold."

"I can see that but hold it anyhow. It's our direct course to New York and I want as short a run as possible, especially if the captain becomes ill. We'll tack when we have to, but two hundred fifty-two is our course! Sable Island be damned!"

* * *

"A full month we have now been at sea, and it seems that we have not moved from the same spot in the ocean but a sailor said that we are more than half way to America," Fergus said to Pierce as the two stood at their places in line to use the grate for the first time in more than a week.

Under now sunny skies with winds from the southwest, the Primrose, keeling to starboard, moved through choppy waves with the sun at its zenith. The canted deck made it difficult for the two, and others about, to stand with their hands full of the tins of water and bags of oatmeal and the wood chips and shavings for the fire.

"It would indeed be nice," Pierce called over the wind, "just for once to be able to have a bowl of hot mush and not the cold gruel we have been having."

"Ach. It would be indeed, and a hot cuppa tea too," Fergus agreed, as the two moved to take the places of two others who were leaving.

"It was well that the representatives were able to get a schedule, and us lucking out to be together for our cooking times," Pierce said as he placed some chips on the embers in an open spot between other water tins heating. "It was hell those first days with the fighting and anger amongst us. The ship's crew didn't seem to care so it was up to us to settle our differences and so far it seems to be working."

"And with another number of weeks still to go, it had better work." Fergus said as he fanned his hands over the embers for warmth in the sunny but chilly air.

"How is your hand now?" Pierce asked seeing Fergus massaging his right, middle knuckle.

"It is getting better. It still hurts when I try to hold something. The bone," he pointed, "has healed but with a bump I'll have the rest of my life."

"It was a grand thing you did in stopping the blaggard but it was too bad that you had to hurt yourself in doing it."

Fergus nodded his head in agreement, "But at least I have my own teeth which is more than the thief can say."

"True. He will be on pap for a long time yet . . . " Pierce looked up to hearing a shout from above them on the spar deck.

A sailor called down to the gathering around the grate, his mouth cupped with his hands, "Grab your tins. We are coming about to tack to port. Watch the fires. We're going to keel." A frantic effort was made by those attending their tins to keep them from tipping and splashing the precious water and contents as the Primrose hoved to port, the sudden wind shift catching the grate fires and spewing the embers and sparks into a swirl about the crowded deck, the tins and their cooks all atumble.

"Damn! There has to be a better way that we can do than to cook a meal like this," a disgusted William Waters, cursed as he crawled across the deck to retrieve his tin, now empty of its contents of potatoes, grabbing of them what he could save.

"It is a wonder the sails don't catch on fire when they do this," an equally upset Joseph Wildes echoed, as he too scampered along side William·and picked up a tin, not his own, but a tin as all the others now mixed together, their food and water contents strewn about the deck.

"Or the tarps with our goods beneath," William added.

"I too have wondered about our goods," Joseph grunted as he pulled himself up to the port gunwale, looking down at the water racing past only a few feet below. "With the rains this past week, I am sure much of our wares are soaked and will be rotting unless we can get them to sunlight."

"How?. . .When?. . ." William questioned, joining him. "It will have to be in a calm sea with plenty of sunshine and that we haven't seen much of these past weeks. I now know why we were told to take only what we really needed." He looked to the mounds of the tarpaulin-covered collections of the worldly goods of so many desperate people. "They have just piled things all together and there will be hell to pay when we try to sort out that which is ours. When and if we get the time."

"I don't know. I don't know," Joseph said dejectedly as he moved with others as they headed for the booby-hatch. "I must get back to my Julia and the baby. It will be potatoes alone for a meal this day and without water until they dole it out tomorrow."

"Your wife, she is not taking this well?" William asked knowing from Hilary that the women of the group were all concerned about Julia and the baby.

"No, she is not. She has a chill and the babe has a rash. It is in the air we breathe, a miasma, your Mr. Gray calls it. With the hatch doors closed most of the time, the air does not move in our quarters. I am sure that when the weather gets better, she will get over it. She is a strong,young person but may not have been ready to travel so soon after Gwen's birth. Nevertheless, she insisted."

"Yes, I am sure it is our crowded conditions," William agreed. "I am sure, too, that it is the air and now the water they are adding vinegar to, that all adds up to our great discomfort and the arguing and bickering among those of us who should know better."

"Like the two from Ely who came to blows over one's child crying. And they've known each other all their lives, I was told." Joseph added.

"Well, now let me give you a hand," William said as they came to the booby-hatch where others were crowding about to enter.

"I'll take your tin and will hand you both when you get to the bottom. With the boat hopping about as it is now, we'll want both hands on the ladder and nimble feet on the rungs."

The Primrose, on its new tack, began listing at a great angle, now plunging into a rolling swell, sent ahead by a storm still over the western horizon now under a slate-blue darkness, sending tumbling, crashing water over the bow surging along the port-half of the main deck, sweeping the steerage people into piles against the starboard gunwale which took the full blow of the avalanche of water foaming and raging in its intensity. William held fast to the hatch door jamb, while Joseph, half-way down the ladder, clung tightly to the rungs as a burly man below him lost his hold and dropped upon another who was scampering into the steerage compartment, now a scene of screaming and wailing as in the near darkness, water from the huge wave cascaded down into the hatch carrying Joseph and William and the third man into a heap at the bottom.

Waddling in the trough between another swell higher and more mountainous than the first and bearing down on it, the Primrose sidled with sails slack into a broadside of the towering green wall descending upon it.

* * *

"Mother! . . . Mother! . . ." both George and Stanley Hall called out as they clung to Sophia who in turn clasped Regina and Peggy as they lay huddled between the bunks of feted water from the bilge below mixed with the salt water drenching them and their trusses.

In the now complete darkness, Sophia answered, "Yes. Yes, my darlings. I am here. We are all here."

"Where is Father?" Regina's voice pleaded.

"I don't know but am sure he is safe. He will be all right and will be with us soon." Sophia trying to be reassuring to her children while she herself was alarmed at her husband's not being with them in this terrible time. "He went to see Brenden Foster and I am sure he is with Brendon. They'll be all right," she added.

"It seems to be calming down," Peggy's voice said. "The boat is settling down."

"Yes, it does seem so," George added in a reedy tone.

The noise of babbling voices and calling about by the others became almost deafening as the first moments of relative quiet and calmness was now lost on the aroused immigrants as they began to take stock of their situation.

"We need light!"

"We need a lamp!"

"Thomas! Where is my Thomas?"

"Open the hatches! We need air."

A gaggle of voices, tense and wondering, began calling out the oppressive darkness now a more feared enemy than the random sea surge which being followed by a second, now raised the Primrose on its foaming crest at such a rapid rise that the crew and passengers all were as glued to the decking and then as soon were sent all tumbling together again gasping, crying, sprawling . . . as it swept beneath them and moved on into the North Atlantic on a course for Iceland.

234

"As God is my witness! If I live to be a thousand, I will never again sail on a boat! Never!" a desperate and aching Honora near wept as she wiped Noreen's nose with a damp rag, rung from the knee-deep water sloshing about the compartment space of the steerage 'tween decks.

"Ach. Yes, and we were told by that it would only be a few weeks to cross the Western Sea. I heard, with Fergus, that we still have maybe another two or three weeks of this and we have already come three weeks and two days," Pierce grumbled as he arranged the sodden straw in the truss to make a bedding for his alana. "How is Noreen?" he added.

"She is still coughing but her eyes are clear and she is a little rambunctious and wants to move about."

"That is good for I have seen others, and older ones, who are not well. We must stay by ourselves as best we can . . . " he started to explain.

"My God! How can we stay by ourselves? We are all crammed together here in this hell hole of what they call steerage. Steerage we are! Like cattle we are!" Honora fumed.

Pierce looked about the faces in the dim glow of the relit lamps and found them in varying degrees of being comatose, some seeming interested in her raging, others oblivious and concerned only with their own fates.

Honora settled Noreen into the bunk. "I must use the water closet. Watch her," she said as he edged in beside her and knelt at the bunk and smiled at his macushla.

"Ah, my little darling," he whispered. "If only you knew what has been happening these past weeks." He paused and kissed her forehead. "It is well though that maybe you don't know. I hardly know myself what to make of it all. It is all new to me and your mother as well. God bless her for putting up with the likes of me. But we will be together, the three of us, in a new land. . ."

He raised his head and heard a wailing banshee cry from a number of bunks down and across the aisleway.

"My baby! My little Gwen! Please God! No!" an anguished wail pierced the confines as a woman clutching a baby staggered into the aisle beneath a lamp as others parted to let her through. Julia Wildes, holding the limp body of her baby girl, knelt and bent over the little corpse in convulsive sobbing.

"Stay back! Stay away!" Robert Hall demanded of a number of other passengers who went to attend Julia. "I have just come from up forward and there was a young Irish girl, the one with red hair, who has also just died and a number of others as well this past half-day."

"What is it? The babe seemed well earlier. It was her mother I have been worried about," Elly Hall said as she herded Laura and Edith back to their berths. Edith retching at the sight of the dead infant.

"We must get help from the Captain. I am sure he will know what to do," Louisa Taylor said as she ignored Robert's command to stay away, and went to Julia, now prostrate with grief. "Where is Joseph? Her husband?" she asked aloud as she took the baby from the mother's still holding arms.

"He went to get their water and it takes so damn long to get it," a voice stated angrily from the gloom.

"I'll go get him," Ethan Wilcox said as he crawled out of his bunk. "I'll take his place for water."

"But what about you? You, yourself, have not been well these past days," his mother, Hilary, questioned, now alarmed that the baby's death could lead to others.

"I will go with you and inform the Captain and the Mate what has happened," Robert said to Ethan as he took Sophia aside. "Take the children back from the others and away. We do not know yet what it is. Maybe nothing but on the other hand, with the other child dying and any number not feeling well, we must take care."

* * *

"There are five that you know of this day?"

"Yes, sir. Three infants, a young girl and an old man."

"Well now! Isn't that just great! We have come this far with no problems and now in one day we have five. Five that we know of. What does it look like to you?"

"I don't know, sir. I'm afraid to say. I'm not sure."

"Afraid! Damn it man! Speak out! I cannot play fools games with you over something as serious as this. What in the hell is it?"

"Cholera!"

"Cholera? Damn it anyway. You know what cholera is. Why are you guessing?"

"Yes, I know what cholera is, but this seems—from my quick glance at them—it seems to be cholera with complications."

"My God man. Cholera is bad enough to contend with. What complications?"

"The three children all had rashes on their faces with pimples."

"Pimples and a rash! My God man," the captain gasped. "We've got the pox as well." He strode across his cabin to the transom window and looked out on a calming sea, a rain squall moving past them, eastward, agitation in his actions.

"Secure and batten the hatches. Let no one out or in the steerage," the Captain barked an order to his Mate as he reached for his southwester. I want no contact between the crew or the passengers with those of the steerage." He paused. "What of the cabin passengers?"

"Nothing yet. But sir…"

"Keep them away from each other. Confine them to their cabins. We will work out a system for their meals," the Captain said bending over his map table. "Damn it! And only three weeks more."

"Sir. We will have to allow the use of the deck toilets and the burying of the dead. If we have five today, what will we have

237

tomorrow or the next three weeks?" a pleading mate asked of what he knew was a terrified captain of a ship that could well get the name of a 'coffin ship'.

Captain Devine rubbed his forehead and placed his southwester on. "Allow, then, only those who will be to enter the dead on deck. We will pass them in 'tween decks, victuals and water, but with no personal contact. Work out an arrangement. Pipe all hands. Mr. Grayson, I want full canvas every day. The sooner we get to New York the better for all of us. And pray we can bypass the port authorities in quarantine. It can get very messy."

* * *

In the growing darkness, the Primrose, waves curling white from her bow and sloshing past, angled into a stiff westerly wind and keeled into a trough as three bodies were hurled over the starboard gunwale of the main deck. "How many is that now?" Oswald Moran, Marquis of Westport, asked his companion, Jack Sutton, as they huddled hidden from view at a vantage point they had found to observe the main deck each evening at burial time.

"From what I have seen, I would say seventy-two but some surely have been cast over without our knowing."

"Seventy-two and more. My God. What a calamity against God. Whyte was certainly right in his diary of the conditions on the brig he sailed and they were no different from here on the Primrose only a few years later."

"But what is to be learned? We do not know what brings these things about and upon us. God's curse, they say, but why would God curse a babe in arms, a young mother or even an old man and then by the dozens?"

"Oh, indeed. We will never know God's ways or intentions but at least the numbers seem to be less each day. Today only three, yesterday five and the day before nine. Let us hope tomorrow there will be none."

"Yes. Let us hope but it might be only wishful thinking," Jack said as he turned to follow Oswald back to their cabin in the now all enveloping darkness without stars or moon, a cloud filled sky their shroud for the night.

In the cabin Jack looked about and commented as Oswald lit a lantern. "We are indeed fortunate in our cabins of not having to come into contact with the steerage unfortunates who are taking the brunt of the deaths of this voyage. Only the old woman in cabin four and she from the palsy only a week out and being alone. It has to be, certainly, the putrid air they breathe in the steerage that causes their great sickness. It is the gathering of the foul air and the rats that run loose with their evil bodies that has much to do for the conditions they live within."

"We at least have no rats that I know of and the air we breathe blows free all the time." He stopped and realized he had been on a tirade of sorts. "Well, enough of that. It is time we picked up our dinner from the galley. What is it tonight? Do you know?"

Oswald looked up from where he had been writing his notes at a small table, "I was told we are to have a specialty of the cook, a rarebit, which he has been only waiting the opportune time to present—and this is about that time—along with Madeira and assorted pastries. It sounds good does it not?"

"Ah, it sounds good," jack agreed. "We have really been fed well on this voyage but I am afraid at maybe the expense of our steerage people." He looked to Oswald and nodded to the open diary before him. "The Captain? How do you have him written in your notes?"

Oswald leaned back in his chair and replaced the cork on his ink well. "He is a knave as are so many in his chosen field or endeavor. He is an opportunist who wants only to line his pockets with gold at the expense of those less fortunate than himself."

"And the Mate, Grayson?"

"About the same only a follower of his Captain until such a time as he will have learned all the tricks of the trade, as the saying goes, and then have a ship of his own." He yawned and shook his head as to clear his thoughts. "I am sure our notes will do much to dispel their sort and make the lives of the immigrants a better and safer place on God's green earth . . . Or His oceans."

"Stephen de Vere and Robert Whyte both have written of the excesses they saw so much as to have them outlawed in the Passenger Vessel Act of three years ago, but we find no following of the law's provisions on this vessel or others we have heard of. The shipowners have too much of the ear of the port authorities and the enforcement of the law's requirements. Do you still believe we can do more?"

The Marquis of Westport arose and reached for his Chesterfield topcoat. "I not only believe. I pray to our God in heaven in His infinite wisdom to see it changed and as soon as possible. Come let us get our dinner. I am famished."

* * *

"How is Joseph?" Hilary asked of Sophia as she knelt beside Ethan and fed him a bit of hard biscuit soaked in molasses.

"He is the same. He sits and stares and cries. He is within himself," she answered, "as he has been these past ten days."

"He hasn't again tried to . . . "

"No. Not with the booby-hatch, dogged as they call it, from the outside and he has no strength to climb the ladder alone. Has he tried to kill himself again by wanting to jump into the sea to join Julia and the babe?"

"How many days does Robert now have notched on the bunk side?" Hilary asked pointing to the bunk beside Sophia where indentations were made to show each days passage.

"Today gives us thirty-eight days we have been at sea, though he thinks he may have missed a few when he was sick. I never thought to do it for him at the time."

Hilary wiped Ethan's chin, "And they told us in Liverpool

that it would only be a few weeks to America and here it is now over five weeks... Oh, Elly, you're back," she noted as Elly Hall and Laura Anne made their ways in the dimness to their bunks. "And how is the line and the stench?"

"The line is still long for those who can wait and no line at all for those who cannot and the stench is as it is here." Elly responded as she made her way to the table to sit beside Laura. "How much more of this can we take?" she added wistfully.

"From Robert's marking it should not be too much longer," Sophia answered quietly.

"Well, let us pray it will not be too long," Elly said as she took a hard biscuit from a sack and crunched on it, her teeth aching. She positioned herself and looked about the hold with its humanity, which to her seemed so much out of time and place. This was not the fens of Anglia East . . . this was not home. All these weeks, she thought, now hopefully to come soon to an end. She had seen all the hardships and the deaths of so many. She herself was haggard and drawn and had lost weight; she did not know how much but her hands, once plump and with trimmed nails, were now gnarled. Her nails split and ragged. Her auburn hair once coiffed and her crowning glory, was now matted and full gray.

She looked to her family about her. At least they were still alive and seemingly as well as could be expected but all were, as all of the others in the steerage, emaciated and suffering from diarrhea from the now foul water thick with an alga and the vinegar all used up days ago.

Her children once so robust and full of life, all were now as shadows of their once selves, almost strangers to her. The girls, Laura and Edith, their hair and clothing disheveled and unkept and her once handsome sons were once clean shaven, or as with Murdoc, his mustache always trimmed neatly, were now scraggly bearded and bushy headed with sunken eyes, their clothes hanging on them. The Primrose rolled from what she knew now was what was called a swell. The water in the bilge immediate below

241

her gurgled and as the boat now seemed to rise and fall and roll, it seemed to her, all at the same time. She knew she would never get used to it.

Robert, our oldest, our strength, our hope. He has been so strong. Not to just us, his family, but to all of those from Ramsey who except for Emma Foster, were still all together although Kenneth Thayer and Paul Lawford from Ely had died of what anyone could guess was called the Irish fever because one of the first one to die was an Irish boy.

Her reflections were broken as she heard Sophia in the dusky somberness, ask of Robert, making his way through a maze of figures strewn about lying or sitting about helter-skelter, "What have you learned?"

Robert grabbed the table edge for support and sat down hard on the bench. "The Bo-sun says that if the weather holds and the wind keeps, we should be in New York in two or three days!" he exclaimed excitedly.

"Oh, my God!" Elly cried.

"Did you hear that?" Hilary said to Ethan and Lorna who was wiping her brother's brow. "Only two more days. Three maybe at the most."

"That calls for a fiddler!" William Waters called.

"Ah, if we only had one." Sophia laughed for the first time she could remember.

"Let me tell you. Here. Gather round." Robert called stilling the group's jubilation. They quieted and hushing and smiling gathered as close as they could to him. "First, he says there is a lot to be done by us."

"What's to be done?" Hosea Clement of Ely incredulously asked. "All we want is get off this damn boat and be on our way to this place in Ohio."

"He says," Robert continued, irritated at the interruption, "that if the weather promises, we are to clean our quarters by washing and airing and to get rid of our bedding and pots and pans and even the clothing we are wearing. We are to receive our fresh clothing and other needs from the storage on deck and replace what we have been wearing as they are to also be thrown into the sea. It must be done for we might be stopped and have to go into quarantine…"

"Quarantine?" two or three voices asked in awe.

"Yes. We must pass an inspection of our health and living quarters before we can be allowed to land."

"Are we that bad that we must meet their demands?" Hosea again questioned. "I, and yes all of us, have seen worse conditions in Liverpool and earlier in Coventry when we passed through. We have had our deaths and sickness but who hasn't."

"Ah, but you must remember that we are not in Liverpool or Coventry or even in Ely. We are now to be in America where they have their own rules and we must do our best to comply to their demands and requirements. Otherwise we could spend days or weeks in quarantine according to the Bo-sun."

"Aye, Robert," William Waters agreed. "We will do what we must. Anything to get us ashore and on our way to journey's end. It is only fitting that we do as bid."

"Indeed!" Robert nodded, acknowledging William's support and understanding. "The other representatives have also been told as I of what must be done, and the other groups will do as well. We will all do what is asked of us and do it willingly. So be it!"

* * *

"There is America. The United States of America," George Hall said in awe as he and others on the main deck looked out across a tranquil sea to the mainland of North America, low on the horizon to their north as the Primrose headed on a course parallel to the south shore of Long Island in a direct line for the Lower Bay of New York Harbor. The noon sky, a brilliant blue with fluffy clouds chasing the packet, gave the low island profile a fresh spring green cast, lighter than the deep sea green that cumbered upon its sandy shores.

"Yes," Stanley agreed. "America. But I don't see any of the high mountains that we have been told of."

"Oh, it's a big land," George assured Stanley. "This is only the beginning. I am sure that we will be seeing the high mountains soon."

The boys then turned their attention to the task at hand, along with many other steerage passengers, of sorting out their wares and salvaging what they could from the ravages of the past forty-four days' weather.

"Father says that we have been fortunate that our goods are still able to be saved," George offered as they sorted through their clothing. "Most of it is mildewed but a day or two in the sunshine should do wonders he says and I will be happy to change. Even I cannot stand myself any more."

"How is. . ." Stanley asked hesitantly. "How is your book?"

"I don't know. I am afraid to ask Mother. I put it in the clothes' hamper and she and the girls are sorting through it now. From what I could see when Father and the others undid the tarp, the hamper seemed to be all right and altogether, not like some that have been smashed and soaked. I am sure though that Mother will let me know."

For the past few days the weather, as the Captain had hoped, held and the beat south of Nantucket across Long Island Sound to along the south shore of Long Island was under clear skies with warm west winds. The steerage and cabin passengers soaked up the late May spring zephyrs as best they could. It was the task of the women to sort out their families clothing and other wares much of which they realized was more than necessary for their needs while others still had to wear the clothes on their backs they had come aboard wearing so many weeks ago.

The men, under the direction of Bo-sun Fanshaw and with some of the sailors, turned to the steerage and gutted it, giving it a cleaning with sand and water. The booby-hatches were thrown open so that the drafts of fresh air for the first time in weeks coursed through the quarters. The bilge was bailed out with the same tins as were used for cooking and water stores.

Aft on the spar deck at the taffrail, the Captain and First Mate surveyed the preparations for landing the next morning at the South Street wharf. "We should pick up the pilot off Rockaway Point before dark and be ready to be underway by daybreak," the Captain stated. "I don't want us to be the first in or the last. If we can get by quarantine, so much the better. They always seem to want the first and last in line."

"Aye," the First mate agreed. "They cannot take us all so they shoot for the first and last and maybe grab at one or two in between. But we are cleaned up, as best we can be, and with the fine weather we have had the past days, the cabin and steerage all look much better than they did a week ago. And we have had no deaths four days now."

"Yes. What we have had, the cholera and the pox and my runs, let's hope they are in the past now." He paused. "How many do you count?" the Captain added as he motioned to a number of other packets and assorted vessels milling about all awaiting a pilot for tomorrow's entrance through the Narrows to their final berths along New York's bustling harbor.

The First Mate took a quick glance about. "We've got quite a few. It has been a long spring . . . I'd say about . . . " he counted, "fifteen." He put the long glass to his right eye. "Ah. There is the Wanderer from Bremen."

"Ah. The Wanderer . . . We should have a good time with her Captain . . . What was his name?"

"Eberhard. Klaus Eberhard."

"And his First mate?"

"A very funny fellow. Ah . . . "

"Wolfgang."

"Ah, yes. Wolfgang. I don't remember his last name."

"No matter. If I do remember they might just stay long enough to discharge their immigrants and be off for Savannah the next day and a load of cotton which, if we were smart, we would do too. But I am sure we will be seeing them tomorrow night if they don't go into quarantine. They and their women . . . Which reminds me."

"Sir? Ah, yes. I know what you mean."

"So?"

"Nothing. There was this wench who when she first came aboard . . . I thought. But she was never out of the sight of three others. So I gave up. I'll just have to hold myself until tomorrow night."

"And for me. I'll have to hold myself for my wife. I am sure she knows we will be in by noon. The news travels fast on South Street."

CHAPTER FOURTEEN

Buffalo

The tolling of church bells carried over the city as a warm, yellow sun rose on a now subdued and quiet Buffalo. The hustle and bustle of the Saturday night now took on a near silence with the occasional clopping of horses hooves on the deserted streets. Captain Roby looked to his watch, then wound it. Six o'clock. He then took a sip of his coffee.

"Can I fill your cup, Captain?" the cook asked with a motion of the coffee pot.

"No, thank you, Abraham. But I will have another helping of your grits and bacon."

"Yes, suh. Coming right up...Mr. Stebbins...?"

"No. No, thank you. I am fine," the Chief Engineer shook his head as he wiped his mouth with his napkin.

"I saw you last night with a very attractive lady, David."

"Oh...?" he thought. Who? When? "Ah, yes. She is Barbara Gaynor, a widow who is Henry's aunt. She is going to visit his mother, her sister, in Toledo. And yes, she is a most attractive woman. And speaking of Henry..."

"Good morning, Captain. Good morning, David," a haggard Clerk greeted the two.

"Good morning, Henry. Would you join us for breakfast?" the Captain asked.

"No. Thank you, sir. I have already eaten. I just wanted to know when you wanted the immigrants aboard?"

"Are all the cabin passengers aboard?"

"Yes and all cargo is stowed."

"The wine and the Lovelace trunks?"

"Yes, sir. All taken care of."

The Captain studied his Clerk for a moment. "You look bushed, Henry."

"As with all of us I suppose. These past few days have been really something else. I didn't sleep too well after the boy's death."

"Yes, indeed," David agreed. "I am sure we will all be glad when this trip is over. The deaths of the old man and the boy were bad enough but I hear from George Jefferson that Larry Dana was attacked by a street gang and was beaten up trying to protect our cabin maid Christine." He looked aside to the Captain who gave a quick wink.

"Oh, yes. He is really hurting. I saw him when he came back last night and just a little while ago in our cabin," Henry agreed.

"All I would need now is to have my bituminous oil, the full six kegs, not be delivered," David added.

"Ah, but that is my next report. They were delivered by a special messenger just a few minutes ago. All six kegs," Henry explained to a now beaming Chief Engineer.

"Ah, yes. That Winslow fellow knows that if I didn't get my full six kegs that I would have really raised hell," David stated emphatically. "He's charging enough."

Captain Roby took his plate of grits and bacon from the cook, "Thank you," he said. He then said to Henry, "If you have all the preparations made for the cabin passengers and the cargo, you may allow the immigrants aboard now. I want them all assigned to their places and for us to be ready to leave at ten o'clock but no later than ten-thirty…Oh," he paused, "have you seen Mr. Evans?"

"No, sir. Mr. McCoit helped me with the loading."

A concerned Captain frowned. "I'll check on him myself. He wasn't feeling too well when I saw him last evening. I'll tend to him."

"And I'll tend to my oil and get us ready for our departure," the Chief Engineer said rising and putting on his cap.

"And I will get to the immigrants and have them start boarding," the Clerk said as he and David took leave of the Captain.

Charles Roby sat for a few moments, picking at his breakfast . . . Emily . . . the children
. . . his mother . . . Albert . . . his mind roamed and took on the same thoughts that crowded his thinking most of the night. Emily . . . she is not well.

The past winter has been too much for her and now these past three days . . . too much? But what? What can I do? He forked a now cold piece of bacon to his mouth. "Ah, what the hell!" he exclaimed so loud that the cook heard him in the galley.

* * *

"Well, you two look a lot worse for wear," Jack Cooper said sarcastically to John Paulding and Bill Tillman as they hoisted a barrel of beer up from the dock to the saloon deck. Both grunted obscene replies.

"Well, one has to pay the piper," John said as he steadied the barrel from turning while Bill hauled on the rope.

"You both look as weak as kittens," Jack continued, enjoying their hangdog attitude toward their early morning labors after a full night in a brothel on the south side.

"Oh, it's a small price to pay for some good drinking and some floosies who know what they are doing," Bill explained between exertions of pulling on the rope hauling the barrel aloft where John Chichester and the assistant cook, Marshall Gantry, wrestled it to the deck.

"Where are you going with your duffel bag?" John asked Jack as he rolled another barrel into position for hoisting.

"I've quit. No more namby-pamby Roby for me."

"Quit? You just started," John said surprised.

"The runs are too long and too slow. I've signed up with the America. Its home port is here and so is my wife and our baby to be this fall."

"Well, good luck to you," Bill called.

"Yeah. I'll see you around," Jack said as he waved to the two and took off through the now gathering immigrants who were being lined up by Albert Tiffany and the Clerk where they stood at the barricade fence in the early morning bright sunshine that warmed the faces of the smiling and jovial immigrants as they waited patiently for their names to be called and their assigned spaces on the deck to be given.

"As usual they are mostly family groups," Albert stated as he scanned his master list of names and destinations before him. "I have two-hundred fifty-six immigrants and forty-five cabins."

"I see we have quite a few Germans again. They must all be leaving Europe," Henry said looking over his manifest. "And our usual Irish."

"We have more than I had really hoped for. The break in the canal wall near Seneca Falls has backed up a large number who should have sailed last Sunday but I suppose as long as the weather holds, it shouldn't be too crowded or uncomfortable in eating arrangements." He shuffled his papers. "Here is the list of cabin passengers. The cabin . . . The one where . . . ?"

"Oh, hell yes. It was cleaned as soon as we knew about it. Captain Roby would have had a fit if it hadn't been. He also doesn't want anyone talking about it either."

"Yes, I know. His family is back and mum is the word. He says he just wants a quiet trip, to be able to get his wife and family back home. This trip has been especially bad on his wife."

"On all of us. I have even had some second thoughts on a number of things but after thinking about them, I thought while we have had some ups and downs at least we are all together in one piece and with good weather and calm seas we can put all of this behind us in a few days."

"Indeed," Albert agreed as he looked to the immigrants

patiently waiting their instructions. "Let's hope so. Well I'm ready if you are to get them aboard."

Henry shook his head and raised his right hand with his list to get the attention of those closest to him who in turn hushed others about so that in a few moments all were attentive to his instructions.

"Ladies and gentlemen," he called over a shrill boat whistle. "Ladies and gentlemen. Please listen carefully for your group name, of your own name and where you will be assigned. We have crew members who will take you to your places for the short trip to your cities of arrival." A low hush of foreign tongues drifted over the gathering repeating his instructions. He paused for them to listen again. "The names are not in alphabetical order so you will have to listen carefully. Now then listen!. . . Heth! The Franklin Heth family!" The name was echoed by others.

A voice called from off to the right, "Here. Here we are! We are coming!" the crowd parting to let a family of four through to the ramp.

"Follow this fellow; he will take you to your assignment. Forward on the hurricane deck, Richard."

"Yes. This way. Follow me," Richard Mann motioned to the family.

"Money!" Henry called next. "The Money group!"

"Yes, we are here. We are coming!"

"Bohling! The Gustav Bohling family!"

"Ja! Ja!"

Henry waited for the family of nine to make its way through. He looked to Albert, "They are moving along. It shouldn't take us too long." He turned and continued calling names.

* * *

"You're looking a little better. How do you feel?" Marie asked Christine as she felt her forehead for a possible fever.

"Terrible," Christine replied through puffed lips. "My mouth

251

is so sore I can hardly drink from a cup."

"Ah, yes. You will be in great pain for a few more days. Will you want some more opium?"

"Oh, no. I don't want to become too used to it. I have a cousin who cannot now be without it and I don't want to become as bad as he is," Christine winced just from having to talk. "I'll take my time with the pain. How is the loading of the immigrants coming?"

"They are now coming aboard. We will have a full boat load. More than our usual, I understand."

"How are the cabins? I will help you as best as I can."

"No. I want you to stay here in our cabin. I'll manage. I'm going to ask if Clara Gantry can help me. At least in making beds. Captain Roby has enough on his mind now without cabin people wondering about a beat up cabin maid and his other problems."

"Oh?"

"The Indian boy. He's dead. He drowned."

"Oh. I'm sorry. How...?"

"Never mind him. What happened to you? I still don't know the whole story. Did Larry...?"

"No. We did nothing. At least I can say that honestly. I am not even sure if I would have let him. As it is, I am without my front teeth but he did not put himself into me. My baby is still...George's ...Oh, oh," she moaned.

"All right, honey. I'm sorry for everything. But I am sure things will work out for the best. They usually do. Christ, at least I hope so. You can always tell George that the boat took a sharp turn. Which it really did and that you were thrown headfirst into a bedpost or whatever."

"Do you really think George will believe that?"

"Why wouldn't he? Why would he think otherwise? If he loves you, as you say, he'll believe you if I am the one who tells him what happened."

"Oh, would you? But what about Larry? I don't even want to see him again."

"I don't think you have to worry about him. You'll be off the boat and I am sure he will not want anyone to know what really happened. Especially, if he wasn't able to score with you."

Christine rubbed her eyes. "I am so hungry. We really didn't have that much to eat. Just some pretzels and wine. Too much wine."

Marie picked up some soiled washcloths, blood soaked, I'll throw them overboard when we leave port, she thought. She'd had the dress burned by Abraham. She moved away and looked at the now frail and pathetic figure lying on the bed curled into a ball. "Try to get some sleep or rest. I'll close the cabin window and pull the curtains. The immigrants are mostly aboard but they keep to their own so you should still be able to rest. I'll be back as soon as I can. I'll bring you something to eat and drink. Take care."

*   *   *

"Sam, I have been with Bill."

"Sir?"

"He is in no condition to take the watch so I will take it for him. I will have Robert Davis on the wheel so you can have Richard tonight. I want both of you well rested. I want the return down the lake to go without a worry or a hitch."

"I understand, Captain," the Second Mate nodded to his Captain knowing full well that the First Mate was heard raging in his cabin and that he threw a tray of food brought to him by the Captain to the deck. "I am truly sorry, sir, for Bill. I have known him for years from when we both sailed on the . . . I am sure that it was his wife's death, Carrie, that has led to his crazy actions. It will pass with time."

"Yes. Let's hope so," Captain Roby answered, knowing that the two had been old friends. "It is a shame what a bottle can do to a man now in the prime of his life and with a great future before him." He cleared his throat. "This is between us."

"Yes, sir."

"I have talked with my brother-in-law, Billy, and I have recommended Bill for the captain of the Niagra which Billy has just purchased, in May, and wants to put into the Detroit-Chicago run next spring : . . ."

"Ah, sir. That is good news . . . "

"And that you would be my new First Mate with Richard Mann as Second."

"Oh, that is great. A fine choice. For Richard, I mean as well as Bill and myself. Richard is quick to learn and quick to act. I am sure it was his reading of the shoal water that saved us the other day."

"Yes. I know. But now with Bill's problems, I just don't know."

"I'm sure, sir, that with your help and the understanding of the rest of us, that we will be able to bring him back to his old self in only a few weeks. He could use a rest ashore. Maybe take a passage or two to Chicago to get to know the lay of the land as the saying goes . . . "

"I hope so, Sam. We will see. But," he slapped the map table top, "we have a boat to get underway now. Will you please ask David to see me. I have a few things I want to talk with him of."

"Yes, sir. And, sir, thank you for your confidence in me. I will do you proud."

CHAPTER FIFTEEN

"Good morning, Mr. Tremaine. I trust you slept well last night."

"Ah. Good morning, Captain. Yes, I certainly did. Your accommodations are fine and the fiacon of claret to help make the night pass was excellent."

"The ship is now yours and in your good hands," Captain Devine said as they made their way to the wheelhouse where the Harbor Pilot took command of the Primrose by ordering the Bo-sun to weigh anchor. The anchor detail sprang to the task and in a few minutes the anchor was off bottom. With a southwest, offshore wind catching the reefed sails, the Primrose moved into a line of other jockeying ships, vieing for position to enter the Lower Bay of New York Harbor from around Norton Point.

"Mr. Grayson, I want the cabin passengers to be on deck and promenading in their best bib-and-tucker and no sluggards in the rigging and as many from the steerage as you can have to be on the main deck waving and having a good time. I want the quarantine people to see that we have people up and about," the Captain commanded his First Mate.

The Primrose moved into a position behind the Wanderer, putting itself into seventh place in the fleet of fifteen assorted ships, all trying not to be one of the two or three that would be picked at random for inspection at the quarantine station on Staten Island now to the port-quarter as the Primrose, under a steady south wind, moved past Fort Hamilton on its starboard beam and entered The Narrows.

The First Mate pointed to a quarantine cutter, its yellow flag signaling its intent maybe to board, beating its way toward them. "There it is, the quarantine boat," he called to the Captain who had turned to acknowledge two of the cabin passengers who had made a request earlier to see him.

"Good morning, Mr. Moran . . . Mr. Sutton . . . " the Captain nodded cordially. "I was told by my First Mate that you wanted to see me prior to your departure. How may I be of service, gentlemen?"

"Thank you, Captain, for your time. We know you are busy," Oswald Moran stated, "but we feel that we must talk with you regarding some concerns we have come up with before we leave the ship."

"You have concerns?" the Captain asked with an arched right eye motioning to the two to follow him as he moved out of hearing of the pilot, who was calling orders to the helmsman and Bo-sun Fanshaw. The Primrose, taking a port tack, falling in behind the Wanderer, they and the others snaked their way into The Narrows. "Mr. Moran, sir. We all have concerns. I am concerned that this vessel reaches the South Street Wharf just as soon as I possibly can. I have concerns that my cargo of immigrants and trade goods be deposited ashore as soon as possible upon our landing with the greatest dispatch and least amount of lost time." He folded his arms and stared at Oswald. "I am also concerned that you are Oswald Moran, Marquis of Westport, County Mayo, Ireland, and that Mr. Sutton is your aide-de-camp. You both boarded my vessel with the prime purpose of finding fault with the manner of my, and my crew's methods of bringing your country's castoffs to the United States."

"Sir!" the Marquis of Westport stated emphatically and now angry. "I am sorry, sir, that we had to resort to a form of chicanery to see for ourselves, first-hand, what transpires on an ocean voyage. And, sir, we do not regard these poor souls who have been kept in a form of bondage for so many weeks as castoffs!"

"Oh ho! Bondage you say! I am sorry, sir, but I do not have to tell you of the bondage of the Irish peasants to the English overlords these past hundreds of years. My own people came from Ireland. From Tralee, I've been told. I know, sir, of what bondage means," the Captain almost snarled as he turned to see the preparations being made for docking.

"Captain, sir, I did not come here to argue. I know that would be foolish. But I wanted you to know that Mr. Sutton and I have annotated and documented day by day of the number of deaths. Of your mistreatment of the steerage passengers by your erratic sailing procedures... and the returning of foodstuffs to your broker before you were even out of sight of land at Liverpool..."

"My dear Marquis," the Captain interrupted, his eyes leveled with Oswald's. "I too have an accounting of the deaths aboard this ship. This trip, seventy-four. My last trip, sixty-eight. No more, no less than those of other packets carrying immigrants from Liverpool or Cork or ...Bremen. They — the immigrants — bring their pestilence with them...cholera...the pox...whatever! We have had them before and we will have them again. It is God's will, or curse, and we have to learn to live with it, or die in the attempt."

"I can well understand that," Oswald said agreeing in the Captain's assessment. "But I cannot excuse your selling back to your broker food that was destined to be used by your charges."

The Captain again turned to the pilot who with the First Mate seemed more interested in the goings on between the two than in berthing the ship. "Avast there!" he called angrily. "Get on with your duties!" He turned again to the Marquis. "I sold back only what I knew would rot and not be used at all. Others could, and I am sure were able to make use of them and if I was able to make a small profit, so much the better," he continued glaring now at a now too glaring Marquis. "You did not see one person on this vessel ever in need of food. In fact, my Bo-sun reported last night that we have an excess of potatoes and rice which I intend, sir, to give to the Borough of Queens for use in their soup kitchens."

"It was only, sir, that you had a surplus of food because we made better time in the crossing . . . "

"So! Damn it, man!" the Captain cursed. "That is a plus! That, sir, is why I am a captain. I am the one who has to read the stars, to cozy the winds, to drive my crew. Damn! You should be applauding me rather than finding fault in my handling this voyage."

The Marquis and Jack Sutton looked to each other in almost helpless rage as the Captain motioned to the quarantine cutter passing to starboard on a line for the packet behind the Primrose. "Do you see that?" he pointed. "If that officer thought for a minute that something was amiss on this ship, he would have been aboard and had us hove to for inspection, just as he is now doing, as you can see, to the packet astern of us." He paused, savoring his victory over the odds of being one of those not selected for inspection and possible delay of days and maybe weeks in quarantine. "As it is, we are now free to tie up just as soon as the pilot gets his clearance to a berth . . . "

"Captain Devine," Oswald almost stammered. "I fully intend to report this ship's voyage and the despicable behavior and attitude that you and your crew had toward the steerage passengers..."

"Report? To whom?" the Captain fumed. "This, sir, is an American vessel. A ship of the United States of America. I follow my nation's rules and regulations for the care and well-being of my human cargo, not those of England or France or wherever. You . . . " he looked disdainfully, "are an English aristocrat with no legal recourse here in America. And may I remind you, sir, that it has been only a few short years that our two nations were almost at war over the Oregon Territory. I do not think you will find much support for your concerns from those who may have had to go to war only too recently."

"In London, sir . . . "

"Aye. London. I am well aware of the so-called Passenger Vessel Act of 1848. I know of a Whyte . . . another one with concerns who presented a cry baby's list to your Parliament only to have it acted upon and then forgotten by your own countrymen. Please, sir," he paused for effect, "Your Grace, do not let me suffer any more of your recriminations of my handling of this vessel. We are here. We made it in six weeks. Sir, as you can see, a steam tugboat is now approaching us so you will have to excuse me as I must attend to the pilot and my crew as we will shortly be docking in New York City, the United States of America. Good day, sirs."

* * *

"Oh, my dear God. I cannot believe it! Land! We are again on land. No more moving about. No more being sick," Honora almost sobbed as she knelt and touched her hands to the ground of the wharf as they disembarked the Primrose and joined others showing the same elation of finally arriving in America.

"Aye," Fergus agreed as he hefted Noreen to his left arm and took up his bag as the four worked their way along with the surging crowd of immigrants as they made their way from the bustling wharf area and to the open city of New York before them. Voices called in a babel of tongues of the immigrants now in America but in many ways still alone and confused—but still in America.

Pierce looked about in almost near panic. "We are here but now what?" In his wildest dreams of imagination he never really gave their arrival too much thought other than having Thomas Meagher meet them when they came ashore and they would get on with their lives in a new land where one could do his own thing and have plenty of food and peace of mind. But then, Thomas was in a city called Boston and this was New York. It was only the past three days that he and Fergus had any really serious talk of what was to become of them. Fergus to the city

259

of Cleveland and him and Honora and Noreen to New York. No. They agreed that they would accompany Fergus to Cleveland. Fergus knew his brother would find work for Pierce just as his brother had found work for him. They had also talked to other Irish immigrants, many in the same situation as they, desperate to leave Ireland but not at all too sure of what they would find in America, other than it had to be better than what they had left.

"How will we know how to get to this Cleveland?" Pierce asked Fergus as they stopped to rest Honora and Noreen and themselves and to take stock of where they were and where they were going.

"In his letter to me, Hugh said I was to go to O'Brien's Saloon on Lexington and Twenty-third Street where an agent was to help me to gain transit to Cleveland, like we did in Liverpool with Terrance Gallagher."

"Only our money is almost gone. We may not have enough to get us another distance." Pierce asked discontentedly, "And this place, how do we get to it?"

"We ask." Fergus replied as he looked about. "See. There are people who are talking to others," he added as he motioned to other groups being attended by earnest young men gesturing and moving about taking the groups in hand and heading off in different directions. Fergus remembered one of the groups as being the Hall family, the ones who had been so kind to him when he broke his hand on the rogue who stole from one of the young lasses in their group. He just realized that he had never, in the six weeks at sea, even spoken to her or any other member of the group.

"Hello," a voice called to them as they started to follow the Hall group, not knowing to where but at least moving out form the dock area.

"Hello," Pierce answered looking quizzically to a young man approaching them with a big smile.

"Do you speak English?" the young man asked.

"Aye. We do," Pierce answered.

"Can I be then of service to you? For only a few pennies, American money, I'll help you find lodging or food or do you wish directions? The Melville House on Broadway is a fine lodgings or the..."

"We want to find a saloon called O'Brien's on a street called Lexington and Twenty-third Street," Fergus interrupted the fellow's spiel. "We are to find an agent to help us get to Cleveland in Ohio."

"Oh, yes. John O'Brien. A fine a man as you will ever meet" the street runner exuded. "I know him well. Come . . ." he looked to the foursome, "I will take you there. It will only cost you two bits . . . an American quarter, and you will not have to wander about in this morass or be picked upon by charlatans who will steal you blind."

"Fergus, what is a quarter? Two bits?" Pierce asked, ignorant of the terms.

"I don't know but he seems to be willing to take us for whatever it is in American money. I am sure we will soon learn its value as we will with everything new in America."

"Sir? Young man?" Fergus asked hesitantly.

"Yes? My name is Northy. John Northy at your service, sir. I am what is called a runner. I help people like yourselves."

"Ah. Aye. John. We do not know of American values. We know we need your help in finding our agent but we do not know what you want. What is a quarter? We have only a few pounds, some shillings and pence or two and little of that."

"Ah. It is lucky for you that you found me," the runner said grandly. "You will not have to wonder about your paying me. John O'Brien is also a hiring agent for the Erie and Wabash Railroad Company that is building a railroad in Ohio and needs strong backs and the determination to get ahead. It is he that you will want to meet and he will make your payments to me if you sign up with him."

"Sign up with him? For what?" Pierce questioned, uncertain of the man's intentions.

"As I said. To work for the railroad. It is a great and wondrous thing that has been happening here in America. This country is like nothing you have ever seen. The railroad needs men of strength and courage and will pay to take you to Cleveland and provide you and your family with living quarters and a decent wage paid once a month."

"If it is such a great and wondrous thing, why then are you, a young man, doing such as you are and not helping build the railroad?" a now understanding Fergus asked the fellow.

"Ah, but you see, I am too going. I signed only yesterday and a steamer is leaving tomorrow from the Chamber's Street dock. I will be taking transit on it to a city up the Hudson River called Albany and then on to Buffalo on a canal boat as you will be also doing if you sign up for working on the railroad. But you will see on a map at O'Brien's just where you are now, where you have been and where you will be going . . . to Cleveland, in Ohio." The runner motioned to them as he wended his way through a group that seemed so all alone in an alien world without any guidance or support. "I have been trying for these past weeks to move out and continue my own way west to a place called California, but only yesterday learned of the need by the railroad for manual laborers to lay its tracks in Ohio and them heading west like me."

"I know not at all of what is needed by the railroad, but I do know that I want to get to Cleveland and if this means to do so, I will sign and be happy to work for the railroad." Fergus exclaimed with a sense of relief.

"Ach. And I too," Pierce added as he looked to Honora and Noreen, both exhausted.

"All I want," Honora said wearily nodding to Pierce's decision, "is a good night's sleep without any ship's movement for both me and my baby . . . Pierce . . . Fergus . . . let us get to this O'Brien's saloon as fast as we can."

* * *

262

"Are we all accounted for?" Robert Hall asked William Waters as the Ramsey-Ely group assembled in a small vacant lot a few blocks from the wharf.

"Aye. But we had to chase after Brendan again. He is getting to be quite a handful," William answered looking over the group.

"Getting to be . . . He has been a handful ever since Emma died." Sophia Hall sighed as she set her bundle of goods to the ground. "George . . . Stanley. Help your sisters with their belongings. They are too much for them." The two boys set their goods down and made room for their sisters. "And how is Joseph?" she asked, seeing him forlorn and so all alone.

"He is still with us—but just." William answered. "But he is no problem, now. He seems to accept his wife and baby's death. Especially after seeing so many others dying as well. Time will heal his hurting for them."

"Isn't it amazing that we have so much less than when we started." Ada commented as she joined the others.

"Yes. With what we had to leave behind after Min died and then what was wet or stolen on the boat." Sophia nodded.

"And what we had to throw overboard because of the stink and dirt. It is lucky that we have the clothes on our backs," Hilary Waters added as she fanned her face with her right hand, the warm spring midday sun shimmering over the city with a hint of summer.

"How is Ethan?" Sophia asked Hilary.

"He seems to be better but he is still weak. What he needs, and what we all need, is some good hot food. We must seek out a place to eat."

"Oh, indeed we must," Sophia agreed. "Hot food and a full stomach will do wonders for us all . . . "

"Now then," Robert called to the group. "We must all stay together. We cannot go wandering away. The city is crowded like Liverpool and we must be on our guard all of the time." He waited for the passing of a rumbling coach to continue. "We are to go to a place called O'Brien's where we are to get passage on a steamer…"

"Oh. More water," a voice called almost wailing.

"But it is on a river. No waves or storms," another voice answered.

"This young man," Robert continued, pointing to a lad who had joined them, "says he knows where O'Brien's is and will take us there for a few pennies, American. So let us stay close together and we shall soon be having something to eat and get some rest for the next part of our journey."

The group gathered their belongings and as a procession set off after the runner through the narrow streets. "This reminds me of Liverpool," Louisa Taylor said to Laura Hall, as they scurried along the crowded sidewalks trying to keep the rapid pace the runner set.

"Yes, but thanks to God, we do not have the rain and cold that we had there," Laura answered, now panting and her feet hurting. "And let us hope we do not meet up with the likes of the one who stole your valise."

"Let us hope not, ever again," Louisa agreed, casting a wary glance around to passersby hoping to never again see a beggar boy or a rogue as the other two.

* * *

John O'Brien's Saloon and Bar occupied the southeast corner of Lexington Avenue and Twenty-third Street and on this May day was hosting immigrants, mostly Irish, recruited by runners to sign on the dotted line for work on the Erie-Wabash Railroad in Ohio, the steamboat Oswego leaving in the morning at seven o'clock for Albany and connections to the Erie Canal in Troy.

John Northy looked up from his meal and saw another group of immigrants — English — as they passed by his table in the rear of the saloon, next to the doorway that led to the hostelry next door through a passageway connecting the two buildings.

Just like the others, he mused: excited, scared, nervous, all spent and exhausted from the weeks and months at sea but still with a vitality that would carry them to their final destination. But not all. In only his few weeks in New York, he saw many who gave up and became wards of the city or county that didn't want them, but they had no choice. He reflected on the past two days and the changes that had been made in his own situation. It was fortunate for him and others, who arrived only these past few days, that the Erie and Wabash Railroad in Ohio was needing labor, cheap labor, but at least he and they would have more than they have now. His taking to being a runner after receiving no help from George's uncle but only a hand shake and a 'good luck.' It was the realization that he must find some way to get money if he ever hoped to get to California that he put in with others in his plight of also trying to make some quick money as a runner to be able to move on. The need for the help came to him as a godsend and tomorrow he would be on his way again to California and the gold fields.

He noted one of the young women in the group passing, a comely lass, though a little stern looking but with a fine tall build. She was with a group that came in off the Primrose and while they had no one sign up with the railroad, they were proceeding to Albany tomorrow on the Oswego with him aboard and then on to Buffalo. Maybe he would be able to get to meet her. He wondered.

CHAPTER SIXTEEN

"How are you doing? I hope the sleep did you some good," Marie said as she entered the darkened cabin, the bright morning sunlight casting a shaft of light across the space to where Christine lay, now shading her eyes from the glare.

"My mouth is still very sore. I don't know how much I slept but I know I had some terrible dreams. What time is it?" Christine asked as she sat up and accepted a mug of coffee and a bowl of grits from Marie.

"A little after nine. They're still loading the immigrants but are just about done. We're to sail about ten."

"What of the cabins?"

"Clara is helping with making the beds. I do all the rest with no thanks to Larry.

"How is he?"

"He's still hurting. But he'll get over it. His kind do."

"Has he said anything about me to the others or . . . asked about me . . . ?" Christine asked hesitantly.

"No. But I would stay here in our cabin if I were you. I'll bring you your food and it is lucky we have our own commode so you don't have to share the water closet with the cabin passengers." Marie paused as she looked to the tragic figure before her. "Here, I'll help you to the commode and then I must get back to Clara and our duties. She wasn't too happy to help but she is a good woman and I appreciate her stepping in."

"Marie," Christine spoke softly, her gums burning from the coffee, "I want to thank you so much for helping me . . . "

"Ah, don't thank me. My God! It was my insisting that you go along with Larry that brought all this about. I'll try my best to help you as I am sure you would help me if the tables were turned, and they well could have been. But! I am off. I must get back to my work or Larry will raise hell and I do need the job. Please try to rest."

Marie left leaving the cabin window open slightly to allow air to circulate in the now warm and humid cabin. She was mildly surprised with the large number of immigrants as from the lesser number of earlier sailings. She had heard of the break in the canal wall that caused a backup of shipping on the canal barges and packets and was the reason for so many extras on this trip. Just about all the deck space, she noticed, was taken up as she made her way to aft on the main deck to gather sheets from the linen room. She was intrigued by the many foreign voices about her. The guttural German. The English with their clipped accents, except for those from Wales whose voices were lilting but so hard to understand. The Irish with their singsong and then her own heritage, the French-Canadian, her father's language. She really hadn't spoken the French Canuck since she was a child in Laval. But now, after all these many years later in Cleveland, she and her French friends spoke a bastardized version of what she had been born to and was changing rapidly to become American. Oh ho, she thought, Marie, you had better get a move on. You have a lot to do. Get with it.

* * *

"Ah, Sergeant Robinette, Good morning," Captain Roby greeted the Buffalo police Sergeant as he entered the pilothouse.

"Good morning, Captain. I have some papers to be signed and since I saw you last evening, I have another problem which maybe you can help me with."

267

"Another problem? Oh ho. Join the club," the Captain said looking down to the bow of the main deck below him with its crowding of immigrants.

He was a little worried of possible heavy weather and wondered if he should have reassigned them, but to where? The boat was filled up and all spaces taken on the main and saloon decks and he wanted the hurricane deck for the use of the cabin passengers. He glanced to the Sergeant. "How can I help you?" he said taking an envelope tendered to him by the Sergeant.

"We have taken another body from the river a few blocks north."

"Oh. How can I be of help?" the Captain questioned.

"I have been told that you had a death aboard when you were just out of Cleveland on Friday."

"Yes. That is true. We had a Mr. Lovelace who died but we had his body attended to by Friday evening as soon as we docked."

"Do you know by whom?" the Sergeant asked opening a memo pad.

"Sergeant, my boat's agent is Albert Tiffany of Tiffany and Lockwood. He is the one who made the arrangements for the disposition of the old man's body."

"Oh yes. I know Mr. Tiffany."

"Well, I think you would want to talk to him. I don't know who the undertaker was. But what makes you think it was my passenger? Surly, there are others that drown on any given weekend."

"Oh yes, certainly and I don't mean to imply anything," the Sergeant offered, sensing the Captain's wariness in his questions. "We do have our share of drownings. Almost every weekend and during the week as well and it could have been some one other than your passenger. I am just interested in knowing who the undertaker was that was used."

"As I said, you will have to take this matter up with Albert. As you can see, I am in the process of getting my boat ready to get underway," Captain Roby stated emphatically as he signed the release form.

"Yes, sir, and I understand. I will see Mr. Tiffany tomorrow morning. I am sure that all will be explained and that we will find out who the poor soul was."

"Yes, I am sure you will. Now, sir, I must attend to my wheelsman and my First Mate in preparation for our leaving within the hour. Good day, sir."

* * *

"I want these kegs stored in the forward locker away from anything inflammable." David Stebbins told Eddie Thatcher and Howie Crown as they tended to the loading of the six kegs of bituminous oil from the dock.

"Aye. And these are the answer to your needs. These little kegs," Eddie stated as he rolled one of the coopered kegs into the sling with the others.

"Yes, indeed and as soon as we get to Toledo, we will make the necessary changes in our new lubricating system and you two, and the others, can take it easy and not have to work double shifts," the Chief Engineer exclaimed happily.

"Good morning, Mr. Stebbins," a woman's pleasant voice called to the threesome from above on the main deck.

David looked up, shading his eyes from the bright morning sun with his cap. "Good morning, Mrs. Gaynor," he answered. What a fine looking woman and so attractive so early in the morning, he thought.

"I see you received the oil you were speaking of last evening," she stated.

"Yes, indeed and I'll feel a lot better once I get them to Toledo just as I told the boys here."

"Will you be able to join me for breakfast?" she asked gaily.

"I have already eaten, Mrs. Gaynor, but I will be happy to join you for a cup of coffee," he replied as he bowed to the two

269

oilers who looked at him in a new light. "Gentlemen," he noticed their reaction to his new found lady friend. "Please excuse me. I have a date."

"Well. What do you know about that?" Eddie said as the Chief Engineer took leave with a spritely step.

"Damn, but she's a good looker," Howie acknowledged as he gathered the sling ropes together and hooked them on the hoist catch. "Pull away, Eddie." He then cupped his hands and called up to the main deck. "Here they come, Hiram."

"What do you know?" Eddie repeated to Howie. "I hear she's Mr. Wilkinson's aunt. For an older gal, she's really something."

"And good luck to Mr. Stebbins. He seems to be a different man this morning."

"Do ya suppose . . . ?" Eddie began.

"Ah. Nah. She just came aboard yesterday and knowing him, they just met then. But you know the old saying 'In the spring a . . .' "

"Yeah. Only now it's an old man's fancy."

* * *

CHAPTER SEVENTEEN

Erie Canal

At the command of Captain Billy Seguin to cleat up, the canal-packet, Sam Adams, edged its way from the snubbing post on the wharf at the foot of the Rome Pike Road in Utica and continued its way westward after a brief rest stop for his more than one-hundred passengers, mostly immigrants, and to watch a horse relay. The towpath driver yelled "Giddy-ep, Susie; Katie," to his new tandem team of mares as the tow line lost its slack and tightened to the weight of the canal boat and its passengers, crew and mail. The horses' hooves now clopped in a rhythmic beat as the momentum of the pulling lessened the dead weight of the packet in a row with others all moving westward on this Tuesday morning, June 11, 1850. The past three days, since leaving New York for Albany then to the canal at Watervliet, had been uneventful for which the immigrants were grateful as it gave many time to recoup their senses and physical beings and to enjoy the late spring weather without the tossing and rolling of an ocean packet with its squalls and howling winds.

The break in a canal caused by heavy rains near the town of Lock Berlin in Wayne County had been repaired and now hundreds of canal craft, from swift packets who could make better than four to six miles an hour, to freight boats, called line boats, which plodded along at about a mile and a half per hour and pulled by oxen, mired the line of water craft back for miles going both east and west. With the heavy spring rains now about over, Captain Seguin hoped to make up for lost time and would be using every trick in his trade to get around slower craft and to get to Buffalo by Friday afternoon as he had plans to see the Christy Minstrels Saturday night come hell or high water.

Robert Hall stood with William Waters at the forward part of the packet's cabin roof with others of the Ramsey-Ely group and looked out upon the passing countryside. "The agent, Mr. Lockwood, back at the saloon, was right in his saying we would be seeing some grand and wonderful country in this America. This land is still new, it seems, with so much yet to be opened up as they say," William stated as the packet passed through a bower of trees covering over a length of the canal.

"Aye, it is hard to believe that we are here at all. It is so quiet and clean and yet so much alive even with the forests, which come to the canal walls in many places," Robert added motioning about them. "After New York City, this is really a pleasure and while our stay was short there, I was not unhappy with our moving on as we have."

The rolling hills of the Mohawk Valley stretching from the distant Adirondack Mountains, now under an arch of a cloudless blue sky, to the north and the Catskill Mountains to the south with only streaks of high cirrus, were now in full spring blooming of mixed hardwood and pine forests. Farms along the canal path were in their first greening of crops of wheat, corn, vegetables and orchards of apples, all with a promise of a full harvest in the fall. Cattle, pigs, goats and chickens crowded pastures and farm lots on both sides of the canal. Barking dogs on each homestead greeted the canal travelers.

"And if it is like this here in New York state, what must it be like in Ohio where it is still a wilderness, as some call it," William wondered aloud as he contemplated what would have to be done in the next few years to bring his land patents as well as the others in the group to the same fruition as these prosperous farms they were passing by.

* * *

John Northy looked about his surroundings and almost
wished he was back on the Ambrose. For the past three nights,
it was all he could do to get a good night's sleep. He had just
returned with other men and boys from a stop along the canal
bank long enough for them to take leave ashore for their needs
before they turned in for the night. The women and girls had
taken their places forward in the dining cabin and a heavy red
curtain was drawn between them and the men and boys. John
had been assigned a middle bunk on the opposite of the towpath
side of the cabin which matched up with the twenty-four other,
making a total of forty-eight in the cabin. The bunk was a canvas
cover over a wooden frame attached to the wall on hinges with
small link chains linking two other bunks to the ceiling. The
snoring, coughing, the insects and rats that scurried about did
not allow him to sleep hardly at all each night. He looked toward
the arrival in Buffalo hoping it would be better on the steamer,
the Griffith, he had been told its name, that would take him to
Cleveland. His one consolation, however, and a hope for his
future was that today he had talked for the first time with the
beauty he had seen in O'Brien's in New York. He laughed at the
remembrance of it but... then it could have been more serious
than it had been. He shook his head. Her name is Louisa, he had
heard her called by one of the girls that was always with her.
He had been on the cabin roof talking with a young fellow he'd
met in New York when he took the Irish couple with the baby
and another man, from the Primrose to O'Brien's. The fellow's
name was Ethan, a nice sort of a guy who had become quite
sick on the crossing from Liverpool. He was still not up to par
but seemed to be getting better each day and even smiled once
in a while.

The two got to talking of their mutual desire to move on to
California once they reorganized themselves in Ohio; Ethan to
help his stepfather clear land in a place called Litchfield, while

273

John, who had no wish to work as a track worker, as the laborers were called, would stay over in Cleveland just long enough to get enough money as a runner, if need be, then to move on to another city, maybe Chicago or St. Louis. He really didn't know but he would be on his way as soon as he could.

Because of the slow pace of the packets due to the crowded waterway, any number of the more energetic or athletically inclined passengers, both male and female, would step off the packet and walk or trot beside as it moved along. Many of the faster ones would run ahead of the packet and wait at what was called occupation bridges. These were bridges constructed with little space to spare between the packet cabin top and the bridge underside and were made for farmers to cross over their divided holdings as well as travelers over the canal. As Louisa and Lorna were able to move faster than the packet, they ran ahead and waited on one of the bridges to drop back aboard when it passed underneath, a distance of about two or three feet. John and Ethan and others crouched to get below the bridge bottom, some having to stretch out flat on the roof, others more nimble jumping onto the bridge and dropping back aboard as the packet passed beneath. With the packet approaching the bridge, John saw Louisa and Lorna, preparing to come back aboard. She hitched up her dress skirt as John took his eyes away for a moment to check Ethan who gave a weak cough when he heard. "Louisa!" A shout went out from one of the girls. John turned to look and saw the bow of the packet pass under the bridge span with Louisa's dress caught on a rusted bolt on the bridge, causing her to be held to it as the packet moved under her as though she was being dragged along the cabin roof, her arms and legs and shoulders thumping along. More voices called out. "Stop! Stop the boat!" as John, seeing the situation, leaped to the snared dress and slashed at it with his Bowie knife.

* * *

"I heard the captain tell one of his men that the boat will be in a place called Albion by night fall and that we should be in Buffalo tomorrow afternoon at the latest." Pierce Hill remarked to Fergus and Honora, who with Noreen, were in a line with others to the kitchen at the rear of the main cabin with their trays.

"Aye, and it will be glad that I am," Honora replied. "This crowding is no better than the steerage on the big ocean boat we just left."

"True. But the food!" Fergus said beaming as he looked over the offerings before them. "After weeks of almost nothing fit to eat, I cannot believe the food that I have seen before us."

"Oh, yes. The food these three days is grand and so much of it," Honora agreed. "It is all so new. The only food I recognize is the potatoes and they are cooked differently from what I know."

"There is the lass who was hurt yesterday at that bridge," Pierce said, motioning his head to Louisa as she waited in the line with a number of people behind them. He remembered the young man she was talking with as the same fellow who had been the runner who took them to O'Brien's in New York City. He was also the one who had saved the girl by his quick action.

"A fine couple they make," Fergus said as he took Noreen's tray and motioned to her to move to an open space at the table before them. "It is lucky that she only has bruises. She could surely have been more hurt," he added as he took a space beside a burly, blond, curly haired man who was riding herd on a large group at the table who spoke a tongue he did not know.

"It is indeed lucky that we can speak English," Pierce almost whispered to Honora. "It is the language of America and these poor souls will have a hard time of it I suppose."

"No more than ours did to learn the English that was forced upon us against our will. But these will want to learn so let us not worry about them," she replied as she sat closer to Noreen to make room for the young couple to be able to sit together

275

next to her. They both spoke English but each had a different way of speaking. She didn't particularly want to hear their conversation but she had no choice. The young man spoke in a higher tone than the girl and at a faster pace. But they seemed to understand each other and Honora soon tired of their talk and turned her attention to Noreen.

* * *

"You say you are a carpenter," Louisa Taylor said to John as she cut a slice of roast beef.

"Aye. I was my father's apprentice as a boy and then his assistant these past two years. We had great hopes… but he died only this last March."

"Oh. I'm sorry."

"And as there was no work in Ashburton … That is where I am from. Ashburton near Plymouth in Devon. Do you know where that is?"

"Yes, I know where Plymouth is but…"

"No matter. I am gone and wonder if I will ever again see my mother and younger brother."

"You left your mother and brother. I left my da… my father. He is a weaver in Ramsey, in Cambridgeshire. And I too have my fears of never seeing him again. But as with you, there was no work," she laughed, "nor any hopes of marriage. All our young men had left for Birmingham or London or wherever, even some earlier to America."

"Your plans. What are they?" John asked as he sipped his cider, pleased to be so close beside her.

"I am to go into the household service of a Mr. Burnswick in a place called Medina, in Ohio. What are your plans?"

John liked what he saw now up close. What a beautiful woman… "Oh," he caught himself. "I… I had hoped to go on from Cleveland to California. To find gold and make my fortune. But now…"

"To California? To find gold? Then that makes two of you."

"You mean the young lad, Ethan?"

"Yes. I know of his plans and I saw you talking with him. But with his being so sick on the voyage and still is. I don't know."

"Aye. He is not well and I have been told and warned that it is a long trek across the entire continent of America. There are deserts and high mountains and wide rivers and that it will take weeks and months to get there." He looked to her profile, her head slightly bent forward as she ate. He again sipped his cider. "But now. I don't know. It was probably wishful thinking all along. A silly boy's dream."

Louisa's face lit up with a smile. "You say you are a carpenter."

"Yes. Since a boy of nine but really a jack-of-all-trades, I suppose."

"Mr. Burnswick, my da said, is a rich man. He knew him as a boy and that is how I got my position with his family," she explained. "He makes his riches by making mills at river falls for sawing lumber or grinding grain." Her eyes sparkled as she faced him. "Maybe he would hire you to work for him."

John sat up straight and gazed up at the ceiling and shook his head faintly. "Ah, that would be grand."

Louisa touched his left arm gently. "Yes, it would," she agreed softly looking with new thoughts for this young man, a hero he had been called for his saving her yesterday. She now saw him in a different light. A young man with a needed trade and a handsome one as well. "Please give it some thought. Let California wait for a while and maybe…"

John turned so that their eyes met. "Louisa…" John said surprised at his using her name for the first time. He liked its sound.

"Yes?" she replied, her voice almost inaudible, her heart racing.

"Louisa, You are alone, I have been told, except for your friends. I am too alone. If I were to see your Mr.…."

"Burnswick."

"And get employment," he cleared his throat, "do you suppose…"

"Yes. I am alone," she nodded. "My friends from my village will be going to another town and we will all lead our separate lives and go our own ways."

"Do you suppose," he repeated, his heart thumping so loud he thought she might hear it, "that if I do get employment that you would…"

She laughed softly. Never she thought did she ever believe she would be so taken by a man and so quickly. The rouge in Liverpool had given her great cause not to trust any man, especially after remarks and gestures made by some of the sailors and a few steerage passengers on the Primrose. But this man, an older boy really and about her age she guessed. "That we become friends. Yes, I would like that. But we do have an unknown future ahead of us. All of us," she motioned to the crowded cabin. She paused. "So, now then. Tell me of your mother and brother."

* * *

CHAPTER EIGHTEEN

Buffalo

"This is where you and your family and friends will be accommodated until you get to Cleveland tomorrow. If you need to use the commode, or nettie as you English call it, it is on this deck behind the pāddle boxes. The men and boys use the one on the port side and the women and girls use the one on the starboard side," Robert Davis, a Wheelsman, said as he directed the Ramsey-Ely group to their spaces on the port side of the main deck just forward of the cabins. "We will call you for meals by groups so be together at all times and stay away from the railings as best you can."

Sophia Hall, Elly and the children crowded together with others of the group as Robert and other Griffith personnel gave directions to others of their assigned spaces. "What a great difference between the people on the Primrose and these," Elly said as she stood next to George and gave him a hug. She surveyed the others. Robert and William talking with Murdoc and Albert Reynolds who, she was pleased to see, looked quite chipper for all his ills and discomfort these past months. She thought of the others still all massed together, one on top of the other it seemed; but soon to end. Oh yes, soon to end. The man said Cleveland tomorrow. She remembered the map on the wall in the saloon in New York City... O'Neil's... No... O'Brien's. Oh yes... O'Brien's, showing Cleveland so far to the west then and now it is only another day away. Not the end of their perilous journey but close. Only a half day of travel beyond to Medina. The voices about her now caught her attention. It was not the English or the bastardized English-Irish of the Primrose, but now a mixture of languages she had heard called Dutch and French. So strange but yet so exciting to hear. She never heard either language before and yet they seemed to tell her of the new world that she and hers would now be entering. May God protect us and save us, she asked, her eyes imploring as she gave George another hug. Her musing was interrupted by a movement through the crowd by two of the boat's sailors who went to a post on the main deck at the bow and threw off a heavy rope attached to the dock below. At the same time, the boat seemed to shudder as the paddle wheels in their housing began slowly to turn with muffled churning of the turgid waters between the boat and the dock into foaming bubbles and swirls backing it away into the main channel of the Niagra River. Other steamers, arriving or departing blew salutes to the Griffith as she made her way in a wide turn starboard to take her to a position for a heading of two-hundred degrees on a course for the Lackawanna bell-buoy six miles distant to the south.

"Well done," Captain Roby commended his Second Mate, Sam McCoit, and Wheelsman, Richard Mann, as the Griffith began to pick up speed and headed for the open water of Lake Erie, paralleling the shoreline on its port side. The pleasant sunshine and a warm southwesterly wind, gentle on a smooth lake surface, provided a panorama of the shoreline with hills, grape arbors and farmlands stretching from the water's edge far back into the hinterland to the south.

"We're making good time," Sam McCoit stated as Captain Roby noted the time of departure and the course setting on his map and in the log book.

"Yes. I'll want flank speed as long as the weather holds and is still daylight and the water is calm. I want to get to Sandusky by tomorrow evening. I don't want a delay in Erie or in Cleveland. The sooner I get rid of that damn wine the better I will feel."

"Aye, sir. I've heard. The word has gotten around."

"Yes. I am sure that it has," the Captain nodded, knowing damn well it had.

"Captain Roby," David Stebbins' voice called from the pilot-house doorway.

"Yes," he replied seeing David and the woman he had seen him with last evening approaching from the hurricane deck. He stepped outside to greet them.

"Captain, sir," David said motioning to Barbara with a slight bow. "I would like you to meet one of our first class cabin passengers who will be with us to Toledo. Captain... Mrs. Gaynor. Barbara Gaynor."

Captain Roby smiled at the thought of David with a woman and indeed a very attractive woman. "Ah yes. Good morning, Mrs. Gaynor. It is a pleasure meeting you."

"Captain Roby," she replied and curtsied. "Thank you and it is so nice to meet you. I have heard so much about you from David."

"Oh. You will want to watch what David has to say. He is good at exaggeration," the Captain laughed. "I trust we will meet later so that I can introduce you to my wife." He paused and spoke to David. "You have your bituminous oil all stowed away?"

"Oh yes. All six kegs. Stowed away until we can make good use of them in Toledo."

"Captain Roby... David. I see that you are both busy with your boat's just getting underway," Barbara said, realizing the timing of meeting the Captain was a little awkward for him. "I will leave the two of you to your work. David, I will see you later. Perhaps for lunch?"

"Yes, Barbara. I will look forward to it," David answered as she took leave of them.

"Charles, what of Bill Evans?" David asked, now serious with Barbara out of hearing.

"He is a problem. No doubt about it. It is his drinking now

that I am worried about. He has whiskey in his cabin."

"Cannot we take it from him?"

"No. It is only for the one night and I don't want to antagonize him. I will confine him to his cabin so that he doesn't interfere with the crew or passengers."

"Ah yes. It hurts to see him this way. But let us hope it is only passing," David said as he stretched and stifled a yawn. "Well, I must make my rounds. I want to check the shaft."

"If you see Henry, tell him I want to see him," Captain Roby asked as he reentered the pilothouse.

The Griffith was outbound just passing the entrance light to the Buffalo Harbor. A gentle breeze still came from the southwest and to the far west the sky was a majestic blue. "The weather seems to be on our side this trip," Sam McCoit said making room for the Captain at the map table.

"I certainly hope so," Captain Roby said, scanning the map. "Good enough. I will be going to see my wife and family. I appreciate your taking this time to get us out of Buffalo. We should make good time to the Lackawanna buoy then take a heading of two-three-three degrees. I should be back by then to relieve you until this evening. You'll want to get some sleep. Both of you," he pointed to Richard.

"Aye, sir," Sam replied as he positioned himself to the right of the Wheelsman. For what seemed to be the hundereth time, Sam reflected back on his promotion to First Mate and to have Richard as his Second. Ah. Sally will be glad to hear of his good fortune when he gets home. For how long has she wanted him to leave Studdiford and sail for the Monroe Line. But now as First Mate, she'll finally be happy and who knows what might come about in the next few years? Maybe a captaincy. Aye. Maybe. His attention was drawn to hearing the voices of Larry Dana and his crew as they began assembling the portable lunch table ahead of the pilothouse on the saloon deck. He looks a little better than he did when last I saw him last night, Sam thought, as the First Porter and his bartenders, John and Bill, set up the table and installed a beer keg on the deck at the far end of the table toward the bow. He then saw the Headwaiter, John Chitchester, and the cook, Abraham, and his helpers, Marshall and Clara, along with the Cabin Maid, Marie, pushing and pulling food carts ladened with platters of fish, sandwiches, cookies, salads, coffee, tea and skimmagig, the buttermilk he so liked. The bartenders then toted trays and stacked them beneath the table. Cafeteria-style, he had once heard the headwaiter call the system of feeding the large number of immigrants as they lined up for the cooks to dole out the food as they passed by.

And this was the main meal for them until tomorrow. He hoped they would have enough. He looked for but did not see the other Cabin Maid, Christine. Oh well. "A sloop is bearing off the port-quarter," he informed the Wheelsman.

Captain Roby wended his way aft on the hurricane deck, nodding and acknowledging the looks of the immigrants and was pleased with himself for the on-time departure and the benevolence of the weather. He did feel a great relief with the concerns of old man Lovelace and the Indian boy behind him. Let Albert worry about them. When I return in another week or two, it will all have blown over. But then… the wine and his concern for Emily, he now had the thought that her depression of late had been caused by the death of Carrie. But she had not let on or said anything beyond her original reactions to her friend's horrible death. Well, he'll have a talk with her brother, Billy, when they get to Toledo. Maybe he can be of some help to her.

"Captain, sir. You wanted to see me?" Henry Wilkinson asked as they met at the foot of the companionway to the main deck just starboard of the cabins.

"Yes, Henry," the Captain said as he led Henry aside from the main aisleway. "Yes. I want you to be sure the wine is ready to unload with quick dispatch as soon as we dock in Sandusky. I do not want a delay."

"Yes, sir. I understand. The wine is stored forward next to

David's oil. It will be easy to get off."

"Good. Now I have something I want to ask of you."

"Sir?"

"I am confining Bill Evans here in his quarters." He motioned to his cabin. "I have asked him to stay in his cabin until we reach Toledo and he has agreed, but I would like you and David, as well as myself, to occasionally look in on him, and keep an eye on him."

"Is he still drinking?"

"Yes. He had whiskey. I don't know who got it for him, but he had it. I don't know if he has any now."

"I am afraid that some of our people have been too quick in Buffalo to make a fast quarter eagle to provide him with his needs," Henry noted.

"I suppose," Captain Roby agreed shaking his head. "But I am off. Keep an eye on Bill. I'll see that he gets something to eat," he said as he resumed his walk of inspection of the placement of the immigrants.

Ada Roby greeted her son with a wide smile as he approached his cabin. "Charles, you'll never believe the change in Emily since only last night. She is a new woman."

Charles looked about the cabin, his mother the only one there. "Where is she?" he asked.

"She's with Candace and Tom. It seems some of the immigrants saw them together and have taken a liking to Tom and Candace and are showing them great attention."

Charles nodded knowingly. "Ah yes. I have seen this before with other children, especially from those who have lost children on the crossing, the passage over as they call it."

"Emily is pleased as punch with the attention and is now with a group from England. I was told they lost a mother and her baby girl. Candace has also become a friend of a young girl her own age, whose brother almost died. How these people must have suffered," she offered in retrospect as she thought of losing Tom and Candace to forces beyond her control. Oh, Jesus no.

"Ah yes. They have suffered and will probably still much more. Many have a long way still to go before they reach their final destination. I have been told there are those who want to continue to the gold fields of California," Charles offered, then added, "Ah, that I should be so fortunate," he offered with a grin.

"Well, I am off to be with Emily and the children, but... Be thankful that you have what you have in your family and being the Captain of this beautiful vessel. You don't need a dream of the gold fields," Ada admonished her son.

"Yes, Mother, I know," her son admitted ruefully as he kissed her on the cheek. "I am very happy with my Emily, my children... and you."

"Will we be together for dinner?" Ada asked. "At seven-thirty. David and his friend are to join us."

"I hope so, but I want to make the best time I can for Erie. When Sam takes over for the night run to Fairport and Cleveland, I'll take a break if all is well. If only to join you in a dessert."

Ada nodded, understanding her son's responsibilities and gave a small wave of the hand to him. She then proceeded on her way forward on the main deck where she found the English group they had met up with earlier with Emily holding forth in animated discussion, the talk being of Emily describing the passing scenery of the shoreline so near at hand along with a history of the area. Her mention of the Battle of Lake Erie in eighteen-thirteen brought a wistful smile from Abram Clement whose father had served in the British Navy in the ignominious defeat and now here he was with his family to settle in this same land. Father, forgive me, he asked silently.

The first group to be fed was trailing past, each person, young and old, with a tray. The air was filled with gaiety and pleasant laughter as they moved along. The group with Emily broke up as their names were called by the Headwaiter. How organized and efficient John is, Ada thought. To move so many so quickly, she noticed. Even to the point of having one of the Cabin Maids, Marie, she remembered her name, carrying a tray to one of the cabins. What fine service under such crowded conditions she thought.

"How are you feeling," Marie asked, as she entered hers and Christine's cabin. "I've brought you some food." She looked at the pitiful being before her. "I hope you can eat it. Or at least drink the tea."

"I think I am better. My mouth is still sore. It hurts like hell," Christine answered as she arose from the bed and took the tray from Marie.

"It is boiled perch and soft bread with butter. It should be easy to chew and I have some tea. Strong tea, but without the gin. If you want more, I'll get it to you later."

"Oh no. This is fine... Where are we now? The boat seems to be moving along."

"Oh, we're somewhere off Silver Creek. We're supposed to be in Erie by six o'clock. The Captain has a stick up his ass and wants to break all records from Buffalo to Toledo. From the way things are going, he just might! But... I've got to get back. We have a lot of mouths to feed and then do the dishes."

"I wish I could help. I feel like such a damn fool... about everything," Christine said discontentedly as she nibbled on a piece of the fish.

"What's done is done. Forget about it," Marie replied as she pulled aside the curtain from the window and then opened it a crack. "You need fresh air in here. Now then, I'll be back as soon as I can."

Christine carried the tray to the dresser below the cabin window. The sounds of the immigrants, their mixed languages, the hustle and bustle of their moving about was overshadowed by the surging and gurgling of the paddle wheel as it turned in its housing only a few feet away. Its pulsating rhythm was steady and gave her a sense of life, the life of her baby pulsating within herself. George's baby... Oh George. May God forgive me for my actions. But it is our baby and I will make it up to you to be a good wife and mother. I really will. Her bittersweet thoughts were interrupted by the sound of voices just over the sound of the paddle wheel almost yelling to be heard coming from just outside her window. English but strange. Even among themselves the English spoke so differently but this was different. She cocked her head to hear more clearly and stepped back from the window a few inches to the side.

"Ach. I am so full I could bust." Pierce Hill burped as he and Honora and Noreen stood on the deck by the window, with Fergus Kilbane.

"And we didn't have to cook the food as we did on the Primrose." Fergus added as the foursome looked out across the dark, blue waters of the smooth lake to the not too distant shoreline.

"I cannot believe we are on a body of water... a lake... Erie, and not have the heavy seas and winds of the ocean. My prayers have been answered," Honora said as she shaded her eyes from the bright mid-afternoon sun crossing in a clear sky. "I hope that this beautiful day will be an omen for our future."

"Aye. We have had enough bad cess these past weeks and months to be in need of a change," Pierce added as he made room with Noreen to allow for a group to pass by for their meal call.

"And I am ready to put myself back to work. The weeks and months have taken their toll on me. I need the work. To do something with my hands," Fergus added.

"Your hand," Pierce pointed to his right hand, "and how is your hand?"

"Oh," Fergus flexed his fingers. "I'll have the nub the rest of me life. But it works fine now. It had to take its time."

The three stood silent as in one thought. The journey was about over. Only another day and they would be in Cleveland. Fergus with his brother Hugh and his family. Pierce, Honora and Noreen to still an unknown future. But with a promise of a place to stay while Pierce worked his way west with the railroad to make money to bring them to him. They had asked about

287

a Catholic church to join and were pleased that a St. Malachi's, with a large parish in a part of Cleveland called Irish Town, was there. They were told not to speak Irish in public. Many Americans were determined that the Irish, and other immigrant groups, especially the Irish, must speak English only. But because most already spoke English, it would not be too much of a problem to live with. Perhaps the church would keep their language alive although the Latin Mass was its base. Ah, a new country indeed.

To the left of the foursome, two young boys worked their way through the maze of humanity. George and Stanley Hall, with their father's permission, were allowed to explore the deck area but only within sight of the group. To them the G. P. Griffith was so much better than the Primrose. It was so sleek and fast. The two smokestacks poured forth so much smoke and ash, leaving a trail in the sky for what seemed miles behind. The paddle wheels especially intrigued them. How they wished they could go into the part of the boat where they were told was a large steam engine and actually see the way the engine drove the huge wheels. George remembered as a little boy one time when he went with his father to Newmarket and saw a steam engine on a small railway car but he didn't know how it worked just that it made a lot of smoke and noise. He did know that a Scotsman named Watt had something to do with it and that he was a great man. Maybe he had something to do with the steam engine on this boat? The boys' attention was drawn to one of the groups in which a young man began playing a small hand accordion to whose accompaniment others in the group joined him in singing some rousing songs. The music was energetic and seemed to move some of the groups' members to want to dance in jig form but the space was too crowded and they had to content themselves with singing and body gestures. And father thought my book was too big to take along and look at the man with an accordion much larger and heavier than my book, George thought as he stepped aside to let a boat crew member pass.

Larry Dana was making his way along the crowded deck when he saw Marie leaving her and Christine's cabin. He touched the nape of his neck. Still sore. Ah, that bitch, he thought. Well, she got what she deserved. A bashed face for fawning over that black boy. Well, she's through with this boat or any other if she tries. He pondered. At least she is staying out away from everyone and she gets off in Cleveland. Goodby, sweetie. And good riddance... Marie? What the hell! Why not? Somehow she had never turned him on but now who can be choosy. Yeah, maybe I'll make a play for her... but what of the Clerk? They seem to be pretty cozy. Nah, he's a funny one and besides he has an aunt aboard. Ah, what the hell. I'll bide my time till tomorrow night or maybe in Toledo. Marie? Why not, indeed! Damn, but I miss Gail. Now there was a woman!

He continued on his way through the chattering and happy throngs who, for the first time in months, since the previous summer in their homelands, were able to enjoy the warm sun on their pale faces and a mild breeze tussling their hair. A large convergence of gulls seemed to come out of nowhere as they dove and fought with each other for the garbage scraps of the Griffith which the cooks were not throwing overboard. Their cacophonous screaming and crying caused many of the immigrants to cover their ears and cower from the display of birds seemingly gone amuck in a scavenging frenzy.

Jesus! What a mess, he thought as he maneuvered his way through the packed decks. That damn break in the canal. God! What it brought about. Instead of the normal hundred-eighty or two hundred, we have more than a hundred on top of that. What in the hell was Tiffany thinking when he booked so many and Captain Roby allowing so many aboard? Shit! Money! That's what! Only one meal was promised. And now they've had it. Now what? Ah, tomorrow Cleveland, where most will be getting off... The sharp tones of the Griffith's bell caught his attention. He checked his watch and found it was now a few minutes past six o'clock and looking forward he saw, in the not too far distance, the riprap breakwall that protected the entranceway into Erie's harbor. "Damn. That man is good," he admitted remembering that the Captain had wanted the Griffith to get to Erie by six and here it was almost on the button.

William Evans peeked out from behind his cabin window curtains. "Ah," he whispered to himself, "there goes Dana... A busy man on a busy boat. Everyone running, everyone pushing so they can all reach their destinations and get on with their worthless lives." He turned and half stumbled to his bed. He sat on the disheveled mess in the semi-darkness, the only light coming from a halo of light from around the cabin window curtain and a crack from under the door. "God, what a lousy trip," he half moaned. He looked about the cabin and saw the results of his violent actions of throwing the breakfast tray that Charles had brought him that morning. Its contents were strewn about the floor as garbage. His bed clothes were half off and half on the floor. His pillow a sodden mass in the far corner. He turned again to stare at the picture of Carrie, now askew on the wall. He cocked his head to study it. "Well, my lady. What do I do now?" he asked as he wiped his stubbled chin. "I am to stay here in my cabin until we reach Toledo and then I take leave of the boat. Then what? I get my walking papers. That's what!... Crap!" He rose unsteadily and made his way to the washstand against the far wall. He pulled it away from the wall and took a pint bottle of whiskey from behind it... He studied it. "Good ole Monom... Monongahela," he stuttered. "Only one bottle left to get me through another rotten night." He'd heard the Griffith's bell strike six o'clock. The stop over in Erie wasn't long. No time to have gotten anymore from Johnny Paulding. Maybe it would last to Cleveland where he could get some more from Johnny. "Ah, that bastard," he said to the bottle. "He'd do anything to make an extra levy but I can't complain, he brought me three bottles in Buffalo, he and his pal Bill," he giggled a slurpy laugh. "When I make captain, I'll have to remember never to hire those two thieves. They're not to be trusted."

He uncorked the bottle and took a long drag. The burning of the almost pure alcohol caused him to gag but he gritted his teeth and swallowed hard. The burning caused him to cough and he spewed a spray of whiskey and saliva. "Oh my God!" he gasped as he staggered back and fell on the bed, still holding the bottle erect. "Whew!... What the hell. Ah. Bill... Take it easy. This has to last ... Settle down. You've got a long night," He raised himself on his right elbow and listened. A noise. "Who?... Who is it?" he asked to a thumping on his cabin door.

"Hello... Bill..." He heard muffled through the door. "Bill this is David. Open up. I would like to talk with you."

"Go away. I don't want to talk to you."

"Bill, I don't want to yell. Let me in. Charles wants me and others to see how you are doing."

"I'm here you know that. I'm doing fine. Go away."

"Bill, can I bring you some food? You haven't eaten since breakfast."

Bill looked at the tray on the floor and the food strewn about. No, he hadn't eaten since breakfast and even earlier... Last night? He couldn't remember. He was hungry as hell though. "I have food. I'm not hungry... Go away."

David shook his head and stepped back from the door. He looked about and saw that he had been listened to by a number of immigrants who were looking at him and his talking to a closed door. He touched his cap's visor and bowed to the closest ones and took his leave.

Well now, he thought. What's to be done? He sounded reasonable and isn't hungry. Maybe we should just leave him alone. He knows what is expected of him. A good night's sleep will do him some good and tomorrow he'll be his old self. He checked his watch. Oops! I'd better hurry and get Barbara. Emily wants her to join us for dinner at seven-thirty. I'd better hurry.

The Chief Engineer wended his way through the throngs packing the deck, moving in and out among them as he made his way to her cabin. He stopped for a moment and listened to the sounds and felt in the deck the pulsing paddle wheels as they pushed the bow of the Griffith in a white froth of waves curling back along the hull sides to mingle in a crescendo of paddle buckets chopping the water, then flowing back to form double wakes disappearing in the distance on a deep blue water surface under a clear sky. He thought of the brief stopover in Erie. Not really worth the stop. Only a dozen or so barrels of cargo and six passengers. Charles didn't waste any time there and soon cleared Misery Bay and rounding Presque Isle Point made a beeline for Fairport.

He continued his way. Ah what a pleasant evening this will be. The weather is perfect. The boat is moving along at a steady rate, the shaft is holding, and Barbara and I will be enjoying a fine dinner with Emily and Charles' family. He had seen Emily earlier with a group of immigrants and was happy to see she was smiling and visiting with them. Such a wonderful wife for Charles and mother of their beautiful children. He approached and tapped lightly on Barbara's cabin door which opened in a moment.

John and Louisa stepped aside from the railing from where they were looking out over the lake to the shoreline to make room for Barbara and David to pass by on their way to the dining salon. The mid-evening brought high thin clouds from the south-west and a light breeze which tipped small crests with flicking white foam. In the east the waning full moon paled against the darkening sky. The immigrants, after the ordeals of the canal and taking passage on the Griffith, settled down for the night in quiet groups with talk and activity hushed and muted. Lines for the water closets moved along orderly with an occasional plea to those inside to hurry.

"I've been doing nothing of thinking what the next few days will be bringing us." Louisa said as the two huddled together, their newfound friendship growing with each being together and the realization that they were star born, their meeting being fore-told long ago, they liked to believe.

"Aye. We can just hope your Mr. Burnswick will be in need of my trade. I have never worked on a mill but I am certain I will be able to learn and be a help to him."

"Oh, John. I know you will. I just hope that we will be able to see each other often and make our plans. I am to live in his home with his wife and family. It was the cost of my passage to attend to them for three years…"

"We'll see to that when the time comes. If I cannot get work with him, I'll try others. It seems that all the immigrants have work for them already lined up, even the Irish on the railroad. I gathered from hearing some of the Germans talking that a young lad in one of their groups is going to Cleveland to work in a brewery. If they need one to help make ale or beer, they must also need one to build the mill to make the staves to make the kegs. That one is me!" He laughed.

"Let us hope that Mr. Burnswick does have a place for you." Louisa smiled as they clasped hands and looked into each other's eyes.

"Ah, my Louisa. I am so glad that we have met, even under the terrible circumstance," John whispered as they hugged gently. The Griffith gave a slight heel as it began a wide turn to port and made a course for Fairport whose night lights were now guiding the steamer to its main dock.

"The wind is freshening and moving around more to the west," Captain Roby informed Sam McCoit as he relieved the Captain and Richard Mann replaced Robert Davis. "Keep her out. I don't want any unknown shoals to hinder us tonight," he half jested. "If we make the time we want, we should be in Cleveland by four-thirty… five at the very latest. Head her out and then take a two-three-zero degrees or would you rather have the designations of southwest by west?"

"Oh, sir, I know the old terms only too well. I was weaned on a sailer as were you. But the new ways are more precise. I feel much more secure knowing that a heading can be followed by degrees than by wild guessing at times. I never did feel, especially after learning the new means, that west-by-west meant the same to me as it did to you or whoever captain I was with. It is lucky that we never sail much out of the sight of the land."

"Ah, yes. Our times are changing, Sam. This new oil for lubrication. No more fretting about a bearing burning out. New ideas, new inventions that is the way it is now and will be. I'm glad that David has the foresight to see the change coming. Already he has plans for a bigger and better steamer... But enough for now. We will talk of this again. I am off now to see my family. It has been a long day and I feel the want of the bed. You are now in command, Mr. McCoit." He turned to the Wheelsman and nodded his head. "You and your new Second Mate. Welcome aboard, Mr. Mann."

"Thank you, sir." Richard answered as Sam rang the engine room to build up a head of steam for departure of Fairport.

Captain Roby left the pilothouse and made his way through the now slumbering and quiet immigrants. An occasional sound of a child calling or low voices was heard. Thank God it is only one night to Cleveland, he thought. Where most of them will depart. Another day or two with so many could prove to be too much. The toilet facilities alone were way over worked. Ha. He remembered, David has a new plan for that situation as well... Yes, he'll be glad to be in Cleveland in another three hours but first he must get some sleep. Damn! Bill! How is he doing? David and Henry were to check on him. He hadn't heard from either so things must be all right with him. I'll check with him myself... No. It is in the middle of the night and besides Emily must be wondering when I'll be getting in. Ah, I am sure he is all right. I know David and Henry have looked in on him and his needs... God, I'm tired. And still a full day tomorrow to Toledo... and Sandusky too. Ah, well. To my Emily and bed that is what I need now.

"That man is the captain," George whispered to Stanley as the two stood in line to use the nettie.

Stanley looked at the man in a dark suit with a visored black cap working his way among the crowded deck. "He seems to be quite young to be a captain," he answered. "He doesn't look like the captain of the Primrose. He was an old man."

"Maybe this is part of being an American. Everyone seems to be so much younger than we knew back home."

"Well, it is called the New World," Stanley said as he danced mincing steps because of the urge to pee growing stronger within him.

"Excuse us please. Excuse us. We would like to get by," David Stebbins asked the boys and others as he and Babs made their way past. "It will take me only a minute to check my stacks and see how the shaft is holding. I should be back in a trice," he said as he gave her hand a squeeze as they approached a space and he took a passageway to the engine room.

She nodded in understanding of his having to leave and took the time to look about her in the now full of the night. It was a serene setting. Lard peg lamps cast limited lighting along the deck. It was strange for her to be on a steamer, especially at this time of night. For having so many people round about the decks, it was quiet. In Buffalo before leaving, the noise in the streets and on the dock was something else. But now here, under a clear sky with millions of stars across the cosmos, it was so different for her meeting with David, only two days ago and she had no idea of who he was or if she would ever meet anyone like him. And now… She had loved Ernest. He was good and kind… But David. Ah, he has so much more to offer. His talk of building another steamer. He would build it himself if need be, he said. He also had hinted that he might call it the Lady Barbara. Oh David. May God grant your wish and may he also see us together.

Her attention was drawn to a young man who was intently listening to an older man who was talking in low tones as they sat huddled under the faint glow of a peg lamp.

"Sophia and I would like you to stay with our group until you will be able to get back on your feet. I am sure that this Medina, where we are going, will need your skills as well as those in Amherst where you say you are going."

The young man rubbed his forehead. "It is that I thank you, Robert. You and the others in your group have been so kind to me since Julia and…" he choked… "Gwen dying. But" he paused. "I do have friends in Cleveland I am to see. It is they who got me a position as a mason in a quarry in their Amherst." He paused again. "You also are caring for the old man." Joseph Wildes motioned with his head to Brendan Foster asleep with his back to the boat railing, his chin on his chest. "I am sure you will have your hands full with him as I have already seen that you have."

"Aye. We have indeed, but it is almost over now. He has a son living in a town called Akron. It is not too far from where we will be in Medina, I've been told. I am sure he will come to take him with his own people," Robert explained.

"But," he emphasized by pointing his right index finger, "always remember that you have us as friends. Let us know whenever we can help you."

The Griffith's bell tolled three times as Robert returned to his group after his turn at the nettie. The bell's intoning meant nothing to him, just an interesting way of telling time on the boat just as it was on the Primrose. His mind raced. This morning in only a few hours now to Cleveland and then a good days walk, maybe two and then… Medina. Then What? So many times these past weeks… months really, he had wondered. Had they, he and Sophia, done the right thing for their children?… and themselves? At times, yes! Ramsey and the rest of England was in great trouble. America offered work and a chance for a new life… Other times, No! Their heritage, all that they knew to be forgotten in an alien land. To die and be buried among strangers. But it was done. He shook his head. Aye, it is done…

He still had his keys. Ha, he laughed silently. The damn fools. They didn't take them from him. He shook his head. They probably never thought of it. So if it's locked! So what! But, he had thought, Would I be able to see if there were no lights? Ah, ha! He had that figured out too. He would just take his peg oil lamp with some loco-focos and make his own light. He was nobody's fool. He descended through the hatchway from the main deck to the locker forward of the crew's quarters. He looked about. Good. No one was about. He moved cautiously, feeling his way in the passageway to the closed locker door. "What do you know?" he whispered softly. "It's unlocked! Damn. If I was the captain and some dumb-ass left the door unlocked, I'd really raise hell," he added as he eased the door open and stepped into the darkness. He reached out and felt around. I'll need my light. I can't see a damn thing. He closed the door behind him and knelt on the deck where he placed his lamp and fumbled for the loco-focos. He scratched one on the deck and it burst into flame but then went out. "Crap!" he growled. He scratched another. This one lit. He cupped it and then touched it to the lamp. "Well, now that's better," he sighed in relief as he held the lamp high to see about the closed compartment.

The locker was filled with various Griffith's supplies of cleaning goods, spare parts, coils of rope and other items needed on a cruise. In the confined quarters, the lard oil lamp gave off thick fumes causing him to gag. "Ah. There's the wine," he said with a wide grin as he saw cases of wine bottles stacked in a pole. "Ah, what luck. A couple are already open. Ah, yes," he remembered that Henry had opened a few bottles to check for the supposed sabotaged wine. But not all the bottles, only a few. Hell, spoiled or not, they won't miss a couple. He reached into a case and took out a bottle, throwing the excelsior packing to the deck. Shit! The cork. He didn't have a bottle cork opener. But wait! Ah, my penknife. That'll do it. But it's in with my shaving gear in the cabin. The smoke and fumes from the lamp caused him again to cough. I'd better hurry and get a few and run, he realized as he pulled two bottles, the packing to the deck and atop a small keg of highly polished oak, bound with bright copper bands alongside a number of others, all neatly stacked together.

He stuffed two of the bottles into his front waist band and carrying a third, moved with the lamp toward the door. One of the bottles slid down his pant leg causing him to stumble. The peg lamp fell into a loose pile of packing causing it to flame. "Damn!" he bellowed as he stomped on the fire. "I'd better be more careful. He checked the spot and was sure he snuffed out the fire. "I'd better go." He looked around. "Yeah, I'd better go."

CHAPTER NINETEEN

Holocaust

"With the lake as calm as it is, we should make the Cleveland light in about three hours," Sam McCoit informed Richard Mann as he went to the map table and measured the distance between Fairport and Cleveland.

The Wheelsman nodded his head and glanced at the chronometer, a little after two. Plenty of time. The boat is moving along at a good steady rate. He checked his heading. Two-three-zero. Right on the mark. He thought of the Captain and Sam talking earlier of the changes in sailing from the old sailers to the steamers. What luck I have in being now on my way in a good company with a fine captain. He continued, twenty-two, soon to be twenty-three. Ach. My father would be proud of me. Father. Mother and Gertrude and Hedda. They must be fine young ladies now. Hmm. It has been over three years since I last saw them. Ah. With the lay over planned in Toledo to work on the shaft and change over to the new oil, maybe I could get a few days to be able to see them again. Yes. That is what I will do. His attention was taken by Sam.

"I'm going below to check the mooring lines for docking in Cleveland. I forgot about Jack Cooper quitting us in Buffalo. So I'll give ole Teddy a hand in readying up for our getting in. I'll be only a few minutes."

"Aye. I'll keep my eye on things," Richard answered as he took a quick scan about the horizon. The moon, in a haze of high thin clouds, was at its apex in the star-filled sky. The dark waters of the lake, with a shimmer of silver on its surface, was smooth. To the south he could determine the darker shoreline along the horizon. Captain Roby had set the course so that the Griffith paralleled the almost even shoreline from a distance of a little over two miles. He turned to look aft. Over his shoulder... "Mother of God! Oh my God! Fire! We're on fire!" He gasped in almost a scream as he saw a cloud of sparks trailing up from between the waterjacket and the starboard stack spewing into the night sky. He quickly reacted and gave the helm a sharp turn to port causing the Griffith to surge into a tight left toward shore just as Sam raced into the pilothouse.

"I saw it from below. We're on fire between the stacks!" he yelled. "Keep her steady for shore. I'll get the captain," he added as he rang the engine room for full ahead. The sparks changed from bright, lurid red to full-blown crackling sheets of flame.

* * *

"How are you doing?"

"Terrible. I can't sleep."

"Me neither. I wonder what time it is."

"A little after two. I heard the bells. You haven't learned to know them. Have you?"

"No, not really... Marie?"

"Yes."

"I'm afraid to see George... I... I just don't know."

"Aw, honey. It'll be all right. He'll believe you... and me. I know he will. I'm sure that things will work themselves out fine. I'll bet on it."

"Oh, Marie, I hope that..."

"Ah! What! Oh my God another shoal!" Marie cried as the cabin made a sudden lurch and she grabbed her bunk side and held tight from falling out.

Christine above in her bunk screamed as the Griffith plowed

its bow through calm waters because of the sudden thrust of its paddle wheels and made a sharp turn to port.

"Oh no. Not again. This is too much!" Marie continued more angry now than afraid.

Christine jumped from her bunk and sat huddled on the deck as Marie crawled from her bunk and the two hugged each other in the darkness.

"What. Oh what?" Christine muttered, tears welling in her eyes.

"There. There," Marie now consoled trying to sooth and calm herself as much as Christine. "Settle down. Yes, let's settle down. The boat is moving... Maybe another boat got in our way... Yes. Let's settle down."

"What's that?" Christine tensed and sat up. "It's someone yelling... Oh my God. Jesus... Fire... We're on fire."

* * *

"Grandmother!... Gramma! Where are you?"

"Yes. Yes, my darling. I am here." Ada Roby answered as she groped her way back to the bed.

"What happened?" Candace called as she reached out in the darkness to find her grandmother, who had fallen out of their bed due to the abrupt turn of the Griffith, lying on the deck, disoriented between the toppled commode cabinet and the settee. "Is it another shoal?" she asked excitedly as she took her grandmother's extended hand as she returned to her granddaughter's voice.

"I don't know... I... Maybe another boat in the dark. But I am sure someone will be here to tell us what is happening." Ada was now able to adjust to their situation and clasped Candace in her arms. "Come we must get out of here," she now gasped from pain in her right rib cage.

"Oh, Grandmother, I hope Mother and Father are all right... and Thomas."

301

"Yes, dear. I know… Hurry we must see what has happened. Here give me your hand. Hold tight and follow me." Ada wheezed as the pain in her chest made her almost double over.

"Are you all right?" Candace almost screamed.

"I hurt my side when I fell from the bed. Come. Hurry… We must leave."

"Grandmother, there is someone yelling. Listen!"

Ada Roby raised her head and looked to the blackness of the ceiling. "Fire!" she heard. "Fire! The boat is on fire! Oh my dear God. My dear God. No. No. Please no," she moaned as she reached and opened the cabin door.

* * *

"It is a beautiful night," Sophia Hall whispered to Robert as he returned from his talk with Joseph and made way for him to sit beside her. "I can't sleep," she said as she snuggled into his waiting arms.

"Aye. A lot of us are not sleeping. It is the excitement. Only Brendan is sleeping and only because he is old and the journey has wasted him." From their space along the starboard side of the main deck, forward of the lower deck cabins, Robert and Sophia were able to see the crowded deck ahead and behind them, the paddle wheel sponson, housing the thumping paddle wheel as it pulled the Griffith along. He looked down into Sophia's upturned face reflected in the low lantern glow and kissed her gently on the tip of her nose. "I know of George's book."

"I know you know."

"Which one is it?"

"The Life and Adventures of Robinson Crusoe," she giggled, giving him the books full title, as her right hand caressed his left cheek.

"I should have known. He must have read it a dozen times back home… Where does he keep it?"

"In his front. Under his shirt and trousers. Tied with a cord."

"That little imp," Robert laughed. "That is why these past few days he has been walking so stiff and tall."

"He did so want to take it with him. It was a gift from Mr. Tomlinson. It had been given to him when he was but a lad and George cherishes it. I was upset myself when I found out at first..." Sophia raised her head to better hear calling from the deck above. "What is it?" she asked Robert with a tremor as he bolted upright, just as the Griffith made a sharp turn, the shift causing them to be thrown together roughly then parting into a tumult with others who were now crawling and rolling about in dismay and terror.

* * *

"This damn wine is putrid. Charles should take it back and make the bastards who did this to him, drink it all. What crap!" Williams Evans ranted as he finished the second bottle and threw it in the corner. He wiped his chin stubble and belched a bitter bile and grimaced, when he heard a muffled cry of "Fire!" coming from without. Fire? Where? There's no fire. He remembered. There was no fire. I put it out. It was only a little one anyway. So shut up! There's no fire... He was spun around and crashed to the deck of the cabin as it turned suddenly. Damn! Not another shoal! Not this close to Cleveland. What the hell is going on. I'd better... Fire! A fire! He knew the procedures for a fire on the water and the course they were on was less than two miles from shore and we will head straight for it. He knew. He crawled swiftly to his bed and from beneath it pulled a life preserver which he donned in a moment. "Over the side my bucko. Now! No need to be asked," he shouted as he threw open the door and bolted out onto the deck to see a stream of sparks soaring into the night sky followed by a tremendous whoosh of flame. It was all that he needed.

* * *

"Mother! Mother!" Shirley Waters screamed hysterically as her mother stumbled and fell atop Laura as she arose up at the shrieking of those about her who had heard the call of "Fire" and turning of the boat upsetting them.

"William! What do we do? William! Where are you?" Hilary called as panic coursed through the totally distraught and terribly frightened immigrants, as now dense smoke poured from the stairway between the saloon and main decks, followed in an instant with a rush of flame which raced along the cabins, engulfing those within in a fiery tomb, their screams not heard by those of the screams and yelling on the decks trying to avoid the onslaught of flames as the Griffith charged at flank speed toward the unseen shoreline. The flames fanned by the forward motion raged mid-ship and blew back upon the massed souls, many who were now jumping overboard.

* * *

"John! What is happening?... Oh my God!" Louisa wailed as he held her tightly trying to figure a way of getting to the railing through the hysterical, surging mass of immigrants and some cabin passengers caught in a vortex of despair wanting to survive but not knowing how. "Oh my Louisa," he cried as smoke and flame blinded him and he felt the tremendous heat enfold them. "We're dieing too soon. I hardly got to know you," he said just as they leapt off from the boat into the thrashing and flailing bodies of others who too, took to the waters of the lake for their salvation only to find death there as well.

* * *

Ah, what a wonderful woman, David Stebbins sighed as he pulled back his bed sheet and fluffed his pillow. How can a man

304

possibly have such a beautiful person enter his life and in only two days have asked her to marry him. He laughed as he relaxed in his bed. You old fool. Who would have ever believed that I, or she for that matter, would ever do such a thing. It is unheard of… But it has been done… I asked and she said yes… He paused in his rapturous thoughts. Carol. I've almost forgotten about Carol. What will she say? He lay in the darkness, the steady thumping of the paddle wheels assuring him of the return to Toledo to work on the boat. And Charles. To have him perform the marriage on our next trip. Carol. Ah, I am sure she will be happy for me. One less to worry about in the winter months with her and her family in Curtice. He continued his reverie. Toledo tomorrow night. Then about a week for the shaft and a new lubricating system… and then our wedding. He smiled.

"What the!…" The cabin seemed to lurch to aside as he rolled out of his bed unto the deck in the darkness. It can't be another shoal, he wondered fearfully as the Griffith swung into a turn and he felt the increase in thrust as the paddle wheels pulled the steamer in a headlong dash. "My God. What?" He crawled to the commode and found his lamp and loco-focos and was preparing to strike one when he heard the yelling. "Oh NO! NO! NO!" he screamed as he raced for the door.

* * *

Pierce Hill held Noreen in a tight death grip as he shouldered his way through the jammed and milling hoard, followed by Honora who became separated from him and was being trampled underfoot by the crazed mob. He stumbled and caught himself, kicking at others to stay clear but to no avail. The frenzied crowd overwhelmed the narrow deck space, sending dozens of them with him and his baby over the side railing into the swirling waters off the bow where they were washed among the hull to be crushed by the thrashing paddle wheels of the starboard paddle wheel.

* * *

"Mother… Candace… Thank God I've found you."

"Charles. Oh my Charles. What has happened? Oh your beautiful boat. Oh…"

"Not now, Mother. We must get to Emily. She is at the pilot house with Thomas. Come!" Captain Roby pushed and pulled his mother and daughter forward to the stairway leading to the hurricane deck. Flames and chocking smoke tore at them. Their hair singed and clothing smoldering from the now intense heat. He clawed at and pulled away from their path, a young boy who stood screaming, "George! George! Where are you?" who was then caught up in the maelstrom of humanity fighting for their lives. The crushing throng seemed to break for a moment allowing the three to dash up the stairway, then to close again, sending others over the side railing in a wild melee.

* * *

From his view from the pilot house, Richard Mann looked down in horror between the billows of smoke and flame and saw Hades. Flames were now totally enveloping the Griffith's superstructure; its whole upperworks now browned, and blistering, soon to be torched. He tore his eyes away and stared intently at the compass needle. "One-Eight-Zero!" he cried aloud in pain and terror… Straight south… Not south-by-east or south-by-west but straight south, one-hundred-eighty degrees to an unknown shore. Below him, the screams, the cursing, the praying of the damned could be heard even above the roaring of the flames now encircling the pilothouse. "Oh God! How soon? How soon!" he pleaded as the Griffith's forward motion began to slow as the steam pressure in the destroyed engine room was lost. He stared again to the south. Nothing but inky blackness beyond the reaches of the inferno's glare, the blackness soon lost in a now towering cascade of fire as the Griffith ran aground,

the hull grinding onto a shoal, then skewing it portside parallel to it, with a list to starboard. With its motion stopped, the steamer was totally engulfed in a burning carnage. He tried the door almost unable to breathe and found the door handles were red hot. "Mein Gott!! Oh mein Gott," he cried as with his last vision in life he saw Captain Roby below him, lift his wife and baby and throw them over the side as he did then to his mother and daughter and then followed after them. None to rise from the now steaming waters.

Larry Dana and Henry Wilkinson both heard the yelling of a fire at the same time as they leapt from their beds, the smell of acrid burning already permeating their cabin. Larry ran to the door and swung it open to a deck jammed with immigrants who blocked any exit from the cabin. Henry joined him and they both thrust themselves into the screaming swarm. The Porter was knocked to the deck and trampled, while the Clerk wrenched his way to the railing and jumped overboard. The water of the lake was cold and shocked him into sensibility of his frenetic action. His reaction to the call of "Fire" was instant, to escape. Oh... Aunt Babs. Oh no. From his view from the water, the Griffith moved on... To where? Flames shot high into the night sky, smoke rising and obscuring the almost full moon. Thank God he could swim, he realized as he treaded water and looked about him. The noise and the crying of others about him, thrashing and struggling to stay alive and afloat was agonizing to hear. He panicked and fought off a young woman who tried to catch hold of him and pushed her away to see her sink in front of his eyes only a foot or two away. He saw two others locked together sink from his sight only a few moments later and no more than two feet away. The Griffith, lit up like a funeral pyre, moved on into the darkness leaving behind its wake a growing stillness as one by one or in small groups clinging together in death grips, the survivors gradually becoming victims as they slipped, some thrashing, others quietly, into the shallow depths less than a half mile from the northern Ohio shoreline.

"My God, I am tired," Henry lamented as he looked about his narrow range of vision, the light from the Griffith no longer a candle to that about him, "I need something to help me float. Maybe a life preserver? No. Only bits of cloth or a hat, or some small objects floated about. Nothing. He remembered. Each cabin had four and each yawl, six. The yawls! Why aren't they about? John Chitchester and… damn… Oh yes… Jack Cooper were to man the yawls in the event of a need. But where were they? Damn! And for the immigrants… None. No life preservers for them. I'll have to look into that when I get back to Toledo." He swallowed a mouthful of water and gagged as he struggled to see above the parameters of his small watery world in a now silent and mournful state. He paddled and prayed. Oh God. Please God. Help me. He wondered, all the others he had heard pleading and begging for help from God, why should he expect to be a chosen one. Old man Lovelace. Hell… I was ready to steal his trunks and not even knowing what was in them. And now I ask God to save my life… Marie. A married woman screwing around with the likes of me and her with a husband, a damn sick husband… What's that? A board… No a bench! A damn bench from Larry Dana's lunch table. A bench! Oh God. Thank you! he gasped as he tried his best to climb onto the floating bench with only his arms and upper chest being supported. He raised his head as far as he could to get a better view of his surroundings. The overhead sky was awakening in the east with a faint glow on the horizon telling him, at least, in which direction land would be available to him. East. That is east he said at the glow on the horizon which was being obscured by the smoke from the Griffith its upperworks now in a convulsion of flames and the smoke drifting low on the water, drifting east he now knew.

Fini

EPILOGUE

The Cleveland Weekly Herald
Cleveland, June 27, 1850

The Steamer *G. P. Griffith,* which took fire and ran aground only miles from its Cleveland goal on June 17, was examined this past week in the shallows off Willoughby Township where it had been towed earlier. The charred hulk, which was burned to the waterline, attested to the fury of the fire. What it must have been like to have been one of those who lost their life cannot be imagined. As best as can be ascertained, there were three-hundred-twenty-six persons on the boat: of these only about thirty-one were saved, including only one woman, a cabin maid, Marie Walrath. Every child, which number composed almost half of the passengers, perished. The *Griffith's* books were all destroyed in the inferno, thus only a small list of the victims can be given but it is known that the tragedy of the *Griffith* will live in the annals of Lake Erie sailing history. Partial List of Killed: Captain C. C. Roby, his wife, mother and two children; Mrs. Gaynor; George Jefferson; Abraham, a colored cook; William Tillman; Clara, cook; Christine Hood; Hiram Faulks; John Paulding; a boy, George, had a book strapped to his body, his name on the flyleaf; Howard Crown and many English, Irish and German immigrants. Partial List of Survivors: Robert Hall; Brendan Foster; John Chichester, who is credited with saving the lives of seven by swimming ashore, securing a small boat and returning to pick up others from deeper waters; William Evans; William Waters; Fergus Kilbane; David Stebbins; Henry Wilkinson: the Clerk of the *Griffith*; Edward Thatcher; Sam McCoit; Robert Davis; Marshall Gantry, cook. A hearing as to the cause of the calamity will be held this Monday, July 1, at Empire Hall at ten-thirty. Mayor William Case, presiding.

the hull grinding onto a shoal, then skewing it portside parallel to it, with a list to starboard. With its motion stopped, the steamer was totally engulfed in a burning carnage. He tried the door almost unable to breathe and found the door handles were red hot. "Mein Gott!! Oh mein Gott," he cried as with his last vision in life he saw Captain Roby below him, lift his wife and baby and throw them over the side as he did then to his mother and daughter and then followed after them. None to rise from the now steaming waters.

Larry Dana and Henry Wilkinson both heard the yelling of a fire at the same time as they leapt from their beds, the smell of acrid burning already permeating their cabin. Larry ran to the door and swung it open to a deck jammed with immigrants who blocked any exit from the cabin. Henry joined him and they both thrust themselves into the screaming swarm. The Porter was knocked to the deck and trampled, while the Clerk wrenched his way to the railing and jumped overboard. The water of the lake was cold and shocked him into sensibility of his frenetic action. His reaction to the call of "Fire" was instant, to escape. Oh... Aunt Babs. Oh no. From his view from the water, the Griffith moved on... To where? Flames shot high into the night sky, smoke rising and obscuring the almost full moon. Thank God he could swim, he realized as he treaded water and looked about him. The noise and the crying of others about him, thrashing and struggling to stay alive and afloat was agonizing to hear. He panicked and fought off a young woman who tried to catch hold of him and pushed her away to see her sink in front of his eyes only a foot or two away. He saw two others locked together sink from his sight only a few moments later and no more than two feet away. The Griffith, lit up like a funeral pyre, moved on into the darkness leaving behind its wake a growing stillness as one by one or in small groups clinging together in death grips, the survivors gradually becoming victims as they slipped, some thrashing, others quietly, into the shallow depths less than a half mile from the northern Ohio shoreline.

"My God, I am tired," Henry lamented as he looked about his narrow range of vision, the light from the Griffith no longer a candle to that about him, "I need something to help me float. Maybe a life preserver? No. Only bits of cloth or a hat, or some small objects floated about. Nothing. He remembered. Each cabin had four and each yawl, six. The yawls! Why aren't they about? John Chitchester and... damn... Oh yes... Jack Cooper were to man the yawls in the event of a need. But where were they? Damn! And for the immigrants... None. No life preservers for them. I'll have to look into that when I get back to Toledo." He swallowed a mouthful of water and gagged as he struggled to see above the parameters of his small watery world in a now silent and mournful state. He paddled and prayed. Oh God. Please God. Help me. He wondered, all the others he had heard pleading and begging for help from God, why should he expect to be a chosen one. Old man Lovelace. Hell... I was ready to steal his trunks and not even knowing what was in them. And now I ask God to save my life... Marie. A married woman screwing around with the likes of me and her with a husband, a damn sick husband... What's that? A board... No a bench! A damn bench from Larry Dana's lunch table. A bench! Oh God. Thank you! he gasped as he tried his best to climb onto the floating bench with only his arms and upper chest being supported. He raised his head as far as he could to get a better view of his surroundings. The overhead sky was awakening in the east with a faint glow on the horizon telling him, at least, in which direction land would be available to him. East. That is east he said at the glow on the horizon which was being obscured by the smoke from the Griffith its upperworks now in a convulsion of flames and the smoke drifting low on the water, drifting east he now knew.

Fini

EPILOGUE

The Cleveland Weekly Herald
Cleveland, June 27, 1850

The Steamer *G. P. Griffith,* which took fire and ran aground only miles from its Cleveland goal on June 17, was examined this past week in the shallows off Willoughby Township where it had been towed earlier. The charred hulk, which was burned to the waterline, attested to the fury of the fire. What it must have been like to have been one of those who lost their life cannot be imagined. As best as can be ascertained, there were three-hundred-twenty-six persons on the boat: of these only about thirty-one were saved, including only one woman, a cabin maid, Marie Walrath. Every child, which number composed almost half of the passengers, perished. The *Griffith's* books were all destroyed in the inferno, thus only a small list of the victims can be given but it is known that the tragedy of the *Griffith* will live in the annals of Lake Erie sailing history. Partial List of Killed: Captain C. C. Roby, his wife, mother and two children; Mrs. Gaynor; George Jefferson; Abraham, a colored cook; William Tillman; Clara, cook; Christine Hood; Hiram Faulks; John Paulding; a boy, George, had a book strapped to his body, his name on the flyleaf; Howard Crown and many English, Irish and German immigrants. Partial List of Survivors: Robert Hall; Brendan Foster; John Chichester, who is credited with saving the lives of seven by swimming ashore, securing a small boat and returning to pick up others from deeper waters; William Evans; William Waters; Fergus Kilbane; David Stebbins; Henry Wilkinson: the Clerk of the *Griffith*; Edward Thatcher; Sam McCoit; Robert Davis; Marshall Gantry, cook. A hearing as to the cause of the calamity will be held this Monday, July 1, at Empire Hall at ten-thirty. Mayor William Case, presiding.

the hull grinding onto a shoal, then skewing it portside parallel to it, with a list to starboard. With its motion stopped, the steamer was totally engulfed in a burning carnage. He tried the door almost unable to breathe and found the door handles were red hot. "Mein Gott!! Oh mein Gott," he cried as with his last vision in life he saw Captain Roby below him, lift his wife and baby and throw them over the side as he did then to his mother and daughter and then followed after them. None to rise from the now steaming waters.

Larry Dana and Henry Wilkinson both heard the yelling of a fire at the same time as they leapt from their beds, the smell of acrid burning already permeating their cabin. Larry ran to the door and swung it open to a deck jammed with immigrants who blocked any exit from the cabin. Henry joined him and they both thrust themselves into the screaming swarm. The Porter was knocked to the deck and trampled, while the Clerk wrenched his way to the railing and jumped overboard. The water of the lake was cold and shocked him into sensibility of his frenetic action. His reaction to the call of "Fire" was instant, to escape. Oh... Aunt Babs. Oh no. From his view from the water, the Griffith moved on... To where? Flames shot high into the night sky, smoke rising and obscuring the almost full moon. Thank God he could swim, he realized as he treaded water and looked about him. The noise and the crying of others about him, thrashing and struggling to stay alive and afloat was agonizing to hear. He panicked and fought off a young woman who tried to catch hold of him and pushed her away to see her sink in front of his eyes only a foot or two away. He saw two others locked together sink from his sight only a few moments later and no more than two feet away. The Griffith, lit up like a funeral pyre, moved on into the darkness leaving behind its wake a growing stillness as one by one or in small groups clinging together in death grips, the survivors gradually becoming victims as they slipped, some thrashing, others quietly, into the shallow depths less than a half mile from the northern Ohio shoreline.

"My God, I am tired," Henry lamented as he looked about his narrow range of vision, the light from the Griffith no longer a candle to that about him, "I need something to help me float. Maybe a life preserver? No. Only bits of cloth or a hat, or some small objects floated about. Nothing. He remembered. Each cabin had four and each yawl, six. The yawls! Why aren't they about? John Chitchester and... damn... Oh yes... Jack Cooper were to man the yawls in the event of a need. But where were they? Damn! And for the immigrants... None. No life preservers for them. I'll have to look into that when I get back to Toledo." He swallowed a mouthful of water and gagged as he struggled to see above the parameters of his small watery world in a now silent and mournful state. He paddled and prayed. Oh God. Please God. Help me. He wondered, all the others he had heard pleading and begging for help from God, why should he expect to be a chosen one. Old man Lovelace. Hell... I was ready to steal his trunks and not even knowing what was in them. And now I ask God to save my life... Marie. A married woman screwing around with the likes of me and her with a husband, a damn sick husband... What's that? A board... No a bench! A damn bench from Larry Dana's lunch table. A bench! Oh God. Thank you! he gasped as he tried his best to climb onto the floating bench with only his arms and upper chest being supported. He raised his head as far as he could to get a better view of his surroundings. The overhead sky was awakening in the east with a faint glow on the horizon telling him, at least, in which direction land would be available to him. East. That is east he said at the glow on the horizon which was being obscured by the smoke from the Griffith its upperworks now in a convulsion of flames and the smoke drifting low on the water, drifting east he now knew.

Fini

EPILOGUE

The Cleveland Weekly Herald
Cleveland, June 27, 1850

The Steamer *G. P. Griffith,* which took fire and ran aground only miles from its Cleveland goal on June 17, was examined this past week in the shallows off Willoughby Township where it had been towed earlier. The charred hulk, which was burned to the waterline, attested to the fury of the fire. What it must have been like to have been one of those who lost their life cannot be imagined. As best as can be ascertained, there were three-hundred-twenty-six persons on the boat: of these only about thirty-one were saved, including only one woman, a cabin maid, Marie Walrath. Every child, which number composed almost half of the passengers, perished. The *Griffith's* books were all destroyed in the inferno, thus only a small list of the victims can be given but it is known that the tragedy of the *Griffith* will live in the annals of Lake Erie sailing history. Partial List of Killed: Captain C. C. Roby, his wife, mother and two children; Mrs. Gaynor; George Jefferson; Abraham, a colored cook; William Tillman; Clara, cook; Christine Hood; Hiram Faulks; John Paulding; a boy, George, had a book strapped to his body, his name on the flyleaf; Howard Crown and many English, Irish and German immigrants. Partial List of Survivors: Robert Hall; Brendan Foster; John Chichester, who is credited with saving the lives of seven by swimming ashore, securing a small boat and returning to pick up others from deeper waters; William Evans; William Waters; Fergus Kilbane; David Stebbins; Henry Wilkinson: the Clerk of the *Griffith*; Edward Thatcher; Sam McCoit; Robert Davis; Marshall Gantry, cook. A hearing as to the cause of the calamity will be held this Monday, July 1, at Empire Hall at ten-thirty. Mayor William Case, presiding.

DATE DUE

MAR. 10, 2000			
MAY 2 7 2005			
FEB 1 5 2007			
DEC 1 6 2009			

The Library Store   #47-0102